WORTH EVERY
Risk

HAWKSTON BILLIONAIRES
RAE RYDER

Worth Every Risk

Book Three of the Hawkston Billionaires

Copyright © 2025 by Rae Ryder

The right of RAE RYDER to be identified as the author of this work has been asserted by her in accordance with the Copyright, Designs and Patents Act 1988.

All rights reserved. No part of this publication may be reproduced, transmitted, or stored in a retrieval system in any form or by any means without permission in writing from the copyright owner, nor otherwise circulated in any form of binding or cover other than that in which it is published and without a similar condition being imposed on the subsequent purchaser.

This is a work of fiction. All characters in this publication are fictitious, and any resemblance to real people, alive or dead, is purely coincidental.

PB ISBN: 978-1-915286-06-2

www.raeryder.com

Cover by GetCovers

Editor: Sarah Baker

To anyone who has ever needed someone to hold them through their pain.
This one's for you.

Author's Note

Please note this book is written in British English and will include British variations on spelling and vocab where applicable.

You'll find pavements, lifts, tubes (as in metro/subway), boots (of the car), a lot of S instead of Z, and an extra U in places you might not expect. Sometimes an E for an A, too.

Finally, Mr and Mrs appear without the .

Trigger warnings can be found on my website at www.raeryder.com/content-warnings. Please note that this book contains a terminal illness plotline.

This book contains mature content and is intended for those over 18.

1
ARIES

In the back of the black cab, racing through the streets of London's most exclusive postcodes, I take out the note Mum gave me when I left last night. At the top, in handwriting that's more spindly than it used to be, she's written *Aries' London To Do List*. It's a very short list, and I've already read it about a thousand times.

1. *Live*
2. *Dream*
3. *Live the Dream*
4. *Fall in love*

I roll my eyes at the last one and scrunch up the piece of paper, clutching it in a tight fist. I'd throw it away—I'm here to work, after all, not fall in love—but one day, much sooner than I'd like, Mum'll no longer be here, and I'll want to keep every scrap of paper she ever wrote on. If I throw this away, I'll have recurring nightmares about it. I flatten the crumpled paper against my thigh, fold it up neatly like the treasure it is, and slide it back into my wallet.

The taxi rolls to a stop outside a huge white Palladian mansion that's set back from the street beyond a set of intimidating cast-iron gates. *Holy hell, it's a palace.* I jump out before I lose my nerve. The driver opens the boot and lifts out my enormous suitcase, setting it next to me on the pavement. He nods at the monolith. "You'll be all right to get it up to the house?"

I can't tell if his concern is on account of the size of my case, which is so big I could probably fit inside it if I curled up really small, or the fact that I've directed him to a building that's so unlikely a destination for an ordinary girl like me it might as well be Buckingham Palace. From the way his wary gaze keeps darting to the mansion, I suspect it's the latter, which is doing nothing to settle my nerves.

"I'll be all right." I keep my voice light and friendly as I check the back pocket of my jeans with a light tap. *Yes*, the piece of paper with the housekeeper's number is still there.

Once the cab driver is gone, the nerves I've been striving to control bubble in my stomach like a pot of boiling water that could overflow at any moment.

Deep breath. You can handle this.

But—*shit*—the house is bigger than any I've ever been inside, other than those *National Trust* properties Mum used to take me to visit when I was younger. I didn't realise people lived in houses this big in central London. No wonder Mr and Mrs Hawkston were offering such an enormous salary for a nannying job. It was much more than any other role I looked at.

I take another deep, fortifying breath, and drag my suitcase up to the pedestrian gate, which is just as solid and intimidating as the one meant for cars. There's a large post box and a sign in aggressive capital letters that reads NO JUNK MAIL, and another that says BEWARE OF THE DOG.

I press the buzzer and wait, aware that I'm in the sights of the camera. I feel a little self-conscious. *Is anyone watching me?*

No one answers. I check my watch. It's just before midday on Saturday. I'm a bit early, but not much. The housekeeper, Mrs Minter, expressly said she would be in to show me around and help me settle in.

I pull the piece of paper with her number from my pocket and dial it on my phone. It rings out. I dial again, just to double-check I have entered the right number. Same result.

I try to stave off the panicked thoughts that rise up. *What if she changed her mind? What if they don't need a nanny anymore? What if it's me they don't want?*

I peer through the gate. A man wearing noise-cancelling headphones is pushing a lawn mower over the grass. He's so large that the machine looks like a toy in his hands. A pair of worn jeans hang from his hips, revealing the waistband of his boxer shorts. A plaid shirt hangs open over a broad chest, and beneath it, a white t-shirt hugs his pecs.

Thick dark hair arches off his forehead, plastered back with what I assume is sweat. It's a sweltering June day, which I hear is unusual even down south. Up where I'm from, on the west coast of Scotland, it's unheard of. This man is wearing far too many clothes for the weather, and as if he realises it at the same moment I do, he stops what he's doing and peels his shirt off, tossing it onto the driveway.

I can't take my eyes off him, because what I had assumed was a t-shirt is actually a tank top, and this man is ridiculously ripped, like he should be chopping wood in a forest with his bare hands, not mowing a lawn in West London. What does he do in his spare time? *Nope, don't go there.*

If I'm going to keep this job, as the nanny to Mr Hawkston's four-year-old daughter (and I *really* want to, because that little girl, Lucie, was adorable when we spoke on the video call), then I can't be hitting on the gardener. But I'm not made of stone; the man is gorgeous. He might be the best-looking man in the whole world, or at least in *my* world.

Hope flurries in my belly, scattering my nerves. Not only am I going to be working alongside an absolute specimen of a man, but if he's on the other side of this gate, then the chances of me getting through it just skyrocketed.

I wave. "Hey. Hey there."

He looks up, wipes his forearm across his forehead, and takes his headphones off.

A confused expression passes over his face and he glances back towards the house as if to check I'm not talking to someone else.

"Yes, you," I yell, with another wave.

He stalks towards me but keeps his gaze on the ground. He does not look friendly; his glower alone is menacing but, paired with his large, muscular body, it's all I can do not to turn and run. He raises one arm to push a lock of hair back off his forehead, making his bicep bulge even more.

When he reaches the gate, he drags his eyes up my body slowly, taking his time about it and glaring like I've interrupted him from something incredibly important. *How important can cutting grass really be?* Not that I want to dismiss his job or get in his way, but it's not far to the gate; letting me inside will only take a minute, tops.

Whatever his problem is, I'd rather be on good terms with everyone I work with, so I flash him a big smile and offer him my hand, sticking it through the metal bars. "Hi there. I'm Aries. The new nanny."

He glances down at my hand, and for some unknown reason, I start waggling my fingers, like Thing from *The Addams Family*. *Ugh. So uncool.* His eyes flick up to mine, and there's a ferocity in his gaze that makes me feel like I've just stuck my hand into the lion's cage at the zoo. I want to yank my hand right back again. Instead, I grit my teeth and leave my hand dangling, fingers still waggling. I'm pretty sure I've lost control of them. *Come on, Aries. Get your shit together. Just because this man is freakishly handsome, it's no excuse for acting like an idiot.*

He wipes his hand on the back of his jeans and clasps mine in his. It's warm, slightly damp and calloused, like he works with them a lot. And it's massive. My hand is completely swallowed by his. *At least my fingers can't move anymore.*

I'm suddenly struck, full force, by the pure masculinity of the man before me, and any concern about my fingers, other than the fact *he's touching them*, ceases to matter. It's like he's emanating pheromones. They're in his sweat and pooling out in the air between us, causing heat to rush my body.

"Aries," he repeats, dropping my hand.

Is that a question? People normally think my name is odd, but the blank expression on his face is unnerving. By now, I'd have expected some sort of human reaction. A greeting. A smile. But this guy's giving me nothing. Maybe if I opened up his chest, I would find only grinding metal and computer circuits. *And a dash of hot pheromones to fool us into believing he's real.*

His face is a bit perfect. Maybe I'm not far off the mark with this robot idea.

"Like the Zodiac sign," I offer, hoping he might latch onto this tidbit and start making conversation.

Fat chance.

He blinks at me. "Right," he says slowly, and for some reason, it feels like a response to *me* rather than my name. As though I'm the oddity. "You look young. How did you get the job?"

I frown. *Why is he asking? Is it any of his business?* My thoughts are a swirling mess—I'm too befuddled by his face—but one thought wins out. *What if all the previous nannies have been older, and when Mr and Mrs Hawkston see me, they won't want me because I look too young?* My stomach clenches, but somehow I manage to sound calm when I say, "Same way most people do. I applied. I had a couple of video interviews with Mrs Minter. She said Mrs Hawkston wasn't available, so she took the interview."

He stares for a moment. "How old are you?" *Oh, God. Really? I must be the youngest nanny they've ever had.* I need to lighten the mood before I start panicking about being under thirty.

"Didn't anyone tell you it's rude to ask a woman her age?" My tone is teasing, but not even a glimmer of a smile cracks through his veneer. Awkward silence descends, and beneath his stony gaze that shows no sign of shifting, I blurt the answer. "I'm twenty-six, but my mum had me covered in SPF50 as soon as I popped out of the womb. Fair skin, you know."

I thrust my arm further through the bars, clenching my fist and brandishing my pasty, freckled forearm so he can see it. His eyebrow shoots up, his lips curving in distaste. Safe to say my appreciation for this man is *not* reciprocated, but the pure disgust he's displaying is unwarranted.

"All right, Mister," I begin, my voice hovering somewhere between annoyed and jocular. "Just because your forearms are perfect and tanned from all this outdoor work you're doing, it doesn't excuse that repulsed expression on your face."

He looks even more perturbed after my outburst, and I feel a flash of guilt at having taunted him. He clearly can't take a joke. His arms hang at his sides, but he flexes his fingers, causing the muscles and tendons in his forearms to stand out in perfect formation. *I want to touch them.*

I retract my hand, just in case it does something crazy like lurch further through the gate in an attempt to do exactly that. "Do you think you could let me in?"

He grunts and presses a button on his side of the gate, releasing the lock with a mechanical clink so he can open it.

"Thanks," I mutter, fixing my handbag tightly over my shoulder and dragging my huge suitcase up the garden path. I expect him to follow me so he can get on with his mowing, but I don't hear him move.

I glance back to find him staring at me with a really strange look on his face. It's as if he's never seen a woman before, and I'm wondering why a guy who looks like *that*—tall, muscular, and with a face that strikes a perfect balance between beautiful and manly—would ever have cause to stare at a woman the way he's looking at me. It's like I'm an alien or something. After a beat too long, he lets the gate swing closed on its slow-release hinges and paces behind me.

I roll my suitcase up the path, heading towards the five stone steps that lead to a black front door with brasswork so highly polished it gleams like gold. The knocker is so clean that I don't want to touch it.

First things first though. I have to get my enormous case up the steps.

Standing on the first step, I turn around to haul it behind me, only to find the gardener still staring at me. For someone who appeared so resentful to be disturbed from his work, he sure is taking his time to get back to it.

"Where are you going?" he asks, in a tone that suggests what I'm doing is not only wildly inappropriate, but certifiably insane. *What is with this guy?*

"What does it look like? I'm going inside. Mrs Minter is expecting me any minute now. I don't want to make a bad impression." He scowls and my nerves return in full force. If I can't charm the gardener, what hope do I have with the housekeeper? Or the rest of the family? *Shit*. My urge to babble takes hold, as it always does when I'm anxious. "I had no idea she lived in a house like this. Have you ever seen a house this big? I haven't. Well, other than when we went to Dunrobbin

Castle on a school trip. That was mega. Huge. Like a fairytale castle. But in cities, I didn't think there were houses this big. Not really. Guess I never thought about it, actually." I gaze up at the house. "It's really something, eh? I wasn't expecting this."

One of his thick eyebrows arches, a pale white scar running through it. Paired with his grumpy demeanor and unwavering stare, it makes him look a little sinister. *Maybe this guy has a dark side.* "What were you expecting?" To my surprise, it sounds as though he's genuinely interested, which calms me a little.

I shrug. "Not sure. I didn't think about it much."

He stiffens slightly, then fixes me with those dark eyes that bristle with something I can't read. "You didn't Google your employer?"

"Nope. I've worked for several families and never googled them. I go by gut feel. You know... my intuition." He frowns, looking like he doesn't know what I mean at all, or at least doesn't approve of it, but I refuse to be put off. "Mrs Minter gave me all the info I needed. I liked her. Lucie I particularly liked. What a sweet kid. The cutest smile. She kept kissing the screen when we spoke online." I can't help the broad grin that spreads over my face. I've always loved kids. "Apparently there's a son too, Charlie, but he's away at boarding school, so I don't know what he's like yet. Oh, and the pay! This was the best offer I've ever had. Do you reckon they know they're paying well over the average wage?"

I smirk and wink, waiting for him to smile, or acknowledge that he too is being paid well above the average salary, but all he says is, "If they're paying more, they're expecting more."

A wave of self-consciousness washes over me. *Why can't I keep my mouth shut?* He's probably thinking I'll exploit the generosity of my new employer by doing the bare minimum, and I can't let that stand.

"I'm going to work hard. I'm very good at my job, even if I do look young. I'll be worth every penny they pay me."

He draws back slightly. "Okay."

When it's clear he has nothing more to say on the matter, I turn my attention back to trying to heave my suitcase up to the next step, but under his judgmental gaze, I'm getting stage fright. It takes a concerted effort to keep my voice casual when I glance at him and say, "Give a girl a hand?"

"Staff entrance is round the side." He nods his head towards a path down the side of the house that I hadn't noticed.

"Oh. Right." I guess that explains the way he was looking at me earlier, but I can't help feeling a touch annoyed that he didn't tell me *before* I began this lugging-the-biggest-case-in-the-world-up-the-steps endeavour. I blow out a breath and begin the process of getting my bag back down.

The gardener makes a move, quick and nimble, grabbing the case from me. "I'll take it."

"Thank you. That's so kind." *Finally*. Maybe he can be a gentleman, after all.

He huffs, shunts the retractable handle down and picks the bag up using the one on the side instead. The enormous case shifts orientation in one smooth movement. If I had tried that, it would have pulled me right to the floor along with it.

He strides past me up the steps to the front door.

"Wait, don't we go in the side? You just said that's the staff entrance."

He stops and glances over his shoulder at me. "I don't have the keys to the side door."

Before I have a moment to query him, he's off again, and I get the most glorious view of his arse in his jeans as he takes the steps ahead of me. There's tight muscle in there that begs to be squeezed. His thighs, too, are dense. I can see the shape of his quads through the denim.

Just as I'm thinking how much I'm going to appreciate working here for the next few months—even if the guy is laconic, at least he's good to look at—he reaches the top step and taps the suitcase down.

There's a faint clicking noise and my stomach plunges. *Oh, shit.* The latches fly open and one side falls open, spilling the contents down the pristine stone steps. Balled up socks roll like boulders in a rock-slide onto the path, while the top step is splattered with my underwear and clothes. The gardener stares at the mess with a repulsed look on his face, as though I've vomited at his feet.

Thank goodness I put my dildo in the zip pocket.

"Ah!" I scoop up the runaway socks and scamper up the stairs, gathering items as I go. "Shit, sorry. It's so old, this case. It does that sometimes if you set it down sideways. I should have mentioned it."

My arms are bulging with clothes, but I can't get them all, and I really don't want this man seeing all my crappy, washed-out grey underwear. I should have bought some new stuff, but I figured I'd wait until after my first paycheck. Now, I'm wishing I'd planned in advance.

Oh, holy hell, he's bending down, picking up my clothes. *Helping me.* His large hand hovers over a pile of faded knickers, his eyes widening a fraction as he realises what he's about to grab. I freeze too, and for a few panicked moments everything moves in slow motion until his hand shifts over to a safer pile of t-shirts, and I sweep up the underwear and stuff it deep in the bag.

"You should get a new suitcase," he says. "What if this happened on the flight?"

God, this guy is a real energy drain. But boy, does he have one luscious voice. It's like melted chocolate dribbled all over a naked body. *Yummy and hot.*

"I didn't take a flight." My Scottish accent sounds even stronger compared to this gorgeous man's dulcet English one. "I took the train from Edinburgh. The scenery is better."

"Hmm." He busies himself with stuffing clothes back in my bag, and we do that together until everything's back in.

He lets me click the suitcase shut.

"Thanks," I say.

"You're welcome."

My heart does a funny pitter-patter. *Wow.* How does he make *'you're welcome'* sound like a pickup line? If he didn't look so grumpy, and his energy wasn't so uninviting, I'd say he was doing it deliberately. But I suspect it's accidental. The man is so sexy he's doing it without effort.

I turn to him, one hand on my hip. "You could be one of those audiobook narrators, you know. You have a voice I could listen to all day. In fact, you should talk more. Waste of a great voice if you don't."

The front door clicks and he shunts it open with his shoulder as he heaves my bag inside. I glance around, wondering how he opened it. I didn't hear a doorbell and there's no one waiting inside for us. Must have been a keycode or something.

My breath catches at the sight of the inside of the house. The entrance hall is like a gymnasium, it's so big. But with a marble floor, panelled walls, and modern art in sleek frames. A wide, carpeted staircase spirals up through the house, rising goodness knows how high.

"Audiobooks?" he repeats.

"Uh-huh. You have a voice so hot it could deep-fry a Mars Bar."

He stares at me like I'm a dog that's started talking. "You don't know when to shut up, do you?"

Rude. But I refrain from objection because he has a point, and his comment is so close to sounding like a command—*and this man giving orders would be sexy as hell*—that a nervous giggle slips out my mouth.

"I've been told that. It's my thing. When I'm nervous, I get verbal diarrhoea. Doesn't mean it's not true though. That you have a really... great voice." I nearly say sexy, but catch myself just in time. I don't want to come on too hard; I've only just met the guy. "You're also older than you looked from the street. When I saw you through the gate, I was thinking maybe you were thirty. But up close, I can see the lines around your eyes. And you have greys in your hair. Just over the ears. So I'd say..." I stop talking, aware his expression is narrow and there's something close to disgust in his gaze. *Crap.* I've just analysed his face out loud, which is so much worse than him asking me how old I am.

"Go on..." he says, and I sense he wants to hear what else I have to say as much as he doesn't.

"I don't know. Sorry. I'm being really rude. I don't even know you. Oh, wait..." There's a pair of my knickers attached to his shoe. How did that happen? I don't know how I missed them, or how the hell they got stuck there like a bit of loose toilet paper, but before I can question it, I dip to the ground and snatch them.

They don't move. *Shit.* He's got them pinned beneath his huge foot.

I tug them again. "Erm, excuse me..."

The toe of his boot shifts and my panties are free. I stand up to find him looking at me like I'm crazy, and in response, I flick them around my finger and stuff them in my back pocket. "My underwear.

Sorry. I mean... not that it's a big deal. You look like you've seen a lot of women's underwear."

I am talking absolute rubbish now.

He fixes those dark, humourless eyes on me. "You make a lot of assumptions."

"Oh. Yeah. Sorry. I just say what I see. You're a really handsome man. Like, freakishly so, actually. If all men around here look like you—"

"Kitchen's downstairs," he interrupts. "Mrs Minter will show you around when she gets back. Your room will be up on the top floor with Lucie, so you might as well leave the case here for now."

"Oh. Okay." I feel a little dejected at the way he cut me down, and I hold his gaze as I gather the courage to try and rectify the situation. "Look, I think maybe we've got off to a bad start. I'm getting the sense that you don't like me much, and really I'm not that bad. I'm nervous. That's it, mostly. Sort of. I mean, I like talking. Human beings are interesting, you know?"

"They are. Which is exactly why you should Google your employers in the future. It always pays to be prepared."

"Right, okay. Will do. I mean, I prefer meeting in person than over a screen, but yeah. Maybe." For want of something better to do, I stick my hand out to him again. I'm behaving like an idiot, but he doesn't comment on it, and takes my hand, as if us shaking hands twice in the space of fifteen minutes isn't really weird and awkward. "I'm glad we've met."

He releases my hand and lets his arm fall to his side, flexing his fingers. "You are?"

"Yes. I don't know anyone in London. This is the first time I've ever been here. I'm completely alone." I force a smile, which is hard because admitting I'm alone in a huge city doesn't feel like a good thing. And for all I'm trying to break down this man's exterior, he's chock full of resistance. If he'd been even a tiny bit friendlier, maybe I wouldn't have been so nervous, and then I wouldn't have made such a fool of myself. By this point, what with my pasty forearms and waggling fingers, I'd have had a lesser man at least smirking by now, but I'm not even causing a chink.

I'll give it one last shot. "I could really use a friend, and I can sense there's a cool guy that's worth getting to know underneath the big-burly-gardener-hunk thing you have going on." I sweep my gaze over him, trying to get a decent read on him. On impulse, I reach out and tap his chest with my knuckle. "I reckon you've got a kind and caring soul under there somewhere." This gains me no reaction other than the furrows between his brows deepening, so I snatch my hand back and change the subject. "Do you live here too?"

A hint of amusement sparks behind those dark eyes. I sense it more than see it, because his face remains stone cold. "Yes."

"Great. Then we'll definitely see one another. Do all the staff live in?"

"No. Not all."

A tense beat of silence fills the large entrance hall.

"Okay, I'll see you around then..." I leave my sentence hanging, waiting for him to add his name.

"Matt," he says. "It's Matt."

"You can call me Aries. Matt and Aries. That's nice. Not really the same type of name though, is it? Matt is very ordinary. No offense. At least there's an edge to Aries. You know, a conversation starter. Icebreaker. 'Why are you called Aries?' type thing."

My babbling has reached epic levels; I blame Matt. I can't even tell if I'm flustered because he's so gorgeous, or embarrassed because the responses he's given me are so minimal I feel like I'm talking to a brick wall. Either way, I'm making a fool of myself.

"I'm not going to ask," he says, and for some reason, I feel like I've propositioned the guy and he's slapped me away like a mosquito. Itchy heat spreads beneath my clothes.

"Right. Okay. Bye," I mutter, feeling so awkward that I almost run in the direction of the stairs that lead to the basement. But, despite our bizarre first encounter, I'm already plotting how I'm going to break down the defences of the most handsome man I've ever seen.

Maybe this summer might be fun.

2
ARIES

A clattering of pans greets my ears as I descend to the kitchen. There's also a radio blaring. I peek into the room; it's so vast it looks like it could cater for an entire restaurant. The surfaces are steel, and I half expect Gordon Ramsay to spring out from behind one of the enormous fridges and give me a mouthful of abuse. Instead, there's a slim young man in a chef's white coat flapping around.

He looks up when I take another step into the room. "Can I help you?"

He's a sweet-looking man, maybe in his late twenties. Blond, blue-eyed, and doesn't look like he could grow a beard, ever.

"Hi. I'm Aries. The new nanny?" I don't know why it comes out like a question. Probably because I'm still recovering from the ordeal of trying to maintain a normal—*ugh, nowhere near normal*—conversation with the hot-but-grumpy gardener. "I'm waiting for Mrs Minter. She should be back soon."

"Ah. Aries. Like the Zodiac?"

Here we go. "Yup. I'm an Aries. And I'm Aries."

He chuckles at my lame joke. "Fiery and passionate rams, right?" He nods at my hair. "You look the part." *Thank God he didn't nod at my tits. I've had that before.*

"Thanks, I think."

"Welcome to the madhouse," he says, smiling even wider. I can already tell I'll like this guy. So much friendlier than the gardener.

"That bad, eh?"

He chuckles. "It's all right. Been a bit rough since Mrs Hawkston left. We've been scrabbling to keep the place ticking over."

"She left?"

"Last summer. They're divorced."

"Oh. Mrs Minter didn't mention that. Just said that Mrs Hawkston wouldn't be able to speak to me, and that Mr Hawkston was too busy, so he delegates all household employment decisions to her. He's always at work, apparently."

"Sounds about right, although Mr Hawkston's been around a bit more recently. For the kids. But between you and me, I don't think he really knows how to care for them. Never put in the time. Workaholic." He wipes his hands on his chef's coat. "Not that I can talk. The hours he's got me working here, I'm worse than he is. I'm Alec, by the way."

He points a knife at me rather than shake my hand, then continues chopping up an onion with a precision and speed that nearly blows my mind.

I take a seat at a large granite island in what appears to be the more homely part of the kitchen. I glance around to find there's also a wooden kitchen table, a cushioned window seat, and a sofa area across the other side of the room. Overall, the place looks like it's having an identity crisis, but in a very stylish, deliberate way.

"Were they together long? Mr and Mrs Hawkston?" I ask.

"Oh, yeah. Years. Since they were teenagers, I think."

Wow. I can't even imagine being with someone that long. "How old are they now?"

"I dunno. Mid-thirties? Somewhere around there. Far too old to have stuck out a marriage like that."

Alec keeps chopping like he hasn't just dropped a gossip bombshell. I'd love not to pick it up, but I don't have that kind of restraint. Plus, I'm feeling a bit off-kilter, given I've entered an entirely new environment and, as Matt the grumpy gardener reminded me, I haven't done my research about where I'm living. *Surely, information from a member of staff is more reliable than Google, anyway.* "What was wrong?" I probe.

Alec scratches his eyebrow with the back of his wrist, still holding his knife. "It's not my place to say this, but they were bloody miserable. You could hear them fighting almost every time they were in the house together. Charlie, that's the son, he used to come in here when he was little and hide under the kitchen counters when it got really bad. I came in one morning and found him sleeping in the cupboard over there." He points with the knife at a double-doored cupboard. "Said he'd come down in the night because his parents were fighting upstairs." Alec inhales deeply and blows out the breath. "Sorry. That's a bit much, isn't it? It wasn't a nice place to work. You could feel the toxicity in the air."

I wince. "Sounds awful."

He closes his eyes and shudders, then snaps them open again. "Yeah. Like I said. Better now. Quieter."

"Happier?"

Alec stills, his eyes glazing over like he's remembering something. "I don't know about that."

For a moment, I hold my tongue. My parents were stuck in an unhappy marriage until I was six. I know what it's like to be the kid hiding.

Alec focuses on his chopping, as if realising he's said too much. For a while, we fall into an uncomfortable silence. Not that silence is ever comfortable for me. It's part of the reason I talk too much. I feel obligated to fill the void, but after the intensity of our conversation about the Hawkston's, I feel it even more so.

Soon, the weight of the silence becomes more than I can endure. "I met the gardener out the front. He's a peculiar guy. Not very friendly."

Alec's eyes narrow, but he doesn't look up, focusing on his chopping. "Really? I've always liked Steve. Really cheery guy. I didn't know he was in today."

"Steve?" I frown. "He said his name was Matt."

Alec's knife pauses mid-chop. "Matt?"

"Yeah. Tall guy. Huge. Really broad." I hold my arms up to span the distance of the guy's chest. I exaggerate, hoping to make Alec laugh.

He doesn't, and unease prickles my spine. "Why are you looking at me like that?"

"Matt's not the gardener."

"Huh? But he was cutting the lawn."

"Ooh, you want to stay out of his way when he's doing that..."

I'm about to question him further when Alec's eyes shoot over my head, obviously catching sight of someone behind me. A tingling pressure erupts on the back of my neck, telling me that someone's standing there.

I turn on my stool, which conveniently—or perhaps not conveniently—spins round far too easily. I nearly fall off, managing to stabilize myself at the last second, fixing my gaze on the man in the doorway.

Oh, crap.

It's the gardener. Except—*holy shit*—he doesn't look like a gardener now. His dark hair is wet, thick, and combed back off his forehead, making his dark eyes appear even more intense, and the way he's fixing them on me has me swallowing nervously, but I can't stop staring at his face. *That bone structure is insane.* His cheekbones are so sharp they look like chipped flint. He's just had a shower, and the realisation brings a whole host of—not entirely unwelcome—images into my mind. Water, skin, muscle...

I blink to focus on the real-life man before me, rather than the imagined showering version. A charcoal grey suit hangs from broad shoulders, fitting him perfectly; the phrase 'like a glove' suddenly takes on a whole new meaning. I've never really noticed suits before, but this one is different. It looks expensive, so I guess you get what you pay for. His white shirt is a burst of light in the otherwise dark impression of the man, and the pale blue silk tie is a river of calm down his chest. He's breathtaking, and very, *very* corporate.

His dark eyes flit away from me as he directs his attention to Alec. "I'm going out for lunch. I'll be back for dinner. Just me tonight. 8 pm."

"Absolutely, boss."

Whatever spell this man has me under splinters, leaving the unbearable truth.

This is *the boss.* Lucie's dad. This is Mr Hawkston, who's always working and never home and who I was highly unlikely to *ever* meet.

Oh, my God. I'm dying.

His unflinching gaze lands right on mine and he steps towards me. "Aries." He holds out his hand. "Matt Hawkston."

We're not seriously shaking hands a third time, are we? I glance at it like I'm not sure what to do with it, but then I pick my jaw off the floor and grab his hand *again*. It's so big he could crush me with it.

"I'm so sorry. Really. I had no idea that you were *you*, outside in the garden." I press my free hand to my temple. "And now you've gone and done a Superman—"

There's a noise behind me. Did Alec just *snort*? Matt's irises dart from me to Alec, and I know he heard it too. The silence that follows that small shift in Matt's attention is enough to make my heart rate peak. He might not be snorting, but he probably thinks I'm a complete idiot too.

Matt drops my hand, but holds eye contact. It's so intense that I want to screw my eyes shut. "Superman?" Matt finally says.

"Yeah. You know. You've stripped off the disguise." *Oh, fuck. Why can't I stop talking?* "Fifteen minutes ago you were working that sexy gardener thing and now you're all suited-up like a corporate superhero—"

"Stop." His command has my mouth sealing shut. *Shit, shit, shit.* "I assume Mrs Minter selected you because you're the best for the job, but I'm not seeing that right now. If you're caring for my child, you need to do your research. Any time you take her anywhere, you need to know who you're meeting. You make sure it's safe. You might trust your gut to make decisions that affect *your* life, but I don't want you using it to care for my daughter. At least not until I know you better. No more mistakes. Three strikes and you're out."

For once, I'm speechless. Then I say, "Out?"

"Yes. Out. Home. Back to Scotland. If you put my daughter at risk in any way, I'll put you on that train myself."

And with that, he's gone, leaving nothing but a hot, uncomfortable embarrassment filling my body, and the lingering scent of expensive cologne hanging in the air.

I'm still staring at the doorway when I hear another snort from behind me, or perhaps it's the other half of the one Alec had to stifle earlier.

I spin to face him. "What?"

"Looks like you made a good first impression."

I exhale a curse. "Was he being serious? Just because I didn't look him up, doesn't mean I would put his daughter at risk. Would he get rid of me because I didn't know who he was?"

"Maybe. Everyone knows who Matt Hawkston is. Like... *everyone*. Especially people he employs. How... I mean, *how* did you not know?"

I shrug. "I'm interested in the kids, not the parents. And when I interviewed for this role I only spoke to Mrs Minter, and she was lovely. I got a really great feel from her. She said she was my point of contact, and that Mr and Mrs Hawkston were always away. I didn't feel the need to know more than that."

"Hmm. Curious." Alec's lips twist like he wants to laugh, but he doesn't. "That's like me saying I only want to know where they do their food shopping."

I chuckle. "That's important information, though, right?"

He breaks into a broad smile. "Yup. Crucial."

Laughter bubbles up and flows out of my mouth like a riot I can't control. It's verging on hysterical, and I think Alec knows it, but he's laughing too, and I am seriously wishing I'd met him first. Then I might not have made a prize fool of myself in front of my boss. Who, I might add, looks even better in a suit. Matt Hawkston is one very, *very* good-looking man.

The thought pricks some idle hope I didn't realise I'd been entertaining, deflating it like a sad balloon; the gorgeous gardener, who I'd already anticipated would be the friend I needed to show me around London, doesn't exist.

"Oh, God." I drop my forehead into my palm. "I told him he could narrate audiobooks."

"That doesn't sound like the worst thing," Alec says slowly, as though he's trying to work out if he believes what he's saying. He tips his head to one side and adds, "A bit odd, but not the worst."

I scrunch my eyes closed briefly before looking back at him. "I said he had a voice that could deep-fry a Mars bar."

Alec's lip curls. "Yuck. And I say that as a man who tries to accept all food on an equal basis."

I try to laugh, but can't summon enough humour to drown out my humiliation. "It was a joke. You know, a Scottish thing. Everyone thinks we eat deep-fried Mars bars, but actually you have to search pretty hard to find one. I meant... I meant he has a smoking hot voice. One that women love to listen to because it turns them on."

Turns them on? Please, Aries, stop talking.

A large smile breaks over Alec's face. I think it's amused, rather than mocking. *Thank goodness.* "Yeah, I got that. I'm pretty sure Mr Hawkston would've understood it too." He tosses another onion in the air and catches it, then winks at me. "You also called him Superman."

I let out a groan and bury my head in my hands. *How can I come back from this?*

By the time Mrs Minter arrives with Lucie, I'm almost beside myself with worry. *Should I even unpack my bag? If I'm going to be fired soon, maybe I should save myself the effort.*

As Mrs Minter runs me through details about the house, I try to stay focused and listen to her instructions, but I can't help wondering if I ought to fess up and tell her I've already made a dreadful first impression on the boss, so I might not be here long.

I decide to hold my tongue, because Lucie, Mr Hawkston's daughter, is staring up at me the whole time, peeking out from behind Mrs Minter's legs, where she's clinging as though she hopes no one will notice her. She's a gorgeous, dark haired four-year-old, who has definitely inherited her father's good looks, but without the grumpy exterior. I can't wait to get to know her better.

Once Mrs Minter has finished the introductions and explanations, she leads the way upstairs. She's wearing a simple cream blouse and jeans, which surprises me. I expected the housekeeper to wear a uniform of some sort in a house like this. She must be in her mid fifties, but her figure is as neat as a woman of twenty. She has highlighted blonde hair and a pretty face with even features. Lucie grips her hand, shooting glances back at me and whispering to Mrs Minter, but I can't make out what she's saying.

I smile in the hope it'll make her warm to me, but when I do she hides her face by burrowing it against Mrs Minter's thigh.

"The lift is this way." Mrs Minter points down the corridor, her face impassive, as if having a lift inside a private house is normal. I try my hardest to mirror her expression, whilst in my head I'm screaming, *'Lift? There's a fucking lift in here?'*

I grab my suitcase from where I left it in the entrance hall and drag it along behind Mrs Minter and Lucie. Moments later, the three of us are crammed into the lift.

"Mr Hawkston's rarely home during the day, even at the weekends," Mrs Minter says. "He works long hours. He's a very busy man. The Hawkston Hotel Group has forty hotels in the UK alone."

"Hotels?" My stomach cinches, like someone just pulled a too-tight belt around it. "He's Hawkston like the Hotels?"

I feel like a prize idiot. I do trust my gut, and my gut was screaming like a fire engine telling me to take this job. But maybe it's naïve to make all your decisions that way. My mum taught me to do it. She always said our intuition is the greatest superpower most people don't know they have. She was a tarot reader and reiki practitioner, so reading people's energy and letting her intuition guide her readings was her thing. It became like a game for me; letting my intuition choose my clothes for the day, or which book to read, or any number of other things. And it was fun to see how everything panned out.

I never felt really stupid about it until I was confronted by that unforgiving glare that Matt Hawkston sent my way in the kitchen. It has me questioning all sorts of things, and near the top of the list is whether my reading on him in his ripped jeans and tank top was completely off. Was I thrown by his casual appearance, or is there really a kind and caring soul buried deep inside? If we'd first met in the kitchen, him all stiff in his suit and tie, would the possibility even have crossed my mind?

Maybe all my practice hasn't honed my intuition at all, and I'm as easily influenced by appearances as the next person. Those jeans and tank top had me believing there had to be a casual, relaxed man in there somewhere. Maybe it was nothing more than wishful thinking. Either way, relying on my gut meant I wasn't prepared to meet my employer, and that's got to be an almost unforgivable employee sin.

"Your mother didn't tell you?" Mrs Minter's voice pulls me back into the tight space of the lift. Of course, they've spoken, but Mrs Minter doesn't know Mum well enough to know she wouldn't give a crap about whether someone had money or not, let alone how they made it.

"No," I say. "She wouldn't have considered that important information." *Was that rude?* I just dismissed Mr Hawkston's family business as though it meant nothing. "She's been too ill," I add quickly, although that has nothing to do with her omission.

"Ah. Yes, of course. I'm so sorry." She's frowns, and Lucie stares up at me, still nuzzled into Mrs Minter's side. "Your mother is a wonderful healer. All those sessions she did for my father online... it made it all so much easier."

My stomach drops a little. Mum told me Mrs Minter's father died last year. She had been doing distance reiki sessions for him to help with the side effects of chemo. After he died, Mum and Mrs Minter kept in touch, and that's how I found out about this job. I always wanted to live in London, at least for a while, and after Mum's diagnosis, she started getting all worried about how my refusal to leave her alone meant she wasn't going to see me live my dreams. So here I am, living the proverbial dream as a nanny in West London. Or at least satisfying my mother for a while.

"I'm sorry for your loss," I say, and Mrs Minter nods, giving me a sympathetic glance. Fear stirs in my belly, knowing how likely it is that people are going to be saying those exact words to me in the not too distant future.

"What's wrong with your mummy?" Lucie asks. "My mummy's not well either. That's what Daddy says."

Mrs Minter gives Lucie's hand a tight squeeze. "Your mummy is absolutely fine, honey. Daddy's wrong."

Lucie's tiny features crumple inwards, looking confused.

"My mother has cancer," I say, and immediately wish I hadn't, because Lucie looks even more confused, but for whatever reason she doesn't ask a follow-up question. *Thank goodness.*

Mrs Minter gives me another compassionate glance, but I can tell she's holding something back, as though she's on one side of the gulf and I'm on the other. The before and the after. I repress a shudder at the thought and focus on how thankful I am that Mrs Minter was so eager to help when she found out Mum was ill. The pay for this job is so good that I've already appointed a private carer to look after Mum while I'm here. And I've always loved working with kids, so this is perfect.

The lift stops and the doors open behind me.

"This is the fourth floor," Mrs Minter announces. *The fourth? Wow. How big is this place?*

I back out with my suitcase and when we're all out in the corridor, Lucie tugs Mrs Minter's hand. "She does, doesn't she?" she hisses, obviously continuing an earlier conversation.

I kneel down, fixing my gaze on Lucie's huge dark eyes. "What do I do, Lucie?" I keep my expression open and non-judgmental. I know it sounds weird, but I always remind myself to speak with love when I'm working with kids. It sets my energy system up correctly, and the day goes much better from there. They respond better too, but then we all respond best to love, don't we? Sometimes, though, when everything feels like shit, it's hard to remember.

Lucie looks up at Mrs Minter for approval. She, in turn, glances down at Lucie with an appreciative smile on her face.

"Go ahead," Mrs Minter says, and Lucie fixes her eyes on mine, more sure of herself now.

"You look like The Little Mermaid. From the cartoon. You have orange hair."

I smile, but make sure not to laugh. I don't want her to think I'm making fun of her. "Shall I tell you a secret?" I whisper, and she leans in, eyes wide. "I reckon it's actually red." I twist a strand of it around my finger and hold it out toward Lucie, who stares at it like it's made of gold.

"I'd say it's a mixture of the two," Mrs Minter interjects, sounding as though she's really considered the issue. "Reddish-orange."

"I love it," Lucie coos, still transfixed by my hair. "Mine is boring. It's dark brown, like Daddy's."

"You have great hair," I say, ruffling the top of her head as I stand. *And so does your dad.*

Damn. I kind of hate that my thoughts went right there.

When it's apparent Lucie has nothing more to say, Mrs Minter directs me to a room at the end of the corridor.

"This is Lucie's floor. There's a separate kitchen up here for you, a bathroom and her bedroom. Charlie's room is on the floor below."

"Ah, right. And Charlie is Mr Hawkston's son?"

"Yes. He's sixteen. Nearly seventeen. He'll be home for the summer in a few weeks."

Sixteen. So he's a decade younger than me. And his father is maybe ten years older. I wonder to what extent Charlie will be my responsibility when he's home.

I drag my bag into my room, with its plain white walls and single bed. I'm in the eaves, so the ceiling slants harshly over the headboard. There's a dresser, a wardrobe, and a dormer window that looks out onto the street below.

"Can I show you my room?" Lucie says, her tiny hand slipping into mine.

Mrs Minter smiles. "Shall I let you two get acquainted? Lucie can show you around the house."

Lucie bounces up and down. "Yay. Let's start with my room and the playroom."

"Don't go into Daddy's room though. Or his study," Mrs Minter says.

"Yes, Mrs Minter," Lucie replies, clipping the heels of her shoes together and standing bolt upright. She looks like she's used to obeying rules.

"Have you had lunch?" Mrs Minter asks me. I shake my head and she checks her watch. "Twenty-minute tour of the house and then come back to the kitchen in the basement. I'll get chef to make Lucie's lunch and we can all eat together."

Lucie jumps on the spot and claps her hands. "Come on, Ariel. I'll show you everything."

"You can call me Aries," I say. "It's nearly the same."

"Oh yes, I know." Lucie's gorgeous little face pinches into a serious expression. "But I don't want to."

Right. I guess that's that then. Ariel it is, for the foreseeable.

She shows me her room first, opening her cupboards so I can see her rows of beautiful designer dresses and shoes. I try to fake the enthusiasm she's expecting, rather than the shock I'm feeling at the opulence of the contents of her wardrobe. I suspect there are going to be multiple opportunities for me to be shocked at the wealth on display in this house. My mind is already blown, and I'm conscious of how my body is reacting to it. Mum always said if displays of extreme wealth make you uncomfortable, then it's like sending a message to the universe that you don't want money.

I try to keep that in mind, but it's almost impossible when Lucie parades me through the house, which is decorated like no home I've ever seen, with plush fabrics and sleek lines, and furniture that looks too good to touch, let alone sit on. There's not a spot of dirt on anything, anywhere, and I can't help but feel a little bit overawed.

Lucie proudly takes me to the basement to show me the full gym, sauna, and indoor pool. It's like a luxury spa, with mirrored walls. I can see myself from every angle, and it makes the space feel even bigger than it already is.

There's music playing from speakers hidden in the walls, even though no one's here. It's as if the ambiance is set, just in case Mr Hawkston decides to take a dip. *Unbelievable*.

We take the lift to the very lowest level, where the doors open into an underground car park. There are five cars parked down here: a red Ferrari, a black Bentley, a McLaren, a Lamborghini, and a sleek silver Mercedes, which is the most discreet of the lot. There are two more spaces, perhaps in case they have visitors. Safe to say Mr Hawkston likes his cars.

"Which would you choose?" Lucie asks. "I like the red one."

I huff out a little chortle of laughter. "I'll take the McLaren," I say, pointing at it. "Because I bet it goes really fast."

For some reason, an image of Mr Hawkston sitting behind the wheel, a pair of dark sunglasses perched on the bridge of his nose, his large hands gripping the wheel, cords of muscle flexing up his forearms, flashes in my mind.

Am I drooling?

Lucie giggles, and I check my watch. "Let's go to lunch. Mrs Minter will be waiting."

3
MATT

I let myself back into the house, loosening my tie as I take a moment to shed the stress of the day. I don't like to take business meetings at the weekend, but sometimes it happens. It's nearly 7 pm, and Mrs Minter will be heading out. I want to catch her before she leaves.

The house is quiet, but that's no guarantee it's empty. The playroom is on the fourth floor, so if Lucie is up there, I wouldn't hear her. I briefly wonder if the new nanny is getting on all right and an odd burst of amusement ripples through me as I remember what she said earlier.

A voice that could deep-fry a Mars Bar.

I'm assuming she meant it as a compliment, but what kind of woman says that sort of thing to a man she's just met? And what kind of woman has no idea she's talking to her new employer? It's not as if I have a low profile. I'm easy to find online with a quick search. Maybe she was serious when she said she goes off her gut, and all that she needed was to talk to Lucie to know she wanted the job. But how the fuck could she even hear her gut over all that nervous chattering she was doing?

Gut instinct, indeed. To my surprise, a low chuckle works its way up my throat. It's absurd, but I'm willing to give her the benefit of the doubt, because although her constant chatter was irritating, it was also somewhat endearing. What made her so nervous? *Was it me?*

A curious flicker of satisfaction ignites at the thought, and I quickly snuff it out.

If Mrs Minter thinks Aries is right for the role, then she likely is. The woman is a fantastic judge of character, which is probably why she and Gemma, my ex-wife, never got along that well.

Something in my chest tenses at the thought of Gemma. I try not to think about her if I possibly can. Our son caught her cheating in this house, on the kitchen table no less. We have a new table now... I made sure of that. And Gemma... I try to see her as little as possible, even though she bought a house almost identical to this one just down the street. Far too close, in my opinion. But Gemma figured it would make life easy on all of us if Lucie's experience of spending time with her parents separately was as similar as possible. Even the decor is the same. Home, but not home. It's as though Gemma is trying to trick us all into thinking we still live in the same house.

This summer, Gemma has asked for time away from the kids. She wants to be free to take as many holidays and foreign trips as she pleases. I didn't ask why. I don't care. But I needed someone here permanently to care for Lucie if I'm to have her all summer.

I get that Gemma can walk away from me, but to walk away from Lucie too? That, I can't understand. I might not be the most present father, but I love my kids more than anything in the world.

It's only one summer, I suppose.

The click of heels on the floor draws my attention and I look up to find Mrs Minter standing before me, buttoning up her camel trench coat.

"Mr Hawkston," she greets, and I nod. "Is there anything you need before I head home?"

"A word, actually," I say, beckoning her to follow me to my office. I hold the door for her to pass in before me, then close it behind us.

"The nanny," I say as I walk around my desk and take a seat behind it. Mrs Minter stands to attention on the other side.

"Yes?" she says, caution evident in her tone. I'm immediately alert. *Does Mrs Minter expect me to have issues with this woman already?*

"She's been fully checked out and vetted?"

"Of course. Background checks run. She has an excellent record. I spoke with her former employers. They all raved about her. Said she's honest and trustworthy and very loving."

Loving? "She's not your usual hire. Not a Norland Nanny."

Mrs Minter's lips purse at the mention of the esteemed agency. *What is she not telling me?* "If you don't like her, I can find someone else. But Lucie's very fond of her. They've been playing together all afternoon. I've just left them doing bath time and Aries is going to put her to bed if you want to go up in half an hour to say goodnight."

Aries. What a fucking ridiculous name. "Thank you. And you're fully behind this hire?"

"I am. I sent you all her details. Her CV. You approved it."

"I did?"

Mrs Minter narrows her eyes on me, but there's a softness there too. She knows as well as I do that I've not been on the ball since the divorce. "You did, sir."

I scratch the back of my neck. "All right. Thanks."

"Will that be all?" she asks, as she fixes her last button, and I nod. "Then I'll bid you good night and see you in the morning. Don't hesitate to call me if you need anything. We did a walk around the area so Aries knows where the nursery is and the routine. If there's anything she doesn't know, she has my number. I doubt she'll need to disturb you at all."

For some reason, the idea of this strange young woman not disturbing me *at all* doesn't feel great, but I don't let it show on my face.

"Great. Thank you. It's an important role, caring for Lucie. But you know that..."

Mrs Minter smiles, and her face wears such a kind expression that an odd feeling of comfort seeps through my chest. Perhaps this is what it feels like to be looked at by a mother who actually gives a flying fuck. I wouldn't know.

"Lucie is a wonderful little girl, Mr Hawkston. And to my mind, Aries is the perfect woman to nurture her, if you can bear to give her a chance to settle in. I know she's a bit... much."

Much? Understatement of the century. "I think I can bear it," I reply, my voice expressionless.

Mrs Minter smiles again and bows her head to excuse herself before she leaves the room.

I sit alone for a few moments, not wanting to rush out after her and appear too eager in my rush to see Lucie and Aries. But I'm itching to go upstairs and I last less than a minute at my desk. I rarely take the lift, preferring the exercise of the steps, and tonight I take them faster than usual.

When I reach the landing the sound of Lucie's giggles coming from the bathroom greets me, frothy and delicate like bubbles. *So fucking easy to pop.* When Gemma and I were together, Lucie's laughter died pretty quickly if she heard us fighting.

Aries' voice, light and full of laughter, stretches along the corridor. "Oh, no, you've soaked me."

I approach the bathroom door and gently tap it with my knuckle.

"Yes?"

"It's..." I pause for a moment, wondering what to call myself.

"Daddeeeeeee!" comes Lucie's excited squeal and I push open the door, to find her still in a bath, half-submerged beneath more bubbles than I've ever seen. The surface of the water is entirely obscured, and still more bubbles dangle from Lucie's chin like a flimsy white beard.

"Ho ho ho, Daddy. I'm Father Christmas." She scoops up more foam in her palm and holds it out to me. "Can I make you Father Christmas too?"

I glance at Aries, who's kneeling by the bathtub, long red hair falling down her back. Her eyes are green, but not pure green—a million colours are swirling in there—*Christ*, I'm far too close to her if I can see that. The thought causes discomfort beneath my ribcage, but even so, I can't stop looking because her eyes seem to glisten with happiness. I've never seen eyes like them.

My gaze falls to her white t-shirt, which is sopping wet and entirely transparent. She's not wearing a bra, and her breasts are distractingly large. The impulse to reach out and cup one in each hand and brush my thumbs over the nipples assaults my mind.

I frown, averting my eyes as quickly as I can, but I've already taken it all in. A longing I haven't felt for years begins to pump in my veins. *Fuck, this woman is attractive.*

Aries' eyes widen and her mouth forms a small O-shape, like she noticed me noticing. A second later, water splashes her from the bath and she breaks into a beautiful smile again.

"Water stays in the bath," she says, laughing.

"Daddy," Lucie cries, leaning over the side with the bubbles in her cupped hands, bath water running in rivulets to the floor from her elbows. "Let me put them on you. You need a beard."

Relenting, I kneel next to Aries, the water on the floor soaking the knees of my suit, while Lucie smears the bubbles over my chin. It strikes me that Gemma and I never did this with either of the kids... we never sat together at bath time. There's a disconcerting rightness to being here with Aries that makes me feel as if I've wandered into a parallel life.

Lucie sits back, admiring her handiwork. "There we go. Now you're like King Triton."

"King Triton?" Aries questions. "Oh, no, look…" Aries grabs a dry flannel from the side of the bath, and before I know it, she's wiping the bubbles from my chin. Her eyes dance with glee, until suddenly they don't, as though she's realised how incredibly inappropriate what she's doing is. Her hand stills for a moment, and worry fills her expression as she raises her gaze to mine.

"What?" Lucie says.

Aries puts the flannel down on the side of the bath. "I was going to say Daddy looks much more like Prince Eric." She smiles at Lucie. "But then again…" She tilts her head, affecting an inspection of me, more for Lucie's benefit than mine. "He's more like a cross between the two. Big and grumpy like Triton, but handsome like Eric. Either way…" She fixes on me now. "You have a face that looks like someone drew you."

I'm completely at a loss with this woman. "You have no filter, do you?"

The light in her eyes dies, the width of her mouth shrinking. Her hands collapse to her lap, where she clasps them tight. I press my lips together to seal in the urge to apologise that crawls up my throat.

"What's a filter?" Lucie says.

"It means I talk a lot of nonsense," Aries replies, still smiling—*does she ever not?*—but there's a strange sadness in her eyes that I'm sorry to see. And to think I caused it… but then, lines have already been crossed here. I'll have to put the boundaries in place and keep them. At least she's only here for the summer.

"Doesn't she look like The Little Mermaid, Daddy?"

Without thinking, I let my gaze travel over Aries again, drinking her in. She might look like a Disney Princess to Lucie, but that's not what I'm seeing. I'm seeing breasts and curves, and full lips and hair I want to wrap around my fist. A prickling heat roars to life low in my hips. *The things I'd like to do to her...*

Aries tilts her head to the side, and her bright eyes narrow as if she knows exactly what I'm thinking. Sparks jump between us like we're two exposed live wires, and my body begins to tingle all over.

"We watch that movie together a lot," Lucie continues, directing herself to Aries this time, clearly getting impatient with my lack of response. "Daddy says Ariel was the first lady he fell in love with. Before he met Mummy."

Aries gets up, reaching for a towel from the heated rail. "Then Daddy has good taste," she states, holding the towel wide while Lucie clambers out of the bath, and then wrapping her up in it.

There's a strange tension in the room, as if something is happening between me and Aries that neither of us has agreed to, and we're trying to pretend it's not there. Perhaps it's those sparks of attraction—*did she feel it too?*—or perhaps it's the uncomfortable remnants of our bizarre first encounter out in the garden. I could have stopped her making a fool of herself; I should have done, but she was so beautiful, so captivating, that I was happy to listen to her babble.

I stand and plant a chaste kiss on the top of my daughter's head. "I'll come and give you a kiss goodnight when you're in bed."

Lucie's arms snake out from under her towel and she hugs my legs, speaking into my knees. "I love you, Daddy. I love you the most in the whole world, to infinity and beyond."

This kid is going to make my heart melt. I definitely don't deserve this much love. I crouch so I'm at her eye-level. She stares at me with those deep brown eyes that are mirrors of my own, and I want to tell her I love her, but it feels strange to vocalise it knowing Aries is standing right there, watching us. I don't know this woman, and having her watch me interact with my daughter feels far too intimate. But this isn't about me or Aries, this is about Lucie, so I swallow down my hesitation and say the words. "Love you too. The most. In the whole, entire world."

"In the whole entire universe?" she asks, her voice small but eager.

I break into a smile, and this time it's 100% genuine, unencumbered by Aries watching. "The universe," I repeat.

Lucie grins and I kiss her cheek, ruffle her wet hair and stand again.

I glance at Aries, who meets my gaze with no embarrassment whatsoever, which is impressive, given she was wiping my jaw with a flannel only five minutes ago, and she's just listened to me telling my kid I love her. But then, maybe expressions of love aren't weird for Aries the way they are for me. I don't remember being told I was loved as kid, so it's been tough to be natural about it with my own children. I've tried, though. "Have you eaten?" I ask Aries.

"Yes. I ate with Lucie. Lunch and dinner. Your chef is excellent."

I give a slow nod, making sure to keep my eyes on her face, rather than the heavy weight of her breasts in the wet t-shirt. "If you're not too tired, join me for a nightcap at nine. There are some things we need to discuss about your position."

A flicker of something shadows her eyes. Worry, perhaps. It's on the tip of my tongue to say something to alleviate whatever concern she's feeling, but I don't. That's not my role.

"About earlier," she says. "I should never have made all those assumptions. All my fault. I'm sorry. I was—"

"Nervous. Yes. You said that. But seeing as you aren't one to Google people, you might as well get to know me face-to-face. Nine o'clock. Downstairs in the dining room."

That hint of worry never leaves her face, but she agrees to the meeting. I give Lucie another kiss and leave them to do the bedtime routine.

Evening light streams in the dining room windows, a hint of orange in the night sky. We're approaching the longest day, and it's still bright outside.

I'm sitting at the head of a dining table that's far too long for one man who lives alone with his four year old daughter. It's like a scene from Beauty and the Beast. I snort at the thought. Aries and Lucie have me comparing real-life scenarios to Disney cartoons. A pretty miserable comparison too.

The house is silent but for the tick of the grandfather clock in the hall. Eerie, but I'm so used to it I hardly notice. I push my plate away and pour myself a glass of wine. I take a sip of the deep red, feeling the tannin hit my teeth.

I let a lot of the staff go after the divorce went through. They're still on the payroll, but I sent them with Gemma. I prefer the house this way. It does mean that I normally clear my own plate after I eat. But not always. Either way, it's gone in the morning; I still have enough staff to make sure that's the case.

Tonight, there's no one in the house but me, Lucie, and the new nanny. Aries.

Who calls their child Aries? An odd hollowing sensation starts in my stomach as her name passes through my mind. *Maybe not hollowing... maybe flipping.*

A tentative knock at the door breaks my contemplation.

"Come in."

Aries, in a fresh, dry t-shirt, enters. She closes the door and stands before it, her hands clasped. The stance is more formal than I expected.

"Yes, sir?"

The question hangs in the air, and something about the way her voice edges up, that soft Scottish accent folding over the sounds, sets me on edge. Or maybe it's her use of the word 'sir'. Either way, I'm unsettled. And when she looks like *that*... so casually sensual, effortlessly sexy, with the breasts and the hair and the lips and the bare fucking feet... I can't help imagining the filthy instructions I want to give her...

I abort the thought and force my face into neutral. It's wrong to think of the woman who's here to care for my daughter that way.

"Take a seat," I say, gesturing to the chair at my right hand side. There's nothing friendly about my tone, and Aries' usually relaxed brow creases, while her full, pink lips pull tight. The smile she so readily brandishes is absent, and I regret that I've frightened it away. I have to smother the urge to apologise, to put her at ease, to do *something* to bring it back. This is a professional relationship, and I need to keep those boundaries in place.

She doesn't look at me as she sits. There's a compressing sensation in my chest, as if she's radiating some kind of force. It's mildly alarming.

She places her phone on the table. I stare at it as I haven't seen a model that old in years. "What's that?" I ask.

She looks up, noticing my focus. "Oh. My phone."

"You can't use that."

She runs her fingers over it but doesn't lift it up. "It works. I use it all the time. Calls and texts. That's all I need it to do."

To my amazement, she appears completely serious. "What if you get lost? You're new to London, aren't you?"

"I am. I'm not worried about getting lost. I'll ask someone."

"You'll... *ask someone?*"

Those large green eyes expand, and I get the sense she's suffering the same amazed bafflement I am, but for an entirely different reason. "Yes. And I have an A to Z upstairs. It's small. I can take it in my handbag—"

"An A to Z?" I blurt. I haven't seen one of the pocket street maps of London for about a decade. They became redundant when the smartphone came in. "Where did you get one of those?"

"Ebay."

This woman is something else. "I'm ordering you a new phone." I lift my own phone, intending to send my PA a message about it.

A small, slim-fingered hand touches my wrist. It's so unexpected that I nearly drop my phone. I don't know if Aries noticed my reaction, but if she did, she doesn't comment on it.

"Please, don't," she says, her hand still resting on my wrist.

Why is she touching me? "Don't?"

She shakes her head, causing locks of red hair to ripple over her shoulders. "I'm a firm believer that we're all too sucked into our screens nowadays. I'm a better person without a smartphone, trust me. And do you know how many nannies I've seen who take the kids to the park and barely acknowledge them? They're glued to their screens, watching something or reading or... something that takes them away from the children they're meant to be caring for. Wouldn't you rather I wasn't distracted?"

"I'd rather you had the discipline to control yourself around a mobile phone."

She holds my gaze, her eyebrows slowly rising. "There's been research that people feel less connected to you if your phone is in view. You don't even have to be using it to sever the human connection."

Her slender fingers are still resting on my wrist and I don't know why the fuck she isn't moving them, or why I'm not saying anything about it. I haven't been touched with tenderness by a woman in way too long. I'm vaguely aware of a strange fizzing sensation in my body, like my blood is carbonated.

"You were the one who put it on the table." I sound sharp, but I'm not sure it's about the phone.

"Sorry."

She still hasn't moved her hand, and the silence is charged like an electric vehicle, as if we could turn the ignition and *something* would race off at a million miles an hour.

"About this afternoon," I say, and her face scrunches, her hand slipping off my wrist. "It's important that this relationship is professional at all times. You'll address me as Mr Hawkston, and restrain the urge to make inappropriate comments. For clarity, that means comments about my appearance. In fact, I'd urge a greater sense of discretion in general. Is that clear?"

"Crystal. No referring to my boss as Prince Eric, or King Triton or—"

"Superman."

She holds my gaze, and her eyes appear to sparkle, her lips tight like she's holding back a smile. Either that or she's waiting for me to smile so she can release her own.

I don't. I'm entirely fucking serious. If this woman is in my house, tossing all that red hair around and calling me *Superman*, then I'm going to be in big trouble. I pull down the cuff of my shirt to cover the area of skin where her fingertips were resting only moments ago, trying to ignore the fact I can still feel her there.

"Also, I ask that you refrain from touching me." She inhales so sharply it's audible. "I'm not implying anything, but I want to be explicit from the outset. This is a professional relationship. I cannot be your friend. Quite aside from the fact I don't have time, I'm your boss. I'm not someone who can help you settle in or show you around."

A rosy redness rushes up her throat and across her cheeks like a rising blood moon. Maybe I've hammered this home too hard. But it's as much for my benefit as it is for hers.

"I'm sorry," I add. "I wouldn't think it necessary to have this conversation, but I don't want our earlier interaction to set the tone for what has to be a professional relationship going forward."

She lowers her head and nods without looking at me.

Silence falls between us like snow: thick and cold, but it doesn't last long before Aries' head snaps up, her eyes flashing at me as though she wants to fight. "You could have told me who you were. You let me go on, knowing you were my boss. You could have put a stop to my humiliation immediately, but you didn't."

I take a sip of wine, eyeing her over the rim of my glass. She's alluring like this, all fired up. I like that she has the gumption to stick up for herself. Hopefully, she'll do it for the kids too, should the need arise. "It was wrong of me. I apologise. But it's rare that someone doesn't know who I am. Your assumptions amused me."

She stands from the table, picks up her ancient phone, and tucks it into her back pocket. "Then, Mr Hawkston, I would ask that in future, you don't allow me to continue making mistakes purely because they amuse you. That way, we'll both know where we stand."

I sit straighter in my chair, a little in awe of this young woman. I give her a nod so slight it's little more than an eye movement. She bows her head like she's excusing herself from the presence of royalty and turns to leave.

"Wait," I say.

"Yes?"

"Tell me how you found this role?"

"I interviewed. I told you that."

Something's off. "That's not how you found it though."

She concentrates on me. "You should make a note of this moment." She nods, suddenly eager as if something exciting is happening. "Because you're doing it. Gut instinct. Right now. That's why you're asking the same question, again. Your intuition is speaking to you."

My skin prickles and it irks me that she's talking about intuition like it's some magic thing. "Gut instinct... or intuition, if that's what you want to call it, is nothing more than fast data processing. That's all. The subconscious mind, analysing at high-speed. It happens so quickly that we're not aware of it." I don't know why I'm engaging in this shit. I drag my focus back to the matter in hand. "Are you going to answer my question?"

"Didn't Mrs Minter tell you where she found me?"

"No."

"I probably shouldn't tell you then."

This is the second time today I've thought Mrs Minter's keeping something from me. "You've started now, so you'd better tell me."

"My mother was her father's healer."

I frown, replaying her statement in my mind. "What does that mean? Is your mother a doctor?"

"No. She's an energy healer. Mrs Minter's father was her client. She gave him weekly distance healing sessions before he died. To help him cope with the cancer treatments. Mum and Mrs Minter struck up a bit of a friendship, so when Mum said I was looking for work—"

"Hold on. Did you say 'distance healing'?" No matter how hard I try, I cannot keep the scepticism from my tone.

"I did. She's a reiki healer. Also sekhem."

"I don't even know what you just said."

Her mouth tilts up in a lopsided smile. "Are you joking? You aren't going to lose alpha points if you know what it is."

"Alpha points?"

She sighs, like I'm the one who's exasperating. She raises her palms towards me in demonstration, as though she's beaming rays of light from them. "Energy is everywhere. We can use the power of our intention to send it across space—"

I scoff. "So your mother waved her hands around in Scotland, while Mrs Minter's father was getting healed in South London. Is that what you're saying?"

"Exactly," Aries confirms, seemingly not bothered by the fact I'm struggling to keep a straight face. "And time. We can send it across time too."

I decide to let this go. There are all sorts of people in the world, believing all sorts of crap. "You are actually a nanny, aren't you?"

She smiles, like she wants to laugh, but is trying to keep it in check. "I have nannying experience. Yes. And I love kids. I've always wanted to work with them. Nothing fulfills me like seeing joy on their little faces and getting to share in that." She breaks eye contact and inhales deeply, as though she has to prepare herself for whatever she's about to say next. "But I needed this job for two reasons. First, the money. And second, because my mother wants me to be here."

"Why?"

There's a lengthy silence, during which an odd foreboding fills my stomach.

"Because she has terminal cancer and we don't have the cash to pay for decent care so she can be comfortable at home. If I'm not there, then someone else has to be," Aries says finally.

That's intense. I frown, hating myself because the first thing that comes to mind is that healing definitely doesn't work if the healer is sick. The second is that Aries delivered the information like she was reading a register. No emotion whatsoever. Maybe it's because this is her first day and she's not keen to expose her entire emotional range on one day. God knows she's already revealed a lot. Or maybe it's because it's too painful for her to make the declaration any other way. "I'm sorry to hear that."

She shrugs. "That's life. What I'll earn here this summer is enough to afford to have someone stay with her at home until…" She swallows and doesn't finish the sentence.

I feel painfully uncomfortable now. Like I ought to be giving her more, offering to pay for her mother's treatment. Her care. But somehow, I think Aries wouldn't want that, so instead I say, "You wouldn't rather be working closer to home?"

"No. She doesn't want me to waste my life sitting at her bedside. She wants to see me spread my wings. Follow my dreams. She wants to live to see that happen. Besides, you know… my gut instinct and all that. Mum's too. We both feel like I'm supposed to be here." Aries looks up at the ceiling and blinks a few times, as though she's hoping to drain tears back into the ducts before looking back at me. "And"—she manages a smile—"you pay by far the most, Mr Hawkston. It's worth it to be here."

I don't know what to say. Luckily, Aries is quick to fill the hiatus. "Your little girl is a delight. I know it's only my first day, but I enjoy her company, very much. She has a big heart. Huge. You can be proud of her."

The comment sends a surge of positive emotion through me and I smile, but the pleasure brings with it discomfort. I don't even know if I deserve to feel good about my kids. *Am I a good father? Have I been present enough?*

"Tomorrow," I say. "I had it scheduled to spend with Lucie, but seeing as you're new, we can all go together. Natural History Museum. You'll want to check the weather; make sure she's dressed appropriately. How will you do that without a phone?"

Aries doesn't bother trying to hide her surprise. "I'll look out the window." She delivers the line like I'm stupid, and for some reason it makes me want to laugh, but I don't. "Have her ready by half nine, then we can be at the museum before opening to avoid the queues."

"Yes, sir."

She turns and lets herself out of the dining room, and I watch her go. That mane of red hair is so long it almost grazes the apples of her arse cheeks, which are concealed by snug-fitting blue jeans. *So round and tempting.* I scold myself for letting the thought occur, but when she reaches out to open the door, the t-shirt she's wearing shifts upwards, revealing a thin strip of what looks to be a thong resting on her hip bone, and I know I'm going to have my work cut out to police my thoughts. She's temptation wrapped up in a perfect package.

Only when the door closes behind her do I realise that I never offered her a drink.

4
ARIES

Back in my room, I close the door and flop on the bed. *So comfy. Just firm enough without being hard.* I nestle on top of the duvet and pull out my mobile phone. Mum will be anxious to hear from me. I dial her number and wait.

"Aries." My name is little more than an excited squeal. "Oh, honey, how is it down there? Is it amazing?"

I relax at the sound of her voice. My mum is my best friend. It sounds weird, but after Dad left, it was me and her. A team. She became this rockstar energy healer, travelling around Scotland. I went with her and she home-schooled me as we went. Looking back, the whole thing was pretty wild. Dad leaving was probably the best thing that ever happened to her. She flourished, and I got to be raised by a mother who was happy and fulfilled by her calling in life.

"It's great." Should I tell her about mistaking my new boss for the gardener? *No.* She'll know as soon as I bring it up that I like the guy. Her intuition is always bang on. She's had enough time to hone it, that's for sure. "The house is amazing. And Mrs Minter seems lovely."

"And the kids?"

"There's only a little girl here right now. Lucie. Really cute. I think we'll get along. There's a teenage boy too, but he's away at boarding school."

Mum tuts. "I always think it's sad to send children away from home. They need to be with their parents."

"I disagree. It sounds like the house was miserable. Lots of fighting. Maybe it's better that he wasn't here." My chest tightens as fragmented memories ambush me. Hiding under the stairs, hoping the yelling would stop. Mum and Dad, screaming at each other...

Mum is quiet for a moment, and her voice is soft when she says, "Let it go, honey. It's over. Breathe it out."

She always knows what I'm thinking, and that soothing tone she uses works its magic. *Everything will be all right.* I breathe for a moment, following the sensations the memories drag through my body, and then, when they've all but dissipated, Mum says, "I love you, Aries. Even back then, when it was tough. I loved you."

A lump forms in my throat, and I swallow around it. "I know."

"Good," Mum says, as though she's closing the matter. "Your father called me."

I'm stunned into silence. *What the hell?* Dad left when I was six, never to be seen again. No birthday cards. No messages. *Nothing.* The idea that he would call is... *insane*.

"No way," I reply, once I've processed the information.

"Yes. It's a thing, apparently. People call when they find out you're dying. A conveyor belt of people you thought you'd got rid of, ringing you up to see how you are." Mum laughs, sounding genuinely amused despite the morbid topic. "It's hilarious really. 'I heard you're dying, so I thought I'd call.' Did I not make it clear enough at the time that I didn't want to hear from these people?"

I bite back a smile, shaking my head. "You're the most bitter spiritual healer I know."

"I'm not bitter." She states it like an indisputable fact. "I've sent them all unconditional love, but I don't actually want to hear from them in the 3D world. How they didn't get that message, I have no idea. I'd disconnect the phone, but then how would I speak to you? I guess we could use telepathy."

"Mum, this isn't funny."

She sighs. "We have to joke about this stuff, Aries. Otherwise, what would we do?"

The comment hangs in the air. I don't know what the answer is, but it feels heavy.

"Anyway," Mum continues, "I can sense something's up with you. How's the job? How's Mrs Minter? How's London? Tell me everything." I'm about to answer when she says, "No, wait. Let me sense it. Hmm."

I can picture her pulling that face she does when she's trying to read information in the ether; the intense focus, her eyelids flickering, revealing freakish slivers of the whites beneath the lashes.

"A man," she announces. "Looks like Clark Gable."

I snort. "There is a man, but he doesn't look like Clark Gable. Henry Cavill, maybe."

"Who's he? You know I only watch Golden Era Hollywood."

In my mind, I start drawing comparisons between Mr Hawkston and Henry Cavill, and I'm pretty sure Henry is losing. "You're missing out."

"Hmm, but there *is* a man... Wait... something else is coming through. A kind soul. Angry. But kind. You have a connection—"

"Mum, please. Enough with the Mystic Meg stuff."

She chuckles. Wheezes. Coughs. At the sound of her struggling, a stinging sensation hits the back of my nose. I'm helpless to ease her discomfort, and not just because I'm so far away. "I'm right though. This is a great opportunity for you."

I bristle. "What does that mean?"

"You don't like men. You don't trust them. And I don't blame you, after your father."

"I do like men. I—"

"Aries." Mum cuts me off. "Liking men for sex is not the same as liking men. Respecting men. Understanding what they can bring to a relationship and your life. Love is more than that. It's more than passion and breathlessness and orgasms that you can walk away from when the night is over. It's feeling completed by another person. Feeling *safe*. Finding someone who can be there for you when you need them. Someone you can rely on." Mum's sigh crackles down the line before she whispers, "I want that for you."

An uneasy sensation that reminds me of heartburn fires up in my chest. *She's worried about dying and me being alone.* "Did you have that? Love like that?"

There's a long pause. "No." There's so much unspoken emotion in that one word that it feels like a weight bearing down on my shoulders. "But it's too late for me."

"You're going to make me cry," I whisper, and that lump from earlier makes a reappearance in my throat.

Mum laughs softly. "Sorry. I don't mean to. I want to know there could be someone for you when I'm not here. That you're at least open to it. That you might be able to build your own family. Find the Yang to your Yin." Mum tuts and I imagine her shaking her head. "Not every man is going to be like your father."

I'm quiet for a moment. Mum thinks this is all about Dad, but it's not, and I can't correct her. I know how it feels to love someone, because I love her with all my heart. But I also know that I'm going to lose her, and that feeling will be unbearable.

Why would I open myself up to more of that? Casual sex isn't going to hurt that way, which suits me just fine.

I make an effort to roll my eyes even though she can't see me. It's easier to do that than to allow the meaning of her words to sink in. *I can't keep talking about this.* I decide to redirect the conversation to where we began. "What did my father want when he called?"

A strained silence falls. "He wanted to know what I'd left him in my will."

I gape. "He did not."

"Yes, he did. Said when he left, he didn't take all his stuff, so I owed him. I said he left twenty years ago and anything he left was long gone or garbage in the first place. And then he said, seeing as he gave me you, and you're the best thing either of us ever did, I ought to leave him something. As a thank you."

I clench my fist so hard that my fingernails dig into my palm. "Unbelievable. I mean, I am pretty great but I hope you told him where to stick—"

"I did. And then I hung up and sent him unconditional love."

Her deadpan delivery has me giggling, and I cover the handset so Mum can't hear, although I suspect she's doing the same on the other end. Thing is, she's also totally serious about the unconditional love.

"You should do it too," she says. "Send him love. Forgiveness."

"No."

"Come on, Aries. It doesn't mean you have to kiss and make up. You can forgive someone without ever seeing them again. Without ever telling them you forgive them. What is it I always say?"

Mum says a lot of things, but I know exactly which thing she means now, so I parrot it back at her. "Thinking negative things about other people only hurts me."

"Exactly. All those bad thoughts going through your head have vibrations, and those vibrations are going through every cell in your body." She doesn't say it'll make me sick, but I hear it as clearly as if she'd screamed it. I wonder what negativity she thinks did it for her, but the thought brings with it such an unpleasant curdling sensation in my gut that I shove it away. "It's within your power to change that. You always have the power, Aries. Don't forget it."

"I won't. I should get some sleep though. I love you."

"Love you too, honey. Speak soon. And be open to it."

"Open to what?"

"Having more than sex from a man."

"Do I look like a Princess?" Lucie asks the following morning as she appreciates her reflection in the pink-framed mirror on the dressing table. She blows herself a little kiss, and the action is so adorable I want to hug her. I've just spent the last ten minutes plaiting her hair and pinning it on top of her head.

"You do. Come on. Let's go. Daddy will be waiting."

Lucie has such a bright smile, it's infectious. But I'm too preoccupied to catch it this time, and I lead Lucie down the stairs on autopilot as my thoughts run rampant.

I'm oddly nervous at the idea of spending a day with Matt Hawkston, especially after my conversation with Mum last night. I told her I was going to sleep after we finished speaking, but instead, I cracked open my laptop and googled the shit out of my boss. It didn't feel creepy; he'd practically ordered me to do it.

He's one of three brothers who run the Hawkston Hotels Group, and there are over 6,000 Hawkston Hotels worldwide. I don't know why I never put two and two together when I read the names of my employers. Although, I've never stayed in a Hawkston Hotel. They're beyond my budget. I haven't even been inside one.

The net worth of the company varies depending on the source, but it's somewhere between ten and twelve billion. Their father heads up the New York office, but here in London, there are three brothers, all in their thirties; Nico, the eldest, then Matt, who I've worked out is thirty-five, and a younger brother, Seb. There are some incredible genes knocking around that family if the photos online are anything to go by, because all of them are drop-dead gorgeous. Like movie stars. And the ex-wife... wow, she's got to be one of the most beautiful women I've ever seen off the red carpet. Absolutely perfect features and long blonde hair. But in all the photos together, she and Mr Hawkston look miserable. No wonder they got divorced. They couldn't even fake it for the cameras.

I dreamt about Mr Hawkston last night too. It's hardly surprising given how long I researched him before I fell asleep. I tried to remember the details when I woke, but once my eyes were open, all that lingered was the sense of having done something wrong. Like I'd accidentally caught a glimpse of my boss in the shower. *And what a sight that would be.*

Mr Hawkston gives almost nothing away. He's harder to read than anyone I've ever met. And somehow I'm still convinced there's a man worth knowing behind the icy facade. Not that it makes a difference, because he let me know pretty clearly that I'm the staff and he's the boss, and that's the only relationship we'll have. Every time he mentioned professional boundaries, it felt like he was hitting my knuckles with a ruler. Or maybe putting me over his lap and spanking me for disobedience. *Naughty, Aries.*

Suddenly, Mum's voice sounds in my head. *You have a connection...*

I wish she hadn't said that. Planting seeds in my mind. Who knows what that one sentence could grow into? I'll have vines and weeds sprouting up all over the place. I mentally chop them all down and then focus my full attention on Lucie, reprimanding myself for being distracted by thoughts of her father yet again.

When we get downstairs, Mr Hawkston is standing in the hall, wearing a casual collared shirt and jeans. Not ripped ones this time. He's so distractingly good-looking that my steps falter. Lucie glances at me, checking I'm still standing. I smile to reassure her, trying not to melt as her father's gorgeous dark eyes take me in with the briefest of sweeps—so brief it's dismissive—before settling on his daughter.

My gaze settles on him a lot longer. His shirt, a pale blue and white striped cotton one, is open at the neck, sleeves rolled to the elbow. There are lines of muscle that run the length of his forearms, and on one wrist he wears a heavy-looking watch. The strap is thick, chocolate brown leather and the face is large. If I was a watch woman, I'd know what brand it is. I'm not and I don't, but there's something about the way he wears it that is undeniably sexy, as if somehow, this man might have time under his control.

I'm three steps away from him when the smell hits me: a wall of exotic cologne. It's layered and delicate and masculine and mouth-wateringly delicious all at once. It's like the best parts of a forest on a warm summer's day, if that forest also included a high-end spa full of half-naked men.

Half-naked men? Where did that thought come from? Was it last night's dream?

I take the final steps towards Mr Hawkston as a hot blush creeps over my face. One of the worst things about my complexion is that my embarrassment or discomfort is scrawled over my cheeks in the form of an aggressively red blush. I once watched an episode of a TV show where the woman went beetroot red if the guy she fancied came anywhere near her. I'm pretty sure she went to hospital for treatment.

My face is so hot right now, I feel like her.

Fortunately, Mr Hawkston hasn't looked back at me since that first eye-sweep. He's crouching with his arms open, and Lucie's running towards him, squealing. It's as if she hardly ever sees him. Just how unusual is it for this man to spend a whole day with his daughter?

He hugs her, then, still crouching, looks over her head at me. "Ready?"

"Daddy, Daddy, do you like my hair? Ariel did it."

Twin furrows appear between his brows. "You should call her Aries. That's her name."

Lucie folds her lips in on one another. She looks upset to be reprimanded, and I feel the urge to speak up on her behalf.

"I don't mind."

"I mind." Mr Hawkston cuts across me. "Your name is Aries."

My teeth tug against my bottom lip. *God, this man is severe.* "Okay."

"Do you like it though, Daddy?" Lucie repeats, touching her plaited hair, clearly desperate to keep her father's attention for just a moment longer.

"It's great," he replies, but the tone is dismissive and Lucie knows it.

There's a crackling tension in the air, and I don't understand why. *Is he angry about something?*

"Are you sure you want me to come?" I check. "If you already had the day—"

"I said so, didn't I?" His tone is sharp.

"Yes. Sorry."

He does the tiniest chin shift to acknowledge my apology, then smiles at Lucie, and this time his full attention is on his daughter. "Ready, champ?"

She grins and slips her little hand into Mr Hawkston's larger one before we head out.

We arrive at the Natural History Museum when the doors open, so we don't have to queue. Lucie is clinging to Mr Hawkston's hand as we step inside the huge vaulted main chamber, and she stares up at the enormous whale skeleton.

He crouches beside her, pointing up at the bones, and whispering in her ear. She giggles and leans into him, and he catches her weight, his large forearm wrapped around her waist. Seeing him tend to his daughter this way makes him even more attractive. She's so happy to have his attention that I linger back, not wanting to intrude.

Why am I here at all? They planned this day together. Wouldn't it have been better to leave it that way? I wouldn't have minded, and from what Alec said, Mr Hawkston doesn't make much time for his kids. As it is, I feel a bit like a third wheel.

Mr Hawkston's phone rings and he pulls it out of his pocket, releasing Lucie from his embrace at the same time. He looks over his shoulder, searching for me, and I step into his line of sight. "I've got to get this. Can you..." He nods at Lucie, and I take her hand whilst he moves away to take his call.

"This whale is really huge, isn't it?" I say.

A serious expression falls over Lucie's face. "She's called Hope. Daddy told me that's her name. She could eat you in one mouthful."

She performs a giant gulp, followed by a swallow, and then rubs her tummy. It makes me laugh, and Lucie smiles widely in response.

We stare at Hope for a while, and I keep one eye on Mr Hawkston, who's pacing up and down not far away, gesticulating with one hand. He looks frustrated, if not downright angry.

Lucie notices where my focus is and pouts her bottom lip. "Daddy's always on the phone."

"Oh, yeah?"

"Yeah. He loves his phone more than me."

I tear my gaze from Mr Hawkston to look at his daughter. "Oh, that's not true. No one loves their phone more than their family."

She rolls her eyes, which looks incongruously adult on such a young child. "You'll see."

And indeed, I do see.

Lucie and I explore the entire blue zone and most of the green zone before Mr Hawkston gets off the phone. At one point I beckon him to join us so we can inspect the creepy crawlies together, because Lucie is so excited by them, but he waves me off with an irritated hand and I feel like an idiot for trying.

I'm beginning to think he just wanted me here today so he could get on the phone guilt-free while convincing himself that he really does take the time to spend with his daughter. I'm making assumptions, but it seems to fit with what I've seen so far and what Lucie has said.

Finally, just as we're about to head upstairs to check out the dodos and the volcanoes, Mr Hawkston finishes his call. He comes back over, face drawn into an indelible frown.

Lucie has her nose smashed up against a display case with what looks like a giant swordfish inside, her little hands splayed on the glass. I'm pretty sure she wants to climb in there, and someone is going to come and reprimand her at any moment, but for now, she's content and hasn't noticed her father's return. Which is definitely a good thing, because he doesn't look happy.

I walk to meet him. "If you need to go home, or back to work, I can take this from here," I say in a hushed tone.

He glares at me. "Did I say I wanted to leave?"

I stiffen. "No, I just thought, given the whole being on the phone... you're clearly busy—"

"Are you judging me?"

Wow, this conversation has spiraled. I've hit a nerve. Backtrack, backtrack. "No. I didn't mean it like that. I'm here to make things easier for you, and if you don't have time—"

"I'm here, aren't I?"

I should stop talking but, of course, I don't. "Not really. This was supposed to be your day with Lucie and it's nearly lunchtime and you've barely put that thing away." I gesture to his phone, which he's still clutching in his hand. I swear I see his knuckles tighten around it. "It's the weekend."

"I'm well aware what day of the week it is, Aries." He runs his other hand through his hair, then drags his palm down his face. "I'm busy, and I really don't like the way you're looking at me right now." My breath stutters. I want to contradict him, but his dark, angry eyes are fixed on me, and he speaks before I can. "You think I'm a shitty father."

Woah. "I don't."

"You do. I've seen that look before." He breaks eye contact, turning his gaze to the floor. His jaw is tight as he presses two fingers between his brows. He's silent for an unnaturally long time, and something about his stance has me holding my tongue. *Is he okay?* "Maybe you're right," he mutters finally. "I have stuff to deal with, and it's better if I'm not here at all than present, but totally distracted."

"That's true." His eyes widen as though he's surprised that I agreed, and my next words pour out in a rush. "I only meant that it's better for Lucie because she can tell your focus is elsewhere. To a little kid, that feels like they aren't important enough to command your attention. And that translates into generally feeling unimportant and growing up with low self-worth."

He frowns, and for a brief moment he looks completely taken aback by the barrage of amateur psychology I've hit him with. "Are you a therapist?" he asks, his voice harsh.

I cower a tiny bit. "No."

"Then perhaps you should keep your opinions to yourself." *Shit. Nice one, Aries.* "I'm going back to the office. The car will take you and Lucie wherever you want to go." He opens his wallet and pulls out a credit card. "Take this. Put everything on it. Food. Tickets. Whatever. Keep it for expenses while you're here."

I take the card from him without a word.

"Daddy?" Lucie must have noticed our discussion, because she's no longer peering into the display case. She's staring up at her father, her eyes welling with tears.

Mr Hawkston winces a little. It clearly pains him to let her down, but he does it anyway. "I'm really sorry, but I'm going to have to go back to work."

"No! Daddy, no—"

"I'm sorry. There's a big deal that's supposed to complete tomorrow and I—"

"I hate you." She stamps her foot and clenches her hands into tiny fists that hang at her sides. "You're the worst daddy in the whole world."

Mr Hawkston stiffens, and although he doesn't look at me, I sense he's acutely aware of me watching this interaction. "Lucie." Her name is a harsh reprimand. "That's no way to talk to your father."

Lucie's face crumples and she lets out a roaring wail, drawing the attention of people nearby. Mr Hawkston's face looks like thunder.

Trying my best not to scowl at him, I place my hand on Lucie's shoulder and crouch down to her level. "It's so disappointing, isn't it? That Daddy can't stay?"

The wailing stops as she stares at me with watery eyes. Her chin dimples, and she bites her quivering lip. Her little arms weave their way around my neck and she sobs into my shoulder.

Mr Hawkston's glare scratches my skin, as if all my clothes have turned to hessian. I try to ignore the discomfort, forcing myself to hold his gaze.

After a moment, his features soften and he touches the tips of his fingers to Lucie's head, but she burrows harder against me, and his fingers slide off, making something in my chest pinch. "I'll see you later," he whispers. "Come find me this afternoon."

Lucie twists her head and glowers at her father. "I'll spend the day with Ariel." Then she sticks her tongue out and blows a raspberry. "I like her more than you."

Mr Hawkston's nostrils flare, but he backs off, casting one last lingering look at his daughter before he turns and marches away, disappearing between display cases and other museum visitors.

"Don't worry," I say to Lucie, whose tremulous gaze is fixed on her father's retreating form. "We're going to have the best day ever."

By the time we get home, it's after 4 pm. I'm exhausted, and Lucie is weary too. I did my best to cheer her after Mr Hawkston's departure. We had pizza in South Kensington, and afterwards we spent a couple of hours in Kensington Gardens. Despite the fact that we had a car to drive us around everywhere, I still spent a lot of time standing and my feet are aching.

"What shall we do now?" I ask, once we're back in the house. I slide off my shoes, unbuckle Lucie's sandals, and leave them in the boot room in the basement.

"Popcorn and a movie," Lucie suggests, flashing me an irresistible smile.

We make our way to the kitchen, and Lucie directs me to a cupboard where there are multiple bags of posh popcorn in every flavour imaginable. She picks the salted caramel, and we take it to the cinema room.

It's entirely dark in here because there are no windows, but when we enter, four elegant wall lights flick on. They cast a golden glow over the room, making it feel like a real cinema. The carpet is a plush deep red, and the cinema chairs are wide and luxurious. The screen is enormous too; larger than any TV I've ever seen in a private house.

Lucie hops up onto what's effectively a large love seat in the front row and taps the cushion next to her. "Sit with me."

We settle on the sofa, choose the newest DreamWorks animated movie on Netflix, and Lucie shouts for the lights to go off, which they obediently do.

She nestles into me, and her hair smells like baby shampoo. Her readiness to trust me, a complete stranger only yesterday, tugs at my heart. She's so innocent, so vulnerable, and I find myself thinking about how harshly Mr Hawkston reprimanded her today at the museum. She'd clung to me after I'd expressed the tiniest hint of empathy.

Does she ever get that from her father? It's clear she loves him, given how excited she is whenever he appears... but how often is he too busy to attend to her emotional needs?

In the cinema room, we share the popcorn until the bag is empty. The room is warm, the seat incredibly comfortable. It's not long before Lucie falls asleep, but I let the movie run. I don't want the sudden silence of turning it off to shock her into wakefulness. In the cosy darkness, it's not long before my eyes drift shut too.

I wake, confused. *Where am I?* The empty packet of popcorn crinkles in my lap as I rouse, and I remember. The cinema screen is blank, and panic shoots through me. I must have fallen asleep. *What time is it?* I fumble for my phone, wishing briefly that I had one with a torch on it.

The screen lights up. 6.07 pm. *Thank goodness it's not too late.*

Lucie is still sleeping beside me, the low rumble of her snoring filling the room. I stretch and yawn as I ease myself out of the seat. I'm about to lift Lucie too, when I hear a noise somewhere further down the corridor. It's the whirring pulse of machinery and the thump of quick footsteps. *What is that?* I creep down the darkened corridor, following the sound.

The door to the gym is wide open, casting a rigid box of light across the dim hall, and the cold air conditioning filters out, penetrating the warmth of the corridor as though I'm standing before an open freezer door. I tiptoe forwards and peer inside, keeping to the shadows. The gym walls are white, and there are multiple high-end gym machines, weights, and everything else you'd expect in a public gym. There are even duplicates of some machines. Perhaps Mr and Mrs Hawkston used to exercise side by side. The idea doesn't sit well, like a film of grease sliding over the contents of my stomach. But why should it bother me? They were married. It's only natural that they did things together. I shake off the odd sensation. *Maybe I ate something bad.*

Mr Hawkston is running on the treadmill. He's wearing only a pair of grey shorts, while what looks like a damp t-shirt hangs on the bars of a standing bike nearby. I don't know how long he's been here, but it's long enough to have worked up a sweat all over. His broad, muscled back shines like he's coated in oil. There's a mirrored wall in front of him, and I can see his chest, which is just as slick and as defined as his back. The ridges of his abs are practically cliffs and ravines. It's the definition of a washboard. Just how much time does he spend down here?

His face wears a pained expression and he's blowing breaths out, his legs and arms pumping hard. There's a raw masculinity pulsing off him that's hard to resist. I tilt towards him, desperate to get closer. What would it feel like to touch that body? What would this man be like in bed? His skin, sweat-slicked, and his muscles firm against me?

Shit. A low, aching pulse of arousal begins between my legs. I should stop staring and leave, but I don't want to. My heart is thumping like a fist beating against a wall.

He presses a button to stop the treadmill, his footfall slowing. He reaches for a nearby towel, wiping his face and the back of his neck. *Holy hell, he is breathtaking.*

I close my eyes and shake my head. I cannot be thinking this way about my boss, but when he's on display like this—

"Can I help you?"

My stomach plunges at the sound of his voice, and I creak open an eye. The treadmill is stationary now. He faces me as he steps off it, holding my gaze. His stare is an accusation, but even though guilt flashes through my system, it doesn't stop my gaze skimming down his body. *Delicious.* The pulse between my legs kicks up a notch.

He pushes his dark hair off his face as sweat trickles down his chest. I can't help but follow the trail down his skin, where the V of muscles is visible above the darkened waistband of his shorts.

I take it all in at lightning speed, but his eyes narrow when mine land back on his. He's fully aware I've checked him out. My face is so hot I think my cheeks could fry eggs. *I shouldn't be here. What must he think of me?*

"How long have you been standing there?" He speaks each word slowly, as if the answer *matters*.

I step confidently into the light of the doorway, emerging from the shadows of the darkened hallway. *Might as well own the fact that I'm here, now he's caught me.* I blink in the sudden brightness. For once, I'm speechless. Mr Hawkston tilts his head and steps in my direction. I can smell him; his cologne mixed with sweat and body odor. I briefly wonder if this version of his scent is even more appealing than the straight smell of his cologne.

I must be losing my mind.

I grapple for words. Excuses. Anything. All the while he's stalking towards me, closer and closer, until he's so close I could run my fingertip—*or my tongue*—through the sweat on his abs.

"Sorry," I mutter. "About earlier, at the museum—"

"Don't mention it. It is what it is." *Holy crap, this man is attractive.* When his eyes meet mine, there's a hint of something there... not much, but definitely a little amusement. "For the record, I prefer this expression"—he nods at my face—"to the judgmental one I got at the museum."

Heat rages through me, and I can only imagine what expression he's talking about. *Is it that I'm mindlessly drooling over him? Am I that obvious?*

"Oh. Ha. Um..." *Speechless.* He's rendered me speechless—*again*—in his sweaty near-nudity.

"Aries?"

I startle, jolting into a more upright stance and yanking my gaze back up to his face from where I was staring at his abs. *Again.* "Yes?"

"What are you doing down here?"

"I..." *Crap. Why am I here?* "I got lost."

Got lost? Damn it. I could have come up with something better than that.

The creases at the corners of his eyes deepen. "Where's Lucie?"

"In the cinema room. She fell asleep during the movie. I was going to wake her."

"Don't. I'll take a shower and carry her up to bed. She'll probably sleep through the night if she's tired enough. Can you wait with her? Give me ten minutes."

I barely hear anything he says after the word 'shower'. *Did he have to say that? Did he have to plant that image in my mind? Him completely naked with water running all over him? Those droplets would get everywhere. Focus, Aries.* "Sure."

"Do you need me to show you where it is?"

"Huh?"

I'm pretty sure he's trying not to laugh at me, but I can't put my finger on why I think it, because there's nothing to suggest it on his face. "The cinema room. You said you got lost."

The heat in my cheeks is furious. *Is my face on fire?* "Oh, right. No. I think I can find it."

There's that slight glimmer of amusement in his eyes again, like a ghost or a spectre; a trick of the light.

Before I can say another word, he disappears into an adjacent room and I pad back along the hall to the cinema room. It's a straight line from here to there. He definitely knows I didn't get lost. And that I was just standing there, admiring him.

This is definitely not good.

5
MATT

I stand beneath the blast of water in the shower. It's so cold each drop is a shock; like a million needles to my skin. It's exactly what I need to settle the racing of my mind.

The way Aries looked at me back there was nothing short of carnal. I'd be lying if I hadn't felt a stirring in response. The way her skin flushed; twin blooms of red on her cheeks... the acute embarrassment that was written so clearly on her face only made the situation worse.

Well, that and the fact that she has the most glorious soft curves I've seen on a woman in a long time. Her breasts are so full, so heavy, that I want to prop them up in my palms. And all that red hair... I want to fist my hands in it and pull her right against me.

I'm not sure she'd say no, either.

These thoughts are totally inappropriate.

I squeeze shampoo into my palm, aggressively rubbing it through my hair, scratching my scalp like I can tear the lingering sexual tension off my body. I really don't want to have to deal with whatever this is between us. *How long had she been standing there, watching me?* She never answered the question.

I scrub down, turn off the water, and grab a fresh towel. Ordinarily, I'd sit in the sauna after a workout, but I don't have time if Aries is waiting for me and Lucie's asleep.

I have everything down here I need, including sweatpants and t-shirts. I run a comb through my hair and check myself in the mirror. I look relaxed, finally. Endorphins are pumping through my system and I feel bloody brilliant. There's nothing like a hard workout to lift my mood and release the tension of the day.

Moments later, I'm in the cinema room. Aries is sitting on the sofa, stroking a sleeping Lucie's head. She looks so maternal that it knocks the breath from my lungs. *Did Gemma ever do this?* I don't remember. I don't want to disturb the scene, and an uneasy sensation swirls through me as I realise what I *do* want. *I want to join them.* I want to step into the room and take a seat, but that would be as crazy as stepping through the frame of a painting. *Impossible.*

As though she's heard my thoughts, or more likely my footsteps, Aries pauses her movement and turns to look at me. *Christ.* Now I'm the one lingering in doorways and staring, but Aries' expression isn't judgmental. She's been waiting for me, after all.

I approach, and Aries moves aside, letting me scoop up my daughter. Lucie groans but doesn't wake, and I head out of the room towards the lift. Aries walks behind me, saying nothing.

When we reach the lift, I step in. Aries hesitates, glancing over the small space as though she's measuring its cubic volume. "I'll take the stairs."

"Nonsense." I shift against the back wall. "There's enough room."

A look of consternation crosses her face, and understandably so. My bulk is considerable and the lift carriage is small. She lingers a moment before stepping in next to me, and the doors close behind her.

Aries focuses on the floor, her chest rising and falling with each breath. There's a rhythmic tremble of her breasts beneath her shirt.

"You're quiet," I whisper, keeping my voice down so as not to wake Lucie.

Green eyes meet mine from beneath fair lashes, her head still angled towards the floor. "Isn't that what you wanted, Mr Hawkston?"

My chest tightens. Maybe it's that soft Scottish accent that slips around my name, or the intention to please in her demeanor, or the fact that her question is so laden with suggestion I'm surprised it doesn't fall to the ground with the weight of it. I grunt in response and I swear her lips tilt upwards, as though she's secretly smiling to herself. Does she know the effect she has on me? Is she teasing me? No, that would be ridiculous. *Wouldn't it?*

Tension creeps into the air between us that feels a lot like a precursor to... *something*. A *something* that should definitely not happen between the boss and the nanny. I'm barely breathing, as though inhaling near her might infect me with some poison I won't be able to withstand.

"I didn't want you to drop your personality like a hot potato," I grit out.

"A hot potato?" she hisses back at me, a mischief sparkling in her eyes. "I'll have you know my personality is infinitely superior to a potato, hot or otherwise."

"Underwear, then."

My body clenches. *How did that pop out of my mouth?* Of all the words I could have come up with... *why that one?*

It lands between us like an unexploded bomb. I grind my back molars, and at the same time, every aspect of Aries' face widens, her pretty mouth falling open. The image of her on her knees flashes in my mind. *I'm losing control here.*

Her eyes light up, and her lips shift into a smile that she cuts short by biting into her bottom lip.

I'm certain I've just exposed something I didn't intend to, and judging by how Aries is currently gnawing on that full, pink bottom lip of hers, she knows it. And is rather more amused by it than I'm comfortable with.

Thankfully, at that exact moment, the lift stops and the doors open, allowing the tension to burst out like shaken champagne from the bottle once the cork pops. Aries exits first and I follow, taking my first full breath since I got into the lift.

Lucie's bedroom is just down the corridor. The carpet is thick and soft beneath my bare feet. Aries's feet are also bare, and each of her footsteps leaves an imprint on the dense pile. It seems oddly intimate that she's already walking around my house without her shoes, leaving traces wherever she steps on the carpet.

We reach Lucie's room and Aries draws the curtains. We're enclosed in the soft light of the sun, barely penetrating the pink fabric; everything in the room loses its edge. It reminds me of being a child, sent to bed in summer before the sunset. It's like a comforting cocoon in here.

Aries turns down the duvet and I tuck my daughter into bed, still fully dressed.

God, I messed up today. This was the first day I'd had penciled in for over two weeks that I was going to spend with Lucie. I'll make it up to her. I kiss her forehead and stare for a few moments. I love her so much that it hurts. It sounds trite, but it's true. I felt the same about Charlie when he was little. Now that he's a teenager, he annoys me more than I'd like, and he can't stand me. But he still owns part of my heart, even if I do want to throttle him more often than not.

I stand and turn towards the door, only to find Aries leaning against the frame, her arms crossed. I don't know when she moved from my side, but our eyes clash and hold. I have time to take at least two full breaths, which is longer than I usually hold a woman's gaze. It's intimate and sensual and it feels like I'm opening a portal, not knowing what the fuck is on the other side.

With one hand, I wave her out into the corridor and follow her out of the room, closing the door softly behind me.

The silence that envelops us begs to be smashed into pieces, exposing unspoken words beneath the surface that hum like the drone of far-distant traffic. I have no idea what they are. I just know that they're there, right below the surface.

This woman has worked for me for all of two days, and I haven't been this attracted to anyone in years. Not since before I met Gemma. Standing near her is like being plugged into an electric socket; there's a power surging through me that has been dormant, and a desire to see how far and how fast I can go throbs beneath my skin. *This is definitely not sustainable.* We're heading for a high-speed crash.

Unable to bear the potent silence any longer, I speak. "In the gym, you said you were sorry. About the museum." I hesitate, unsure exactly what I intend to say, but I forge on anyway. "I'm probably the one who ought to say sorry."

Why the fuck am I apologizing?

Aries pauses, like my apology is something precious she needs to soak up. When she replies, her voice is soft. "You don't need to apologise to me. There's a little girl in that room who needs to hear it much more than I do."

"I know. Thank you for being there for her." There's more I want to say, but, for some reason, it's hard to admit. The words cling to my throat and I have to cough to release them. "Today… when you spoke to her, and she stopped crying… it was like magic."

Long red hair curls delicately over Aries' shoulder. She twists a lock around her finger and I'm mesmerized by the motion. "Not magic. Empathy. You should..." Her voice trails off.

"What?"

She shakes her head like she's decided, for once, to filter her thoughts, but I'm not satisfied with that. "You were going to insult me."

She smiles, looking cautious. "I don't want to overstep."

"That's an affirmative then." We hold eye contact a few moments longer. "If you don't tell me, I'll be wondering all evening what you were about to say."

A tiny laugh tinkles from her lips. "It wouldn't kill you to be kinder. That's all."

My mouth opens and closes. I must look like a fish that someone removed from its tank. I can't remember the last time an employee called me out. In fact, I'm not sure it has ever happened. Aries smiles, lips closed.

"Good night, Mr Hawkston," she says. And without waiting for a reply, she turns and paces towards her bedroom. Then, with her hand on the door handle, she pauses and looks right at me. I haven't moved an inch. "Oh, and just so you know, my personality is fully intact. I haven't dropped anything. *Yet.*"

6
ARIES

My heart is thudding when I enter my bedroom. I close the door and lean against it, letting my head rock back.

Was that a step too far? Too suggestive? I've only just arrived. I really need to tone down my Aries-ness. But he was the one who dropped the underwear bomb into conversation. A sign of what was going through his mind... *Surely?*

Or maybe the man is just that awkward.

But he didn't look awkward... a little bit surprised, maybe. But not embarrassed. In fact, there's something so un-awkward about him that it doesn't fail to be reassuring. Like he could handle any situation. He's... unflappable.

I take a deep breath. Even if the underwear thing was nothing more than thoughtlessness, or the verbal association of words... things you *drop*... the way my heart is still crashing against my sternum is enough to let me know there's definitely something happening here. Even if it is wholly one-sided.

I have a crush on my boss.

Out of nowhere, my mother's words pop into my mind. *You don't like men. You don't trust them.* And I realise it very suddenly. Not only do I find Mr Hawkston attractive, but there's a depth to him that pulls me in. He feels... *safe*. Sturdy. Like he's part of the building itself. Like there's no chance he's going to run away in the middle of the night and desert his home and kids. He's a man you could lean on if you needed to, although he'd probably have to grant you permission first. He's a tad frosty, and even though I don't know him that well, my overwhelming gut instinct is that I *like* him. And I'm not entirely sure it's a good thing.

My stomach rumbles, drawing my attention to more bodily concerns. I haven't eaten anything since the popcorn I had during the movie, but I can't go back downstairs. *Not now*. Not after the underwear comment. I hold my breath, listening for the sound of the lift that will take Mr Hawkston back downstairs, but it doesn't come. Instead, I hear muffled footsteps pass my door.

He's taking the stairs.

My stomach rumbles again. I'm not just hungry... I'm starving. *Crap*. I've also left my handbag in the cinema room.

Well, I'm not going downstairs again. Not when I could turn a corner and slam right into Mr Hawkston. And I already checked the kitchen up here. It's empty. Mrs Minter left a note for me, saying I should make a shopping list and give it to the chef, but I haven't got round to it yet.

I open my suitcase, which I still haven't fully unpacked, and search the zip pockets. There I find a packet of Tunnock's Caramel Wafers and a bar of tablet, that uniquely Scottish crumbly fudge.

I actually have three bars of tablet and some macaroon too, in all its coconutty sugariness... I'd bought extra as token Scottish gifts for the family, but now that I've seen a bit more of Mr Hawkston, I'm not sure he's the kind of guy who'd eat a bar of tablet. He's probably all lean chicken and steamed broccoli. Maybe protein shakes.

Anyway, it's all I have, so I start with a Caramel Wafer, which I gobble in seconds, and then crack off a chunk of tablet. This food might be extremely calorific and nutrient deficient, but Mum always said food is only bad for us if we believe it is. So while I munch, I try to pretend I'm eating broccoli. Which fails, because not even I can imagine cruciferous vegetables when I'm eating this much sugar.

As it's seeping into my bloodstream, I feel a pang of homesickness I haven't felt yet. I take out my phone and check my messages. There's one from Mum asking if everything's all right. I reply that I am. Then, because it's not enough, I type another message.

Me: Are you doing OK?

Mum: Stop worrying about me. Enjoy yourself. Enjoy London. I'll see you in a couple of months. Not long. I'm always here if you want to speak.

I sigh. It's true that it's not long, but mum's cancer is terminal. Terminal, but she could live another five years. But she also might not. Uncertainty screws my insides up like a used tissue. She won't *always* be there if I want to speak.

I go to put the phone down when another message pops up from an unknown number.

You should save my number. ICE.

I read it again. ICE? What kind of sign off is that?

Another message pops up.

It's Mr Hawkston.

Ah, that explains it. My fingers type faster than I can think and I send:

Me: Oh. Cool. ICE cool.

His reply comes quickly.

Mr Hawkston: Not cool. ICE: In Case of Emergency.

Me: Oh. Now I feel like an idiot.

Mr Hawkston: That wasn't my intention.

I save his number and put the phone down, noting that my fingertips are all zingy and there's energy buzzing around my body at the idea that he's downstairs sending me messages. Sitting in my bedroom on a sugar high, messaging the world's hottest boss, is not a good situation to be in if it gets me giddy like this. Especially not when the content of the messages is purely practical.

I'll have to behave. Stop making suggestive comments and staring at him like I want to lick him. I need to keep this job. I can't go back to Scotland with my tail between my legs because Mr Hawkston fires me on account of our weird dynamic.

And it is weird. I don't even know what it is, but bizarrely, it feels more enticing than anything else I've ever felt. Being near him makes me feel hyper-alert in the best way, as if something exciting could happen at any moment.

Maybe it's all in my head. I haven't got laid for six months. Not since my Friday night sex arrangement with Andy, the guy I met at the local fish and chip shop, came to an end. My hormones are doing a double-trot and my body's about ready to jump in the sack.

Maybe I'll get on the dating scene in London while I'm here. That's definitely safer than nursing a crush on Mr Hawkston. I make a mental note to check with Mrs Minter about dating. I assume there's no bringing anyone back to the house, but the alternative would be to go to their place.

Ugh. No. I couldn't do that unless I knew them really well, and that would take weeks. Not that I don't have weeks, but it doesn't sort the itch.

Mr Hawkston is suddenly looking like the only viable option.

I laugh at the idea as I head to the bathroom to get ready for bed. I need to shower and brush my teeth. I just ate more than my daily allowance of sugar for dinner.

The kiss is rough and all consuming, and so real I can feel his tongue against my own, as well as the scrape of his stubble against my chin.

Somewhere, deeper than the consciousness of the dream, I know it's not real. But right now, Mr Hawkston is kissing me and I'm enjoying every second.

A strange noise erupts, but I can't make sense of it. I try to hold onto Mr Hawkston, but he disintegrates and fades away like dust in the breeze.

The noise repeats, dragging me from the dream.

I blink awake. My room is dark, and the clock on my bedside table says 2.33 am.

A small, shadowy figure stands at the side of my bed. Blearily, I sit up, trying to make sense of what's going on. "Lucie?"

She's sobbing and rubbing at one eye. She's still in her clothes from the day before.

"What's wrong, honey?"

She doesn't answer, but keeps crying. I reach out to pull her into a hug, but my hand hits damp fabric.

It takes a moment to register.

She's wet herself. *No wonder.* I can't even remember when she last went for a wee before we sat down to watch the movie yesterday.

I sit up and swing my legs out of bed. "Oh, honey, it's okay. Let's clean you up. We need new pyjamas. Can we go to your room?"

I take her hand and we potter along to her room. Thankfully, there's the orange glow of a night-light which is enough to see by. I strip the wet clothes off her and find some dry pyjamas in the chest of drawers before helping her to the bathroom. I don't want to run a bath or shower at this time of night, so I do what I can with a sponge and towel, and help her into the fresh clothes.

We go back to the bedroom, and I run a hand over her bed.

It's soaking.

Shit. I start pulling off the sheets. Luckily, there's a plastic mattress protector on the bed. *Maybe this isn't such a rare occurrence.*

"Do you know where the clean sheets are?" I ask her, straining to keep my voice calm. It's not Lucie's fault that I feel out of my depth, but a mild sense of panic is bubbling in my gut. I'm not prepared for bed-wetting. This is only my second night on the job, and dealing with this is like sitting an exam without revising beforehand.

Lucie's still half-asleep, but she manages to shake her head. I run through my options. I can search the house for sheets, but I don't know how long it will take, and I don't want to keep Lucie up too long in the middle of the night. I could take her to my room and let her sleep in my bed, but I'm not sure how Mr Hawkston would feel about that. I could put her in one of the many other bedrooms, but that doesn't seem like a good idea.

I could take her to her dad's bedroom.

No. That's the worst idea yet.

Lucie begins to wail again. "I want Daddy."

Oh, crap.

"Daddy's sleeping, honey. You can sleep in my bed."

The wailing gets louder. If this continues, she'll wake him up anyway.

I crouch down and put my hand on her shoulder and a finger of the other hand on my lips. "Shhh. It's nighttime. Everyone's sleeping."

She opens her mouth so wide I can see her tonsils, and the noise that's about to erupt will wake the dead, I'm sure of it.

I hoist her up into my arms, and the scream she was about to release never materialises. Instead, she tucks her legs around my hips. "Okay. Let's go find him," I whisper, stroking a hand down her back.

The tension in her body dissolves, and her head rests against my shoulder as I take the stairs. The lift at this time of night seems excessive and disruptive.

I remember where Mr Hawkston's suite is from the tour of the house Lucie gave me when I arrived. When we reach his room, I knock on the door.

No response.

"He's sleeping," I say.

"Mm. Want Daddy," she mumbles.

This is a really bad idea. Maybe if I wait long enough, she'll fall asleep in my arms and I can put her in my bed. I could sleep on the floor. Problem solved.

"I want to sleep in the big bed with Daddy," she says before she peels her head off my shoulder and looks at me with huge eyes that are way too wide awake for this time of night.

Okay. The big bed. That sounds like somewhere she's familiar with. Maybe this is something that happens a lot. Divorce can be unsettling for a young kid. Maybe she sleeps with her dad sometimes.

But neither Mrs Minter nor Mr Hawkston mentioned it. But then they didn't mention bed-wetting either. I curse them both under my breath.

"No. Sorry, honey. He's asleep. It's too late. You can sleep in my bed."

I back away from the door and as I do, Lucie lets out the most almighty scream. It's blood-curdling. She sounds like she's being murdered.

No. She sounds like I'm murdering her.

The door to Mr Hawkston's room flies open, and he's standing there in nothing but his boxers. I don't know how he got out of bed so fast.

His muscular chest is on full display, and his hair is unruly around his face like someone just had their hands in it. The picture is way too intimate, and I half expect a woman to follow him out of the room.

Guilt spikes as I realise I'm gawking at him while his face is contorted with panic. "What's wrong?" he asks.

Lucie reaches out to him. "Daddy."

"She wet the bed," I explain.

His features smooth over and he audibly exhales. His palms graze my forearms as he takes the tiny girl from my grip, and his touch sends goosebumps spreading over my skin so fast I almost gasp.

Lucie clings tight to him. I can only imagine how safe and comforting it must feel to be held like that.

"Did you change the sheets?" he asks.

"No. I stripped the bed, but I didn't know where to find fresh sheets. If you tell me, I'll do it now."

"I don't know where they are."

"You don't know?"

He bristles, and I realise too late that there's more judgment in my tone than I intended.

"I don't do the laundry," he hisses, looking pissed off that he's resorted to defending himself. "I don't know where they are. Mrs Minter ought to have shown you."

"She didn't."

He mutters under his breath. "Fine. Leave it for now and sort it tomorrow."

"I want to sleep in the big bed," Lucie says.

Just how big is this big bed? Is it big to a little kid, or would I think it was big?

"Sure thing, sweetheart," he says. "Just for tonight, okay?"

She nods against his chest and over the top of her head he shoots me a look which is somewhere between a '*thanks*' and a '*get out of here before you piss me off any more.*'

The door closes, leaving me alone in the hall with a sensation that's beginning to feel all too familiar: *I fucked up.*

7
MATT

"Time to get up, Daddy."

I roll over to find Lucie grinning at me. She looks wide awake, which is impressive, considering she was up in the middle of the night on account of the bed-wetting. I rub my eyes and stretch, as images from last night pour into my head, free-flowing like wine. Aries in those tiny little pyjama shorts, red hair all loose around her shoulders, her eyes wide at the sight of me in only my boxers. I might have been preoccupied with Lucie, but I didn't miss the way she looked at me. She definitely liked what she saw.

I yawn and fling the sheets back, determined to put Aries out of mind. She's an employee. That's it. That's all it can ever be. Lucie watches me as I get out of bed.

"What are we doing today?" she says, all innocent charm and smiles.

"I have to work. Aries is looking after you." I try to keep my voice neutral, but I'm groggy after last night. I hate having my sleep disturbed.

Lucie looks disappointed, but only for a second. "I really like her."

A tightening sensation corkscrews in my gut. It's going to be impossible not to think about Aries if Lucie is going to keep on like this. "I'm glad."

"I want her to be my mummy."

I freeze as pins and needles pervade my entire body. It reminds me of how I felt when I got caught breaking the rules at school. *This is bad.* As much as I hate Gemma, I can't encourage this.

I sit on the end of the bed and tap the covers to indicate Lucie should sit beside me. She crawls down the bed and sits cross-legged at my side. "Aries can't be your mummy, Lucie. You already have a mummy."

"Yes, but Aries is nicer. And she lives here. Mummy doesn't live here. And Aries loves me."

Oh, fuck. "Did she say that?"

Lucie ponders this. "No. But I can tell she does. She has nice eyes. I like her eyes. She looks right at me with them. And I love her."

I scrub a hand over my face as pity for my daughter creates a great gaping vacuum, emptying me out. *How the fuck am I supposed to handle this?* What if she gets attached to Aries, and then Aries doesn't stay? Or Aries goes home after the summer, leaving me with a broken-hearted four-year-old?

I'm catastrophizing. Projecting a future that hasn't happened yet, and might not happen at all. I shift gear and focus on the positives. *It's wonderful that Lucie likes the new nanny. It really is great. Isn't it?*

"I'm going to have a shower. Can you go upstairs and get dressed?"

She pouts. "I can't get my clothes on by my own."

"Aries can help you."

Lucie does a happy little shrug as if this is the best solution ever. "I said she could wear some of my sparkly shoes."

The image of Aries' bare feet slides through my mind. Even her feet are sensual. Delicate bones. *Fuck's sake.* "I don't think they'd fit."

"They would. Aries said she liked them so much, she'd cut her toes off to wear them."

I chuckle. "She did, did she? Can you tell her not to make a mess of the carpet when she does it?"

Lucie hops off the bed. "Yup. I'll tell her. I'm going to tell her I want her to be my mummy too. Bye, Daddy."

"Wait—"

But Lucie is already racing through my suite and out into the hall. I can't let her ask Aries that. The woman has only been here a couple of days. And more importantly, Lucie needs to know what she can expect from a nanny. I don't want her to be disappointed. They aren't mothers...

I race after her, dodging awkwardly between the end of the bed and the ottoman, clumsy in my attempt to stop her. I burst into the hall, and Lucie looks over her shoulder, eyes lighting up when she sees I'm chasing her. *She thinks this is a game.* She runs up the stairs, letting out an adorable cascade of giggles, and something shifts inside me. *Why am I panicking?* I take the steps two at a time behind her, starting to laugh too. I haven't messed around with the kids for far too long. *When did we last play anything?*

"Daddy Monster, Daddy Monster," Lucie yells.

Fuck it, why not? I curl my fingers into claws and slow down, opening my mouth wide and bellowing like a zombie as I continue to chase Lucie up the stairs. She's laughing hysterically, stumbling and climbing her way up ahead of me.

I'm half crawling, half lumbering up behind her like a monster from a seventies horror movie, letting out horrendous lowing sounds that echo up the stairwell.

"Help, help. Ahhhhh," Lucie screams, still looking back at me every so often, nervous laughter exploding out of her mouth. It's hilarious, and I'm barely managing to hold in my own laughter.

Lucie screams again just as I reach her, using my claw hands to grab at her tiny feet and ankles. She kicks at me and I swipe at her, letting out my best monster sound yet.

"Aries!" Lucie shrieks at the top of her voice. "Save me, Aries."

A door opens and slams against a wall, then footsteps run across the upper landing. Aries appears at the top of the stairs, only a few steps above us, breathless and panicked-looking, and wearing only a t-shirt and those tiny shorts. No bra. I can tell from the way her breasts move beneath the shirt.

Her eyes move frantically over the scene before her. "What? What's wrong?" she shouts.

Lucie rolls onto her back and laughs, holding her little belly. I'm still in position, bent over with my claw hands, face contorted and frozen in a zombie roar, wearing nothing but a pair of boxers.

Aries stares at us, total confusion on her face. Her gaze rakes over me, and I feel it against my bare skin as intensely as when she touched my wrist in the dining room.

I slowly straighten up. "Hi."

Hi? How did I make that one word sound like a come on?

Lucie is still breathlessly laughing at my feet.

"Is everything okay? I thought someone was dying out here," Aries says, still panting. "What was that noise?"

"What noise?" I ask as if I wasn't the one lowing like a cow giving birth only a moment ago.

"That dreadful sound. Like a herd of farm animals being slaughtered."

"Daddy Monster," Lucie explains, kicking her feet and giggling. "The noise was Daddy."

"You." Aries stares at me, a disbelieving smile splitting across her face. "You made that noise?" She starts chuckling. "Wow. You really are a man of many talents."

I want to laugh. I want to join in and keep playing this stupid game with my daughter, because I'm feeling more connected to her than I've felt in months. I'm high off the hilarity and I feel so fucking good that I want to run up the stairs and hug the beautiful nanny that Lucie has already fallen in love with. I want to ask her to play with us, to run around this fucking great mansion and fill the place with love and laughter. I'm pretty sure Aries would be up for it too.

But I don't do any of that. I fix a solemn expression on my face and say, "Sorry we disturbed you. Can you give Lucie a bath and help her get dressed? I've got to get ready for work."

Aries' smile falters and her gaze darts between me and Lucie. "Of course. Come on, Lucie."

Lucie scampers up the last few steps, arriving at Aries' feet and pushing herself up to standing. She puffs out her chest and grins. "You can wear my shoes today. But Daddy said not to make a mess of the carpet when you cut off your toes."

Aries' eyebrows shoot up, and I bite my bottom lip as I watch her maintain this conversation with Lucie with a serious expression on her face. "Did he, indeed?"

"Yes. And also, I love you. I want you to be my mummy."

I close my eyes and hold my breath. *Damn.* When I open my eyes, Aries is frowning, fully focused on Lucie.

"I would so love to be your mummy," she says, her voice utterly sincere. "But I can't, because you already have one. But we can be friends."

"We're already friends." Lucie's brow furrows, then relaxes. "Bestest friends?"

"Absolutely. Bestest buds."

Lucie lets out a tiny squeal, bounces on her toes and claps her hands, and Aries ushers her towards her room with an indulgent smile plastered over her face. I watch them go, willing Aries to look back at me. I don't even know why. I only know that I want it.

I wait until they're out of sight, but Aries doesn't even glance my way, making me feel oddly deflated, as though she's stuck a pin in me.

8
ARIES

I wake unusually early, memories of my dreams about Mr Hawkston falling apart like pieces of a jigsaw. They play on repeat every night, fading with the sunrise. It's driving me slightly insane.

I haven't encountered him in person since I found him playing Daddy Monster with Lucie, the morning after the bed-wetting incident, a week ago now. But he has absolutely plagued my subconscious since then. *Who am I kidding? He's plagued my conscious mind too.* I've been wandering around the house, heart thudding, hoping to catch a glimpse of him like a teenage groupie desperate to see their favourite popstar. *Absolutely ridiculous.* I bet he hasn't thought of me at all.

Milky light filters through the windows in my bedroom. I briefly wonder what the time is, but as soon as the thought passes through my mind, hunger hits me, gnawing at the lining of my stomach. *Breakfast time.* If I haul my arse out of bed now, I can eat quickly before my working day starts. It's bound to be a full-on Sunday, same as last week. But damn, this bed is comfy. I don't want to get out from under the covers. It's better than my one at home, although I haven't told Mum that.

I count to five and jump out of bed. *Ready.*

And then I remember I finished off the contents of the upstairs fridge last night. *Damn it.* I need to get better at stocking up. If I want to eat, I'll have to creep to the basement for food. It's so early that I'm pretty sure I'll be safe, and it's a Sunday. *No one else is going to be up now, are they?*

I take the stairs, all four flights, in the semi-darkness. The plush carpet is soft against my bare feet and I relish the feeling of squishing my toes into it with each step.

When I reach the basement, it's quiet, but the air is thick with the distinctive smell of a hot sauna. *Does no one ever turn it off? The energy bills in this house must be huge.*

I'd really love to nip in there. *But, no.* That would be really foolish, wouldn't it?

But the lure of the freshwater pool is too much. *Maybe I can just take a peek.* Calming spa music filters out into the hall, tempting me like a siren call. *Don't they ever turn that off, either? Perhaps they keep it running because Mr Hawkston is a vampire who stays up all night.*

I laugh at this idea. I've seen so little of him, he could well be locked in a coffin somewhere. I'm not even sure he's in the house at all. He could have gone away on business for all I know. He's under no obligation to tell me about his comings and goings.

I figure that, even if he is in the house, it's so early he won't be up. I'm safe. I take the turn to the pool, and as soon as I enter the room, seeing the water calms me. Ripples reflect across the ceiling, giving it a silvery sheen. It's like I'm standing in a mermaid's lagoon.

I allow myself a few moments to absorb the energy. It's pure luxury. Completely breathtaking. I'd have no idea people lived like this if I hadn't seen it myself. I stay close to the walls, as if moving closer to the water poses a danger to my safety. I might not be able to resist jumping in.

A yawn blossoms, and I stretch my arms as my eyes close. Maybe I should have stayed in bed after all. This first week has been grueling;

running after a four-year-old has been exhausting. She goes to a local nursery on Mondays and Tuesday though, so those are my days off.

I turn, smacking right into a huge wall of muscle. A burning hot, sweaty wall.

"Fuck," Mr Hawkston growls.

My mind is a flurry of activity; a swirling mess of thoughts I can't cling to. All I know is he's half-naked yet again, and his hands are on my skin, and my pyjama top is now covered in his sweat.

I push away from him, or he pushes me off. I can't tell because there's a whole lot of skin-to-skin contact going on, and it's impacting my brain's ability to function.

His face is red, like he's hot. Sauna. He's obviously been in the sauna. There's a white towel wrapped around his hips, but otherwise he's all muscle. *Hot, sweaty muscle*. His breaths are coming fast. *Is that because of the sauna too?*

"What are you doing?" he says, his voice sharp, making my own anger spike. My response spills from my lips before I can stop it.

"Don't you ever wear a shirt?"

There's so much accusation in the question, it's as if I'm blaming him for removing his clothes in his own home. I want to stuff my words back down my throat, but they're long gone now. I can't get them back.

His face is carved in stone. "Not in the sauna."

Guilt spears me. All the times I've seen him shirtless it's been in reasonable scenarios. It's me that's been in all the wrong places, creeping around the house when I shouldn't be. I'm so flustered, it takes me a moment to gather myself enough to speak. "No. Of course not. Why would you? It's hot in there. Sweaty." *Sweaty? Oh, my God.* I can't even talk to this man, and saying the word sweaty out loud has my gaze crawling all over his chest again. I blink to refocus. "Sorry. What time is it?"

"5.15."

"5.15. Wow. You're an early riser."

"So are you, apparently." His gaze is unforgiving, but I don't miss the dart of his eyes towards my breasts, lingering over the damp fabric. My nipples tighten. If he doesn't look away soon, they're going to start winking at him. He might as well be tweaking them with his fingers. He drags his gaze back to my face. "I don't believe in wasting time."

"Oh." That sounded way too breathless. A bit like a noise a porn star might make. Not one in the full swing, but maybe one who was revving the engine. *Shit*. My nipples are definitely hard now.

"But sleep isn't wasted time," I say, inwardly congratulating myself on managing to form a coherent sentence. I inhale fast, words flooding my mind, desperate to spill out; anything to distract myself from what's going on in my body and the arousal that's blossoming without my permission. "It's essential to human survival. You know, like food and sex." *Sex? Dear Lord, I'm a mess.* His eyebrow arches and heat rages up my neck and across my face. I force myself to continue, "I ran out of food upstairs. That's why I'm down here. And then I could smell the sauna and I couldn't resist coming in here. The pool is so beautiful. And the music... it's so relaxing. I couldn't resist." *Damn. I already said that.* He'll think I have no self-control.

His features are still hard. "I see that."

I can't stop staring. *Shit*. I haven't seen him for days and *this* is how I see him? All sweaty and half-naked? I need to say something quickly. My thoughts skirt back to the other times I've seen him shirtless.

"I'm so sorry about last week," I blurt. "About bringing Lucie to your room after she wet the bed. I thought she was going to scream the house down if I didn't, and I didn't have clean sheets and I wasn't sure if you would like it if she slept in my bed."

If he thinks it's weird that I'm mentioning this a week later, he doesn't show it because he responds calmly. "Mrs Minter said she left you a note with the details about sheets. She's very thorough. Didn't you read it?"

I wince. Yes, I read it *after* the bed-wetting incident. Well, I read the first half when I arrived, but I got distracted right around the part where I was supposed to make a shopping list of food to stock my fridge. Clearly, I'm failing on that front too. "I found the sheets in the morning."

This seems to satisfy him. "Good. And, so we're clear, Lucie doesn't sleep in my room. Ever. Can you make sure she knows that? If it happens again, I want you to deal with it. Tell her she cannot sleep in my room and hold that line, so I don't have to do it in the middle of the night. That's your job. Please make sure you're doing it."

"Even if she's upset? And only wants Daddy?"

"Yes. I'm busy. My work is demanding. And like you said, sleep is essential. I like mine to be undisturbed."

Wow. I wasn't expecting that. I find myself longing for the version of this man who ran up the stairs pretending to be a monster. Why can't I get him instead of this icy version? "Sure. I can do that."

He holds my gaze for a moment, and the air fills with static that raises the hairs on my arms. *Something is going on here.* Mum would say it's the energetic charge of our thoughts clashing together in mid-air. *What the hell is he thinking right now?*

"I should go," I say, and I skip past him. I aim for a jolly, carefree movement, my knee raised high. But the moment my foot strikes the floor, I know I've made a mistake. The tiles are wet and my heel slides out from under me.

I reach out for something to grab... *anything* to steady me before my bum hits the floor. And my fingers find... towel. Thick, plush, luxurious towel.

Suffice to say, the towel offers no resistance and I plummet towards the floor in a heap of Egyptian cotton. I brace for the jarring of my coccyx on the tile, but a hand grips my elbow, taking all of my weight before I land.

My bare feet are tangled in the towel. I kick at it to free them, but they only end up further ensnared. Another hand comes around my waist, raising me gently to my feet, which are now half-wrapped in the towel.

The towel!

Oh, shit.

If I have his towel, then what is he wearing? The breath halts in my chest and a surge of panic rips through me so strong that my knees weaken. He must feel it because his hold on me tightens. My heart starts to race, and I keep my gaze very deliberately on the towel at my feet, but he's right behind me, his hand still on my waist. His fingers are on the skin between my top and the stupidly short pyjama shorts I wear to bed. *Why isn't he moving them away?* My skin pulses beneath his hand, like the creature from Alien is about to break out from inside my body.

"You okay?" he asks, sounding concerned.

I scrunch my eyes closed, shifting the towel with my toes. "Uh-huh."

His hand leaves my waist and I bend to pick up the towel, patting the ground with my fingers to find it.

Oh, dear Lord, this is messy. I have Mr Hawkston's towel in my hands. The towel that was wrapped around his hips only seconds ago.

My heart stutters as my brain tries to gear up through the fog of panic. I can't move, and I don't dare open my eyes. "Are you naked right now?"

A silence passes that could fill an eternity. "Yes."

His voice is completely calm, with not even the faintest tremor of shame or embarrassment.

"Oh, fuck. I mean... Oh. Shit. Fuck."

Well, that was eloquent. But holy hell, Mr Hawkston is absolutely 100%, hot, sweaty, and naked, standing right behind me. An unmistakable pressure surges to the apex of my thighs. Even if he's not turned on, I definitely am.

Realising I won't see him if he's behind me, I pop open my eyes, only to be greeted by the sight of our reflection in the mirrored wall that lines the room. I can see *everything*.

My mouth falls open and a wave of heat so intense I feel like I'm the one who's been in the sauna douses me. His cock is... huge. *Jesus.* That thing is a weapon. If I reached out with my left hand, I could pull the fucking trigger. Even soft, it's enormous.

Wait, is it soft? Or is it... *semi*?

Is this turning him on too?

As if reacting to my attention, his dick hardens before my eyes. *Hello, penis.* This is nightmarish and ridiculously hot, all at once. I think I'm about to implode. I'm struggling to breathe.

My gaze lifts, snapping to his in the mirror. His expression is so ferocious that my heart misses a whole beat.

"Give me the towel, Aries."

God, that voice. So low, so commanding. *Is this how he talks in the bedroom?* I've lost it. My imagination is running riot, while my body is frozen.

"The towel, Aries," he repeats.

My heart gives a shuddering thump, like water finally making its way through an air-filled pipe. "Here." The word croaks out from a dry mouth, my tongue feeling thick and uncoordinated.

I dangle the towel out to the side, and he snatches it and wraps it around his waist. Then he steps around me. As he walks past, his right arm brushes against mine. The contact is like a lightning strike. There's a falter in his step, the slightest pause, before he proceeds to the exit without another word.

This job has definitely taken a bizarre turn. If I had any alcohol, I'd pour myself a shot to calm my nerves.

I just got a full frontal view of Mr Hawkston, entirely bollock naked. And his dick... that's not something I'll be able to forget.

If I had a smartphone, I'd be googling whether men get situational erections. If I had been Mrs Minter, would he have got hard? Was it to do with me, or was it to do with the fact he was naked with a woman? Not *me* woman. Just generic female with breasts. Maybe it was the cold air after the sauna? But wouldn't that have the *opposite* effect?

I'd really like to know for sure if it means he's attracted to me, Aries, rather than me, the stand-in for any female human being at that particular moment. Because for me, it's all about him. Mr Hawkston. My hot, grumpy boss who rarely smiles and hates to let his kids sleep in his bed. But has the face and body of an A-list movie star.

I must have made my way upstairs in a daze, because I don't remember how I got here. I'm walking into the upstairs kitchen, and there, pinned to the empty fridge, is Mrs Minter's note. Small curling script curves over two sides of A4. No wonder I zoned out while reading it. I pull it off the fridge and read the whole thing again, in case there's anything else I've missed.

At the very bottom of the list it says, *Mr Hawkston plays golf every third Sunday of the month.*

So that's where he's going today.

I read the line again, and as I sound out his name, an image pops into my mind, crystal clear. It's his reflection in the mirror, and his huge, veined cock, standing to attention. A sudden gush of moisture between my legs leaks onto the gusset of my pyjama shorts and my core throbs. I think my clit is actually swollen.

How am I ever going to be able to look him in the eye again?
I'll think about that later.

Right now, I'm exquisitely aroused and I'm going to have to do something about it. My pussy is aching to be filled, and the penis downstairs is very much not available to me. I'll have to sort myself out. Maybe I can orgasm Mr Hawkston out of my system and move on.

Fat chance. But worth a shot, right?

I head to my bedroom and unzip the pocket in my suitcase, pulling out my dildo. Bright pink, eight inches, and all mine. I feel a little safer holding it in my hand, knowing I can fix this situation. I can make this uncomfortable attraction to this man go away using this lifeless piece of plastic.

I head into my en suite and lock the door. A session with the pink beast in the shower never fails.

But there's a first time for everything.

Ten minutes later, dripping wet and exhausted, I arrive like a fricking freight train. I come so hard that I know this attraction isn't going anywhere.

At least not until I get the real man between my thighs and fuck it out of me.

9
MATT

I swing the club and slice the top of the ball. It trickles off the tee. I haven't hit a shot that bad since I was ten years old. Behind me, one of my brothers scoffs. *Definitely Seb.*

"Take the shot again," Nico instructs.

"He can't take the shot again," Seb says. "It's against the rules."

Nico steps in front of me and picks up the ball. He doesn't even glance around to check no one else is around to see. He drops it in my hand, his dark gaze searching my own. "What the fuck is going on with you? Your whole game is off."

It's Aries. The sauna. Her hair. Her breasts. That mouth I want to shove my dick in. But I can't bloody tell my brothers that.

"Is it Charlie?" Nico questions. The mention of my son's name, combined with the concerned expression on my brother's face, wipes every thought of Aries from my mind. I don't like it one bit.

"Why would it be Charlie?"

Nico shrugs, but I can tell by the tightness of his mouth that there's more to it. My heart pinches. Charlie and I don't have the best relationship at the moment. "Kate and I went down to school to see him. Took him out for lunch. He was a bit... sullen."

"Isn't he always a bit sullen?" Seb asks, stepping forward to join us. He focuses on me. "Maybe if you let him dye his hair blue again, that would cheer him up."

I ignore this last comment. Seb knows as well as I do that the school would never let Charlie have blue hair during term time, and I won't allow it in the holidays. Both my brothers are now standing, staring at me, perfectly attired in white golf shirts and pressed trousers. Nico's the eldest, but I'm taller than both of them. Seb, with his blue eyes and one-sided dimple that appears when he smiles (which is often), has more boyish charm than either me or Nico.

I don't need to look in the mirror to know I look like shit compared to them. I'm pretty sure an unhappy marriage does more to age a person than the passage of time. Nico could easily pass as a couple of years younger than me, despite being older.

Nico glances at me, and that look is still in his eyes. He's worried about my son—maybe worried about me too—but he doesn't want to say it out loud. Maybe he thinks I'll take it as a personal criticism. I'm already paranoid about being a shit father. *Maybe I am one.* Gemma screamed it at me so many times over the years we were together that it's an ingrained part of my identity.

"Did he say something?" I ask Nico.

Nico's gaze slides from mine, then locks on again. "Not really. He's your kid, and it's not my place to speculate. But it's probably been hard on him, this last year. The divorce and all that. It might be worth checking in."

Shitty father, shitty father.

I nod, not sure what else to do. "Let's keep playing."

I bend to put the ball back on the tee, waiting for Nico and Seb to move out of the way. Then I take the shot again, but the result is the same. A trickle off the tee.

We're all silent for a few seconds before Nico picks up the ball again. Behind me, Seb tuts. "Who's got your balls in a knot, Matty?"

"Oh, fuck off." My response is so fast it reveals everything.

Nico's eyes narrow. "Is there someone? And if you say Gemma, I'll punch your lights out."

I roll my eyes at his false bravado. Nico's big, but he doesn't have my bulk. "Of course it's not Gemma. Plus, we don't have any unnecessary contact. That woman's getting nowhere near my balls."

"Glad to hear it. She had them in a vice for long enough." He tugs on the wrist of his glove, making it tighten over his fingers. "It's not work, is it? There's nothing huge looming right now. Everything's under control."

"It's not work," Seb says, grinning and pointing his finger at me. "There's a *someone*." He glances at Nico. "He's acting exactly like you did when you first had that thing going on with Kate. Before you did the deed, you were as frustrated as fuck."

Seb's not wrong there, and I curse my youngest brother's observational skills. I was out in the States when Nico started his affair with Kate Lansen, but even over the phone, I could tell there was something going on with him.

Seb looks back at me. "Someone's under your skin. I knew something was up at the first tee. Your shoulders are as tight as a pig's arse. No wonder you can't hit the ball."

"Last chance," Nico says, putting the ball back on the tee for me, then moving out of my swing zone.

I take position and roll my shoulders. Even after the sauna, they're still tense. "There's no one." I swing back, driving the club through to strike the ball, but it doesn't go well, hooking off to the right and landing in the long grass off the side of the fairway.

They laugh.

"Liar," says Nico. He steps up and places his own ball on the tee, swinging effortlessly, arcing the ball gracefully down the fairway.

"That's how you hit the ball when you're getting laid," Seb gloats, smacking me on the shoulder.

"Hmm. How's Kate's spa project coming along?" I ask Nico, desperate to change the subject.

He keeps his eye on his ball, which is still rolling. When it stops, he turns his attention to me. "Don't change the topic. It's great. She's great. Thanks for asking. Maybe you'll have a partner to bring to the plunge pool by the time it's up and built."

My stomach does a weird flip at the suggestion, and an image of Aries in her tiny wet t-shirt and skimpy pyjama shorts flashes in my mind. "I'll give the plunge pool a miss."

Seb steps up to take his turn. "Stop trying to avoid the question. Who's the someone? You know we'll have it out of you by the eighteenth hole, so you might as well tell us now. Maybe we can help."

"Don't pretend you want to help," I say. "You want to have a laugh at my expense. You're already grinning like a fucking monkey."

Seb tries to contain his smile, but fails spectacularly. "Okay. Fine. But we'll have it out of you either way."

I heave a great sigh and my resistance melts. I need to talk about this situation with someone, and my brothers are the only people I can safely chat about this shit with. "It's the nanny."

"Oof," Seb says, putting a hand on his heart and pretending to fall backwards. "Did you fuck her?"

"Is she hot?" Nico asks.

"No, I did not fuck the nanny. And yes, she's hot. Smoking. She looks like *Jessica Rabbit*."

Seb's eyes widen. "Jessica Rabbit? Like... the big tits and the red hair, Jessica Rabbit? The cartoon?"

"Exactly. I feel like the big guy in the sky is fucking with my head. I'm barely through the divorce after the shittiest marriage known to man, and then this? A drop-dead gorgeous twenty-six-year-old walking around my house with bare feet and tiny pyjamas. A Scottish redhead with an accent that goes straight to my dick." I run a hand down my face. "I don't know what the fuck to do with myself."

For a second, neither of them say anything, then they both speak at once.

"Fuck her," Seb replies.

"Fire her," Nico instructs.

I address Nico's suggestion first. "I can't fire her. I dropped my towel in the sauna this morning and she got an eyeful."

"You didn't." Seb laughs, eyes widening. *He's enjoying this way too much.*

Nico shakes his head, lips tight. "You're setting yourself up for a sexual harassment charge."

"Oh, come off it," Seb says to Nico before turning to me. "You didn't whip the towel off deliberately did you? You weren't flashing the poor girl?"

"Fuck's sake. No. She slipped and grabbed my towel."

Seb's eyes dance with amusement, and his lips split into a smile, revealing straight white teeth. "So *she* pulled your towel off?"

"Yes. Accidentally. But then she stared at my dick in the mirror like she'd never seen one before."

"Are we talking shock here?" Nico asks. "Because again, I'm going with potential sexual harassment charges."

"I don't know if it was shock. I have no idea what she's thinking. She just... swore. A lot."

"Did it turn you on?" Seb is barely controlling his amusement. The fucker is smiling so wide, it looks like his head's about to explode.

"The swearing?"

"No." Seb waves his hand in the air like he's slapping the obtuseness out of me. "The whole thing. You being naked, her looking. Did that turn you on?"

"No." *Yes.* "I'm not a horny teenager who can't control himself."

Seb rolls his eyes. "Whatever. If I'm dropping my towel in front of Jessica Rabbit, who's staring at it with her mouth hanging open, then my dick's gonna be enjoying the show."

"That's because you're filthy," I tell him.

His eyebrow twitches upwards and a smirk contorts one side of his lips, as if to say, *You know you're as bad as I am.*

And he's right. But I can't give him the satisfaction. I cannot share that I got a raging hard-on because of whatever the hell is going on between me and Aries, and had to go and sort myself out in the shower afterwards. I pumped my dick like I wanted to punish it. I'm surprised there's any skin left after I beat it so hard. It wasn't even a satisfactory orgasm; it was functional and fast. But I couldn't stop picturing Aries... those full, pink lips around my cock... her breasts, so round, begging me to take a handful. How I wanted to suck on those nipples that were pointing right at me...

Fuck's sake. Maybe Nico's right. I need to let her go before I do something I'll regret. But I infinitely prefer Seb's solution: fuck her. *But I can't do that, can I?*

"Okay, you can't fire her," Seb says, like he's read my mind. He positions himself to take his shot. "So fuck her."

"Is that what you would do?" I ask.

His upper lip curls with distaste. "No. I would never fuck someone who works for me, at home or in the office. I might be filthy, but I keep my business clean." He shoots an accusatory glance at Nico, who rolls his eyes.

"She might quit, you know. I'd probably quit if you came at me naked," Nico replies, entirely serious. "Problem solved."

Seb's still grinning when he swings the club in a perfect arc. The ball cruises into the air, landing even further than Nico's, just short of the green. It's a great shot.

When the ball finally comes to a standstill, he looks over his shoulder at me. "Go have sex. Then you might be able to keep up with us."

10
ARIES

I'm beyond exhausted by the time I get Lucie to sleep. She's been over-excited all day, ever since she padded into my room in the morning, all fresh-faced and wide-eyed. I was a bit disappointed when she appeared at the side of my bed at 7 am. After my marathon session with my dildo in the shower, *thinking about her dad*, I fell asleep again.

And even though the incident outside the sauna left me insanely aroused and gave me plenty of mental imagery for my epic masturbation session, I've been anxious all day, worrying that Mr Hawktson is going to fire me when he gets back from golf. How long does it take to play golf anyway? I glance at the clock. It's after 9 pm. My nerves are wrecked. No wonder I'm so tired.

I could go to bed, but I'm too worked up. I need to move and try to release some of this anxiety. I head down to the kitchen, where I find Alec preparing tomorrow's breakfast.

"I thought you didn't work Sundays?" I say.

He gives me a broad smile, making his youthful face look even more boyish. He's cute, if you're into that kind of thing. Personally, I prefer Mr Hawkston's angular face and the dark stubble that lurks on his jaw and throat, although I wish comparisons between my boss and all other men didn't keep springing to mind. "Hey there," Alec says. "I don't, but I'm only down in the staff block so sometimes I come and finish a few things up here to save me time in the morning."

"Staff block?"

"Yeah, at the far end of the garden, there's a house divided into flats for Mr Hawkston's staff. You haven't seen it yet?" I shake my head and he continues. "Technically, it's a separate house accessed from the parallel street. But we can get there across the garden too. I have a first floor flat. It's lush."

"That's a job perk."

"Yup. Better than living here with the dragon." He rolls his eyes to the ceiling to indicate Mr Hawkston upstairs. Not that he's home right now, but I get the point. "How's your first week been? Did he forgive you for your misdemeanors?"

I feel the colour drain from my face. "Misdemeanors?"

"You know, calling him Superman and all that."

My body sags. *Thank God he doesn't know the rest of it.* "Yeah. I think so. Maybe. But the other night I took Lucie to his room because she wet the bed. I don't think he was happy about it."

"Hmm. He's not exactly the cuddly daddy type."

I slump down on a stool at the island and prop my chin in my hand. "I think he might fire me."

"For taking his kid to him in the night? I doubt that." He starts clearing things away and wiping down the surfaces. "You want something to eat before this is all packed up?"

I shake my head. "I had some fish fingers earlier with Lucie."

He gives me a disbelieving look. Maybe fish fingers aren't real food to a chef. "When? At five-thirty?"

I frown, then nod. "Yeah. Kids' supper time."

"That was ages ago. I'll make you something better."

"Oh, no. Really, you don't have to do that."

But he starts chopping and frying and pretty soon there's a croque madame on a plate in front of me, complete with homemade bechamel sauce and a fried egg on top.

I cut into it and pop a chunk into my mouth. "Oh, my God, this is the best toasted sandwich I've ever eaten," I say, my mouth full of food.

Alec grins and pushes a glass of water towards me before he leans his elbows on the island opposite me, and we spend the next few minutes chatting. So far most of our chats have been surface level, but today I learn a bit more about his personal life. He's from Manchester, but trained as a chef in London. He had a girlfriend from back home, but she broke up with him when he refused to move back up north and chose to stay with Mr Hawkston.

"Said she didn't want to do long distance." Alec grimaces. "But I don't think that was true."

"No?" I query before taking another bite of the delicious sandwich.

"I think she had a crush on my mate. I hear they're dating back in Manchester now."

"Oh, I'm sorry. That sucks."

He shrugs and begins clearing things away again. "It doesn't matter. What's not meant to be isn't meant to be, right?"

"Guess so."

He looks at me funny. "You've got a bit of sauce." He indicates a spot on his face.

"Oh." I swipe my cheek with my hand.

"Wrong side. Here." He points, and I try again, but his grin tells me I've missed. He laughs. He really is quite cute. His expressions are so joyful, it's contagious. "How can you manage kids if you can't even keep your face clean?"

I'm laughing too now, wiping my face with my fingers again. "It's your fault. It was so delicious I couldn't eat with dignity. Did I get it?"

"Nope. I'll get it."

He comes round to my side of the island, sticks his thumb out, and swipes it over my cheek. His hand is still on my face when—

"Good evening."

Alec jerks his hand off me like I've burnt him, and the two of us turn to see Mr Hawkston standing in the doorway.

"Am I interrupting something?" he asks.

Alec's eyes fill with something approaching fear. They widen and fix on me, before darting back to Mr Hawkston. His mouth opens, but no sound comes out. Apparently, I'm not the only one Mr Hawkston renders speechless.

"Oh, no," I blurt. "Alec made the most delicious sandwich for me. I hadn't eaten properly."

Mr Hawkston says nothing, but keeps staring at the two of us. The silence is painful, and this time it's Alec who speaks.

"Nothing happening here, Mr Hawkston. Just food. That's what I do best. Just food." He holds up his hands like Mr Hawkston is pointing a gun at him. "Absolutely no fraternizing among the staff. I don't find Aries attractive that way."

What the hell is he talking about?

A bemused look passes over Mr Hawkston's face before he nods. "Make sure you clean up properly. And Aries?"

"Yes, sir?"

"Try and feed yourself at a reasonable hour so you're not distracting Alec here from his work."

"Oh, yeah. Sure. Sorry, I didn't mean—"

"Join me in my office in ten minutes."

Mr Hawkston's expression is severe. My stomach falls twenty feet. This must be about the sauna. Fear breaks like a storm down the middle of my body, turning all my bones to mush. My fingers gripping the kitchen island, and the stool beneath me, are the only things preventing me from collapsing. I take a few deep breaths as we listen to Mr Hawkston's fading footsteps.

Then I turn to Alec, forcing a smile on my face. "And I thought I was bad for rambling. Why'd you say all that?"

"Crap. I don't know." Alec is furiously wiping down the surfaces and scraping crumbs off into his open palm. "Sorry. You're very attractive. Obviously. But he was looking at me like he was going to murder me for touching you. It freaked me out. I've never seen that look on his face before."

Hope begins to swell inside me, like the sun rising over the horizon. *Shit.* "That's ridiculous," I say, as much for my benefit as for Alec's.

He gives a mock shudder so big that the sleeves of his chef's jacket quiver. "Seriously though, that was not pleasant. He was like one of those King Kong gorilla creatures, staring me down before he ripped my head off."

My mind whirls. *Was he really looking at us like that? Like he was angry at the suggestion of intimacy between me and another guy?* "Is there a rule about staff having relationships?"

Alec shrugs and begins rinsing out the cloth he's been using at the sink. "Not really. But I don't think Mr Hawkston would like it. Or maybe it's you he wouldn't like having a relationship with other people. Did something happen?"

My heart hammers. "What? No. Like what?"

"It just felt weird, is all. And now he wants you to see him in his office?" He grabs a pen from a shelf over the sink and yanks my arm, scrawling what I assume is his number on the inside of my wrist. "I swear I'm not cracking onto you, but if anything happens... or you need someone, call me. And if you want to get out of the house at any point, you can come see me in the staff block. I wouldn't want to share a house with that brooding monster." He jerks his thumb in the direction Mr Hawkston went.

"You're kind of freaking me out. He's not a criminal, is he?"

Alec gives an odd laugh. "No. But he is huge, and he can be grumpy as shit. I wouldn't want you feeling uncomfortable. Just save my number, or wash it off. Up to you."

"Thanks. I appreciate that. I don't know anyone in London."

"No one?"

"Not really. There might be a few of my uni mates who work down here now, but no one I was close to."

"Where'd you go to uni?"

"St Andrews."

"Ooh, like Wills and Kate?"

I laugh. *That's what everyone says.* "That's the one. But they were long gone by the time I went."

"What did you study?"

"Social Anthropology."

Alec screws his face up. "What do you do with a degree like that?"

"No need to look like that"—I wave at his face—"just because there's no food involved." Alec looks abashed for a moment, but I laugh, which seems to put him at ease. "For a while, I didn't know what I wanted to do. I thought about teaching. Or social work. One day, I still might pursue either of those. But I love kids, so for now, I'm happy to be a nanny. I'm not sure I see myself settling down and having my own family, and this lets me experience caring for young kids. They're so full of joy, don't you think?" Alec's staring at me with an odd look on his face. *I've over-shared.* I shrug and direct the conversation back to more practical matters. "Plus, I need to save some money and this role was so much better paid than anything else."

"Aries." Mr Hawkston's voice barks down the staircase, and I jump out of my skin.

"Has that been ten minutes?" I mouth at Alec, who raises his hands in a gesture of helplessness.

I dash upstairs and run towards his study, my heart in my mouth. I have no idea what to expect.

When I get there, the door is closed. I knock and wait.

"Come in," he says.

I step into the luxurious room. Curtains in red and gold hang either side of a huge sash window, and floor to ceiling wood panels line the walls. Mr Hawkston sits in a wingback chair on the other side of his desk, which is an enormous slab of dark mahogany. I've never seen one so large. It's practically the size of a bed. He could lay me down on that thing and screw me senseless, and my feet wouldn't even dangle off the edge. It's that big. A power desk.

He beckons me with two fingers, a gesture which I immediately misconstrue. *Does he want to put those inside me?*

He must read the confusion on my face because his eyes flare and he says, "Come closer," in case I haven't understood what his twitching fingers really meant.

With each step towards him, his dark eyes focused on me, my cells begin to buzz. As if his attention is the thing that completes my inner circuits.

Fuck, this is awkward. My body reacts intensely to this man, and the fact I pleasured myself in the shower this morning while thinking of him feels like a terrible, shameful secret he could unearth at any moment.

I walk up to the desk until I'm about a foot away. He still feels pretty far away, given the width of the mahogany surface.

Tension crackles. No, it *sparks*. My skin feels like a sheet of aluminium foil that's been put in the microwave at the highest setting. *Is he feeling this?*

"Are you settling in well?" His voice is calm, but his eye contact is so deliberate it's as though he's forcing himself not to look away from me. As if that might reveal some inherent weakness.

All I can see in my mind's eye is him in the pool room, outside the sauna. Absolutely butt naked. It was a glorious sight. It wouldn't matter now how many clothes the man wears... I've seen him in the best possible light, and it's with nothing on. The suits are good. Great, even, but naked, this man tops all the rest.

A strange ache sets up in my chest as another thought occurs to me: I'll never see him like that again. Instead, I'll be stuck with this stilted, professional version of him.

"Are you?" he repeats, and to my extreme embarrassment, I realise I've completely forgotten to answer his question. *What was it? Am I settling in well?*

"Oh, yeah. It's great. The house is really comfortable. My bed is so great. Nice and firm. I love a firm bed. It's much better for..." I stop talking because he's staring at me with that puzzled look on his face, as if he's never met anyone who talks like I do. The silence seems to go on forever.

"For what?" he asks. Am I imagining it, or is there a suggestive look in this man's eye? It's hard to tell.

"For my back."

"You're young to have back problems."

"Oh, no. I don't have back problems. I just really like a firm mattress."

He strums his fingertips on the desk for a few tense moments. "I'm not sure you living in the house is a good idea."

My stomach drops, and I swallow with an audible click. *Crap.* He's kicking me out. I knew I'd get fired. "Oh." *This is definitely because of the sauna.* "Why not?"

He lets my question sit for a while, but he shifts in his chair ever so slightly, as though he's drawing his shoulder blades together beneath his shirt. "There's a free room in the staff block at the end of the garden."

He totally avoided the question. "You're not firing me?"

"No."

"But you do want me to move out?"

"I think it would be advisable, yes. If you like the bed so much here, I can have it moved across."

Advisable, why? "What about night-time? What if Lucie wakes and I'm not there?"

He frowns like this isn't something he's considered. He has a plan, but he hasn't thought it through. *He's winging it.*

He sits back in his chair, head turned slightly to the side so he's not facing me dead on. His eyes narrow a fraction, but he keeps them trained on me, while he strokes his jaw with his thumb and index finger. He looks like a model, sitting there like that, as though the photographer told him to 'look as sexy as possible' and he instinctively knew how to do it. I feel a rush of heat expand from my chest and rise up my neck.

Seconds pass as I wait for him to speak. I don't dare look away, even though I know my cheeks are probably flaming.

Finally, he says, "I'm assuming you want to keep this job?"

"Yes. Although not if you don't want me. I don't want to work in an environment where my employer doesn't want me."

"I want you."

His voice is emotionless, his face immovable, but the air sparks between us again, a fission of invisible particles flowing from him to me and back again.

He hasn't broken eye contact with me for minutes now; I'm surprised the weight of his gaze hasn't made my muscles tremble. I can't take it any longer. I plaster a plastic smile on my face that stretches it in ways it isn't supposed to move. "Great."

"Is that all?"

Is that all? "You called me in here. There wasn't anything I wanted to say."

"You didn't want to talk to me at all?"

"Not really."

"You don't want to say anything about what happened this morning outside the sauna? You, who normally can't stop talking, have nothing to say about it?"

My mind races as I try to work out what he wants from me. I didn't have Mr Hawkston down as the direct communication type of guy. I thought we'd brush that excruciating incident under the proverbial rug.

A few moments of my brain scrambling for an answer has me concluding I can't work out what he wants, and he's *still* staring at me. The pressure is too much, so I do the most ill-advised, dangerous thing in this scenario. I start talking.

"When you question me about this, all I'm seeing in my imagination is you, completely naked. I can't talk about this with you and not see it, so if that's something you don't want me to do, then we should stop talking about it."

His eyebrows pull together. "Is this making you uncomfortable?"

Understatement of the century. "A bit. Not in a bad way."

"Good." He strums his fingertips on the desk again. "I don't want anything festering between us, especially if it's likely to render our working relationship untenable, in which case you'd have to leave. And like I said, I don't want that. Open communication generally works best in these scenarios."

Wow. This man is something else. What does he mean by '*these scenarios*'? "Do you often drop your towel in front of people you employ?"

Not even a hint of a smile. *Bloody hell.*

"No. That's never happened before. I'm navigating an unusual situation here. Is there anything else you want to say about it before we put this topic in a box we never discuss again?"

"Oh." *I need to wind this up. What else can I say? I'll apologise. That's a safe option.* "I'm sorry I pulled your towel off and saw... all of you. But honestly, I don't mind. I can forget about it, if that's what you want. Okay, maybe not forget because that was kind of unforgettable. You're unforgettable, especially without your clothes."

I've totally lost control of my mouth-to-brain connection. The words are pouring out as if someone else is talking. Inside my mind, a small, horrified version of me is listening, begging me to stop.

Mr Hawkston's lips are tight, but I'm sure it's humour compressing them rather than anything else. In fact, I'm certain of it, because his gaze is dancing with it. If I didn't know better, and he wasn't so good at locking down any emotional response, I'd say he's on the verge of bursting into raucous laughter.

I'm unbearably hot. My tongue runs riot when this man is near. I fan my face with my hand and try again. "I mean... fuck. It's just... I really like saunas."

"You aren't in one now, so you can stop fanning yourself."

My stomach takes a dive off a cliff as I force my hand to still and slowly lower it to my side. Mr Hawkston watches every movement I make, his focus so intent it's as though he doesn't want to miss a thing. *Too hot. I'm too hot.*

"You can use it," he says.

"Excuse me?"

"The sauna. If you like them that much, you can use it when I'm not home."

"Oh, right. Thanks. That would be great... amazing. So hot. Shit. No. So generous of you." I'm barely concentrating when I answer him. I think I've died and my soul is floating up into the corner of the room, looking down at the poor human version of me trying to dig herself out of this sewer of verbal shit.

I hold both my hands up. "I've definitely said everything I need to say now."

He stares at my arm... no, my *wrist*, and the tortured look on his face wipes away the hint of amusement. "What's that? It wasn't there earlier."

I turn my palm over and stare at Alec's number, scrawled in black marker pen on the inside of my wrist. I blink as if I'm not sure how it got there. "It's Alec's number."

"I thought he wasn't interested?"

My heart thuds. *Why is he asking?* "He's not. At least, I don't think so. He wanted me to have it in case anything happened."

"In here? If it wasn't on your skin before I came into the kitchen, and it is now, was he worried about what might happen to you in here, with me?"

This man is too sharp. I make a mental note that I can't hide anything from him. "No. Nothing like that," I lie. "He meant in general. Like I told you before, I don't know anyone in London."

"You know me."

I say nothing, because I have no idea what response he's expecting, and I've already made enough of a fool of myself. Also, he explicitly drew up the drawbridge on any potential friendship between us. He must know he's talking shit. Knowing my boss is not the same as knowing another member of staff. There's a hierarchy here I can't climb. Me and Alec have a shot at being friends, whereas me and the man before me... I don't know what we have. A screwed up employee-employer thing, where I've already seen his huge, hard cock.

I haven't had that many jobs in my working life, but I'm fairly certain that's not the basis for a healthy working relationship.

"I want you to call me if you need to." He opens a drawer in his desk and pulls out a brand new iPhone, still in its box, with a matching set of wireless headphones. "I know you prefer your old phone, but I want you to use this. If you're navigating an unfamiliar city, and you're looking after my daughter, you'll need it. And if you need anything, call me. Anytime."

He appears totally in control, and he sounds so confident that he could handle any problem I might have that my chest heats. *Could I rely on this man?* My heart thrums at the thought, but I keep my gaze on the new phone, worrying that if I look at him right now, I'll reveal how intensely his casual offer of assistance affects me.

Clearly, I fail at hiding how unsettled I'm feeling, because he adds, "It won't explode. And if you don't want to keep it after you leave this role, you can leave it here." He taps his desk.

"Okay." I grab the phone and headphones. "Thanks."

"Set it up tonight."

I wait for him to add something else. He doesn't, so I say, "Okay..." trailing up at the end of the K. It sounds like a question, and part of me hopes he'll answer it, so I can stay here with him for a few minutes longer.

He stares, tapping his index finger on the arm of his chair.

"That's everything?" I ask.

"Everything. Hopefully no cause for alarm? No need to call Alec for backup?"

"Nope."

"Good."

The stilted conversation feels like it's hit a natural end, so I hold up the phone and wave the box in the most awkward farewell gesture known to man. Mr Hawkston half smiles and gives the tiniest nod, which I take as permission to leave the room.

When my hand strikes the door handle, I realise there's one thing I do need to know. I turn back, but Mr Hawkston's eyes aren't there to meet mine at eye level. He's most definitely staring at my arse.

He raises his gaze, one eyebrow tripping up, inviting me to speak. No sign of embarrassment whatsoever that I just caught him checking me out.

"Where am I sleeping?"

His brow creases. "What do you mean?"

My heart leaps at his confusion. *Does he think I'm propositioning him?* "Am I staying in this house, or are you moving me to the staff block?"

"Ah. Here. Stay here. As you rightly pointed out, it's best if you're in the house. For Lucie. And then you can keep the bed." There's definite heat in his gaze and a teasing uplift to his lips when he adds, "For your back," and I know I need to get the hell out of this room before I take him up on the unspoken offer I can read in his eyes.

I excuse myself, and when the door closes behind me, I tune into the racing of my heart. *Does Mr Hawkston have any idea what he's doing to me?*

11
MATT

I barely see Aries for the next week. I'm in the office most of the time and I'm certain she's avoiding me when I'm home. I get back after Lucie's asleep. I always go to her room to give her a kiss goodnight, but Aries is never there.

Tonight, the light is on in Aries' room; I see the strip of it beneath the door. I don't know why my heart thuds so fucking awkwardly when I walk past. *Two weeks.* Two weeks of this woman living in my house, and I'm like a hopeless kid with a crush.

I shake my head, determined to put the nanny out of my mind. What happened last week outside the sauna was unfortunate. She's over-familiar. Not my type of woman at all. Far too open, unguarded… and yet I can't get her out of my head.

It's Friday night and I have no plans. Really sliding into that sad divorcé stereotype. Nico asked me if I wanted to have dinner with him and Kate, but I don't really want to hang out with them when they're so smitten and happy. Not that I mind. I'm pleased for him, but sometimes it hits home just how fucked up my situation is. All the years I wasted in a miserable marriage.

After a lonely meal at the kitchen island—one of Alec's frozen lasagnas—I head upstairs to bed, but I can't fucking sleep. I keep thinking of Aries, upstairs, that peek of light from beneath her door.

What's she doing right now?

Sleeping, you idiot. That's what she's doing.

I bring up my phone, scrolling through emails. Most are dull, work-related items, but one snags my attention. It's from Charlie's Housemaster, an old family friend called Barney Wentworth, at Marsden College.

My heart sinks. If Aries thinks I'm lacking empathy when it comes to Lucie, she'd have a field day with Charlie. I don't even know where or when it went wrong, but the subject line sinks like a metal weight in my gut.

Charles Hawkston: Disciplinary matters.

I open it.

Dear Matt,

Some matters have arisen in relation to Charlie, which are best discussed over the phone. When might be a good time to talk?

Best,

Barney.

Barney Wentworth must be nearing retirement. He's a contemporary of my father, and he was teaching at Marsden College when me, Nico and Seb were at the school.

I pull out my phone and bring up his phone number. I have no idea what he's about to say, but I know it won't be good, and as the ring tone buzzes in my ear, a chill runs down my spine.

"Matt," says Barney's gruff voice. "Didn't expect you to call so late."

"This email," I reply. "What's it about?"

Barney splutters before clearing his throat. "One of the boys found a bag of marijuana in Charlie's sock drawer."

I wait, and every muscle in my chest tenses until it feels like my entire torso has solidified. The divorce has been hard on Charlie, but for some reason it never crossed my mind that he would turn to drugs. *I'm not prepared for this.* "And?"

"You know the rules. If a student is found in possession of drugs, he's out."

Expulsion. I close my eyes and pinch the bridge of my nose. "Want me to fund a new library?"

Barney is quiet. "This is serious, Matthew."

"Sorry. I know. What did Charlie say?"

"That's the thing. Charlie says it's not his. Said he'd never seen it before."

"You don't believe him?"

"I want to, but his grades have been dropping off. For the last year, he hasn't been himself. Longer, probably. He looks…"

His voice fades as if he's reluctant to pass judgement, but I can't bear the silence so I fill in the blanks. "Stoned?"

Barney sighs. "Not necessarily. But tired. Haunted, even." *Haunted?* "Your son is a wreck, Matt."

I close my eyes again, letting the sentence sink in. *Your son is a wreck.* I'm not sure anything has ever felt this bad. "Who found it?"

"What?"

"The bag of weed. Who found it?"

There's a creaking sound, like Barney is leaning back in his chair. "Hugo Charlton."

For fuck's sake. Hugo Charlton is one of Mark Charlton's twins. And Mark Charlton is Gemma's new boyfriend. Damn unfortunate that she's decided to play house with a man whose sons are at school with Charlie. In the same boarding house, no less. I've even wondered if she had her eye on him before we got divorced. *Her wandering eye.* The seeds were sown, at any rate. God knows, we saw Mark often enough when we went up to the school. "What the hell is Hugo Charlton doing going through Charlie's sock drawer?"

The question hangs unanswered for a few moments before Barney speaks. "I know this is a thorny situation. And I want to believe Charlie. I really do. But the rules are rules—"

"It won't be Charlie's. You can't expel him. He wasn't smoking it. It wasn't on his person, was it?"

"No. In the sock drawer."

"Anyone could have put it there. You cannot expel him for this. And I'm serious about the library. Or science block. Whatever you want. Whatever the school needs."

"Matt..." Barney's voice is low and quiet, and the sad tone of it causes a shattering sensation behind my breastbone and a thickening in my throat. "Focus on your son. Some things you can't fix with money. We'll have to investigate this marijuana situation, but if there's no evidence he's smoking it or sharing it or whatever, then we can dismiss it this time." He breathes down the line for a few moments. "But there's something here that you really need to pay attention to. I'm advising you to take notice of your son, especially with the holidays coming up. He'll be under your care then. Not mine."

It feels a lot like I'm being reprimanded and I have to check the urge to protest. To fight back. "Okay. I appreciate the call."

Silence falls, during which one of us should say goodbye, but the word sticks to the roof of my mouth, and I hang up before Barney has the chance to say it.

In the dark corners of my mind, I can hear a voice, but it's not mine. *What do you mean he's a wreck? Of course he isn't. He's a fucking Hawkston, and we can weather all the shit life throws at us.*

The image of my father fucking our housekeeper flashes in my mind and I wince at the recollection. I was eleven when I found him, and when I told my mother what I'd seen she screamed at me. Told me to mind my own business. To keep my mouth shut and never mention it again, because 'Daddy needs to do what Daddy needs to do'.

I'm not a stranger to fucked-up family lives, and I turned out all right. *Didn't I?* I certainly didn't give the kids a happy home, and Charlie shouldered most of that. I hope Lucie won't remember me and Gemma living together because it was beyond miserable.

I thought I'd be happy once the divorce was finalised, but I'm not sure I am. It wasn't the magic pill I thought it would be. Yes, we aren't fighting all the time, and I don't come home to find a woman I can't stand waiting in the house for me... but I'm not happy. But maybe 'happy' is an illusion. A temptation that doesn't fucking exist. A word used to drive us forward, always seeking that elusive fucking happiness, but never finding it. *Like the pot of fucking gold at the end of the rainbow.*

Unable to relax, I head down to the kitchen in my boxers to get a glass of water. *Fuck it, water won't cut it.* I pour a scotch in a crystal glass and stare at it for a while. Then I take a few sips and listen to the creaks of the house. I move to sit on the sofa, which is tucked away towards one corner of the large kitchen. I sit and place my Scotch on the low level coffee table in front of me. A feeling of hopelessness spreads over me and I hang my head in my hands.

I haven't turned on the lights, and moonlight streams in the basement window. I don't know how long I sit there, drinking quietly in the dark, savouring this one glass of Scotch. Sipping it slowly, hoping it'll take the edge off. Could be twenty minutes, could be an hour. Either way, it's late.

The clink of keys in the lock shocks me, but I don't move.

"Thanks so much, it was so fun. Just what I needed."

It's Aries. I check the time: 2.30 am. I've been in a daze for hours. I forgot she was going out. God knows how it slipped my mind, because

Mrs Minter told me before she left, but... *Jesus*. I'm really not with it at the moment.

A man's voice replies and my heart clenches in the oddest way. Was that Alec? Or someone else? She'd better not be bringing someone down here. I listen, hardly breathing.

They say goodbye, and I hear Aries' footsteps clatter down the stairs. *She's coming.*

I don't move, watching as she stumbles towards the fridge. *Is she drunk?* She hasn't noticed me sitting in the shadows. An illicit thrill runs through me at the idea of watching her without her knowledge. *Is that fucked up? Maybe.* I sink into the sofa, thankful that the kitchen is so large, and she's unlikely to spot me, unless I make myself known.

She's humming, dressed in a gold mini dress that's all sequins, her hair free and messy. Lucie's right with her Ariel nickname. She really does look like a mermaid, covered in shimmering scales. The dress makes her body look like a gift I want to unwrap. Slowly. I'd take my time with it... with *her*.

She pulls the fridge door open, staggering away as though she hasn't realised her own strength, then she totters back towards it to peer at the contents. The glow of the fridge light puts her in a spotlight.

Fuck, she's beautiful.

She slides her heels off, pulls out a block of cheese, and grabs some eggs from a bowl on the counter.

When she kicks the fridge closed the room is dark again except for the moonlight streaming in the window. She grabs a candle from a shelf and a box of matches. She strikes one, and a flame bursts, making her look other-worldly in its glow as she lights the candle. I don't know why she doesn't turn on the full lights, but candlelight it is.

She's still humming. Dancing, even. Her hips sway, and her dress molds to the curve of her arse as it rides up and exposes her thighs.

I don't think she's wearing a bra because her full breasts move freely beneath her dress as she shimmies. But then I've noticed she hardly ever wears one. It's mesmerising, hypnotizing, watching her move when she thinks she's alone. I imagine touching her, sliding my hands over that arse, cupping each cheek, nuzzling my head between her breasts. Heat pools low in my stomach and tingles stir in the tip of my cock. This woman turns me on without even trying.

She begins cracking the eggs into a bowl, whisking them up. *Why the fuck is she doing this down here and not upstairs in her kitchen?* I'd be irritated if she wasn't so pleasing to spy on. But I don't want to be a creep...

"No eggs upstairs?" I say, announcing my presence.

She continues dancing, her back to me.

Didn't she hear me? I peer at her, noticing she's using the headphones I bought her. A burst of satisfaction courses through me, stronger than any reaction I ever had to seeing Gemma flaunt the expensive gifts I bought her.

Aries raises her hands over her head, hips shaking like she's in the middle of a nightclub, and her words from the other day spring to mind. *Don't you ever wear a shirt?* And here I am in only my fucking boxers. Again.

I'm torn. *Do I get up? Slink out? Sit still and wait until she's finished, hoping she doesn't see me at all?*

That's crazy. This is my house.

I push up from the sofa and pace towards her, driven by the urge to slide my arm around her waist, to pull her close, to press my fucking mouth against the pale skin of her neck... *fuck*.

I'll leave. This is insane.

Suddenly, I'm right behind her. I don't know how she can't sense me, seeing as she's all into her gut instinct and whatever other shit she rambles about, but she's oblivious.

"Aries."

She jumps out of her skin, spins one-eighty, and lets out a hair-raising scream as she flings two eggs at me. Maybe three. They crash against my chest, shells splintering on my skin. Aries isn't far behind the eggs, coming at me, arms-whirling, walloping me with clenched fists.

Her attack is thwarted by the slick mess of raw egg that coats my chest. Her fingers are slip-sliding all over me. I don't know if I'm in shock, but this definitely doesn't feel as bad as it should.

She snatches her hands back, and the mixture of surprise and disgust on her face is absolutely priceless as she stares at the strings of raw egg that web her fingers.

She yanks her earphones out one at a time, dumps them on the counter like she's annoyed with them, then steps back and flicks her hands, spraying raw egg everywhere. "Holy hell, where did you come from?" She's breathing fast, like I've scared the life out of her.

"I was here before you were." I point to the sofa.

Glaring at me, she picks up the leftover eggs, still safely in their box, as if she means to continue exactly what she was doing before I interrupted her, but then her eyes slide from my face to my egg-splattered chest, her mouth drops open, and she promptly drops the box of eggs to the floor, right at our feet.

"Jesus, Aries."

"Jesus, me? Jesus, you." She's still panting, and obviously unnerved. "What were you doing? Sitting in the dark like a perv?"

I'm not exactly calm myself, but my voice is level when I say, "My house, Aries. I can sit where I want. You have a kitchen upstairs."

"No eggs up there," she murmurs, with another glance at my chest.

"None here either," I say, gesturing to my chest and the mess on the floor. "Have you been drinking?"

"A bit. Not a crime, is it?" She eyes me like she can't work out whether I'm angry or not. I'm not sure if I am. Under her assessing gaze, everything feels tangled inside my ribcage.

"No," I concede. "But if you're going to smash every egg in the house, it might be."

She laughs, and all trace of her annoyance vanishes, blasting away any trace of my own at the same time, like sunlight breaking through clouds. "I'm so sorry. I'll replace the eggs." She crouches to the floor, trying to sweep the eggs back into the cardboard box. Her fingers are dripping with the stuff.

I kneel to help, the two of us crouching in the dark, shadows being cast by the light of the candle flitting around us. We gather the shells back into the box and scoop up whatever we can of the mess.

"Good thing the lights aren't on. I'd see right up your boxers," she teases, nodding at where I'm crouched.

I stifle a snort. "Did no one teach you not to say whatever the fuck is on your mind?" I say as I stand.

She shrugs and throws the shells and the box in the bin. "Just saying. Crouching in boxers isn't safe."

"For whom?"

She blinks twice. It's hard to tell with the flickering candle as our only light, but I think she's blushing. "People."

She turns away to wash her hands before she grabs a cloth from the sink and begins to wipe the floor. When she's done, she rinses the cloth and leaves it on the side of the sink, and then she gets a clean one, which she wets and throws at me. I only see it coming at the last second and grab it in one hand.

"What the fuck?"

"Clean yourself," she instructs, nodding at my chest. I'd almost forgotten about the mess on me. I wipe myself down as she watches. It's fucking weird, whatever is happening right now, me rubbing a cloth over my bare torso and Aries glued to the spectacle. I want to take a shower, but I haven't seen this woman for a week and I don't want to leave.

The realisation that I want to stay here with Aries is a slow fucking creep that strangles something in my chest: *I'm enjoying being near her.*

As I'm wiping away the last of the raw egg, I notice the eggs she's already cracked in the bowl. She's too tipsy to realise there are any left. I tip my head at them. "What were you making?"

"Cheese omelet. I've had a lot of wine. Eggs and cheese are great for absorbing it."

I grab the bowl and get a frying pan out of the cupboard.

She stares. "What are you doing?"

"Making your midnight feast."

"Oh, no. Please, you don't have to do that."

"I know. But you're drunk and if you lose these eggs"—I hold up the bowl—"then we're out entirely and you'll have to wait until morning, and by then it'll be too late." I point at a stool. "Sit. This will only take a minute."

She does as I ask, propping her elbows on the counter. I feel her gaze on me like a river of fucking fire as I try to focus on the simplest of tasks—making an omelet. I grate the cheese and add it to the mixture. After a few minutes, she speaks. "Hold up."

I glance at her. "Yeah?"

She rubs her eyes with both fists. "Am I dreaming or is my boss half-naked in the kitchen, cooking for me in the middle of the night? I must have had way too much to drink because this can't be real."

I chuckle as I flip the omelet, turn it up onto a plate and push it across to her, along with some cutlery from the drawer. "Not a dream. Enjoy."

"Mmm." She inhales and licks her lips. "Who knew you had a secret talent for cooking eggs?"

"It's not hard."

She scoffs a mouthful. "Mmm, but this is delicious. Yum." I fill a glass of water and give it to her. "Thanks. You do this for all your nannies?"

"No. Never done this for anyone."

Her features widen in amazement. "Now I feel special." She points her fork at me. "You shouldn't go making a girl feel special if you don't mean it."

"It's an omelet."

She licks the side of her knife. "Special omelet."

"You're drunk."

"Yes." Her eyebrows move up and down in unison. "And you're special."

I laugh. Fuck, this woman is funny. She might be the strangest, most beautiful woman I've ever met. No one... and I mean *no one*, has ever spoken to me like this. Especially not an employee. I don't even want to consider why I'm allowing it to happen...

For a few minutes, I watch her eat, which she does with gusto.

"Why were you awake? What were you doing down here?" she asks as she chows down a mouthful.

My mind flits to the email from Barney and the conversation about Charlie. There's no way I'm getting into that now. "Couldn't sleep."

She arches a brow. "I can help with that."

"How?"

"Reiki."

I cross my arms over my chest. I don't miss how her gaze slides over me, drawn by the movement, lingering on my upper arms. She gives a tiny shake of the head, as if to release whatever distracting thought popped into her mind. "Ah, yes. The reiki," I say with a heavy dose of scepticism.

"It's very relaxing. You lie down, I wave my hands over you—"

"No." That sounds way too intimate. I'm not getting on my back for this woman, especially not if she's drunk.

"No? You'd fall asleep in no time. My mother used to do it for me as a kid all the time. I'd fall asleep while she directed healing energy at my body. I felt surrounded with love while I drifted off."

That sounds oddly appealing. "I thought you were a nanny, not a healer."

"I'm a lot of things. Close your eyes."

The air thickens around us, but I'm not sure she notices. She's so bright, so bubbly. Maybe she's completely oblivious to the attraction that's pulsing through me right now.

"Here? Now? Standing up? Not that I mean to doubt you, but I'm not sure even you have the power to make me fall asleep standing up."

Aries laughs, tipping her head back, rustling all that hair like an autumn breeze moving through fallen leaves. God, even this woman's hair has me turning poetic. "I just meant for you to feel the sensation of it. The tingles."

Tingles? That sounds *dangerous*... like it might lead to places I shouldn't go with this woman. "No."

Aries sighs as though I'm a disappointment to her. To think I might be makes me uncomfortable, like my skin has shrunk in a hot wash. "You're such a sceptic. It's written all over you."

I can't help it, but I let my arms fall and glance down at the bare skin of my forearms, my hands, my chest, as if something is *actually* written there, and Aries laughs again. I love the way she laughs... it's so *free*. On the plus side, if she can laugh so easily then perhaps she isn't too disappointed in me. Judging by the way she's smiling at me, she's certainly not holding onto any resentment.

"Thanks for the omelet. I'm going to go to bed. If you can't sleep, message me." She waves her phone at me as she stands to put her plate in the dishwasher. "I'll send you some distance healing."

I say nothing, because the only thing I want to do is tell her to scrap the distance part of that sentence. And maybe the healing part too.

Fuck it. "Wait."

She turns. "Yeah?"

"If I sit down, will you do it?"

She pauses, considering this. "If you lie down, over there"—she indicates the sofa—"then yes."

I suck a breath through tight lips and force it out. *This is probably a bad idea.* "Okay." I pace over to it, intensely aware of the fact I'm wearing very little and she's walking right behind me. The sweetest sense of nervous anticipation bubbles up inside me, and I do my best not to let it show. *What the hell am I thinking doing this?*

And yet, I don't stop. I lie on my back on the sofa, and Aries drags a chair over from the kitchen table and sits next to me. She smiles, a small encouraging smile, obviously designed to put me at ease. She'd be a wonderful nurse. Or a doctor. There's a comforting warmth to her presence, and as long as she didn't start rambling, her bedside manner would be impeccable.

"Close your eyes," she says, and I do, settling into the darkness behind my lids.

She gives me some instructions about my breathing and releasing tension in my body. I breathe slowly in and out, letting her calming voice wash over me, amazed that I can feel so comfortable in her presence. I can't remember the last time I lay down and took a moment, just for myself, to relax.

After a few minutes, a prickling sensation crawls over my skin, *under my skin*, like parts of me are shifting. It's bizarre. The sensation radiates and moves to different areas of my body. My toes tingle, my calves, my shoulders. My chest seems to unlock, and I get a vision of petals opening like a time-lapse flower.

Next to me, Aries breathes quietly. Her knee brushes my thigh, sparks flying from the point of contact. And then, out of nowhere, a huge surge of energy rises from the base of my spine, pooling in my hips. The tip of my dick begins to tingle.

Fuck. I'm getting hard.

My eyes pop open and I sit upright, nearly crashing into Aries who's leaning over me, but she leaps back at my sudden movement.

"Shit. What happened? Are you okay?" she stutters, leaning back in her chair, looking at me like I might attack her.

"Yeah. Great." I grab a pillow and shove it over my crotch. Aries follows the motion with her eyes, eyebrows rising just a fraction, but she says nothing. "I think you should go to bed."

But Aries doesn't move. "Are you sure you want to stop?"

"Yeah, I'm sure."

"It happens," she says, matter-of-factly, nodding at my crotch. "You don't need to be embarrassed."

Heat rages through me. "I'm not." *Liar.*

"I know it's not personal. It's the energies. The way they flow through the body. It depends on what's going on in your life. Where the blockages are. I don't mind if you want to work this one through."

What the fuck is she offering? It sounds incredibly tempting, but whatever is happening in my body right now, it's not 'the energies', whatever the fuck that means. It's her. And me. And the fact that I want to touch her. Kiss her. Fuck her. Have her ride my face until she screams my name.

And I'm a fucking idiot to have indulged myself this way tonight.

"An energy orgasm," Aries clarifies. I grimace at the word 'orgasm', and my stomach feels like a myriad of dominoes are falling over. *She never knows when to shut up.* "That's what we call it when you climax without being touched. I can hold the space for you, if you want. Looks like you need the release."

Some sort of explosion must happen internally, because my body temperature ratchets up about a million degrees, and I can hardly breathe. "Fuck, no." I peel back the edge of the cushion nearest my abdomen, trying to subtly peek beneath it. My dick is rock-solid. Aries needs to get the hell out of this room. "Absolutely not. No, thank you. Please go to bed."

And I'll work this one through alone.

Aries' cheeks are turning a rosy pink. "All right." She pushes her chair away from me, stands and paces across the kitchen. The further away she moves, the easier it is for me to breathe, but then she pauses, hovering in the doorway with a thoughtful expression on her face. I can tell she wants to say something, and I brace for whatever the hell might come out of her mouth. *Something about the sauna, or about seeing me hard before, or about this becoming a regular fucking occurrence...* Thankfully, her expression shifts a moment later, and she merely says, "Good night, Mr Hawkston."

I sag with relief. "Night, Aries."

I listen to the sound of her feet hitting the steps until it fades to nothing. The kitchen is empty, dark and quiet now. I toss the cushion to the other side of the sofa and drop my face into my hands. *What the fuck?* I allow myself a second of self-pity before I admit that there's something more pressing I need to deal with, unable to hold back for a second longer. I get up and brace one arm on the wall as I slide my other hand into my boxers and grip my dick.

So fucking hard. A million recriminations spring up in my mind... *I shouldn't be doing this... I ought to have some self control...* But as I stroke up and down, they fade away, replaced only by visions of Aries. Her long hair, that sultry bottom lip, so soft and pink... I imagine a different ending for tonight's encounter. Her, straddling me on the sofa, bouncing on my dick, red hair flying, breasts heaving...

When I come, I say her name. Quietly groaning it with my mouth pressed into the crook of my elbow as hot spurts of cum decorate my other fist.

And then I go to bed and try and forget about the entire thing.

12

ARIES

The next couple of weeks pass in a flurry of activity. Lucie and I spend a lot of time at various parks—Kensington Gardens, Hyde Park, the Princess Diana Memorial playground. It's non-stop. Mondays and Tuesdays are rest days for me, but I'm exhausted by the time they roll around.

I speak to Mum every few days. I'm trying not to worry too much, but she sounds weaker, as though it takes more effort to maintain a conversation.

Alec and I have settled into a decent friendship, especially after our Friday night out, where he took me to a loud and sweaty club just off Leicester Square. And then the eggs...

Egg-gate. Maybe that's what I'll call it. Even though I was drunk, I can still remember smearing those raw eggs all over Mr Hawkston's chest. And then the reiki afterwards. *Eek.* Maybe it should be reiki-gate. I can't decide which part of the encounter was worse; all of it was bad. Not at the time, of course. Then, I was enjoying myself. Or rather, I was enjoying *him*. But now, in the cold, sober light of day, I'm embarrassed. Not because I think I did anything wrong, per se, but because it's all so weird. *How can we have a normal working relationship going forward? Maybe we can't...* we never did, really, now I think of it. It's just as well I've barely seen him since then.

Until now. He sent me a message earlier, asking me to pop into his office, and here I am, standing outside, heart thudding. *Nervous.*

I knock on the door and his low, deep voice responds, "Come in."

The familiar buzz of attraction fizzes in my veins as I step into the room, catching sight of him behind that huge desk.

"Aries." His eyes flick up to me from the periodical he's reading. He lays it on the desktop and fully focuses on me. I stand awkwardly. He gives no indication he wants me to sit down, so I don't. My hands begin to tingle and I try my best to ignore it. "How are you?"

"Good."

"Excellent. I wanted to speak to you about Saturday." Momentary confusion must show on my face because he adds, "Charlie's Speech Day at Marsden College."

I recognise the name of the school. It's world famous, mostly because extended members of the Royal family and previous Prime Ministers were educated there. "It's a whole day event. There's the picnic, the boat race, and then the speeches and prize-giving." *Wow, this sounds fancy.* "You'll be in charge of Lucie all day. We'll take the car. Alec will prepare the picnic in the morning."

"Right." This is all new to me, but I go along with it in case it has been mentioned and I've forgotten.

Mr Hawkston goes quiet and a warning prickle crawls up my spine. Whatever he's going to say next, he's not happy about it. "Gemma will be there." It takes me a second to register who he's talking about, which he must notice because he adds, "My ex-wife."

Of course. The beautiful blonde woman from the internet photos. "Will she be picnicking with us?"

"No. She has a new partner, and he has kids at the school too. She'll be with them."

"Oh." *That sounds awkward.* "Is Charlie friends with her partner's kids?"

Mr Hawkston pins me with a stare, his gaze dropping from my face down the full length of me, then back to my face. "I don't know. They're older. Charlie hasn't mentioned them."

Something about this conversation strikes me wrong, but I have no idea what it is. Why didn't he ask me to sit down? And why does he keep looking at me like that? Maybe the awkwardness isn't about Gemma or the boys. Maybe it's about me. Or what happened with the eggs and the reiki. Before I can stop myself, I start talking.

"About that night, in the kitchen—"

"No." I take a step back from his desk, surprised by the vehemence in his voice as he cuts me off. "Don't say a word." He breaks eye contact to dip his head, and I wait, the *whoosh-whoosh* of my pulse pounding in my ears as he takes a few breaths. Finally, he looks at me again. "No," he repeats, softer this time. "Just no, Aries. Don't do this to me."

He sounds tormented, as though he's approaching some kind of breaking point, and he thinks I'm the one who's pushing him there. But that's not all I hear in his voice. There's a hopeless resignation there too, suggesting that he doesn't believe he has the power to stop me. That whatever it is I'm doing to him, it's inevitable...

My brain must be crumbling, because I can't work out exactly what he's referring to, and worse, I feel like I can't question him on it. I press my lips together to stop myself from asking, but it doesn't work.

"Do what?" I mutter, but even as I say the words, arousal swirls between my legs and I know that whatever he's agonising over, it has something to do with this weird feeling that keeps sneaking up between us. This *attraction*. "What did I do?"

He props his elbow on the desk and drops his forehead into his hand, rubbing it agitatedly back and forth. He doesn't look at me when he says, "I cannot keep having these conversations with you." *He's changed his tune. What shifted?* He drags his eyes to mine where they lock on. "I'm your boss. Go and do your job. Nothing more, nothing less. That's enough. I'll see you on Saturday."

He waves the back of his hand at the door to dismiss me, and I clench my fists to restrain the urge to retort. If he won't talk about what's happening between us, then that's fine by me. I'll do my best to ignore it too.

But as I let myself out, I'm aware of an inner knowing that *something* is going to break soon, and there's nothing either one of us can do about it.

Saturday comes around faster than I can believe. Despite Mr Hawkston's odd behaviour at our last meeting, I'm having such a good time working here—hanging out with Lucie—that time is flying.

I'm wearing my smartest clothes—a white cotton blouse and a full length floral skirt. Definitely more tourist-in-Tuscany than Speech Day at England's most prestigious boarding school, but it's the best I can do. Apparently, people wear hats to this event, like a proper English wedding. I don't have one, but Lucie has been telling me all morning how beautiful my hair is, so I'm feeling pretty good. There's nothing like compliments from a four-year-old. And who needs a hat when you have actual red hair that's so thick I need super strong hair bands just to wrestle it into a ponytail?

The car is quiet as we ride up to Marsden College. We're all in the back, facing one another like the inside of a black cab. I'm next to Lucie in her car seat, and Mr Hawkston is opposite us. He's wearing a suit, but he's barely looked up from his mobile phone. Clearly, my comments about severing the human connection were ignored. *Perhaps he doesn't want a connection.*

Or maybe he is that important. Maybe this is still a workday for him, much like it is for me.

I pin my hands between my knees, trying to stay as still as possible. I'm nervous about meeting Charlie, Mr Hawkston's teenage son. Mrs Minter alluded to the fact that he's got himself into a bit of trouble in the past, but didn't give me details. And if what Alec said about the Hawkson's marriage being that unhappy is true, then I'm sure the kid has been through a lot. Acting out a little wouldn't be surprising.

My heart is also hammering from being so close to Mr Hawkston for such a long time. It takes about an hour to reach the school and the car is full of the scent of him… expensive, rich, with notes of cedar and sandalwood and a host of other things I don't know the name of. I don't know if the scent itself is a good one, or if it's because it's his, but it turns me on.

I laugh inwardly at the idea that I thought I could ignore my attraction to him. It's so intense that just being near him has the slow thump of a pulse beating between my legs.

Holy hell, this is inappropriate. His daughter is right here in the car. But even so, I can't push it away. I can't order my body not to feel whatever it is I'm feeling for him.

I wonder if he's feeling the tension too, but there's no way of knowing for sure. He's barely paid me any notice.

Lucie falls asleep, but still, Mr Hawkston doesn't look up from his phone. The longer this journey is, the more tense I feel.

Finally, he slides his phone into his pocket and stares out of the window. "You're responsible for Lucie," he says without looking at me. "Keep her out of trouble. She's never been to Charlie's Speech Day before."

"Okay."

"My ex-wife will be here."

Clearly, it's troubling him. "I know. You told me."

"Don't know why she's coming. Gemma doesn't give a fuck about the kids. Never did."

I frown, and my mouth unhinges as I let out a tiny gasp, my gaze shooting to Lucie. *Still asleep, thank goodness. But even so, how can he speak about his child's mother like that in front of her?*

"She's asleep." Mr Hawkston throws the words at me as though he knows exactly what I was thinking, but it doesn't deter him as he mutters, "And her mother is a bitch."

Okay, that I can't ignore. "Shhhh. Her subconscious is wide awake."

He raises an eyebrow. "Her subconscious knows it's true."

I fold my arms over my chest. I'm not about to argue with him while Lucie is in the car. He shakes his head as if to say, '*You have no idea*'. It's either that or '*you're ridiculous*', and I can't decide which is more unsettling. Neither of us speaks for a long time.

"You're quiet," he says, eventually. It's funny how he's always asking me to stop talking, but then whenever I do, he wants to hear me speak again. *He's conflicted.*

I don't oblige him and in the silence, Lucie snores. Mr Hawkston looks sideways at her, makes a grunting noise, and goes back to his phone. "Did you find that friend you were looking for?"

"Friend?"

He holds eye contact. "Yes. When you arrived, you said you didn't know anyone in London. Have you found people?"

The air hums between us and I wonder if he's remembering that very first conversation we had, where I expressed the hope we'd get to know one another. And not as boss and employee. I guess that won't happen now, because we're stuck in these roles.

But then, given what his ex-wife looks like, I'm not sure he'd go for me anyway.

"I've been spending a bit of time with Alec. That's who I was out with the night..." I begin to blush, knowing he doesn't want to be reminded. "The eggs. You know..."

Something flashes in his gaze, and he mutters a curse under his breath. "I remember."

Heat flashes through me. *Awkward.* "He's such a great chef," I continue, sticking to a safer topic of conversation. "The snacks he makes over in the staff house are delicious. Amazing. And the accommodation... That staff block is so nice. So generous."

Mr Hawkston shifts in his seat, and a surly look crosses his face. "It's not generous. It's part of their remuneration. I've generally found staff work better and harder if their other needs are taken care of."

The way he talks about 'staff' makes me wonder if he sees other humans as actual people or useful animal types he can herd and control. Give them greener grass, and they grow better wool type thing...

"Gemma will expect to see Lucie today. I don't want you to leave them alone together."

The change of topic gives me whiplash. It's clear Mr Hawkston is worried, given the way he keeps circling back to the topic of his ex-wife. *Geez.* This sounds unpleasant and like it's beyond my job description. He must read my uncertainty because he says, "Just keep her in your sights, okay?"

"Absolutely. Yes. I can do that."

The car rolls into the quaintest, cutest town, all narrow streets and Georgian terraces. I gawk like a tourist, nose pressed up against the glass. A few minutes later, we park up on the school fields and I get out. The air is warm and smells like freshly cut grass.

The view that greets me is like a scene from a chocolate box. The buildings, some of them at least, are ancient, like something out of Oxford or Cambridge. A spire pokes above the tree line; a church beyond the fields, just out of sight. The school is so grand, and the modern buildings are sleek and ultra-stylish, slotting into place neatly alongside the ancient ones.

Mr Hawkston gets out of the car too, unfolding himself elegantly, like an actor walking onto a set. He barely glances at the view, like this is all so normal for him. But it's not for anyone who isn't used to hanging out in high society. I did actually Google—check me out and my smartphone skills—the school fees here, and it's something crazy for one kid... more than I would earn in an entire year. *Several years.*

Lucie is still sleeping, and I'm not sure what to do with her. It's too hot to leave her in the car, so for a moment, I just stare at her cute snoozing face, a tendril of hair by her mouth blowing back and forth with her steady breaths.

I sense a presence by my side and know the millisecond before I turn that Mr Hawkston is there.

"I'll get her," he says, and I step out of the way so he can unbuckle his daughter and carry her out.

Around the car, staff are laying out tables and chairs. I didn't realise he'd brought staff, but I see more of them getting out of another nearby car, carrying picnic stuff over to us. There's a table and tablecloth and champagne on ice. And the food coming out... how many people is Mr Hawkston feeding here? There are platters of shrimp and smoked salmon and canapes. "Did we drive here in convoy?"

Lucie still in his arms, Mr Hawkston nods. "Something like that."

He's cradling Lucie like she's the most precious thing in the world. It's adorable. He might be a bit sharp with her sometimes, but it's obvious he loves her. He carefully sets her down, still asleep, on one of the picnic blankets. And then he brushes that little tendril of hair that's stuck to her lips behind her ear.

"Drink?" someone offers me.

Mr Hawkston sticks out his hand and takes it. "Not for her. She's working."

He takes the champagne himself, smiling lopsidedly at me like he feels a bit bad for taking my drink. *Does he care what I think?* I wouldn't expect him to make any concessions and I wouldn't have minded if he hadn't. I *am* working, after all. But that tiny smile—a wordless '*I'm sorry*'—warms my heart a touch.

I sit with Lucie on what turns out to be the softest picnic rug ever. *Cashmere?* Nothing like the scratchy woollen one I had as a kid.

While the staff set up our elaborate picnic, I glance around the field, full of highly polished cars, shining like the staff have just finished waxing them. Mixed in, there are a few rustier old estate cars, where the families are sitting on tartan picnic rugs spread out on the grass and tucking into packet sandwiches. It's amazing to me that even at the most elite boarding school in the country, there's still a hierarchy.

I don't know where Mr Hawkston fits in, but I figure it's somewhere near the top, at least on account of the show he's putting on and the amount of people who are coming over to say hello and to join him for champagne. He's surrounded by other couples, men and women, who appear to be hanging off his every word.

Mr Hawkston is polite and attentive to everyone, and I imagine this is how he works the room at corporate events. It's a side to him I definitely haven't seen before. He's smiling and joking and entertaining these people... and it's glorious to watch. He's yummy. Totally in control. It blows my mind that I've seen this composed, gorgeous man entirely naked. I've smeared raw egg over his pecs, and the memory makes my heart beat a little faster.

And yet, there's something about his actions that seems performative, as though everything he's doing is for effect. He must feel my gaze because he glances over. Our eyes meet for only a fraction of a second, but it's long enough to shatter the façade, as though he's granting me a glimpse at the real man beneath. I'm instantly greedy for more of his attention as every hair on my body stands upright and heat spreads outwards from my chest.

I look away, willing my body under control. *Stop being ridiculous. He's your boss.* I stroke Lucie's hair as she sleeps, and try to concentrate on her.

"Hello." A woman's voice distracts me from Lucie.

She's pretty, dark-haired, and wearing a yellow suit and a huge hat that casts a shadow over her fine bone structure. She's peering down at me, and I squint, using my hand as a shield to block the sun. She smiles and crouches opposite me, holding out her hand.

"I'm Kate," she says, but this means nothing to me, so I stare blankly and she adds, "I'm an old family friend of Matt. Nico"—she nods her head towards a handsome man who looks a lot like Matt—"is my boyfriend."

Nico's looking at me with interest, in the way people do when they've heard something about you that colours their view. I don't want to think what Matt might have said to him.

"I'm Aries. Lucie's nanny."

"I know," Kate replies, her beautiful smile giving nothing away. "This must be terribly dull for you. All this old school stuff. Nico loves it. Thinks this place made him the man he is today." A light chuckle spills from her lips. "Can't wait to see Charlie in the boat race though. That's always exciting. Anyway"—Kate strokes Lucie's cheek and then stands, focusing back on me—"it was good to meet you. Tell Lucie I said hi when she wakes up."

Kate wanders back to Nico and when she reaches him, they share a chaste kiss, but he slides an arm around her waist and pulls her a fraction too close. As though, despite the fact that they're in public, he wants her as near as possible, and she doesn't resist. He whispers something against her ear, and she laughs. The way they interact is adorable. It looks like true love. After a few minutes, the two of them say goodbye to Mr Hawkston and wander off.

It's not long before Lucie opens her eyes and looks up at me. "Hello, Ariel," she says, blinking in the sunlight.

"Hey, sweetie. It's lunchtime. You want me to fix you something?"

She stretches and sits up cross-legged. She looks over to where her father is talking to everyone, watching as the adults pick up what look like smoked salmon blinis.

"Smoked salmon, please," she says. "But not with the cream. Or those little black things."

Crap. Does she expect me to pick the canapes apart for her? "Black things?"

"Yeah, the stinky fish eggs."

Ah. Caviar. "Okay. I'll be right back."

I edge up to the elaborate table that Mr Hawkston's staff have set out. There's silver cutlery and actual breakable plates. Whenever I had a picnic, the cutlery was plastic and the plates were paper. Maybe plastic if whoever brought the crockery was extra organised.

I grab a plate and pile it with three or four blinis. Then, checking no one's looking, I start taking them apart, scraping off the caviar and sour cream. I don't want to waste it though... I mean, scraping caviar and leaving it at the side of the plate? That's tantamount to a crime.

So I eat it. Stealthily, checking Mr Hawkston's back is turned as I do it. I feel like a criminal stealing gold or something, but it's bloody delicious. I'm working as fast as I can and fortunately, everyone is too busy socialising and trying to get Mr Hawkston's attention to notice what I'm doing.

I'm licking my fingers and trying my hardest to keep the mess discreet, when I sense a presence right at my elbow.

"Has the nanny got a taste for the finer things in life already?" It's a woman's voice, and it sends a shiver up my spine because it's so dismissive, so *derogatory*, that I feel violated. "I suppose living with Matt does that to a woman."

I spin, dismantled blini in one hand, to find a beautiful blonde woman staring at me. I know exactly who she is. Gemma, the ex-wife. She's even more beautiful than the pictures. Every feature is freakishly symmetrical, like I'm looking at an optical illusion. Straight nose, big blue eyes, cupid's bow pink mouth. She looks like *Blake Lively*, if someone tweaked all her features so the angles mathematically aligned. My breath catches at the sight of her, but her expression is vicious, and the judgment in her eyes blisters my skin.

"Oh, Mrs Hawkston—"

"Please. Don't call me that. I go by my maiden name now. Von Arsworz."

I don't know what the hell she just said, but it sounded a lot like arse-warts. I don't dare risk repeating it, so I smile inanely as Gemma looks me up and down, her nose scrunched in a disdainful sneer.

"Aren't you pretty. Where'd he find you then? One of those clubs? Bad girl gone good, are you? You look just the type." She waves her hands over my breasts, as if my larger-than-average cup size is what makes me 'bad'.

My brain is struggling to catch up. "I'm sorry, what?"

"Is he fucking you yet?" Gemma smirks. "That would be just like him. To screw the nanny. It would be efficient. Someone right on his doorstep so he doesn't have to take any time off work."

I am completely, utterly, speechless. This woman is a bitch with a capital B. But even so, heat rises up my cheeks, fiery humiliation creeping across my face. Mr Hawkston and I might not have had sex, but I've seen him completely naked. And hard. And I am sorely tempted to tell her, just to see how she'd react.

I'm still staring at Gemma when I notice Mr Hawkston's attention on us. He still has half a glass of champagne in one hand, but his gaze is trained on me and he's coming over.

Gemma hasn't noticed. "So, is he?"

"Is he what?" I ask.

"Don't act stupid. Is my husband fucking you?"

"Ex-husband." Mr Hawkston's deep voice demolishes Gemma's rant. Her hand tightens on the stem of her champagne glass and her shoulders squeeze together.

He ignores her, instead leaning towards me and tapping the side of his lips. It takes me a moment to realise he's letting me know I have food on my face. *Again.*

"May I?" he says, and, because I'm stupefied, standing between the two most gorgeous human beings I've ever seen, I nod. Mr Hawkston reaches over Gemma's shoulder to swipe his thumb across the edge of my lips, picks up a trace of caviar and then sucks it off his thumb.

My heart shudders and heat flushes my body. He just ate food *off my face*. He's holding my gaze like he is fucking me, or he might, or he means to... I feel it right down to my clit. It's wholly indecent.

I'm completely in shock, but not as much as Gemma is.

She spins on her heels to face him, her mouth wide, but before she can speak, Mr Hawkston blasts his attention onto her, glaring.

"Whom I choose to sleep with has nothing to do with you anymore."

Gemma huffs. "Oh, you bastard. You're a sly piece of shit, Matthew Hawkston. Employing a nanny that looks like that and then parading her about in front of everyone. Are you trying to embarrass me?"

"Don't be ridiculous. Aries is a valued member of my household staff."

"Oh, Aries, is it?" She sneers, crossing her arms over her chest. Mr Hawkston says nothing and Gemma spits out, "I'm taking Lucie to my picnic. We'll see you at the boat race."

She storms over to where Lucie is sitting on the rug, yanks her up by the arm and drags her to her feet.

"Mummy, ow." Lucie rubs at her arm.

"Oh, don't be silly." Gemma waves dismissively at Lucie. "That didn't hurt."

Lucie looks like she might cry, and my heart breaks to see it. Lucie, attempting to heal the rift, reaches out to Gemma for a hug.

Gemma swipes her hands away. "Don't touch. This suit is *Catherine Walker*. Your hands are grubby."

Lucie withers, and Gemma grabs her elbow and ushers her away.

Mr Hawkston glances at me, and without waiting to be told, I stumble after them, balancing the plate of dismantled salmon blinis in one hand.

"Aries," Mr Hawkston calls.

I turn to see every trace of desire or whatever the hell it was he was looking at me with earlier has gone. The man is a master of deception. He's performing for everyone all the time.

A hollowing sensation occurs in my stomach that I recognise as disappointment, but there's something else there too. *Anger*. He used me to piss off his ex-wife... I want to tell him what I think of that behaviour, but he pins me with a serious, almost threatening glare, and my annoyance vanishes as nerves begin to churn in my gut. "Don't let Lucie out of your sight."

"Yes, sir," I reply, saluting him with my free hand in an attempt to dispel the tension, but Mr Hawkston doesn't smile, and my nerves only get worse.

I turn and run after Gemma and Lucie, still holding the plate of smoked salmon like an over-exuberant waitress, while trying to shake off the curious foreboding sensation that hovers at the edge of my awareness.

What could possibly go wrong on a day like today?

13

ARIES

Gemma's picnic is twice as fancy as Mr Hawkston's, and there are members of staff mingling amidst the other parents that circulate the tables. They're dressed like waiters and waitresses, in dark trousers and white shirts, and they're handing out platters of food from trays and pouring champagne.

There are just as many people, if not more, coming over to talk to Gemma as there were at Mr Hawkston's picnic. She drops Lucie's arm as soon as she reaches the group and, without bringing her little daughter over to speak to anyone, dumps her on a folding chair that's made for an adult. Lucie looks lost, her legs dangling in midair, and her white ankle socks with their frills, and her patent Mary Jane's, add a whole extra level of cuteness that makes my heart ache. When she looks up and sees me, the relief in her gaze is so acute that it softens her entire body, and a small lump forms in the back of my throat.

"Ariel," she whimpers.

At this, Gemma turns back to look at me. I hand Lucie the plate of salmon, and she starts picking at it with her fingers.

Gemma's nose scrunches, and she snatches it away. "You can't eat that. It looks disgusting. Plus, the nanny had her fingers all over it."

What a bitch.

A man comes up behind Gemma. He's tall, with salt and pepper grey hair, looking close to fifty. A lot older than both Gemma and

Mr Hawkston. In fact, Mr Hawkston and Gemma are probably the youngest parents here. Everyone else looks at least ten years older than they do. They must have had Charlie really young.

"Who's this?" the man asks, looking at me but keeping one arm around Gemma. He snuffles his large nose into her hair, and she makes a soft purring sound.

"I'm Aries," I say, sticking my hand out.

The man's eyebrows rise, and though he takes my hand, I get the sense I've done something socially unacceptable without realising, but I have no idea what it is.

"Mark Charlton," he says.

"This is Matt's new nanny," Gemma says, flapping her hand at me. "Can you believe it?"

Mark takes me in, then nuzzles the side of Gemma's head again. "You know we could have fought for custody, and you wouldn't have to deal with this," he murmurs, speaking to Gemma as though I'm not an actual human being with functioning ears, who's standing right in front of him.

"God, no." Gemma rolls her eyes. "I don't want the kids that often. Matt's welcome to them. Honestly, after today, that'll be enough for me for a few weeks. I'll probably need to lie down and recover." She cackles, and Mark laughs too, as if this exchange is the funniest thing they've heard all day.

Lucie's bottom lip begins to quiver, and her big innocent eyes look up at her mother like the woman has punched a fist right through her ribcage and dragged her heart back out through the debris. Which is exactly what I want to do to Gemma.

"Couldn't agree more," says another woman, coming over to join them. She reminds me of an over-sized bird, all dressed in red with a pointed nose and slightly too-large chin. "We've got three nannies at home. One for each child. The less I see of my kids, the better. David"—she waves at a tall blond man, who's shoving what looks like a tiny Yorkshire pudding into his mouth—"wants to have another. Can you imagine? I said to him, 'David, do you really want another child, or is it a status symbol? Because if it's the latter, I'd far rather get the kitchen redesigned or buy a new car'. God knows, the kids cost just as much."

The three of them burst into raucous laughter.

I kneel at Lucie's side, putting my arm around her. "You okay, sweetie?"

"I'm hungry," she says, and I'm struck by the fact this kid has already learned to suppress what she's really feeling. Maybe she is hungry, but it's certainly not the only thing going on.

I squeeze her hand. "I'll get you something."

Gemma is still clutching the plate of blinis I dismantled, so I make my way to the food table here, pick up a plate and start choosing things.

"Did I say you could eat here?" Gemma's at my side, having left Mark and the red-bird-woman discussing how much they hate their kids.

"It's for Lucie," I reply, but I also haven't eaten and I'm starving. *Was I supposed to bring myself a packed lunch?*

"She hasn't eaten yet?" Gemma asks. "For crying out loud, what have you been doing? You know it's the boat race soon?" She thrusts the plate of salmon back at me. "Go on, give her this, then. If you must. Just keep her out of sight while she's eating. She's messy, and it turns my stomach. I'm easily nauseated."

Gemma swaps her empty champagne glass for a fresh one, which she snatches from one of the staff. She takes a sip and wanders away, leaving me wishing I could brush myself off in case any of her nasty energy is stuck in my field. But I figure everyone here would look at me like I'm crazy, so I focus on my task instead.

As I'm filling Lucie's plate with other bits from the buffet, I notice an influx of school boys drifting across the fields between the parked cars.

They're wearing the fanciest school uniform I've ever seen. Long burgundy tail coats paired with striped trousers, and waistcoats over white shirts. Some of the boys have different colour waistcoats, which must signify some rank or position in the school, but I have no idea what. They have little white bow tie type things around their necks. They look like characters from a period drama, and against the backdrop of the ancient, immense school buildings, I feel like I've been dropped into an alternate universe, where everyone is rich and privileged, and no one bats an eyelid at how bizarre it is.

Three boys make their way towards me, heading directly for the food. In the middle is a tall youth, who looks just like Mr Hawkston. He must be Charlie. He's tall for a sixteen-year-old, but nowhere near as bulky and muscled as his dad. Charlie has a lean, almost lanky appearance that suggests he's yet to fill out.

On either side of him are two equally tall blond boys, but they are closer to men; more muscular, their faces more mature. I guess they're a few years older than Charlie.

At first, I assume they're a group of friends, but when I look closer, I notice Charlie doesn't look comfortable. The other two, clearly brothers, are pinning him in, knocking against him. Charlie jolts between them, shoved first one way, then the other, his brow creased. He makes no move to retaliate, and the other two boys are laughing.

"Boys," Mark Charlton shouts. He opens his arms, and I realise these are the kids of Gemma's new partner. The boys openly embrace him at the same time, while Charlie hangs back. Gemma hasn't noticed him, and when Mark draws her attention to them, she greets his children first, only then going over to Charlie.

She's tall and can see almost eye to eye with her son in her huge heels. She puts her finger beneath his chin. "You look tired. Are you sleeping? Do I need to call the school about the quality of the bed? We could get one shipped in for you."

Charlie shakes his head out of her grip. "No, Mum. The bed's fine."

"Why do you look so dreadful then? Look at Ben and Hugo." She points over at the two boys. "They look healthy. You look like you're half-dead."

"I have to train early mornings for rowing. The boat race," Charlie explains.

Gemma laughs, but I'm not sure what she's laughing at, and if the baffled look Charlie gives her is anything to go by, he doesn't know either. But his face falls, and I know whatever the laugh meant, his mother is mocking him, and from the practised movement of his features, it's a regular occurrence.

"The boys are training too," she scolds. "You're not the only one. Maybe we should book you in for a facial in the holidays."

Hugo and Ben start chuckling, having overheard this. "That won't sort his ugly mug," shouts one of them.

Gemma smiles as if this is genuinely funny. A flash of hurt crosses Charlie's face, and he makes his way to the food table and stares down at what's on offer.

"Can I get you a drink, sir?" one of the staff asks.

He looks up. "Just water, please." The waiter disappears and returns with a fresh glass of iced water. "Thanks," Charlie mumbles. He keeps staring at the food, but doesn't pick anything up. Then, drawn by my attention, he looks at me. "Hi," he says.

I give him a big smile, hoping it might induce him to smile back at me, but his lips don't even flicker. "I'm Aries. I'm your new nanny. I'll be looking after you for the summer."

He huffs a hollow laugh. "Great. A nanny. Dad really doesn't fucking trust me, does he?"

I try not to show how taken aback I am. "Should he?"

"Cracking onto the nanny already?" Ben or Hugo, whichever one he is, appears behind Charlie and slams a hand on his shoulder. Charlie jerks forward under the impact. "I'm Ben. This is Hugo," the boy tells me, indicating his brother who's appeared at the table too. Hugo's waistcoat has the Union Jack printed on it, whereas Ben's is plain blue. I try to remember so I can tell them apart.

"I'm not cracking onto—" begins Charlie.

"Best you don't. Can't have a taste of her," Hugo taunts, grinning at me. "Look at that hair. Red as a strawberry. That would bring you out in a rash."

"Excuse me," I snap, realising I sound a bit too prim. But damn it, this kid is *rude*.

Ben gives a hearty chortle. "Relax. It's a joke. Got nothing against redheads. Charlie's allergic to strawberries. Pretty serious allergy, isn't it?" He whacks Charlie on the back again. It's a gesture that could easily be dismissed as friendly, but it's definitely a little too hard.

Charlie shrugs, although I suspect it's mostly to get the boy's arm off him rather than in answer to the question.

Hugo picks up a large bowl of strawberries and shoves one in his mouth, making a noise which sounds vaguely orgasmic. "Delicious," he moans. "I could eat these all day." He gives me a lewd look, which has me physically recoiling. He smirks at my reaction.

"If he's really allergic to those, you should keep them away," I say, wondering why Gemma would even have strawberries on offer if her son is allergic.

Hugo and Ben snort dismissively. "Yes. Of course. Let's keep them away." The two of them wander off, holding the bowl.

"Do you want to sit with us?" I say to Charlie, indicating where Lucie is sitting.

He looks across at his little sister. She waves at him, plunges off the chair and skips over, throwing her arms around him.

He picks her up, and she hooks her short legs around his waist. "Hey, Lulu."

"Charlie." She kisses him on the cheek, and Charlie finally smiles. Thank goodness; I was beginning to worry that he didn't know how.

"I can't stay," he says. "I've got to go change for the boat race. You're going to come and cheer me on, right?"

Lucie nods. "Row fast. Really fast."

"I will. Make sure you get down to the river early, or you won't see anything." Charlie puts his sister down and looks at me. "Bye, Aries. Good to meet you."

He wanders back the way he came, alone. No one apart from me and Lucie appears to have noticed his departure.

I'm struck by the air of melancholy that clings to him as he walks through the parked cars. *Does Mr Hawkston know his teenage son is desperately unhappy?*

I turn to Lucie, who's busy eating from the plate of salmon. "Does your brother really have a strawberry allergy?"

"Yes," Lucie says, her mouth full. "When he was little like me, his throat got all big and they had to take him to hospital."

"Did that happen after he ate a strawberry?"

"No. A jam sandwich." Her eyes light up. "Hey, can I have a jam sandwich when we get home? I don't like this food." She dangles a piece of roasted artichoke between her fingertips.

"Sure. I can manage a jam sandwich. Probably have to be raspberry though. Just in case."

I keep Lucie entertained for about an hour, when all of a sudden everyone starts moving, like a crowd of well-dressed lemmings.

"The boat race," Lucie squeals. "Let's go, or we won't get near the front."

I take her hand and follow Gemma, Mark and the others. I scan the crowd for Mr Hawkston, but I can't see him anywhere. I wonder what he's been doing. Probably being all suave and charming and handsome. *Did Charlie go to his picnic too?*

Gemma, ahead of me, slows down so she's at my side. "I'll take Lucie. It's important that everyone sees us together. You keep out of the way."

Before I can object, or even wonder why it's important people see her with Lucie, Gemma drags her daughter away through the crowd. Amongst all the over-dressed bodies and the women wearing hats that obscure my view, I completely lose sight of them in seconds.

Shit.

I try to reassure myself that it's all right, because Lucie's with her mother. Gemma might be a little lacking in compassion for her kids, but that maternal instinct is strong, right? It's gonna click right into place if there's any possibility of harm coming to her children.

I push my way through the crowd, heading towards the riverbank. People hustle to get a better view, and I edge my way to the front, hoping that if I keep heading in the direction that Gemma and Lucie went, I'll find them again.

A little further downstream, there's a bridge over the river with a wooden railing. It's not high, but it would definitely give the best view. It's already chock-a-block up there, so I don't have a chance of getting a spot.

As I watch, I see Lucie perched on top of the railing. Gemma is behind her, holding her in place with one hand on Lucie's hip. Lucie's staring at the water below, but Gemma is paying her no attention, talking animatedly to another parent beside her.

Nerves flutter in my stomach to see Lucie so precariously positioned, and anxiety whips through me. I wouldn't let her sit like that, if it was me up there. Maybe I'm being paranoid. She's with her mum, and Gemma will keep her safe. *Won't she?*

I try to put it out of mind, but my eye keeps being drawn back to the sight of Lucie perched on the railing. She's not the only child up there, which makes me feel a little better, but I wish Gemma would hold her with both hands.

I look across the river and see Mr Hawkston on the other side of the bank. There aren't many people over there and it's much less crowded than it is here. He stares right at me, his dark eyes so angry that his gaze scorches; a searing heat on my skin. He glances to the bridge where Lucie sits in the middle.

He gestures toward her, then mouths something at me which looks like '*what the fuck?*' but I can't tell for sure. A horrible sensation spirals through my stomach. *What was I supposed to do? Wrestle her off her mother?*

I begin pushing my way through the crowd again. *Better late than never.*

A cheer starts up as the boats come into view, far in the distance but moving fast. Everyone jostles to see. My path to the bridge becomes even more difficult, but I keep going, heart racing.

They're rowing fast. A couple of minutes later and they're passing beneath the bridge. It takes a few moments before I can make out the faces, but I see Charlie clearly. In the boat with him are Hugo and Ben.

People are clapping and waving. Their boat draws ahead of the other, just a fraction. The boys are working hard, the strain showing in their jaws and necks, and their bulging biceps.

People roar on either side of me as the other boat catches up again. It goes on like that, the tip of one gaining speed and drawing out front, then the other. They seem evenly matched, and neither team has the edge.

I glance to the opposite bank, where Mr Hawkston is cheering, his hands raised over his head as he claps. He looks more animated, more excited, than I've seen him. On the bridge above, Lucie is grinning and screaming, but Gemma is continuing her conversation, barely glancing at either of her children.

As the boats reach the crowd, the boys' faces are wet with sweat. The excitement is unrestrained, and even the primmest looking parents applaud and yell, calling out a chorus of boys' names. Even I get caught up in the cheering.

I desperately want Charlie to have something to celebrate. He struck me as such a sad soul.

I'm jumping up and down as Charlie's boat draws ahead, forging faster toward the finish line.

But then all of a sudden, my intuition hits. A voice in my head whispering, *Lucie, Lucie, Lucie.*

I turn back to the bridge, relief flooding me as I see Lucie's still there. *Safe*. But wait... Gemma's not holding onto her at all anymore. Lucie is unanchored, legs dangling off the bridge, while Gemma is completely absorbed in whatever conversation she's having with the woman next to her. At a guess, it has nothing to do with the boat race, or Charlie or Lucie.

My gut twists. There is a four-year-old perched on the rail of a wooden bridge, and her mother is definitely not paying attention.

My intuition hits big time, screaming in my skull. *Go. Go. Go.*

I don't second guess it. Don't hesitate. I launch myself towards the bridge, trying to shove my way through the crowd, but everyone's too excited to pay me any notice. Their attention is fixed on the boats.

"Please, let me through," I plead, but my voice is drowned out by the cheering. No one is listening to me. They don't even know I'm here. All my pushing is dismissed as the regular jostling of a crowd high on adrenaline.

Go, go, go, the voice continues.

I begin to sweat, anxiety exploding in my stomach. I haven't ever felt a call this strong, and I'm powerless to act on it.

"Please, get out of the way." My voice is louder now, but it's still not enough. A few people glance in my direction but only for a second before being drawn back to the river, the race.

As I try to force my way through a horde of full grown men in suits, something catches my eye. A movement, a *dropping* motion, from the bridge.

I look up, glimpsing Lucie, her bright pink dress a blur, as she plunges into the murky water below.

14
MATT

A second before Lucie falls, I know it's going to happen, almost as if my paranoia willed it to occur. I freeze as her tiny body plummets into the river below.

On the bridge above, Gemma's mouth is open, poised in an Edvard Munch style scream I can't hear over the cheering crowd. But the applause quietens, like the red sea parting for Gemma's shrill and panicked screeching.

The sound propels me to action. How much time did I lose glancing at Gemma? A second? Two?

Gemma's hysterical cries continue to tear through the air, but I don't give a shit about her. I tear off my jacket and dive in the water.

It's cold; shockingly so. It spears my skin all over like a thousand tiny paper cuts. I thrash forward, not caring about anything but Lucie. My clothes are heavy and the water is deep. Nearing the middle of the river I can't touch the bottom.

Lucie can't swim without her armbands.

My pulse pounds in my ears. I'm nothing but water and heartbeat. There's no space for thought. My body's acting like it's been pre-programmed to do exactly this.

I can't even see Lucie's pink dress beneath the water. *Fuck.*

I dive under, but I still can't see anything. Not at first.

I can't hold my breath long enough. I come back up, gasp for air and dive down again.

This time I see a flash of red. Or is it pink? I swim fast towards it. One stroke, two strokes. Then I touch something solid. Human. There's a fumbling of limbs. A hand that feels too large to be Lucie's.

Then my daughter's body is pushed into my arms, tiny and limp, and I drag her up to the surface.

Someone surfaces behind me but I don't stop to see who it is. I have no awareness of anyone or anything other than Lucie in my arms as I strive for the bank, hauling her up with me and lying her down on the mud.

She splutters almost immediately, coughing up water, and relief hits me like a drug. I sink to my knees beside her, coaxing her onto her side.

She lurches, gasping for breath, spluttering, coughing, and I sit with her, holding her. She's breathing. She's breathing...

She's all right.

She's bedraggled, her hair hanging in wet strands. Her little body begins to shake and I take her in my arms, clasping her tight to me.

"Daddy," she chokes out before she bursts into tears.

I stand, Lucie in my arms, only now realising there's someone beside me. Two people. Charlie and Aries. Both of them are drenched, and covered in mud. Aries looks like she's about to cry, and Charlie's blowing out breaths, his chest heaving, like swimming in the river was far more intense than the rowing he was doing moments before. His top and shorts are clinging tight to his frame; he's skinnier than I remember.

"Is she all right?" Aries says, one hand covering her mouth, fingers trembling.

Lucie sobs loudly against my shoulder.

"I told you to stay with her," I grit out. I'm so fucking furious, I could explode. "I told you—"

"I'm so sorry."

"It was your one fucking job today." My voice is barely controlled, breaking into pieces, and Aries winces at the expletive. Lucie clings tighter to me, and Charlie's eyes widen.

"She was with her mum..." Aries says, but the excuse is wafer thin and her words crumble away.

I'm about to launch into a barrage of attacks about Gemma when the woman herself rushes towards us. We're on the quiet side of the river, but people are streaming towards us as they cross the bridge.

"My baby," Gemma wails, reaching for Lucie.

There's a crowd of people directly behind her, so I can't lambast the woman in front of everyone. *Or can I?*

As Gemma gets closer, I tighten my grip on Lucie. "What the fuck were you doing?" I keep my voice just low enough that only the group of us can hear.

Gemma stops, her arms falling to her sides. "It was an accident, Matthew."

"That wasn't an accident. That was neglect. Christ, Gemma. Can't you keep your fucking eyes on your kids for more than five minutes? What were you doing up there? Fucking posing so everyone could see you being a 'good mother'? Fuck's sake."

Gemma inhales sharply, her chest popping up. "How can you say such a thing? I'm not the one who was never home when the kids were in—"

"Don't throw that shit at me now." My words are so cold that for a second everyone freezes, and then Lucie wails in my arms. At first I think it's tears, but then I realise she's crying out a name. *Ariel.*

Aries steps up to me, ready to take Lucie. Part of me wants to keep hold of my daughter, to prove I'm the one she needs and to punish Aries for disobeying me, but Lucie is already reaching out to her with both hands, twisting herself out of my grip. I let Aries take her from me.

"Ariel?" Gemma says, looking Aries up and down, disdain distorting her face as she takes in how Aries' skirt clings to her curves, outlining every inch of her hips and thighs. Lucie, cradled in Aries' arms, shies away from the inspection, nuzzling into her chest, but Gemma doesn't notice. "Is that why you jumped in the river? Because you're a mermaid?" She laughs, but Aries faces her off with a stone-cold glare, then turns to look at me.

"I'll take Lucie to the car. I'm going to take her home. You can come with us, or stay and we'll see you later."

Without waiting for me to give a verdict on her plan, Aries presses through the gathered onlookers, heading back towards the car, Lucie's tiny form cocooned in her arms.

Charlie stares at me and his mother, his gaze wary as though he really doesn't want to be here with either of us.

"Thank you." I lay a hand on his shoulder. "For trying to help. But you'll have forfeited the race by diving off the boat."

Charlie shrugs, forcing my hand off him at the same time his jaw tightens. "I wasn't going to keep rowing when Lucie was in the river."

"The boys won't like that," Gemma snaps, and I know immediately she means Mark Charlton's sons, Ben and Hugo.

"Why do you even care what they think?" I fire back. "Your daughter nearly drowned."

"She was perfectly fine," Gemma states as though she wasn't panicking and screaming like a banshee only minutes ago. "I knew you'd get her out." She drags her gaze up my wet body. My suit is clinging in all the wrong places, and the way she's staring increases the discomfort. "You're a mess. You should go home with your nanny. No doubt that's where you want to be anyway."

The last sentence sounds so dismissive that I'm immediately riled. "I will." I pick my jacket off the grass where I left it—now my only dry piece of clothing—and put my hand on Charlie's arm. "Come with me."

He glances at his mother as if unsure for a moment, but then nods and together we walk after Aries and Lucie.

People part to let us through, and it's only now, as we head for the crowded bridge, that I realise most of the people gathered on the other side of the water are watching us too.

What a fucking spectacle. At least Lucie's all right. That's all that matters. But she didn't want me. She wanted Aries. I'd be lying if I said that doesn't sting. It does. My own daughter didn't want me to hold her, even when I was the one who pulled her out of the river.

I know I should be thankful to have a nanny she likes enough to cry out for, but it makes me wonder if I'm failing as a parent. *Am I the same as Gemma? Both of us, just as bad... neither one wanted in the moment of our daughter's distress?* But then Gemma's right too... in Lucie's short life, I've been more absent than not.

I'm so possessed by the guilt coursing through me that I barely notice anything around me. Charlie's by my side, but we don't talk. I know he'll be upset about forfeiting the boat race, and his team won't be happy either. He's one of the youngest rowers on the team, and to get a place was a real achievement. One I'm not sure I've ever acknowledged. To throw it all up for his little sister was brave, in more ways than one. I'm so proud of the kid, but I don't know how to tell him.

"Are you really going home with the nanny now?" he asks once we clear the bridge.

"Yes."

"Aren't you staying for the speeches?"

Shit. Speech Day isn't even over yet. There's the whole speeches and prize-giving affair in the main hall to endure. I stop walking and face him, holding my hands up. "I'm covered in river water. I smell like a stagnant pool of crap."

"You can shower in my room. I can lend you something to wear," he says, and I can see in his face how much he wants me to stay. A shower does sound good, but I'm not sure I'll fit into any of Charlie's clothes. He's tall and lean, whereas I'm broad. "I have a spare school uniform." He gives me a cautious smile, and I laugh, and the strange tension between us lifts a fraction. I want to be the father he needs, but I'm torn. Lucie's had a shock today, and to abandon her doesn't feel right.

"Are you up for any prizes?" I ask.

A brief flicker of disappointment crosses Charlie's face. "No."

I sigh with tormented relief. If I leave now, at least I won't be missing Charlie on stage. "I should go home. Check on Lucie."

Charlie's cheeks redden, and his eyes flash with anger. "It's all about the fucking prizes, isn't it? There's no point staying if I'm not winning anything."

"No. That's not it at all. Lucie fell in the river."

"She's got the nanny."

"And you've got your mum," I say, my tone harsher than I intended. Charlie's face hardens, and I try to soften my voice, but the register barely shifts, and I still sound angry as I add, "If circumstances were different, I would stay. But today, I can't. I'm sorry. I'll send the car for you at the end of term. We'll have the whole holiday together."

"Fuck that."

"Watch your language."

A muscle pops in his jaw like he's clenching his teeth, and his nostrils lightly flare. "I really hope that new nanny is nice, because I'd prefer to spend time with her than with you. Looks like Lucie would too."

The dig knocks the breath from my lungs. He spins and marches towards his boarding house. I'm not having that. I chase after him, grab his shoulder, and force him to face me.

"Don't you dare walk away from me." His eyes are full of rage that makes heat burst in my chest, my own anger simmering right beneath the surface. My voice is strained with the effort of holding it in. "The weed."

Charlie scowls. "What?"

"The weed in your sock drawer. Was it yours?"

"Would you believe me if I said no?"

There's a right answer here, but my mind is too befuddled to work it out. Too flooded with thoughts, concerns, and amidst them all, like the sinister slither of a python, a writhing coil of panic.

Your son is a wreck.

Charlie is a blur before me as my focus shifts inward. *Would I believe him? Wouldn't I have sought out something to help when I was his age? Didn't I do exactly that?* Smoking joints on the back roof with Nico, the asphalt scratching the back of our bare legs, the soles of our feet, while Dad fucked the housekeeper. The babysitter. The nanny. And Mum sat inside, drinking vodka and staring into the mid-distance like nothing fucking mattered anymore.

"I knew it," Charlie says, his voice a cold snap before he turns and paces away from me.

This time, I don't try and stop him.

15
ARIES

I buckle Lucie into the back of the car, which is challenging because my hands are shaking. It takes me three tries before the belt clicks in. *I can't believe what's happened.*

I try to ground myself, not wanting to add my emotional panic to Lucie's upset. I've taken her wet clothes off and wrapped her in the picnic rug. She's no longer shivering, but I'm wondering if we ought to be taking her to get checked out by a doctor.

"Do you need help?" Kate says. I have no idea when she appeared, but she's here now, peering inside the car, and I'm grateful, even though I can't focus on her. "What can I do?"

If only my hands would stop shaking, I could think more clearly. I'm shivering too, my teeth chattering. I kiss Lucie's forehead and slip out of the car to talk to Kate.

She looks me up and down, brows drawn tightly together. "You're freezing. Take my jacket. Please." She strips it off and holds it out to me.

"I'll ruin it," I argue, glancing at my wet, muddy skin and then back at the pristine yellow suit jacket.

"I don't care about that. Please." She shakes it. "Just take it. You don't need to give it back to me."

"You're so kind," I tell her, taking the jacket. Inside the collar is a label. *Catherine Walker*. The same designer as Gemma's suit. The one she wouldn't let Lucie touch. "Are you sure?"

"Absolutely." Kate's phone rings and she gives me an apologetic grimace before she answers it. "I know the speeches are starting," she says to whoever is calling. "I'm coming. Save me a seat. I'm just making sure Lucie and Aries are in the car. Okay. I'll be with you in a minute."

She hangs up. "I've got to go. You'll be all right?"

"I will. Thank you."

Kate pokes her head into the car to speak to Lucie. "You okay, honey? Have a nice hot bath when you get home. You were so brave."

Lucie smiles, then pulls the blanket up over her mouth.

Extricating herself from the car, Kate gives me a final nod and strides back towards the main school building.

I suddenly feel very lost. Out of my depth. And I'm still shivering, in spite of Kate's designer jacket.

I'd call Mr Hawkston to ask if we're waiting for him, but the brand new phone he gave me was in my pocket when I jumped in the river. It won't even turn on. But I haven't told the driver to leave, so I guess I am waiting for him.

I slide into the car next to Lucie.

"Tell me again," Lucie says, reaching out and clutching my hand, dragging it into her lap. "Tell me what happened."

I spend the next five minutes recounting the story of what happened to her. She finds it soothing, and each time I tell her how she fell in the river and Daddy swam in to save her, she calms down even more.

"You got in too," she says. "Tell me that bit."

"I saw a big splash and I knew it was you, so I jumped in the water with all my clothes on. And your big brother jumped out of his boat too. We were all swimming to get you out."

"But Daddy got me. Tell me again."

Before I can, the car door opens, and Mr Hawkston slides into his seat opposite us. His hair is soaking wet and pushed off his face. His jacket, however, is dry, and he lays it on the seat beside him.

He's glowering. He barely looks at either of us, and the flicker of excitement I saw in Lucie's eyes when her father opened the car door quickly vanishes. It's like he's sucked out any positive energy, filling the car with his bad mood, and now we have to sit in here with him.

Lucie closes her eyes, looking drowsy.

"Has she been sleeping?" he asks. His tone isn't exactly angry, but I can feel his fury. He's like a pot that's about to boil over and I'm not going to be the one to turn up the heat.

"No," I say.

"Hmm. Doctor's coming to the house. Just to be sure she's fine. She'll meet us there."

I briefly wonder what kind of doctor is making a private house call, but I figure it's a rich person thing. If I'd fallen in the river, Mum might have taken me to A&E, maybe. But only if she thought I really needed to go. More than likely, she'd have made me drink a mug of sugary tea, wrapped me in a blanket, and put me on the sofa to watch TV. Maybe done some reiki on me. There would never have been a doctor who came to the house. *Ever.*

"That's good," I say. "I think she's all right though."

"No thanks to you."

The bitterness in his tone takes me by surprise, and my body crumples with guilt. I feel responsible, and the fact that Mr Hawkston thinks I am too is unbearable.

I say nothing because he knows I jumped in the water. He knows I tried. I'm dripping a puddle all over his car. I would have got Lucie out even if he hadn't been there. I'm a strong swimmer.

He sits with his legs apart, his trousers plastered to his thighs, which are thick with muscle. His white shirt is tight and transparent across his chest. On any other day, I'd be obsessing over the definition of his pecs beneath it, but I'm too worried about Lucie and anxious that he's about to lose his shit with me.

He pulls his phone out of the pocket of his jacket and scrolls.

For minutes on end, he doesn't look up, completely absorbed by whatever he's dealing with, and I wonder how he has the clarity to do business, or whatever he's doing, after what just happened. Maybe he doesn't. Maybe he's numbing out, distracting himself, avoiding this horrendous present moment by looking at a screen.

I stroke Lucie's forehead, taking wet strands of hair out of her face. She looks up at me through bleary eyes. "Will you tell me the story again?" she whispers.

"Later. At bedtime."

I'm not about to start telling the story about Daddy the hero with Mr Hawkston sitting opposite me, his soaking clothes clinging to his body like a wetsuit.

Lucie nods and makes a sleepy noise. She's still holding my hand, but it doesn't take her long to drift off now the car's moving.

A tense silence fills the vehicle. Mr Hawkston might be focused on his phone, but his jaw is tight, and so angular, so *sharp*, I want to run my fingertip along the edge to see if it would draw blood.

Maybe he's genuinely not aware of me, sitting here, worrying that he's about to lose his shit at me. If only I had a distraction, maybe I could lose myself in it too. If my new phone was working, I might use it to Google things. Although I don't think Google would have an answer for the question, 'Am I getting fired tonight?'

Perhaps I should hand in my notice. This job really hasn't gone well so far. But I look over at Lucie and remember those sad eyes beneath her dark lashes. I can't leave this kid... not now that I've seen what this family is like. And Charlie? I've only met him today, but I can recognise a teenager that's struggling. I wonder if Mr Hawkston can?

His shoe brushes the tip of mine and he shifts his foot away. If this car weren't so big, that contact would have been our legs. I kind of wish it had been.

Is it strange that I'm thinking about touching my boss after Lucie's ordeal? I'm surprised that my body can go through the shock it has today and still feel the simmering attraction to the man sitting across from me. It feels wrong, but I've calmed down enough now that I can't help it. I allow myself to stare, observing every muscle across his chest beneath his shirt; his nipples are dark beneath the fine white fabric, and erect. I wonder what it would feel like to flick one of them with my tongue...

I push the thought away. Maybe he's cold. The air conditioning is on, and that water was bloody freezing. It's hard to warm up. I'm chilled almost to the bone.

What wouldn't I give for a shower and a sauna right now...

His foot nudges mine again. This time he looks up, and when our eyes lock, everything stops. There's a force in Mr Hawkston's eye contact, like he's physically pinning me down with it. My heartbeat ramps up. His lips part slightly as if he's about to say something, but before any sound comes, his eyes slide to his sleeping daughter and then back to his phone, and we drive the rest of the way in silence.

Even after the driver pulls into the underground car park, Mr Hawkston doesn't say anything. I can feel the anger and frustration rolling off him. I'm not even sure if it's me he's annoyed with or himself. Or Gemma. I don't dare look at him in case the mere sight of me sets him off.

It's only when he gets out of the car that he seems to switch back on, realising he has to be here with us, rather than with his phone.

He doesn't speak to me as he lifts Lucie out of her car seat, and again she looks tiny in his arms. She's still wrapped in the picnic rug and only half-awake, but her tiny hands cling around her father's neck, her head lolling against his shoulder. I gather her wet clothes and follow the two of them into the house.

I drop the clothes in the laundry room in the basement, and when I get upstairs Mr Hawkston is talking in a low voice to a woman who's standing with Mrs Minter in the hall. She must be the doctor.

At the sound of my approach, Mr Hawkston turns and passes Lucie to me. "Take her up. Run the bath, put her in her pyjamas. We'll be up soon."

He's talking to me, but there's no emotion. He's like an automaton. Hasn't even looked me in the eye. *He's so mad at me that he can't meet my gaze.* A nervous bubbling feeling starts in my lower belly.

I take Lucie in my arms, but Mrs Minter stops me, her hand on my shoulder.

"I'll take her. You get changed. You need to get out of those clothes."

Mr Hawkston is watching us, and there's a slight narrowing of his eyes at her words, but he says nothing. I can't read him, but I feel like

I'm walking on eggshells. I mouth 'thanks' and shift Lucie into her arms, and she heads to the lift.

Mr Hawkston turns back to the doctor, continuing to whisper so as not to wake or alarm Lucie. Then the Doctor follows Mrs Minter.

Mr Hawkston takes the stairs two at a time. Even the way he walks up the stairs, each thick, muscular leg bulging in his wet trousers, is aggressive. His anger is a simmering fuel that's surely about to blow.

I wait a moment before I follow him up. I don't want to get too close. But my hope that he's not aware I'm behind him is crushed when he turns sharply towards me on the second floor landing.

"What?" he says. "What do you want?"

My heart races, spreading nervous tingles through my torso. I hold my hands up in a gesture of surrender. "Nothing. I... nothing."

He clenches his fists at his sides. "I can feel you judging me. Thinking I'm a bad father."

I stand still. *What does he want from me?* "I'm not judging," I whisper.

He takes one long step towards me, invading my personal space. "You shouldn't be because it's your fault this happened. All you had to do was keep Lucie close. You weren't supposed to leave her alone with her mother. That fucking woman is too worried about her Louboutin shoes and her silk suits and the fucking blow-dry she got this morning to give a shit about the kids. Why don't you judge her instead?" He jabs a finger in my direction and I flinch, but I don't give way, despite the anger that's steaming off him so hot and fierce it's scalding my skin. He starts poking his own chest. "Not me. I'm fucking trying here, and I can't do it with your eyes on me the whole time."

He's breathing hard, one hand fisted in his thick dark hair as he paces back and forth across the landing. I stand, rooted to the spot, watching him. He halts to look at me, his attention blasting like a series of electric shocks through every inch of my body. "All you had to do was look after her." There's a break in voice, and I glimpse a flash of what's beneath the anger, as though he's carved open his chest and exposed the panicked beating of his heart. He could have lost his child today, and the terror in his eyes causes a lump to form in my throat. "That's your job. If you can't even do that—"

My hand on his arm cuts him off. All I want to do is soothe him. "I'm sorry."

He stares at where I'm touching him for a millisecond, and I dare to hope I might have stayed his anger, but he snatches his arm away. "Don't touch me." He's clearly forgotten to worry about disturbing Lucie, because his voice is rough and thunderously loud, and he lets out a furious, rumbling groan, as though he's beyond tormented. "If you touch me right now, I won't be able to think. I can't... *fuck*, Aries." He tugs a hand through his hair, backing away from me at speed. My pulse pounds through my body, and his pain, his *confusion*, resonates deep in my flesh as though it's mine. I can feel the ache of it everywhere. "This is important. It's fucking important."

"I know." I try to keep my voice quiet, but it only increases the impression that I'm breaking too. "I understand that it's—"

"No. You don't." All vulnerability vanishes from his expression as the angry, furious mask slides into place. "It's not good enough. Not fucking good enough."

It's an effort not to crumble in the face of his fury, but I manage it, forcing myself to look him in the eye. "She was with her mother, and Gemma told me to stay back. I'm not your security team. I'm not a bodyguard and I'm not about to wrestle a child from her own mother's arms. I don't know your wife—"

"Ex-wife."

I jerk my head to acknowledge his interruption. "I'd never met her before today. I don't know her. I know nothing about her. This wasn't a predictable event. It was an accident. Any of those kids on that bridge could have fallen into the water."

He steps back, but his eyes are still full of fire. His jaw is so tight it looks like bone might snap. "An accident?" He shouts the words so loud, I'm sure everyone in the house can hear them. One of his hands is fisted by his side, while the other remains in his hair. "You don't need to know her, you just need to obey my fucking rules."

His anger is stirring up my need to retaliate. I want to lash out at him, but I don't even know what I'd say. Maybe he's right. I didn't do what he asked. Maybe I did fail here…

He blows out a breath and runs a hand down his face. "If you'd done what I'd told you to do, all this could have been avoided." The volume of his voice is lower now, but anger is a harsh scrape through his tone.

I drop my gaze to the floor. "I'm sorry."

He closes his eyes for a few seconds before he speaks. "You put the life of my child at risk today." Again, his voice cracks a fraction. "I don't know where we go from here."

I can't disagree with him. Lucie's fine, at least I'm pretty sure she is, but it could have gone differently…

Mr Hawkston nods in the direction of the stairs. "Go. I don't want to see you again tonight. Tomorrow, we'll talk."

The rest of the afternoon passes uneventfully, but I can't think about anything other than what Mr Hawkston said in the hall.

Tomorrow, we'll talk.

I'm getting fired. I must be. It feels unfair and justified all at once. I didn't do what he wanted, but what happened *was* an accident, and how was I supposed to know he didn't trust his ex-wife? But I can't shift all the blame. It *was* my fault. I let this happen. My negligence. Guilt gnaws at my stomach lining like a starved rat released from a cage, ravenously devouring everything in sight.

After Lucie's bath, the doctor checked her over and said she was fine. I washed all our clothes, made Lucie a jam sandwich (raspberry, not strawberry. Apparently Mr Hawkston doesn't have it in the house at all on account of Charlie, even though Charlie's away at school most of the time), and a cup of sugary tea, the same as Mum used to make when anything bad happened to me as a kid. I can still remember how comforting it was to sip that sweet tea, cuddled up next to her on the sofa watching movies.

That's what we're doing now. Lucie is snuggled against me, and we're watching The Little Mermaid.

We've nearly reached the end of the film when I become aware of a presence in the doorway. Not so much a shadow as an energetic prickle that makes the hairs on my forearms stand on end. I don't turn because I know it's Mr Hawkston. I can hear his breathing. And he specifically said he didn't want to see me tonight.

He stands there for about thirty seconds—the entirety of which my breath shallows like my lungs have shrunk to a tenth of normal capacity—then he leaves.

I can't handle this.

"Stay here," I whisper against the side of Lucie's head.

"Where are you going?" she asks, pawing at my jumper to keep me beside her.

"Bathroom."

She nods, releasing her hold on me, and I slip out into the hall. There's no sign of Mr Hawkston, but I can smell him. His scent is strong, exotic, expensive, and it switches on my hormones like no other cologne I've encountered. Maybe it's more *him* than his scent... I've heard that expensive colognes mix with the individual's skin to form an entirely unique scent. And whatever Mr Hawkston's particular combination is, I think it was made just for me.

But there's an edge of fear to my arousal now, and as messed up as it is, I think it only heightens what I'm feeling. I must be messed up if I can summon arousal for a man who screamed at me earlier today. But that hint of pain in his eyes, the vulnerability beneath the fury... I know he's a decent man. An angry, decent, loving man.

Maybe he doesn't love *me* right now, but I know he's not a monster.

I quickly search the basement, but I don't find him. Nor can I hear him. I head upstairs to his office. I don't even know why I'm doing this, especially after he said he didn't want to see me. But I feel oddly compelled, and I've never been one to ignore that kind of gut instinct.

The door to his study is ajar. I knock, and the door opens a bit further. I peek in. The room is empty and I step inside.

I stand for a moment, absorbing the energy in here. It feels like he does; intense and a little threatening, but warm beneath the exterior.

What am I doing here? Searching for my boss who yelled at me? What if he has cameras in here? What excuse do I have? I've been standing in an empty room too long now to pass it off as nothing.

I still have the broken iPhone. It's in my pocket. I put it there after my shower out of habit. I take it out and slide it across his desk. I'd have to admit to him it's broken at some point, so it might as well be now.

I tiptoe out, hoping no one sees me.

16
MATT

I don't know why I linger at the cinema room door. Maybe it's because the two of them look so peaceful, curled up on the big chair like that. Maybe it's because I want to have that with someone.

Fuck. I don't even have that with my kids, and I certainly don't have the companionship of a partner now. Not that I ever really had it with Gemma. I think we hated each other from the very beginning, and we wasted over a decade of our lives struggling to make something work that never, *ever* would.

I've spent so much of my life feeling trapped by other people's desires and expectations that I don't know how to live without them. Always trying to do the right fucking thing. Be a decent man. Be someone my mother could be proud of because she never had that in my father.

I married Gemma because I couldn't face telling my mother I was having a kid with a woman I hardly knew. And I wanted to give my child stability. I failed there. We both did. Our home has never been stable. I don't even want to think about the impact our constant fighting, our unending unhappiness, had on Charlie as a child. Even Lucie has already witnessed too much.

For a long time, I thought we could make it work... I thought the angry, passionate sex we had might be enough. But it never was, and I was as alone while it was happening as I was when it was over. I don't want that again. *I never want that.*

I stand in the doorway, willing Aries to turn and look at me. Maybe if she looks round, she might forgive me for yelling at her.

I don't even know that I want forgiveness.

I don't know what I want from this woman, but I know it's... *something*. Whatever it is, a very deep part of me is afraid I will never get it.

When the fuck have I ever got what I wanted?

It's ironic that my father used to say it all the time. *Hawkston men always get what they want.* It was his mantra, and it's proved true for Nico. Every time I see how he looks at Kate, it pains me. He adores that woman, and she loves him just as much.

I'm happy for him, truly. But why does he get that and I get... *this*? A broken home, a daughter who loves the new nanny more than she loves me, and a teenage son I can't communicate with.

I need space. I need to get the fuck out of the house. I make my way to the basement car park and get into the McLaren. But before I start the engine, I hear tapping. I look up to find Mrs Minter stooping to peer in at me through the window, which I roll down.

"Shall I start the search for a new nanny?" she asks.

My heart stutters, knocked off its normal rhythm. "Why? Has Aries spoken to you? Did she hand in her notice?"

Mrs Minter shakes her head. "No. But I heard you talking to her earlier. If you want me to let her go, I can deal with it. It's my responsibility if it's not working out. I thought she was just what we needed, but maybe I was wrong. There's no reason for you to have that stress on top of everything else. I can find a replacement from one of the agencies in a couple of days."

I frown, gripping the steering wheel with both hands. "No. Don't do that."

Mrs Minter's about to speak again when I roll up the window and start the engine, revving it unnecessarily loud. She backs away, looking only mildly put out at my abruptness.

———

I drive around town for hours with no aim. I make pointless business calls from the car and meaningless arrangements for next week. I check in with both my brothers, which is unusual behaviour on my part, although neither of them call me out on it.

When there are no more excuses to stay out of the house, I head for home. It's almost seven. Lucie will be going to bed soon. I ought to be there before she falls asleep. I'm avoiding my own child, and I don't know why.

My thoughts turn to Aries. Her face when I shouted at her... how fired up she looked at first, and that moment of tenderness when she put her hand on my arm. But the light in her eyes died as I wore her down, and refused to let her in.

I mentally run through the events of the day, from the moment I overheard Gemma abusing Aries at the picnic. Insinuating that I was sleeping with her.

At the moment, I still have the moral high ground. I haven't touched Aries, but that doesn't mean I don't want to. Even before I interrupted her and Gemma talking, I'd been watching her. That long glossy hair falling either side of the pale column of her neck, shimmering over her shoulders like fire. I wanted nothing more than to grab it and force her to her knees.

I shake my head. So fucking wrong to have those thoughts, then and now.

When I get into the house, I head to my office. There are a couple of emails I need to draft and send before the end of the day. But when I enter the room, the first thing I see on my desk is a mobile phone. The phone I gave Aries.

I immediately remember the words I spoke to her in this very room when I gave it to her.

If you don't want to keep it after you leave this role, you can leave it here.

Fuck. My thoughts spin. *Has she gone? Did Mrs Minter speak to her without my approval? Or did Aries leave of her own volition?*

I've fucked up.

I grab the phone and rush up the stairs to Lucie's bedroom. If Aries is still here, she'll be doing the bedtime routine. I have to tell her not to leave. I can't let her go. I don't even want to look at why I know this for certain, but I do.

As I near the bedroom, I can hear low voices. Hope sparks in my chest like an ignition being started. *She's still here.* I linger outside the door—something I seem to be doing a lot of today—and listen.

"Tell me again," Lucie says.

I press the door open a fraction so I can get a view of them. Aries is kneeling at the side of Lucie's bed. The warm yellow of her bedside lamp illuminates their faces. Lucie's tucked up, clasping Aries' hand on top of the covers.

Aries begins to recount the events of the day in a soothing tone. She goes through the details of what happened when Lucie fell into the water.

"And then Daddy jumped into the river and grabbed you," Aries says. "He pulled you out and held you in his arms."

"And you took me to the car."

"Yes."

"And Daddy didn't speak all the way home."

This bit surprises me. I wasn't sure Lucie had noticed; she'd been so drowsy.

Aries pauses. "He was quiet because he was worried about you."

Lucie's lips pucker, eyebrows drawing together. *Her thinking face.* "Does he hate you?"

Aries stiffens. "Why do you ask?"

"I heard him shouting at you." There's a pause. Long enough that Aries should speak, but she doesn't. "He used to shout at Mummy. He hates her."

"Oh. Honey. I'm sorry. I don't think he hates me. I think he was upset. Sometimes grown ups get upset and they don't know what else to do but shout. Mostly, they do it when they can't handle how they're feeling inside."

Ouch.

"I don't like it when Daddy shouts."

Aries strokes Lucie's forehead with the tips of her fingers. Lucie's eyelids grow heavier. "Does it scare you?"

Lucie pulls the covers right up to her chin, and the movement of the sheets tells me she's nodding, her eyes wide over the brightly coloured cotton print.

"No one's going to shout now, honey," Aries says. "Everything's all right."

Lucie mumbles something, then turns over. A few moments pass before Aries gets to her feet and switches off the light.

I should move from the doorway, but I don't. I'm standing in the shadows, frozen to the spot. Aries hasn't seen me. She turns back to look at Lucie, then opens the door.

She's still looking the other way when she takes the final step and slams against me. It takes her a fraction of a second to realise what's going on. Her hands push against my chest. She feels small and fragile, and her hair smells like coconut.

She squeals and steps back, but not before I've caught her, my hands on her upper arms. Her body is warm, and I desperately want to close the gap between us, but I don't dare move in case I scare her away.

She raises wide eyes to me. A little frightened, perhaps, and it pains me to see it. *God, I'm a terrible human being.*

"Shhh," I whisper.

She stills in my grip, her palms resting on my body. My heartbeat surges under her hands, striking so hard against my ribcage that she must be able to feel it.

Electricity fills the air, like it's seeping out of our pores.

Her face is so beautiful, it takes my breath away, even in the dim light of the darkened hall. I pull her away from Lucie's bedroom, leading her further down the corridor.

"Don't leave," I beg, my voice a raspy whisper. "I don't want you to leave."

My hands are still cupping her upper arms, and her muscles tense beneath my fingers. I let go, but she doesn't move.

This fragile proximity is a gift, and I want to savour it. And so, it seems, does she, because the seconds pass like hours as we stare at one another without moving. I'm so desperate not to lose her that I can hardly breathe.

"I wasn't going to leave," she whispers finally.

I can't process this. I was so certain she was on her way out that her words provide no relief. "You left the phone on my desk. I thought that was you handing in your notice."

My words must give her clarity because she chuckles at my confusion as though she understands something I don't. It's a quiet, seductive sound that slips through her full, pink lips. "That's not what I meant. The phone's broken. It was in my pocket when I jumped in the river. I'm so sorry. I've barely had it for a month and I've already broken it."

"Oh." I take a step back, feeling like an idiot. I jumped to conclusions and panicked for no good reason, and then I let her see it. I'm totally exposed out here.

I wait for her to laugh at me, but she doesn't.

"I can take it to the repair shop," she whispers. "I'm more than happy to deal with it. But I assumed you'd have insurance for it."

"Stop talking about the damn phone."

The harshness of my tone severs whatever connection we had only moments ago, and I could curse myself for it. Aries pulls herself upright, but even at full height, she's still a head shorter than me. There's a wariness in her gaze.

"What do you want to talk about?" she asks, and all the subtle softness in her tone is gone. "Why are you here? Do you want to discuss how you screamed at me earlier? How everyone in the house heard you? That your daughter heard you? She's scared of you. You're huge and terrifying, and when you shout like that, it's frightening. Everyone's walking on eggshells in case you lose your shit. I didn't get it at first, but now I do. I completely understand why everyone in this house is half-afraid of you, including your own children."

My body throbs with the embarrassment of being called out, my chest heating until I'm sure I'm sweating. I don't get easily embarrassed; ordinarily, I'd be outraged at such directness from a member of staff, but because it's Aries, I'm not, and the realisation is so surprising that it feels like some benevolent god has deigned to reach down and tweak my view of the world.

I've spent my working life yelling at employees. My brothers are constantly telling me there are other ways to do things, but it's always worked for me. I might have a higher staff turnover than they do, except for the stalwart Mrs Minter and Alec, but there are a lot of people in the world. Everyone's replaceable.

I grit my teeth; the apology sitting right there, heavy on my tongue. *I'm so, so, sorry, Aries. Forgive me. Don't leave me.* "You didn't listen to my instructions."

Anger glints in Aries' eyes. "And I'm sorry. I'm deeply, truly sorry that any harm came to Lucie. If you want me to leave, I will. But"—her gaze warms and a beat of silence pulses in the space between us—"it doesn't seem like that's what you want, or you wouldn't have been hiding out here in the shadows waiting to tell me not to go." Her voice is tentative, as though she needs me to confirm she's right.

Every blood vessel in my chest feels like it's constricting. There's a weight against my ribcage, pressing down. *Could the awkward tension in the air actually collapse my lungs? What is this woman doing to me?*

"What do you want?" she whispers.

The question hangs in the air like the visual imprint of an exploded firework on a dark night. I absorb it, letting it roll around in my mind. I know what I want. She knows it too, I'm sure of it.

"I don't like repeating myself."

She nods. "Fine. But you need to be really clear on what you want to happen here, because this won't work." She waves a hand between us like there's some definable relationship going on. Something that isn't just temptation that's fucking with both our heads. "You used me today, and I won't stand for it."

"Used you? What are you talking about?"

"When you wiped that caviar off my mouth. You did it for effect. You wanted your ex-wife to think you were sleeping with me, even though you aren't. It was manipulative and cruel. To use me as a tool in your fucked up relationship with your ex isn't fair. To look at me like that when it's not real isn't fair either."

My heart gives a stupid, hard thud in my chest. "To look at you like what? How was I looking at you?"

I don't know why I'm pushing this, but I need to hear her say it. To hear what she thought she saw. As I wait for her response, a pulsing sensation fills my arms, my legs, my fingertips... a surge of energy that only Aries could possibly discharge.

She lowers her gaze, then lifts it to meet mine, staring at me like she's resentful I'm even asking. "Like I'm the only woman in the world you want."

A beat of silence crackles in the air.

"You think that wasn't real?"

She swallows and takes a breathy gasp before she speaks. "Was it?"

Fuck it. I'm done talking, and I'm done listening. I've pushed this moment right to the edge, to the fucking tipping point, and I'm ready to fall. I'm powerless to resist the pull between us. I don't know what the hell comes next, but I want to kiss this woman. Every molecule in my body wants it; the impulse overrides every logical thought in my brain as I close the distance between us with one step. I bring one of my hands to the back of her neck, where the skin is warm and soft. The other slides to her waist, my fingers sinking into the flesh of her hip.

The tiniest, sexiest moan pours from between her lips, which I take as confirmation she wants this too. All her resistance vanishes, her body becoming soft, pliable, as I crush her against me, my mouth meeting hers, warm and eager and wet. Her lips are full, and her tongue dances against mine, soft like velvet. She sucks my bottom lip, then nips it with her teeth. The relief of finally kissing her is like the first sip of a cool drink on a hot day. Blissful, but leaving me desperate for more. *Fuck*, I want to swallow her entire mouth in one fucking go.

Her lips break from mine. "Is that a yes?"

I groan, unable to help myself, desperate to keep kissing her. "Fuck, yes."

Her lips meet mine again, as her hands paw at my body, fingers fisting in my shirt. Her desperation turns me on, and arousal surges through me like a tidal wave as her breasts press against my chest.

Kissing Aries is like no other experience I've ever had. It's the satiation of want and need that's been building for weeks, and now that I've begun, I'm greedy for it. Allowing myself this much will ruin me because the wanting of her only expands with each touch of her skin, each stroke of her tongue against mine. It's not enough, never could be enough. My body craves more of her with each passing moment. I want to meld into her and never let go.

She pulls back just enough to whisper against my mouth. "This kiss... *this kiss*..." Her voice is all amazement.

"I know," I murmur, pressing my lips to hers again.

"Your lips," she says. "Your mouth..."

I can't help but laugh, my breath against her lips.

This kiss is everything I've ever wanted from a first kiss. It's exactly how it should feel and how it has never felt with anyone before. Obliterating any negative feeling between us, transmuting it into something that makes my mind explode with possibility...

"This is better than being shouted at," she whispers.

"God, yes. Sorry. Sorry. I'm so fucking sorry. Forgive me. I need you to forgive me." The words tumble out between kisses, and Aries eats them up.

"What do you think I'm doing?" Her lips are barely a hair's breadth from mine, her voice full of a glorious wonder that warms my heart. *This is all right. Everything is all right.*

Her hands are on the back of my neck, then one trails up into my hair, tugging on it like she wants to cause me pain. If that's what she intends, it doesn't work; it only increases my pleasure.

If this is what kissing her is like, what is sex going to be like with this woman?

I run my hand up her thigh. She's wearing those tiny pyjama shorts again; her skin is smooth and supple. I dig my fingers into her flesh and she responds by lifting her leg, hooking it on my hip.

Arousal and disbelief mingle in my head. *Is this really happening?* I want to hold her tighter to prove it's real.

My cock is throbbing and rock solid, and in this position, it's pressed right against the space between her legs. We're separated by only a few layers of clothing, and I want nothing more than to strip them all away.

She moans against my mouth the moment she feels me there and rocks her hips against me, *into* me, like she wants to slide right onto me. It sends me into a heady spin and I kiss her again, devouring her.

A cry from further down the corridor crashes into my awareness. Aries hears it too, and she pushes off me, gasping for breath. She stumbles a little as she regains her footing.

Aries and I stare for a second. Her eyes are wild, like she can't believe what just happened either.

The cry comes again. It's Lucie, but the sound is full of sleep. She's having a nightmare. I want to go to her, but I also don't want to move. As soon as we move, this is over.

Aries is the first to dash towards Lucie's room. I'm about to follow, but I hold myself back. Aries' earlier words ring loud in my memory, and the recollection makes me grind my teeth.

She's scared of you. You're huge and terrifying, and when you shout like that it's frightening.

Maybe Aries is better at this than I am. Maybe I really am failing both my children. Talk about a hard fucking comedown.

17
ARIES

It doesn't take long to settle Lucie back to sleep. She was barely awake when she was crying out.

My heart is hammering, and adrenaline is still surging through me, making my hands tremble. There's no sign of Mr Hawkston when I come out of Lucie's bedroom. I hoped he'd be waiting for me, but I *knew* he wouldn't, so I'm not surprised to find the dark corridor empty. The only evidence that he was here at all is the lingering scent of his cologne. I wish I could bottle it and take it with me.

Shit. This situation is fucked up.

I don't know what to think. He was so angry earlier, and I was angry with him for being angry, but then... it *shattered*. Sure, part of me hated how he'd dressed me down so publicly, but seeing him standing there, desperate for me not to leave... it was too much. I was overcome with wanting, having, touching, *tasting*. Completely powerless to listen to the sensible part of my brain that hated how hard it was for him to admit he was sorry until we were kissing, and then it spilled out like blood from an open wound... *God, yes. Sorry. Sorry. I'm so fucking sorry.* I don't think an apology has ever felt as good as that one did.

On the plus side, I've confirmed I wasn't imagining this attraction between us. It's real, and now we've let it out, it's a wild creature. We can't put it back in the box. At least I can't.

What if that's why he's not here? What if he's already sealed it, locked it down somewhere he can't touch it? If he wanted to kiss me again, wouldn't he have waited? Shit.

I need to talk to someone. Not necessarily to tell them what happened, but just so I don't have to be alone with the crazy thoughts running through my head. I quickly formulate a plan. I head to my room and grab my old phone from the bedside table. I bring up Alec's phone number. It rings twice before he picks up.

"Hello?" he says.

"It's Aries. Can I come over? Are you busy?"

"No."

"No, I can't come or no, you're not busy?" I sound like I'm panicking.

"I'm not busy and yes, you can come over."

"Thanks. Give me ten minutes."

I return to Lucie's room and set up the baby monitor, then go to my room to fetch the other half. I hope the signal reaches to the staff block.

I pull on a tracksuit over my pyjamas and put my phone, house keys and the other half of the monitor in my pockets.

I head downstairs, praying I don't meet Mr Hawkston on the way. I'm not ready to see him. I need to work out how I feel about what happened... and what I want to happen next. If he hasn't already decided it's over.

It's still light outside, which is weird because upstairs, with all the curtains closed, it felt like the middle of the night. It's a warm evening and I traipse across the lawn to the building that's almost entirely hidden from the house by trees.

I ring the bell for the back door. Inside, I can hear footsteps approaching. Alec opens the door with a big smile, but when he sees my worried expression, his face falls. "What's wrong?"

I shake my head. "Nothing. I just don't want to be alone."

The frown that mars his face is enough to let me know he doesn't believe me. "Okay..." He steps aside, allowing me to pass into the hallway.

The house is pristine; every wall looks newly painted in some expensive version of off-white. The floor is wooden with a pale white-washed appearance. Like the main house, everything is expensive.

Alec's wearing a pair of shorts and t-shirt, and his hair is messy like he hasn't brushed it today.

"How come you aren't making dinner?" I ask.

He shrugs. "Sometimes Mr Hawkston gives me nights off. I prepared a lasagna. He only needs to shove it in the oven."

"Oh." Even the idea of Mr Hawkston putting a lasagna in the oven strikes me as wrong. Too domesticated. "You made a whole lasagna for one man?"

"Yeah, but I make it in separate containers. I freeze a bunch of them. That way, when I'm not around, he has food. So he has a one person portion for tonight."

A hollow feeling carves its way through my chest. It's the rich person version of a TV dinner. *Is Mr Hawkston lonely?* How odd that it never occurred to me before that he might be.

"I have some leftover in the fridge," Alec says. "In fact, I was about to eat. You want some?"

"Yes, please."

Alec laughs at my eagerness. "I might start to get worried that you're only after my food."

"I am," I deadpan.

He smiles and leads me to the kitchen. I take a seat at the table and he slides a small ceramic dish into the oven.

An hour later and I'm full. "Best lasagna ever," I declare, patting my belly.

Alec grins. "I aim to please." He shifts in his seat and fixes his attention on me in a way that alerts me to the fact I'm probably not going to like whatever he's about to say. "That look on your face when you came to the door... what was wrong?"

Damn it. I thought he'd let this one go. I'm not a good liar. "Nothing."

"Hmm. Your voice was weird over the phone. I thought something must have happened." He tilts his head and his eyes narrow. "Did it? You only smiled after you'd polished off the entire plate of lasagna. I thought your smile was a permanent feature. Like a mole. But tonight I've barely seen it." He puts his cutlery down on the plate. "Was it Mr Hawkston?"

I shake my head, aware even as I'm doing it that the action is too vigorous. Too emphatic. I try to backtrack by focusing on the baby monitor, carefully positioning it adjacent to my plate. *Casual.* "No."

"I heard him scream at you. We all did."

"Ugh." I push my plate away and cross my arms on the table, letting my head fall against them. "It was an awful day. Lucie fell in the river at Charlie's Speech Day. It was my fault. Sort of. Mr Hawkston told me to stay with her and I let Gemma take her off."

"Gemma as in Mrs Hawkston?"

"Nah. Ms. Arse-Warts."

Alec laughs. "Von Arsworz. It's a very famous name. Her family owns one of the high end jewellers. Best diamonds on the market, apparently. I heard that's the only reason the old Mrs Hawkston didn't lose her shit when she found out Gemma was pregnant. It was like a society match. Rich people, eh?" He pats me on the back. "Don't worry about it. If Lucie was with Gemma when she fell in, it sounds like it was Gemma's fault. Mr Hawkston's more bark than bite. I'm sure he'll forgive you."

I keep my head down and let out a groan. I don't know about forgiveness, but we were only a step away from having sex in the hall.

A noise crackles from the baby monitor. Alec's eyes dart to it, and I sit bolt upright in my chair, but neither of us moves. Because it's not Lucie.

The voice is Mr Hawkston's.

"I'm so sorry," he whispers.

I grab the video monitor and pull it closer so I can see the image. Alec leans over me.

It feels wrong, spying on him like this, but I can't look away. Lucie's still asleep. I can hear her regular breathing. Mr Hawkston is sitting on the edge of her bed, his hands in his lap.

"I wasn't a good father today. I let you get hurt, and I shouted at Aries. I'm sorry I did that and that you heard me. But Aries was right; sometimes adults shout when they're upset because they don't know what else to do." I inhale audibly, realising that he heard everything I was saying to his daughter at bedtime.

Alec raises an eyebrow, but I ignore the implied question.

"I want you to know it's not like with Mummy though," Mr Hawkston continues. "I don't hate Aries. I don't know what I feel for her, but it's not that." He sighs, and the confusion in the sound is evident even over the monitor. He runs a hand down his face. "I like her. I like her a lot. More than I should, probably."

My heart races, hope fluttering in my stomach. I reach out for the monitor to stop it, but Alec catches my hand, shakes his head a fraction. I want to hear what Mr Hawkston says next, so I let him stop me, and pull my arm back.

His deep voice is a soothing whisper. Lucie hasn't moved so she must be asleep, meaning this conversation is more for him than anything else. "Aries is a great nanny. She's thoughtful and caring and kind, and maybe Mrs Minter is right. Maybe she's exactly what we all need." His voice falters and he drops his head into his hands. He lets out a low groan. "Maybe she's exactly what I need—"

"We shouldn't be listening to this." I reach out and grab the monitor, switching it off before Alec can stop me this time. But even after I've shut it off, Mr Hawkston's tortured tone plays in my head. Like maybe I really am what he needs, but he doesn't want to need me...

My limbs feel weak, and if I tried to stand up right now I'd probably fall to the floor.

Alec's mouth is hanging open, and he's staring at me. My hand is fisted around the monitor as I look up at him through my lashes. A hot blush races up my neck and across my cheeks. I don't need to say a word, because my face is doing all the talking.

"Oh, shit," he says. "Something did happen. This is why you're here, isn't it? This is why you looked so skittish at the door, and sounded so weird on the phone." Alec's eyes are so wide they look like they're going to pop. He shakes his head slowly and mutters, "Woah. This is big."

My old phone buzzes and I'm thankful for a reason to look away from Alec's shocked stare. There's a message from Mr Hawkston. I click it open to see five words.

Mr Hawkston: Come back to the house.

He must have seen me leave. Maybe he was waiting for me, after all?

I stare at the phone as another message comes in. It's only one word.

Mr Hawkston: Please.

18

ARIES

Please.

The power of that one six-letter word, coming from a man like Mr Hawkston, is a force I cannot resist.

Alec watches me, no doubt hoping for an answer, but I confirm nothing, and although he looks confused when I get up and leave, he doesn't stop me or press me for more information.

My heart pounds as I walk back across the lawn. Mr Hawkston is waiting for me. That terrifying man, with a perfect face and a sculpted body, who melted me with the most passionate kiss I've ever experienced, wants me to come back.

I don't know what I'm walking into, but I know for sure I couldn't walk away.

With each step closer to him, the tingling in my body increases. My lips throb, like they need to be kissed again, and arousal buzzes through me; an illicit pressure with no release valve.

At least not yet.

The house is quiet when I enter. There aren't many lights on. The hall is dark, but there's a glow falling across the floor that's coming from the formal sitting room.

I'm insanely nervous. I've never felt like this; like every nerve ending in my body has been rubbed raw and left exposed, sparking into nothingness. There is no man in the world who has ever induced this delightfully toxic mix of fear, anticipation and arousal in me. I want it to last forever.

Mr Hawkston is sitting in a chair reading a book. I wonder how long he's been there. He was upstairs with Lucie not long ago, but he looks so relaxed that if I hadn't seen him on the monitor myself, I'd have been convinced he'd been here all evening.

He lays his book down on the table beside him and glances up at me. It's a look that jolts against my body, making my breath catch in my throat. It was intense when we made eye contact before, but now it's a fire that could burn me up from the inside because we both know what it means and where it leads.

We both know *exactly* why I'm here.

He's still wearing the white shirt and pale blue jeans he had on earlier. His dark hair is tousled. *Did I do that?*

He strokes his fingers over his bottom lip as he observes me, as if he's remembering our kiss too. His forefinger pauses and tugs a little on that full lip, pulling it down so I can see the pink inside.

Want is scored across his dark irises. He stands and walks towards me. My heart constricts a little more with each of his steps until he's right in front of me. *I can hardly breathe.*

He holds out his hand, and I place mine in it. His clasp is warm and gentle, almost tender. He leads me out of the room, towards the stairs.

He doesn't speak, but there's no need to. We're united in whatever this is, and right now I'd follow him anywhere.

On the first floor, he stops outside the door to his suite and releases my hand. "Do you want to come in? I need to be sure, because if you say yes, it changes everything."

"We're way past the point of no return, Mr Hawkston."

His eyes sparkle with amusement—it's a good look on him. "It's Matt. Call me Matt."

I bite my bottom lip and smile at him. "Okay, Matt." The name feels weird on my tongue, and he smiles as I say it, encouraging me. "If you think the way you kissed me earlier hasn't already changed everything, you're really underestimating your skills."

He laughs quietly. The sound does strange things to my insides. "I'm not underestimating anything. I want your consent, that's all."

"You have it."

He gives me a sexy smile that causes a rush of arousal to pulse between my legs. I'm already soaked, and he's barely touched me.

He opens the door to let me into a large dressing room that's bigger than my bedroom and Lucie's together. A dim yellow light glows from beneath the dark wood doors of the wardrobes that line the room.

"Wow," I say.

He follows me into the room, closes the door and the lock clicks in place, but he pauses a moment before he turns back to me, his hand on the handle. I have no idea what he's thinking, but hesitation doesn't feel like a good thing.

"Are you about to change your mind?" I question, words bubbling up before I can stop them. "Because if you are, I'll have to resign. There's only so much humiliation a girl can take."

He spins to face me, and there is nothing appropriate about his heated gaze. "No."

Relief floods me, and the anticipation of what's about to happen is so sweet, I can almost taste it. Every inch of my body is alight, glowing from the inside. My skin is so sensitive that each rub of my clothes is abrasive.

Mr Hawkston steps closer, his eyes blazing with desire. No one has ever looked at me the way he's looking at me now; it's so raw, so intense. I've never felt more wanted.

He lifts my hair from my shoulder, his fingertips grazing my neck. "Can I?" he rasps.

"Anything. You can do anything," I reply, and his exhale is a barely disguised laugh, but it doesn't last long before he lowers his lips to the same spot and kisses me there, so gently and with such reverence that I can't move. Lust is firing through me. I want so much more than he's giving me, but at the same time I want to appreciate each thrill his touch elicits.

His lips move up my neck all the way to my jaw. He groans, and the rumble of it vibrates along the side of my face, sending a shiver of desire all the way down my spine. A breathy moan escapes me.

"Fuck." He releases the word on a desperate sigh, as if this is more than he can handle. For a second, I worry he really will change his mind, but then he grabs me, harder than before, pulling me against him, pressing our bodies flush.

His lips crash against mine, and his kiss is ravenous. It's both hard and soft at once, and if it's possible, more charged than the first one. His hands are in my hair, cupping the back of my head, my neck, drawing me deeper into him. We kiss passionately for what feels like forever, but when we finally slow, I suck his bottom lip into my mouth and bite down on it gently. When I let go, a deep rumble vibrates in his throat.

"Shit," he whispers, his breath hot against my skin.

I cling to his broad shoulders, needing to catch my breath before I speak. "Are you going to swear all night?"

He shakes his head, and I can feel him smile against my mouth. "I'm encouraged that you're planning on being here all night." His hands slide down my back to grip the bottom of my tracksuit top. "But you're wearing far too many clothes."

I lift my arms to let him pull off my jumper, which he throws to the floor. Underneath, I'm wearing the skimpy pyjama top, without a bra. My breasts suddenly feel huge and sensitive against the cotton. My nipples are hard and easily visible and, as if he knows what I'm thinking, Mr Hawkston stares at my chest, a look of utter amazement on his face as he draws in a few slow breaths.

His gaze drifts upward to my face, his eyes widening just a fraction before his arm slides around my back and he's pulling me towards him again, his mouth latching onto my hardened nipple through my top. He moans against my breast, and I feel it between my legs.

I gasp as his fingers dust against the skin of my stomach. He releases my nipple from his mouth so he can lift up my top and take it off. I raise my arms and he eases it over me. He flings it to the floor to join my jumper.

I'm topless for only a second before his mouth is on my other breast, sucking it into the warmth, flicking my nipple with his tongue, while his other hand gently kneads the flesh of my other breast. "These are beautiful," he whispers, his voice sounding heavy with want.

My back arches, and a noise that can only be described as an erotic moan slides over my tongue, escaping between my lips.

His teeth graze the length of my hardened nipple, tugging on it. A shot of white-hot desire jolts right to my clit.

The attention he gives my breasts is the most exquisite foreplay, and the slickness between my legs increases.

I run my hand into his thick hair, dragging him off me. My breast leaves his mouth with a slick pop.

He looks up, a question in his eyes.

"I need more," I almost beg.

"And you'll get it," he reassures me, his voice so low I could lick it off the floor. "But I want to appreciate every second of this."

A flutter of unease breaks through my arousal. Does he want to savour this moment because it's a one-time thing? Is this my only chance with this man? I hope not, because it feels like there is no end to my wanting him. If he denies me, I'll never be able to satisfy this endless craving alone...

He draws me into another kiss. His fingers tease at the waistband of my tracksuit bottoms, but he doesn't pull them off or order me to. Instead, he slides his hand beneath them and my shorts, his fingers trailing through the hair. *Fuck*, I should have waxed.

I hold my breath, expecting some hesitation on his part. I bet his ex-wife was completely hair-free. *Shit*.

"What?" he asks, obviously sensing my tension.

"I didn't wax."

"Do you think I give a fuck about that?"

My clit throbs as his fingers graze over it, and then he goes deeper. His finger pushes inside me, sliding with ease, and I inhale sharply. He lets out the longest, deepest moan so far as his finger sinks to the knuckle.

Mr Hawkston's mouth is on my neck again, pressing kisses up to my ear, sucking my earlobe between his lips as his finger thrusts in and out of me. The slick sounds of my pussy welcoming him fill the room. It's so loud I'd be embarrassed if I cared. But I don't, because my body has taken over, my hips thrusting against his hand as another finger joins the first.

"So wet, Aries. So fucking wet," he groans in appreciation. "If I knew you wanted me this much, I'd have done this earlier."

"I've only been here a few weeks. You couldn't have done it much earlier."

"I'd have taken you out there on the lawn when you first arrived."

I giggle. "The sexy gardener thing really did it for me. I'd have said yes."

"I know."

His fingers curl against the perfect spot inside me as I grind against the heel of his hand, seeking my release. The pressure building in my core is so hot, so insistent, that I can't hold it back.

I grip his shoulders, digging my fingers into his shirt as he finger-fucks me so perfectly that I'm a breath away from orgasm. "Oh, oh, fuck," I cry. "So good, it's so good. Don't stop."

I ride his hand unashamedly, chasing the orgasm that's spreading from between my legs through my entire being. It bursts with a power that shakes my whole body, my feet lifting from the floor as Mr Hawkston holds my weight with his other arm.

That was fast.

I moan against his shoulder, gasping for breath as he continues to work me. The pleasure lasts longer than I've ever experienced, tingles spreading to my fingers and toes for what feels like minutes on end.

As the height of my orgasm ebbs, he strokes me more slowly, bringing me down until the post-orgasmic jerks running through me ease off and my breathing returns to normal.

I'm completely spent, hanging boneless in his arms.

"Thank you," I murmur, the words little more than an exhalation against his chest.

"My absolute pleasure," he replies. "But we're not finished yet."

He lifts me into his arms, and I bring my legs around his hips. His erection presses against me, and a shot of pleasure fills my core. I could come again in seconds. I've never been this turned on before.

He carries me into the bedroom, where there is the most enormous bed I've ever seen. *The big bed.* The sheets look like they've never been slept on. *Does he have them changed every day, like he lives in a hotel?* When he lies me down on them, they're softer than any I've felt before.

"These sheets," I purr, spreading my arms over them like I'm making a snow angel. "So soft."

He smiles as he kneels at the end of the bed to remove my shoes and socks. He does it with such reverence—kissing my ankles, then the arches of my feet—that watching him is unmistakably sensual.

I can't bear the tension. I'm so aroused I want to wriggle out of his grip, just so I can push him to the floor and straddle him, but before I can move, he yanks down my trousers and pyjama shorts. I raise my hips to let him slide them off, and he doesn't take his eyes off me as he drops them in a heap on the floor.

I'm spread out on his bed, entirely naked, with nothing on me but the heat of his gaze. And it's the hottest thing I've ever experienced.

He stands at the end of the bed, dragging a hand through his hair as his gaze roves hungrily over my naked body. "I want to remember this forever. You're so unbelievably beautiful. Where the fuck did you come from?"

I've never been looked at this way, and his handsome face displaying such awe is incredibly sexy, but the hint of disbelief there, as if there's a chance I'm a figment of his imagination, makes me laugh, and he briefly closes his eyes.

"I love the sound of your laughter," he tells me, a dazzling smile breaking over his face. "You always sound so happy."

"I am happy." I sit up and crawl towards him. His eyebrows rise, his irises twinkling with excitement. I rise up to unbutton his shirt, sliding it off his shoulders. His pecs are so defined, the ridges of his abs so perfect. I could play his torso like a musical instrument. For a few moments I stroke his tanned skin, kissing the muscles, flicking his nipples with my tongue. *I can't believe I'm doing this.* His breaths are quick and shallow.

Then I sit back and tuck the tips of my fingers into the waistband of his trousers. "I want to see that beautiful dick of yours."

He grants permission with a slight nod of his head. I loosen his belt, but he does the rest, removing his trousers and boxers in one swift motion.

His cock is huge and thick, and so fucking hard. The tip is already beading with pre-cum. It's even more magnificent than it looked in the pool room.

"Wow. Your dick would make a perfect dildo." He frowns, a confused smile tugging at his lips. I grin up at him. "I'd fuck myself with it every day."

His mouth drops open. I think I've shocked him, just a tiny bit, and the idea thrills me.

Still kneeling on the bed, I lean forward and run my tongue along the underside of his cock until I reach the tip. I flutter my tongue there, tasting the pre-ejaculate. His cock jerks against my mouth and I take it deep inside. He groans, and I try to take more, but he's too big. I fist my hand at the base, focusing my mouth on the tip, running my tongue over it, sucking on it like I want to inhale it. That he's giving me unrestricted access to his body is exhilarating.

Mr Hawkston's hands come to the back of my head, his fingers wrapping in my hair, but he doesn't fuck my mouth, although I sense he wants to. He holds back, letting me pleasure him first.

"Wait." I'm still bobbing my mouth up and down his hard dick, but his command makes me pause. "I want to come inside you," he grits out. "The first time I come, I want it to be inside you."

"You can come in my mouth," I say.

There's a spark of fire in his gaze at my words, but he shakes his head. "No. I want to come in that beautiful cunt."

Wow. Hearing him put it like that has my pussy aching to be filled. I haven't a single objection to anything this man might want to do. I crawl back up the bed and lie down. He follows me, nudging my legs apart with his until he settles between my thighs.

"I can't promise I'll last," he says.

He reaches across me to get a condom from the top drawer of the bedside table, tears the packet open with his teeth and rolls it over his gorgeous cock. Then he lines his body up with mine, letting his dick slide up and down the lips of my wet pussy. It takes all my self control not to squirm with need.

He holds eye contact, propping himself up on one arm, his body hovering over mine. *Glorious.* "Ready?"

"Fuck, yes," I mutter.

His mouth twitches with a tiny smile, and he nudges his tip inside me. I bite my lip as I feel the stretch, even from only a small part of him.

I shift my hips a little to encourage him. "You don't need to be gentle," I tell him, feeling desperate for all he has to give me. "You need to fuck me. Ruin me."

"Ruin you?"

I nod. *God, I want it so bad, so hard. If he holds back, it won't be enough.*

Still holding my gaze, he quirks an eyebrow and thrusts deep into me in one go. It's pleasure and pain and everything I need all at once.

He pulls out again slowly, then pushes in again. I'm moaning, noises coming from my mouth I can't control. I've never had a dick this big. It fills me in ways I never knew were possible. My orgasm builds in deep inside me, gathering intensity with each thrust.

The sounds of our bodies slamming together is an erotic cacophony that heightens my arousal.

And Mr Hawkston... his eyes... Never before has a man looked at me this way during sex, like he's not only fucking my body but making love to my soul. Even as he pounds me, I know I'll never get over this. *Ever.*

Orgasmic bliss ripples through me, rising to a crest I can't control. "Fuck, fuck, I'm coming."

He groans, his jaw tight, his face contorted with ecstasy as he comes with me. I feel the jerk of it deep inside me. It lasts longer than I expect, his body rigid between my legs, all the tendons in his neck standing out as his cock pulses.

Finally, his muscles slacken, and he slumps against me. But he doesn't let his full weight fall on me; he keeps himself propped up on his elbows. His face hovers above mine, our noses almost touching. We're panting, our chests heaving, my breasts rising and falling against his pecs, our sweat mingled between us.

"That was fast. Was that fast?" I say, suddenly nervous. "You make me come so fast. Shit."

His brow creases. "Was it too fast for you?"

The answer comes easily, soothing my anxiety. "No. It was perfect."

"Perfect," he repeats the word slowly, sounding out each syllable like it's a new concept. "Yes. That's exactly what it was."

A strange warmth that has nothing to do with sex ripples through me. He holds eyes contact a few moments longer, our hearts so close they're almost beating as one.

"You're definitely not real," he says with a throaty laugh.

I smile up at him and kiss him. "You're a dream too, you know."

He holds me as our breathing returns to normal, still staring into my eyes as if he thinks I'll disappear if he looks away. It's a look that sinks right to the core of me, like he's embedding himself into my memory. Into my *soul*.

This is way more intimate than I expected, and all of a sudden I can't bear it. This was supposed to be *just* sex, a release of the crazy attraction I have for this man, and somehow it feels like way more. More than I've ever felt with any man. It feels like too much. My overwhelm must be apparent on my face because his brow creases as though some unpleasant thought is passing through his mind.

And just like that, whatever spell we were under is broken. He slides off me and pads out of the room, leaving my skin cold with the absence of him. I watch him head towards the bathroom, and I'm gripped by the unnerving sensation that I'm looking at a stranger.

19
MATT

I tie up the condom and toss it in the bin. I grip the edge of the sink and stare at myself in the mirror.

What the fuck just happened?

I think my world has been blown apart by a woman, and I have no idea what to do now. *Should I pretend I'm unmoved? Pretend this was just sex? Pretend she was nothing but a good fuck?*

My heart feels raw, like that orgasm stripped layers off it. I can feel the beat of it everywhere; the rush of blood in my ears is deafening. It *never* felt like this with Gemma.

"Mr Hawkston?" Her voice is soft and there's a hint of sadness to it. Even after what just happened, she's not using my name. "Was this a mistake?"

My body heats uncomfortably at the question. I look up and see her in the mirror. She's standing naked in the bathroom doorway.

"Does it feel that way to you?"

Her brows draw together. "Not at first. It felt right. So right. The most right thing in the world. And then…"

I turn to face her, leaning back against the sink. "Then what?"

"Then it scared me, feeling that way. Being so open to you. I shut down the connection. I didn't mean to. And then you noticed, and it felt like you thought it was all a mistake. All of it happened in the blink of an eye, and then you walked in here like you were trying to escape."

I blow out a breath. She saw *everything*. In seconds, she had me all figured out. *This is intense*. And also ridiculous, the way we're both naked, discussing what ought to have been nothing more than a quick and satisfying fuck. And Aries is only making it worse with her talk about connection and openness and all that bullshit. Only it's *not* bullshit, because I know exactly what she means...

I did this. I fucked this up, and I don't know how to unfuck it.

Moments ago, our bodies were so in tune, so perfect together, and now there's an insurmountable gulf between us.

"Is this a one-time thing?" she asks, her voice full of pain. "Should I leave?"

I rub the heels of my palms against my eyes and let out a frustrated groan. "No. I'm sorry. It's just... I wasn't expecting it to be the way it was either. I wasn't—"

"I know. I get it."

"You do?"

A tentative smile pulls at her lips. "I was there too, remember?"

I laugh, but without opening my mouth to release the sound. "Shit."

She takes a step towards me, cautious at first, but then with more confidence. "There's one thing I really do need to know," she says, looking at me seriously. "Am I going to get more time with that huge dick of yours? Because if not, you're going to have to clone it for me."

I laugh aloud now, unsure what the hell she means, but grateful that she's making light of whatever just happened. "Huh?"

"Make a model. Turn it into a dildo. So I can fuck myself with it every day."

This woman is full of surprises. I smile, shaking my head. My dick is hardening again at the thought. She nods knowingly at my growing erection.

I don't know how she did it, but she dispelled the tension like it was nothing more than morning mist. *Maybe she's the sun.* She shakes that mane of red hair and laughs, and for a second my heart stops beating. *Definitely the sun.*

I step towards her, meeting her in the middle of the bathroom. I wrap my arms around her and kiss the top of her head. "You don't need a dildo. You can have the real thing. It has to stay attached to me, though."

Her cheeks fill out as a broad smile splits her face. "Thank you. That's all I needed to know. We can forget about all the other stuff."

I lean away from her. "What other stuff?"

"All the stuff you were saying to me with your eyes."

I purse my lips, giving her my best sceptical look. "You think my eyes were speaking to you?"

"The eyes are the window to the soul. They're always talking. You can't hide anything from me, Matt."

It's only the second time she's said my name, and the raw ache of my heart heals a fraction at the intimacy it conveys, as though, right now, I'm not her boss at all. "I don't know whether to be reassured or disturbed by that idea."

She tilts her head up, meeting my concern with unflinching directness. "Then don't think about it. Let's just fuck again instead."

I burst out laughing and she wraps her arms around me, pressing her cheek against my chest.

I hold her tight. "You are definitely a dream."

It's nearly dawn and we've barely slept. Aries is insatiable.

"It's one of my favourite things." She's in the middle of telling me about her penchant for dildos and masturbation. I'm stroking her stomach and breasts with one hand as she lies on the bed next to me, our legs intertwined, and I love the intimacy of it. I'd say I'd missed it, but the truth is, I've never known it. Not the way it feels with Aries. "Any time I'm not feeling great, I set aside time for self pleasure. Nothing shakes up your energy system like an orgasm."

I tilt my head in agreement. I certainly feel thoroughly shaken up.

She rolls onto her side, facing me, propped up on one elbow. "I thought of you, you know. Every time I've masturbated since I arrived, I thought of you."

A wave of heat rolls through me. "You did?"

"Sure." She shrugs like it's no big deal. "I figured we'd be sleeping together sooner or later."

"I don't believe that for a moment. I didn't think we would."

"Why not?" She waggles a finger in my face. "You do that sexy eye thing all the time—"

"Sexy eye thing?"

"Yeah. Do you always think about sex? Because you look like you do. Sex appeal pours out of you. It's pretty hard to ignore."

I huff a laugh. "I don't think about sex all the time. I think about it every time I look at *you*. There's a difference."

"That explains why I always think of sex when you look at me, then. You've been sending me telepathic messages."

I roll my eyes and shift onto my back. "You're full of shit."

She slaps my chest, grinning all the while. "It's true."

"Maybe you did it," I say. "Maybe you sent them first."

She idly flicks my nipple with one finger, and the tip of my dick gives a corresponding throb. "Maybe. Who knows? The point is, we're in sync." She sighs heavily, then all the amusement is gone from her eyes. "I don't want to get in the middle of things with you and your wife."

"I'm divorced. There's nothing to get in the middle of."

"Hmm." She sounds thoroughly unconvinced. "What happens now, then?"

"We do more of this," I say. "We enjoy the summer. I'm booking a last minute holiday. I want to take the kids away when school finishes. You're coming too."

"It's my job. I'd expect to."

"Now you have other duties." I give her a mock-salacious wink and she laughs. "I'm afraid your workload has increased significantly. Longer hours, more physical labour."

"Are you going to increase my pay?"

I stiffen. "Seriously?"

"No, stupid." She sounds affronted. "I'm doing this for free, because I want to. And because you're the best sex I've ever had. I'd like more of it. Lots more, please."

I can't wipe the grin off my face. "Thank God. I was worried you were just after money."

She's quiet a moment too long, as though whatever she's thinking needs careful deliberation. "It must be horrid worrying that people only want you for your bank balance." An uncomfortable tension spreads in the air, but then Aries slides a hand between my legs. "Whereas I only want you for your huge dick."

Her eyes glint with mirth, but beneath it there's something far deeper. I understand what she means about our eyes speaking. She's making light of the situation, but we both know this is more than sex. More than her hand on my dick. The fact that we got here so fast is insane. I've never felt a connection like this.

We're so comfortable, it's like we've been together for months, not hours. Laughing, I pull her in for a kiss, relishing the sweetness of her tongue against mine. Our kisses have grown softer, gentler, as the night has gone on. To me, it feels like we've known each other forever.

A strange sound comes from somewhere in the room and we break apart. Aries scrambles off the bed, sifting through the heap of discarded clothes we threw off last night.

"What's that?" I check.

She holds up the video monitor and flashes it at me. "Your daughter."

Lucie's waking up. I glance at the time on the alarm clock at the side of the bed. 6.22 am. *Shit*.

"You had that half of the monitor all night?" I ask.

She nods. "And yes, before you ask, I heard you talking about me."

"Hmm. That's a bit invasive."

She's pulling on her clothes, dragging her jumper over her head, covering her beautiful full breasts. I feel an ache in my chest. *When am I going to see them again?*

"It's my job," she says. "Don't feel bad. It's the reason I came over here when you messaged me. You sounded..." Her words fade and a puzzled look crosses her face.

"What?" I ask.

She looks hesitant before she says, "Lonely."

I sit up. "Lonely? You slept with me because you thought I sounded lonely?"

She's got one leg in her trousers and she's hopping on one foot when she pauses to level a serious stare at me. "Stop fishing. I slept with you because I saw your enormous cock that day outside the sauna and I haven't stopped thinking about it. That, and I was bored of my dildos. They have a limited repertoire." She winks and bites her bottom lip;

the mixture of cute and sexy is almost too much to handle. "The fact that you sounded lonely was by-the-by."

I'm already propped up by the pillow, but I put my hands behind my head. "Phew. I was worried I was a pity fuck."

Her face scrunches. "You worry about a lot of stuff. Let's have fun. Where are we going on this holiday?"

"The Mediterranean. On the boat."

"Sounds great."

She flips her head upside down and ties her long red hair into a ponytail with a hair-band from her wrist. There's something so sexy about the way she does it, and how it swings down her back when she rights herself, that I'm immediately hard again.

She gives me a suggestive smile, like she knows exactly what I was thinking, but just then, a noise comes again from the monitor. She checks it, then slides it into her pocket. "See you later. I've got to get back to my day job." She blows me a kiss and leaves the room.

She's officially the sexiest damn woman I've ever met. And she lives in my house. To say I'm elated is an understatement.

20

ARIES

Later that morning, I walk into the kitchen to find Alec already there, chopping up fruit. He stops and gives me the once over. His eyebrows rise far too high up his forehead as he waves the knife at me and says, "You look like you had a good night. Did you get *any* sleep?"

I can't stop smiling. I'm normally cheery, but this is next level. My face gives everything away, but I hold my index finger against my lips to *shh* him, my eyes dropping to where Lucie is following me into the kitchen.

Alec straightens, lowering the knife to the chopping board. "Hi, Lucie."

"Hello." She grins and hops up on a stool at the island.

He pushes a bowl of mango at her. "For you, Princess."

"Is there any for me?" I ask.

He slides another bowl over to me. "Only because you're a great nanny." He imbues his words with so much inflated emotion, I know he's being facetious. "So kind and caring. And because I like you. Maybe a little too much."

I roll my eyes, trying to look like I'm not affected by his repetition of Mr Hawkston's words from last night, but I can already feel the heat rising up my cheeks. "Stop it."

Alec turns his attention to Lucie. "You're very lucky to have such a great nanny." The jocular tone is gone, and I can tell he means it. "You know that, right?"

"Yup. I know that. Daddy said so."

Alec gives a satisfied smile and nods his head. "Too right."

"What did Daddy say?"

I spin in my seat to see Mr Hawkston—*Matt. How strange to think I can call him that*—standing in the doorway, his shoulder leaning against the frame. Holy shit, he looks like a different man. He's so relaxed, his smile so warm. He looks sexy as hell... if it's possible he's *more* handsome this way. I cannot believe I spent all night having sex with this specimen.

I immediately want to do it again. And again. And again. My heart is beating like it has a million tiny wings, and every cell in my body heats up. If I don't hold it together, there's going to be a puddle on my chair when I stand.

"You said Aries was a great nanny," Lucie repeats. "Last night, when you came to my room and sat on my bed."

Matt frowns, then looks up at me, a wide smile spreading over his face. "It seems everyone was listening."

Alec keeps his head down, furiously chopping way more fruit than we need. If he's making assumptions about my night based on how I look, there's no way he won't draw the same conclusion from witnessing his boss this at ease.

Matt walks into the kitchen and kisses the top of Lucie's head. Then he pauses beside me. It's a tantalizing moment of static sparks. His hand twitches like he's about to touch me, but he lets his arm drop.

Alec catches my eye, and I know he noticed. *So awkward.*

Matt sits on the stool at the island on the other side of Lucie so she's pinned between us. "What are we eating?"

"Mango, currently," Alec answers. "But I can make you anything you want."

"Hmm. Fruit's not going to cut it this morning. I'm starving." Matt pushes his tongue into his cheek and looks at the ceiling for a second before focusing back on Alec. "Can you make Eggs Benedict? There's a cafe just down the road—The Belmont—that does the most fabulous Eggs Benedict."

Alec smiles. "I know it. Those are my favourite."

"A man of good taste," Matt replies.

The exchange is cordial, but it makes me wonder how often Matt has taken the time to talk to Alec before this. And if he loves the Eggs Benedict from The Belmont so much, how come he's never asked for them from his chef before?

We all sit making slightly awkward conversations while Alec makes breakfast. When he's done, he places the plate, with perfectly symmetrically arranged Eggs Benedict on it, in front of Matt.

"Tell me, Alec, what are your aspirations?" Matt asks as he spins the plate as though he wants it to face a certain direction before picking up his cutlery. He's still staring at his food when Alec throws me another *'what the fuck?'* look as though he's amazed at the change in his boss.

"Actually, it's to be the head chef at the Mayfair Hawkston Hotel. And to get at least one Michelin star."

"Really?" Surprise echoes in Matt's voice as he loads his fork with a bite. He pops it in his mouth, his eyes wide as he chews. Then he swallows and says, "God, those eggs are better than The Belmont. Why did I never know you could do this?"

Alec wipes his hands on his chef's coat. "You never asked, sir," he admits, but I hear no resentment in the statement.

"What other talents are you hiding from me?" Matt asks, and Alec blushes as he rolls off a list of his favourite dishes to cook.

"You'll have to have a trial at the Mayfair Hotel then," Mr Hawkston says. "Although I'd be damn sorry to lose you here."

Alec looks so ecstatic that he might float off the ground. I smile, enjoying the repartee between them. I'm sensing it's new, given Alec's continually surprised expression.

"Where are we going today?" I ask Lucie, because at the moment no one's paying either of us any attention.

Matt breaks off his conversation with Alec. "You can have the day off," he says to me. "I'm taking Lucie out."

"Yay," Lucie cries, wrapping her arms around her father's neck. "Daddy-Lucie day."

I raise a brow. "Are you sure?"

"Absolutely. Take a nap. You might be up late." Matt's voice doesn't waver, but Alec's eyebrows rise so high, it looks like they're trying to hitch a lift with his hair.

Heat flares in my cheeks as images of last night flood my mind. Arousal pulses between my legs, and I lean forward on the stool, pressing my thighs together in an attempt to dampen the effect, but it only makes it worse.

I really hope I'm up late. I want to be up late every night. I'd be raw, but fuck it, I'd be sated. And then there's that other thing... the contented warmth I felt after we shed the roles of employer and employee last night. I want more of *that* too.

When Matt finally finishes eating, he takes Lucie off for the day, leaving me and Alec staring at one another in the kitchen.

"What the hell did you do to him?" Alec hisses. "I've never seen him like that. He's normally a moody bastard. Did you fuck another personality into him?"

"Alec. Shut up." I press my lips together, then bite the bottom one and tilt my head to the side. "Maybe."

He places his hands flat on the kitchen counter and leans across the island. "Tell me *everything*."

I shake my head and motion zipping my lips. "Nope. I don't do gossip. Not about this, anyway."

"Damn. This is the most interesting thing that's happened in this house since Mr Hawkston busted Gemma having the affair."

A pang tweaks my heart. "She cheated on him?"

Alec nods. "Yeah. But their marriage was over long before that. And really, I wouldn't feel too sorry for him. He was never here, and when he was, they fought. I know he works hard, but he was very absent, and when he did show his face, he was grumpy as fuck and barely said a word." Alec wipes the back of his hand over his forehead. "I've honestly never seen him like he was just now. He seemed like a real human being."

I'm struggling to compute what Alec's saying, because the man I spent the night with was not just a real human being, but one that's kind and passionate and tender and... *Shit. I'm already feeling far too much for him.*

I suddenly remember the conversation I had with my mother, when she accused me of only liking men for sex. One night with Matt Hawkston, and I'm re-writing every previous opinion I've held about men. I've played up the whole 'I love your dick' thing because I don't want him to freak out... and I don't want to freak myself out... but if I'm honest, whatever this is between us, it's *big*. Emotionally big, not just physically. I like him. *A lot.*

But then I recall the man that shouted at me in the corridor yesterday, and I wonder if I like him *enough* to make my peace with that. I'm so attracted to him that any real concerns about his behaviour flew out of my mind as soon as he kissed me. But now, in the cold light of day, with Alec staring at me over the kitchen island, I find it hard to reconcile the two versions of this man. How can he be so kind, so passionate, but also sharp, cold and closed off? I could excuse the shouting as stress... not only is he working hard, but he was worried for his daughter's safety. But not every man would have lost his temper the way he did.

A strange wave of discomfort ebbs low in my belly.

No matter how wonderful it was to be in his arms last night, how connected I felt to him and how certain I was that this is more than just lust... I'm still not entirely convinced I haven't made a big mistake.

The thought sits like a dead weight in my gut, but as I observe the sensation, it shifts. And to my surprise, I find I don't care at all. It might well be a mistake, but it's the best mistake I've ever made.

I spend the afternoon strolling around the west end. I walk the river from the Houses of Parliament all the way to the Tower of London. It's beautiful and vibrant, and I love being able to do it, but I have an acute sense of loneliness. I ought to be sharing this experience with someone. And truthfully, there's only one person I'd want to do it with, and he's my boss.

My attention is intently focused on my old mobile phone, weighing down my pocket like a boulder. I'm waiting for it to ring, or buzz, but it doesn't.

I try not to be disappointed. After all, Matt is with Lucie, and he's probably too busy to be sending messages to me.

When I finally get home, my feet are aching, and I'm tired. I ate dinner alone, waiting on the text message that never arrived. I creep up to my room. The lights are low, and I can see the soft glow of Lucie's night light. Matt must have already put her to bed.

And then it occurs to me; I know exactly what I need right now—a sauna. He did say I could use it, so I'm taking him at his word.

I strip off my clothes, wrap a towel around me, and head down to the basement in the lift.

A few minutes later, I enter the pool room and approach the sauna. I can smell the hot wood before I open the door. When I step inside, the heat blasts me like I'm stepping into hell; an impression that's only accentuated by the dim red lights beneath the wooden slats of the benches. *It's wonderful.*

None of the staff will be in the house because it's Sunday night, so I'm feeling totally relaxed. I don't know where Matt is. I assume he's home, but he hasn't contacted me and I don't want to appear too eager. Although it's possibly too late for that...

I take a seat on the wooden bench and close my eyes.

Fuck, it's hot in here.

I breathe slowly, allowing the heat to penetrate my skin, reaching the deeper flesh. Sweat begins to pearl all over me and I lie down, still wrapped in my towel.

But if no one's here, shouldn't I be able to have the full sauna experience? I open my towel, spreading it on the bench, and I lie back down on top of it, fully naked. It's glorious, allowing the heat to touch every forbidden part of me.

I'm immediately turned on, and I run my hands over my breasts, touching my hardened nipples, imagining it's Matt doing it. In my mind's eye, I see his large hands strumming my body. I see his face, his jaw, his dark eyes, that thick hair that begs to have my fingers twisted through it. His body... those muscles... that huge, hard dick...

My arousal zooms to one hundred per cent, and I feel a gush of wetness between my legs. I part my thighs, letting the heat hit my pussy.

After last night, I've been semi-aroused all day and haven't done anything about it. But now, lying here naked in the safe cocoon of the sauna, it seems like the perfect moment. Before I get too hot and can't take it anymore...

I slide my hand down to my pussy, which is already soaked. I laugh to myself. If Matt can get me this wet when he's not even here, then I'm in deep trouble.

I raise my knees a little, digging my heels in to the bench beneath me as I drag my wetness up and over my clit. With my other hand, I knead one of my breasts, teasing the nipple. The images in my head are so vivid, I can almost smell Matt, feel his body pounding against mine, taste the salt of his sweat on my tongue.

Holy crap, this is unbelievable. I lift my hips a little off the bench, rubbing my clit, which swells beneath my fingertips. Pleasure zips through my body, little ecstatic buzzes ripping through my cells. I move my hand faster, needing my orgasm to break before the sauna gets so hot I can't breathe. I moan in the heat, teetering right on the edge.

The door to the sauna clicks open, cool air flooding the small space. *Fuck*. I open my eyes, raising my head, using my hands to cover myself.

Matt stands in the doorway, a towel wrapped around his hips. He's so huge that he dominates the space entirely. I'm surprised he doesn't have to duck to stand in here.

He stares at me, desire smoldering in his dark eyes. The air crackles with electricity. "My sauna's never been this fucking hot." A laugh bubbles through my lips, but he crosses the sauna in two steps and presses a finger to my mouth. "Don't stop."

I raise an eyebrow at him, but he doesn't look away. "Let me see you," he says, as he sits by my feet.

His gaze lowers to my very wet, very exposed, very *hot*, pussy. With one large, warm hand, he nudges my bent knee so it falls outward. "You're drenched." His eyes widen with what looks like awe. "Tell me what you were thinking about."

God, this is so fucking dirty. I'm not used to this unabashed sexuality when there's another human being present, but the longing on his face is so exquisite, and the commanding tone of his voice so authoritative, that I can't disobey him. "You. I was thinking about you."

He lets out a groan, and the sound resonates with desire. It infuses me, and an internal heat roars through my body, mingling with the heat of the sauna. I'm slick with sweat; every inch of my skin is shining. My tolerance for the temperature is running out, but with Matt's eyes on me, I know it won't take a moment to come.

I begin to touch myself again, and in a couple of strokes, I'm exactly where I left off, teetering on the edge of orgasm. "Fuck. Oh, fuck," I say. "Please, Matt. Touch me—"

He growls in response, his hands clamping around my ankles.

"That's not what I meant," I bite out.

"Keep going," he orders.

I squirm and writhe, my hips shifting against my towel as I touch myself. "Please, Ma—"

His hands tighten, cutting me off. His breaths come hard and fast, his eyes glued to where I'm now slipping my fingers inside myself.

I'm desperate to feel him there instead, deep inside my body, to have that delicious fullness that only he can give me. It's clear from the fierce grip he has on my ankles that he's not going to give me what I'm asking for, but the low, frustrated groan that he lets out suggests he's denying himself too.

"You have no idea how much I want you," he rasps, confirming my suspicion. "But watching you touch yourself...*fuck*. It's almost as good." He lets out another of those groans which only increases the need humming between my legs. I won't be able to hold back much longer and I work my clit harder. Matt's eyes flare with desire as he notices the shift in my movement. "Come for me, baby," he whispers, deep and greedy. "Let me see you come undone."

His words send me plummeting over the edge into an orgasm that makes my legs shake against his hold. My back arches, my head thrashing against the bench, hair spilling loose around my shoulders.

It goes on and on and on, cresting and sinking and cresting again, Matt's eyes on me the whole time, eating me up, drinking me down. *So greedy.*

When my orgasm finally dwindles, I lie still, my chest heaving. I'm seeing stars, my head is light from the heat of the sauna and the mind-blowing orgasm.

I cover my eyes with my hand, and blow out a loud breath. Matt chuckles, bringing his lips to the inside of my shin. He kisses his way up my leg, stopping at the knee. I creak my fingers apart so I can see him.

"How the fuck did you get to be so hot?" he breathes.

I smile. I can't help it when he's looking at me like I'm the most delicious thing he's ever seen. "It's a sauna. It's ninety fucking degrees in here."

He snorts and looks me over, assessing and appreciating. He squeezes my thigh, then hops off the bench. "Let's get you out of here before you pass out."

His hands are lifting me, entirely naked, from the bench, and he's pushing the door open with his hips.

The heat is deep in my flesh by now. I think I'm partially cooked. Not even the cool air out here makes a difference.

Matt lies me down on one of the loungers by the side of the pool. They're huge and anchored to the floor. It's warm against my back, a gentle soothing heat.

"Is this thing heated?" I ask.

"Yup."

"Wow."

There's a fresh towel rolled up at the end of each lounger, like the house is a high end hotel. Which I guess isn't surprising, given where the Hawkston money was made.

He sits at the end of the lounger, and his eyes sweep over me, taking in every inch of my bare skin. His gaze is like a soft caress; reverent, yet laden with longing.

He raises a small bottle of what looks like massage oil. I don't know where he got it, but he pours a little in his palm, sets the bottle on the floor and rubs his hands together. I eye him warily, watching those huge, oil-slicked palms rub against one another.

"Relax," he says. "You did a lot of hard work in there." He nods at the sauna.

I lie back, unable to forget that I'm completely at his mercy. He's huge and strong, and I'm lying here naked and helpless. If he wanted, he could do anything with me. And yet I feel completely safe as he begins, working his way up my body in long, deep strokes that tenderize my muscles.

The oil has a calming scent, like lavender and bergamot. In other circumstances, I might drift off and fall into a relaxing sleep. But with the most gorgeous man I've ever met stroking oil into my naked skin, I can't possibly.

There's a fire in his eyes, like all he wants to do is bend me over and fuck me raw, but he's taking his time, sliding his hands up my thighs.

My breath catches in my throat as his hand finally reaches the top of my leg. I clench my fists at my sides, and bite down on my lip. He must notice the sudden tension in my body, because a deep moan rumbles in his throat.

"Please," I say, my voice a breathy whimper.

"You like to beg, don't you?"

I nod as he teases the edge of my pussy with one thick finger, his eyes shining mischievously. I shift my hips, seeking friction, hoping I can somehow tempt him to slide inside me.

"Please, fuck me." I cover my face with my hands, embarrassed that I want him so much I'm *still* begging. "I can't bear this."

"I don't tend to bring condoms to the sauna," he replies, still stroking the edges of my pussy, gradually increasing the pressure around my wet entrance.

I let out a needy moan. "I'm on the pill," I say. "Please—"

"Are you sure?"

I gasp as his finger finally comes to rest right at my entrance, and he runs it around the edge, sensitizing every cell in the area until my need reaches fever-pitch.

"Yes, I'm fucking sure," I bite out. "You're a cruel man, Matt Hawkston."

Laughter rumbles in his chest, such a sexy sound that I'm barely managing to control myself. I shift on the lounger in an attempt to sit up, but his hand comes to my shoulder easing me back down. "Nuh-uh," he says. "We're going to do this my way."

That deep, commanding voice does things to me that I never knew were possible. My body is vibrating with anticipation. I lie back as he stands, the towel around his hips doing nothing to hide the huge erection that tents the fabric.

Hanging on hooks on the wall are four towelling robes. Matt removes the belts from them and returns to where I'm lying on the lounger.

My heart is in my throat. *Fuck me, he wants to tie me up.* I didn't think I could be more turned on than I am right now, but as he grips the belts in both hands, pulling them taut between his fists, arousal buzzes through me like an electric current.

"Arms over your head," he says, and I obey instantly. "Anything you don't like, tell me and we'll stop."

I nod, and he begins to tie one of my wrists to the leg of the lounger. Then he moves to the other and secures it so I'm unable to move my arms. Then he moves to my feet and ties my ankles to the legs at the bottom of the lounger.

My arousal is soaring as I let him splay me out, and my mouth dries as Matt holds eye contact, his gaze burning me up until I'm nothing but the intensity of my desire. I don't give a fuck what this looks like, or what anyone might think. All I want is to feel his body on mine... *in* mine.

He stands at the end of the lounger and surveys his handiwork, a smug grin tugging at his lips.

My hips jerk of their own volition, my back arching as if my pussy can jump off the lounger and reach him. "Please, let me see you," I breathe.

He tilts his head in consent, then lets his towel drop to the floor.

"Oh, my God," I moan, as he stands there, his dick huge and hard, rising to his navel. His abs are beautifully defined, his thighs dense with muscle, and the definition of his quads is so deep I could slide my fingers in the ridges. He is a perfect specimen.

And his face... that jaw, those eyes... I cannot believe this is really happening.

He bends so his forearms are on the lounger, his torso hovering over my lower half. He trails his tongue up the inside of my thigh, and my leg twitches like his touch is charged.

"If you don't fuck me I'll—"

His tongue slides inside me, thrusting deep.

"Oh, shit." I begin to writhe on the lounger, my hips pressing upward, into his mouth. His jaw is hard, and his stubble rasps against me.

I thrash my arms, but the ties hold tight. I had no idea what sweet torment it would be to be unable to touch him. I have no control, and it makes the wanting that much more desperate. And Lord knows, it was desperate before. I want to grab his head, tug his hair, force his face deeper, but I can't do any of those things.

He slides one hand under my arse so he can tilt my hips, giving him better access. When he has me where he wants me, he feasts, his tongue alternately lapping in long strokes, then flicking in short ones as he teases my clit before he sucks on it. Pleasure builds as he works me with his mouth, and sparks fly through my body, making my toes curl. No one has ever given me so much pleasure before.

He lowers me, then slides one finger into my wet slit, then another, pressing against that deep spot within. His tongue continues to tease my clit, which is full and swollen and eager for release.

The pleasure intensifies until not even the rigidity of my thighs against his shoulders can hold it back.

And then he stops.

"What the fuck?" I yell, the tingles of my imminent orgasm beginning to fade.

"Hold it. Keep it right there." He grins at me, his lips and chin wet with my juices. Then, in one swift motion, he's on top of me, the reassuring weight, the heat of him, pressing against me.

He lines us up and then—"Now," he commands, as he thrusts deep inside me.

My orgasm breaks with such force that I can't control my body. I'm shuddering and jerking against him, moans and screams slipping from my mouth.

I'm so consumed with pleasure I'm not even here. Every cell of my being, every fibre is alight, burning with more ecstasy than I've ever experienced.

Matt rides out my climax, fucking me hard, each thrust shooting another burst of pleasure through me like the strike of a whip.

"Fuck, fuck, oh, God—"

"Not God," he growls. "Me."

I tug at my restraints, desperate to touch him, to feel him, to claw at him, but I can't. Somehow, it only makes the pleasure last longer, the repeated crests of my orgasm pulsing through me; up my forearms, my hands, right to the tips of my fingers. It's unlike anything I've ever known. My whole body is buzzing.

Matt pumps his hips, his huge cock filling me so completely, touching the deepest parts of me.

"Come again, come for me," he says, his voice a desperate rasp against my ear.

And I do. My climax rises to meet his words, my pussy clenching around him, dragging his orgasm out.

"Oh, shit," he groans. "So good, so fucking good." Tendons in his neck stand out, every muscle in his arms and chest tense as his cock jerks inside me and the warmth of his seed fills me up.

He lets out a final shuddering moan before he lowers himself against me, pressing my breasts against his chest.

For a few moments, we breathe, waiting for our inhales and exhales to return to normal.

"What the fuck are we doing?" he mumbles, his voice soft, his lips pressed against my neck.

"Having fun," I reply, still breathless. "I don't know about you, but I'm having the time of my life here."

He chuckles against my throat. "Don't leave. Don't ever go anywhere. I need this kind of fun in my life forever."

Forever.

I say nothing, letting him slowly kiss my breasts, caressing my nipples with his tongue. I don't know what to say, because I don't know what this is. He's still my boss, and I'm in a role that was never meant to be permanent. I need the cash, and I need to go back home at the end of the summer to be with my mum.

And then what?

I push the thought out of mind, focusing on the gorgeous man whose hands and mouth are slowly worshiping my body in the wake of our conjoined orgasm. But there's a sense of sadness fluttering in the darkness that I can't shed.

Matt stops touching me, his body going tense and still. Concern creases his brow. "What's wrong?"

I debate telling him how I feel, but what's the point? This isn't a normal situation. We aren't two people who met as equals, with a viable future ahead of us. He might have said forever, but I'm certain he doesn't really mean it.

"I should've checked that you've been tested," I say, hoping to dispel the intense emotion of the situation by bringing us back to more practical concerns. "You know, because of all those women you've slept with before me." The words I said to him on my first day pound in my ears, *You look like you've seen a lot of women's underwear.*

He quirks his head. "I got married at nineteen. What kind of husband do you think I was?"

"You've been divorced for a year. That's a lot of days. A lot of potential—"

"You should stop talking," he says, a playful smirk on his lips. "Gemma was my first. And you..." His words fade along with the expression on his face, and the silence is burdened by whatever he's about to confess. He looks so uncertain that I know exactly what he's about to say. *I'm the second.*

Fuck me. This is a big deal. A big fucking deal, and I don't know how to handle it. I feel a bit like I might faint, I'm so surprised. I had this man pegged all wrong, and my concerns about whatever this is between us shrivel, sucked dry by the new knowledge that whatever this is to me, it's something else to him.

You make a lot of assumptions. That's what he'd said when I made the underwear comment on my first day. I force a smile onto my face, trying not to show how overwhelmed I am by his almost-admission. "Can you untie me?"

He sits up and moves to the leg of the lounger to release me, but his face is creased with concern. "Is everything all right?"

The belt falls away and I rotate my free wrist. "Yes." I lie, focusing on my wrists so I don't have to meet his gaze. "Yes. Fine."

He dips his head, easing himself into my field of view, forcing me to look at him. "You'll tell me if I do something you don't like, won't you?"

"Of course."

"Good." He tips my chin up with one gentle finger, making sure I'm really looking at him. "I'd never take a risk like that with your health, Aries. I hope you know that."

The way he says it is so gentle, so full of care, that my heart starts quivering in my chest, the regular rhythm going haywire as if he'd said something else entirely. "I know that, Mr Hawkston." My voice is soft, but I mean the words so completely, that it feels like the most important thing I've ever said.

He grins. "Matt. Call me Matt."

And for now, that's enough.

21
MATT

I'm at my desk early on Monday morning. I know I'm not going to be effective; I'm too distracted with thoughts of Aries and how the hell I manage whatever this is. I very nearly told her that she's the only woman I've slept with aside from Gemma, but that felt like a risky admission. It might have freaked her out, and I certainly don't want to do anything that might scare her off.

There's a knock on the door, and before I can answer, my brother Seb opens it. He stands in the doorway, one hand on the door handle, and stares at me. His lips purse, his eyes narrow. "What?" I ask.

He continues staring for a few seconds more, then says, "Holy shit, you did it."

"Did what?"

But he doesn't answer. Instead, he backs out into the corridor and yells, "Nico! Get in here." When he looks back at me, he's grinning so wide, his face looks like it's made of plasticine, and I catch sight of Nico approaching over Seb's shoulder.

"What's going on? What happened?" Nico asks, alarm clear on his face.

Seb turns from his position blocking the doorway, so Nico can see me. He slaps a hand on Nico's shoulder. "Relax. It's not an emergency."

Nico frowns. "Why the hell did you shout like that then?"

Seb tilts his head at me. "Matt fucked the nanny."

Nico's irritation morphs into intrigue as he slowly turns to me for confirmation. "Did you?"

I push my chair away from the desk, lean back, and steeple my fingers. Might as well try to look calm about this, although my heart is pounding at the mere thought of Aries. And hell, do I want to tell someone how I've spent the last two nights.

"He did. Look at his face." Seb waves his hand. "That is the face of a man who's been royally fucked all weekend."

Nico squints at me, like he's trying to see whatever Seb can see and comes up wanting.

"Where do you get this shit from?" I ask. "You can't tell anything about my weekend from one glance at my face."

Seb crosses his arms. "You're underestimating my powers of perception. Put me out of my misery and admit it. You got laid, didn't you?"

I shake my head and blink to conceal my eye roll.

Seb laughs. "I'm taking that as confirmation. You fucked the hot nanny."

"Stop saying that. Her name is Aries," I snap.

Nico's eyes widen, and his strong jaw goes slack. "Fuck," he mutters, looking away from me to stare at Seb. "You're right. How the hell did you know?"

Seb gives a smug smile and crosses his arms. "I'm a genius."

Nico shoots me a serious look. "You realise you just shat on your own doorstep? That was seriously dumb."

"Says the man who slept with a colleague," I throw back.

"That's different. I've known Kate all my life. It's different," he repeats, as though it's really important to him to make this distinction known. "I want to marry Kate. You're not going to marry the nanny, are you? You hardly know her."

I feel a pang in my chest at his accusation. I might not have known Aries long, but I feel more of a connection with her than I have with anyone... probably ever. Certainly more than I felt for Gemma and I ended up married to her for over fifteen years.

I sigh. "Aries. Her name is Aries."

Seb laughs. "Next he's going to be telling us he didn't fuck her. He made love to her."

Nico stiffens, looking at me. "Are you?"

"I'm not going to tell either of you anything." I stand and usher them back towards the door. "Get the fuck out of my office and go back to work."

"Okay, okay," Seb says. "But when am I going to meet this woman? If I'd known you were going to bring her to Speech Day, I'd have come along."

I frown, unsure whether I want Seb to meet her at all. She's still my employee, first and foremost. "Do you just want to ogle her, or do you want to meet her like a woman that's of interest to me?"

"Jesus," Nico says, running a hand through his hair. "You need to sort your shit out. This is going to get messy. And Gemma will find out and cut your balls off."

"Gemma's not getting near my balls. Ever." I blow out a breath.

"What is this nanny to you? This" —Nico blinks, looking confused— "Aries, sorry. What is she to you? An employee you're messing around with, or something more?"

My heart thumps so hard it's choking my throat. *I don't fucking know. Why is Nico pressing this? Do I need to know the answer to this right now?*

I clear my throat. "The boat. I'm taking the kids on holiday. Why don't you both come?"

"We can't all take time off like th—" Nico begins.

"Of course we can." Seb replies. "I haven't been on the boat in way too long. Email me the details, and I'll clear our diaries."

"You can't do that," Nico begins. "We—"

"Fuck, Nico. Chill out," Seb admonishes. "This place will still exist if you take a break. Get Jack Lansen to cover. You're always going on about how great he is. He's more than capable of filling your shoes for a week or two. And God knows, we deserve a break."

Nico considers this, his head to one side. "I could use some sun. Kate would have to come too, obviously."

"Obviously," Seb says, with mock sincerity. "And I'd bring... probably no one. But maybe I'll find someone at the last minute."

"No last minute dates on a holiday where my kids are involved," I warn. "That's where I draw the line. If you want to come, you come solo."

Seb looks irritated for the first time since he entered my office. "Fine. Solo it is. You aren't getting rid of me that easily." He slaps a hand on Nico's shoulder. "Let's leave lover boy to his daydreams."

"Fuck off," I bark, watching as the two of them disappear out into the hallway. I close the door and lean against it.

Was asking them to come on the boat really fucking stupid?

The next week passes in a blur of sex and Aries and dark nights and soft sheets. She's always ready for me, her soft pink pussy so wet... every fucking time I touch it, she's soaked. And the taste of her. *Fuck*.

I can hardly work because this obsession is taking over most of my brain space. I got her a new phone, but when she's with Lucie, I don't hear from her. It's a good thing she's not staring at a screen when caring for my daughter, but it makes the anticipation more acute. I'm always waiting for some word…

My phone buzzes on cue. It's half seven, so Lucie's already in bed. I'm working late.

I click open the phone.

Aries: *My body misses you.*

Before I can reply, a photo comes through.

Fuck me.

It's a selfie of Aries. Her face is obscured and she's wearing only underwear. She must have put a bra on just for this. Her full breasts spill out of it, and she's tugging the cup down on one side, revealing a tight, pink nipple. *Fuck me, again. I want to suck it.* The curve of her waist is so feminine, so irresistible as it fills out to those hips, that arse… dimpled and soft, and those thighs that fit so perfectly around my neck when I eat her.

Aries: *Want more?*

Me: *Yes. But this is a work phone. That wouldn't be a good idea.*

Aries: *I thought you were the boss.*

Me: *All communications are called in if there's an issue.*

Aries: *So no sexting?*

Me: *No.*

Aries: *Come home then, before I change my mind and decide you're too old and boring to fuck.*

I chuckle before sliding my phone into my pocket and powering down my computer.

When I open the front door, the house is quiet. I pace into the hall in breathless anticipation, my dick already semi-hard at the thought that Aries is inside, waiting for me.

I walk into the drawing room to find a woman on the sofa. But it's not the one I want to see.

Gemma is sitting in the midst of the designer cushions she chose, her long legs crossed, looking elegant in a trouser suit. Her shoes, with their stiletto heels and toes so pointed she could use them as weapons, poke out beneath. Her tight smile makes bile rise up my throat.

There is no way she should be letting herself into my home like this.

I hold out my hand. "Your key," I demand. "I'll have it back."

She curls her fingers through the air. "My biometrics are still in your system, Matthew." The way she says my full name makes my hackles rise.

"They won't be after tonight. You can't show up unannounced."

Gemma rolls her eyes. "You think so little of me. I rang the bell. Your nanny let me in. She really is a very pretty girl. Young though. She must be ten years younger than you."

"Why are you here? I thought you wanted a break from the kids all summer?"

She laughs. "Not the special occasions." She uncrosses her legs, springing to her feet like a long-limbed gazelle. "Charlie's coming home soon. And it's his birthday. I'd like to throw the party at my house."

"You do yours, I'll do mine. He can have two separate parties."

"No. We'll combine. He's turning seventeen. That's a big deal, especially after last year. We barely acknowledged his sixteenth, given the divorce and all that." *Fuck, she's right about that.* "This year, I want us all to be together, like a family."

"We aren't one."

A sour look crosses her face. "Maybe we should be. For one afternoon."

We glare at one another, the air awkward and thick.

"Did Barney Wentworth call you?" I ask.

"Charlie's housemaster? No. He didn't call me."

"Email?"

"No. Is something wrong?"

Part of me doesn't want to elaborate, but Gemma is still the mother of my children. "He's worried about Charlie."

Gemma laughs again. "Oh, the weed. Under his bed. Mark told me about it. Hugo found it, apparently. Stashed away with Charlie's underwear." She wafts a hand in the air. "So what? A little weed never hurt anyone. Takes the edge off." She nods at me like an idea has just occurred to her. "You could do with some. You're so edgy nowadays you're like a shard of broken glass." She walks towards me, and I instinctively back away, but her hand rests a moment on my shoulder as she passes. "I'll send you an invitation, but we'll host it here. Your place is bigger, after all."

I rub my thumb and forefinger across my eyes. "Fine."

"Night, Matthew. Don't stay up too late. You look awful."

I don't escort her to the door, or turn around once she's left the room. I stand still until she's gone. The front door slams, and her heels click down the steps outside the house.

"Sorry," comes a soft voice.

I turn to find Aries standing in the doorway. Her long red hair is tied in a messy bun, strands falling about her face. She's in a loose-fitting white t-shirt that does nothing to hide her voluptuous, now braless breasts. Pale blue jeans skim her hips, and her feet are bare. She's breathtaking in her casual perfection.

"I didn't know what to do when she showed up," she says. "I wasn't going to send her away. She said she'd only take a minute of your time."

"That's all right. You did the right thing."

I blow out a breath, letting the irritation Gemma infused into my blood diffuse, enabling me to focus on the only woman I want to see right now. As I stare, the air buzzes with energy swarming between us. It feels a little like my heart might explode.

She must see the appreciative look in my eyes, because a seductive smile breaks across her face. She steps into the room and closes the door with her foot.

We're alone amongst the luxury furnishing. Her toes sink into the deep pile of the carpet. I suddenly think of Gemma and how she picked out all this fabric with our interior designer; chose these sofas, these fucking cushions. It's all so perfect and stylish and I fucking hate all of it.

"Bad day?" Aries asks.

"Not really—"

"Let me make it better."

She crosses the room, my mind ablaze with ideas of what she's going to do to me. But she halts a pace away, staring above my eye-line. She holds my gaze as she runs a thumb over my brow, like she's smoothing out my frown. Her thumb lingers over my eyebrow; the strip where there's no hair. "This scar," she whispers. "How did you get it?"

"A fight."

"In a bar?"

"No. At home."

"Who—"

"Gemma. We argued. She hit me with a wine glass. There was a fuckload of blood. A few stitches."

Aries inhales sharply. "Did you—"

"I didn't touch her, if that's what you're about to ask. We fought a lot, but I never hurt her. She broke things. Smashed whatever she could lay her hands on." I cover her hand with my own, where it still hovers over my eyebrow. "But that was the only time she physically hurt me."

Aries nods. "I'm so sorry."

I shake my head. "Please, don't be. It's over."

She rises on her tiptoes to kiss me. Her lips are soft, and the kiss is soothing in a way most of our kisses aren't. But it only takes a moment before it deepens. Her tongue slides against mine in a relentless, ravenous way that has my dick hardening in my suit. I greedily suck her mouth, her lips, driving away the memories of my tormented marriage.

Aries breaks the kiss, her hands going straight to my trousers. She undoes the buttons and unzips the fly. *No messing around.*

I hold my breath, growing harder by the second as this goddess' fingers graze against my cock. Sweet anticipation coils through me as she deftly pulls my trousers down. She slides a hand into my boxers, her lips quirking with a delighted little grin as her fingers curl around my girth. She nibbles her bottom lip and raises those green eyes to mine, her gaze swimming with lust that's impossible to ignore.

"Such a big boy," she whispers. "I love your cock."

Her words prickle against my skin as she drags her fisted hand up my shaft, and a shock of arousal blasts through my body from the tip of my dick.

I huff a laugh. "I know you do."

"And it loves me," she says, amusement sparkling in her eyes as she eases my boxers down to join the trousers on the floor.

My breathing shallows as Aries drops to her knees, her hands on my bare hips. She runs the flat of her tongue along the underside of my dick, which jerks in response

"Fuck my mouth until you feel better," she purrs.

"You're a dream," I murmur as I thread my fingers into her hair to tug out the band that holds it up and throw it to the floor. Red waves fall around her shoulders as she runs her tongue across the tingling head of my dick, her tongue curling over the bead of pre-cum.

She eases her mouth over the tip, sliding down my shaft, sucking as much of it as she can manage, while her hand fists at the thick base.

For a few minutes, she sucks, licks, and laps at my dick like it's the tastiest thing in the whole damn world. It's blissful, erotic, *un-fucking-believable*, and I want to sink into the warmth of her mouth over and over again, but I hold back until she releases my dick with a soft pop, her fingers digging into my hip.

"Didn't you hear me?" she queries.

The question throws me into confusion. I'm so turned on I can barely think. "Hear what?"

"Fuck my mouth, Matt."

Does she mean what I think she does? "You sure?"

She nods and opens her mouth to take me again when I grab her head to hold her back.

"Take your clothes off. I want to see your tits while I fuck your mouth."

A slow, knowing smile spreads over her face, and her eyes are full of a heat that scorches my skin, filling me with anticipation. She could tip me over to orgasm so easily, and we've barely started.

She pulls off her t-shirt, and her full, glorious breasts fall out, each mound crested with a pert pink nipple. No bra. *I knew it.*

I want to sink my teeth into that pale skin, but I don't trust myself not to bite her, drawing deep red blood across her skin. I want her that damn much.

She stands, undoes her jeans and slides them down her thighs along with her panties. My cock throbs, a hard beast rising to my navel, the head seeping pre-ejaculate.

Entirely naked, Aries sinks onto the floor and takes me in her mouth again. She sucks once, twice, rolling her tongue around my tip, and then she stops. She doesn't suck again... she *receives*, and it's bloody exquisite.

I fist my hands tighter into her hair, and slide my cock in further, expecting her to gag, but she doesn't. Encouraged, I withdraw and thrust again, using my hands in her hair to move her exactly the way I want.

Fuck. This woman is ready to take as much of me as I need, allowing me to drag my pleasure from her body. It's a fucking turn on and I tug harder on her hair, using the strands like reins to control her.

My thick dick passes in and out of her full lips, again and again, her breasts bouncing with each of my thrusts.

A moan vibrates along my cock, and I pump harder, faster, until I'm fucking her mouth relentlessly, hitting the back of her throat. Her eyes are watering, her moans growing more desperate. Each choked gurgle has my arousal crescendoing to new heights.

Sweet Jesus, this is something else. I watch my dick disappearing into her mouth, bucking my hips to meet it until my balls hit her chin. The slapping sound, flesh-to-face, combined with Aries' garbled noises and my own grunts of angry desire, is a sensual mix that has tingles spreading from my dick and up my spine. Pleasure coils at the base, like a tightly wound spring.

"Fuck, Aries. That's so fucking good," I say, as tension builds in my torso and my neck as I maintain my thrusts. "Take every inch. Every"—*thrust*—"fucking"—*thrust*—"inch."

She moans, and one of her hands moves from my hip to between her thighs.

"Don't touch yourself," I command, with one more powerful thrust. "That pussy belongs to me."

Her hand falls just as my orgasm breaks, and I pull her head towards me again, my dick vanishing between her lips.

"Oh fuck, fuuuuuuck." I groan, letting a hot spurt of cum spray into the back of her throat. There's so much of it, it feels like I'm ejaculating forever, but Aries takes it all.

My legs feel shaky as I let the last of my orgasm fade away. Aries swallows and eases back on my dick, swirling her tongue up the length and around the tip, licking up every last drop of cum, making me jerk as though each agonising swipe of her tongue is electric.

Then she sits back on her knees, her hands on her naked thighs. She looks like a vision from a Rubens' painting, all that red hair flowing loose over her shoulders, and her soft curves.

"If you hadn't drained me, I'd come all over those tits," I say.

She laughs and wipes her mouth on the back of her hand before she brushes away the tears from her eyes with her fingertips.

"You all right?" I ask. Her throat must have taken a pounding. I feel a flash of guilt mingle with the post-orgasmic bliss that's coursing through my body.

"I am."

"Your lips are swollen..."

She sucks her bottom lip inward, biting down on it. "Worth it," she whispers.

I take her in, waiting naked on the carpet. "You give head like a pro."

"Like a pro, eh?"

I nod, pulling up my boxers and trousers.

She eyes me. "I can't work out if that's an insult or not."

I sink to my knees and press my lips to hers, tasting the remnants of *me* on her mouth. "Compliment. The word you're looking for is compliment. Now lie back."

22

ARIES

Matt gently presses my shoulders to the floor and eases my legs apart. I sink back onto the plush carpet, and he crawls between my legs where he stops to stare at my pussy.

The force of him fucking my mouth was more than I bargained for, but I've been able to open my gullet since I was a teenager. I trained myself to do it so I could beat the local boys at downing pints of water. A rather useless skill, except when you want to shock men in a pub by finishing beer quicker than they can. And giving great head.

Matt slides his finger through my slick pussy lips, eliciting a moan of pleasure.

"You're dripping," he says.

I shrug a shoulder against the carpet. "What can I say? My ridiculously hot boss just stuck his cock down my throat. I enjoyed it."

He gives the slightest shake of the head as though he can't believe what I just said. His eyelids lower a touch, and he smiles as he dips down and runs his tongue along my slit, lapping me up.

He moans against my entrance, heaving me towards him with both hands on my hips. "I'd fucking tie you up and leave you here for my pleasure if I could," he says, chuckling against my clit. His breath is warm, like a teasing caress.

He grabs a cushion from the sofa and slides it under my bum. I'm going to ruin it, but if he doesn't care, then I don't either. I'm not about to stop him doing what he's doing to save a piece of silk.

His thick tongue caresses my throbbing pussy, with long, tender sweeps that send sparks ricocheting in their wake. He drags my juices up to my clit, but he doesn't stop there, instead continuing to lick me all the way up my stomach to my nipple. He flicks it with his tongue, then takes the whole thing in his mouth, giving it a sharp suck before raking his teeth over it.

A whimper of pleasure escapes through my teeth, and Matt slides two fingers into my wet pussy. I'm so slick there's almost no resistance, and the sound of sucking wetness as he plunges in and out is obscene, but in the most delicious way. Filthy, yet so hot...

I grind against him and he licks all the way back down until he tugs my clit in his mouth, and then replaces his fingers with his tongue, spearing me with it, twisting it inside me, licking my walls.

The familiar fizzing pressure grows at the base of my spine. I curl upwards, peeling my spine off the carpet so I can grab fist-fulls of his hair with one hand and push his head deeper between my thighs. My other hand rests on the carpet behind me, levering me off the floor as I ride his tongue, taking my pleasure from his mouth.

"Oh, God, I'm close... so fucking close..." I throw my head back as I thrust my pussy into his face, my moans mixing with the wet slurping sounds as he eats me out. The arm I'm using to prop myself up begins to shake, the lactic burn too much.

Matt gives a long, hard suck on my clit, pushing me right over the edge, and all of my senses blaze in a bonfire of orgasmic bliss. I'm nothing but ecstasy and Matt Hawkston between my thighs.

I can't hold myself up as my orgasm crashes through my body, my thighs trembling around his ears. He tilts my hips up, an arse cheek cupped in either hand as he devours what's left of me, pushing my orgasm right to the edge, punishing every last tingle from my clit and cunt.

When I'm nothing more than a boneless, quivering mess, my breaths heaving, he lowers my limp body. My legs shake violently.

"What's wrong?" he asks, his handsome face drawn into such an expression of concern as he eyes my quivering thighs, that I almost laugh. The dark stubble over his chin gleams with my juices.

"The tension. The orgasm," I murmur, as my legs continue to shake violently. "So, so good. You've made my ears ring."

He laughs. "Thank fuck. I thought I'd broken you."

I cover my eyes with my forearm. "You have."

A door slams.

I jerk to an upright sitting position, pulling my knees in to restrain the shakes. "What's that?"

Matt's eyes are wide with alarm as he gets to his feet, pulling himself up with one hand on the back of the sofa.

"Mr Hawkston?" comes a deep, male voice. "I'm going to head home now."

Matt slams a hand to his forehead. "Fuck. My driver. Charlie's home," he says. "I forgot he was coming back tonight."

"Dad?" Charlie yells.

I scrabble for my clothes, pulling on my t-shirt. My heart is hammering. This is horrendous. At least Matt's fully dressed. *Thank God.*

Matt grabs my jeans and knickers off the floor and throws them at me. I catch them and begin to haul them on. Matt kneels to help me, the two of us behind the sofa.

"Hurry up," he hisses, as my foot gets stuck in the hem of the jeans.

"I'm trying," I whine, pulling out of his reach. His haste isn't helping anything. I have half a leg in when the door opens.

"Dad?"

Matt springs upright, swiping his hair off his forehead. His other hand, hidden from Charlie's view behind the sofa, presses a flat palm to the air, signaling me not to move. I must be losing my mind because the wordless command sends a fission of sexual energy through my core.

"Welcome home. Good journey?" Matt sounds so cool that there's no way Charlie would suspect anything if he hadn't popped up from behind the sofa like a Jack-in-the-box. I wish I could see Charlie's face, because then I'd have some idea of whether he's surprised or not.

"Traffic was bad," Charlie replies. His tone is level; no indication he thinks his father's actions are weird or out of place. *Phew.*

Matt walks around the sofa, and I can no longer see him. I'm trying so hard not to make a sound that I'm barely breathing. I run through a list of excuses for my presence on the floor behind the sofa, but come up wanting. The sofa shunts towards me, a nightmarish hulk of designer fabric on the move, as one of them—*Charlie?*—slams himself down on it, and I cower.

"I haven't eaten," Matt says. "Have you?"

Charlie makes a sort of grunting sound. "No."

"Let's go out?"

"Only if we can get fusion at Los Mochis."

"Whatever you want."

The sofa creaks and I assume Charlie's standing again. I hold my breath, waiting for them to leave the room. A few minutes later, I hear them walk out the front door. An acute sense of abandonment bites into my skin. I might be fucking Matt Hawkston, but he's not taking me for fusion food at Los Mochis, wherever the hell that is. He's not taking me anywhere but his bedroom. His sauna. His fucking drawing room floor.

Not that I resent him spending time with his son. It's what he ought to be doing, and I should be glad he's doing it, especially after he missed Charlie's prize-giving because Lucie fell in the river.

No, I'm pleased he's taking Charlie out. But there's a hollowness in my chest, an empty ache behind my breastbone, and a dark sensation that hovers somewhere between panic and fear seeps in to fill the space.

23
MATT

Charlie hardly speaks at dinner. Or maybe it's that I'm so distracted by thoughts of Aries that I'm not inviting conversation.

I stare at Charlie, his thin face, the hollows of his cheeks, the dark circles under his eyes. Barney's words blast through my head. *There are some things you can't fix with money. Your son is a wreck.*

I'm a terrible, terrible father.

"How was the end of term?" I ask, keeping my voice neutral to conceal the worry behind the question.

"Yeah, all right." He scratches his eyebrow and doesn't look at me. "Same old."

"Sorry about Speech Day."

He shrugs. "No worries."

This is excruciating. "School okay? Your friends?"

"Yup."

"What about the piano? Are you getting to practise much?"

"Some."

For a few minutes we eat in silence. The happy noise of people socializing at nearby tables, *enjoying themselves*, is jarring. My ribs contract, squeezing at the air in my lungs, making my heart ache. *Do we even fit in here?*

"We're taking the boat to the Med," I say.

Charlie examines the taco on his plate, probably debating whether to attack it with his cutlery or lift the whole thing in one and put it in his mouth. He picks option two. "Mmm," he replies with his mouth full. "When?"

"Monday."

His eyes widen, but he says nothing, continuing to chew thoughtfully.

"Uncle Seb and Nico are coming too," I add.

"Mmm," Charlie mumbles, wiping his mouth on the back of his hand and swallowing roughly. "Great."

"And Lucie and Aries."

"Aries?"

"The nanny." My heart thuds. *Fuck.* The mere mention of Aries in regular conversation makes my palms sweat. *Pathetic*. I rub my hands down my thighs.

"She's still here then?" The sarcasm in Charlie's tone has me stifling a wince. "Figured she wouldn't have lasted long with you yelling at her."

I stiffen. "If you're referring to the boat race, I was angry because of what happened to Lucie. When you have kids, you'll understand."

Charlie scoffs. "Because I'll love them as much as you love me?"

His words hit like an uppercut to the jaw, but I conceal their impact, keeping my voice even when I state, "I do love you."

He tilts his head down, but his gaze rolls towards the ceiling.

My chest tightens, and I desperately want to reprimand him. To tell him not to roll his fucking eyes at me, but I hear Barney's voice in my ear again. *Your son is a wreck.*

"You gonna make me spend the rest of the summer in the office doing work experience, like last year?"

I take a gulp of my beer. "We'll see. You could do tennis camp or—"

"Yes. Tennis. I'll take that over the office."

"Fine. I'll get Aries to book it for you."

My thoughts are drawn to her, lying back on the carpet in the moments before Charlie came home. *What's she doing now? And more importantly, how the fuck are we going to keep sneaking around, now there's a teenager in the house?*

Last year, Charlie found his mum in the kitchen with a man he didn't know, doing things he should never have seen. I can't do that to him. I can't take a chance that he'll come into a room and find me with the nanny... it doesn't bear thinking about. I shudder involuntarily at the thought. This evening, we were so fucking close to that exact thing happening. *What the hell am I doing here? Are these risks worth taking?*

"What?" Charlie says, clearly perturbed at my withdrawal.

I force myself to focus on my son. "Nothing. Let's finish up."

After I've helped Charlie to his room with his belongings, I hear Aries in the basement kitchen, talking to Alec. They're laughing, and envy spears holes in my chest at the sound. There are no barriers for them to overcome... Aries can relax with Alec in ways she never could with me... in public too. They could go out to restaurants, go on dates... have a normal fucking relationship.

The two of them stop talking as soon as I step into the room. Aries sets down her cutlery. Alec's made her something for dinner, and the vision of the two of them together is so intimate, so *domesticated*, that the piercing sensation in my chest only increases. I can't be with this woman in my own home the way this man can.

Not that it matters because I've come to a decision. *Better pull the fucking plaster off quick because this one is going to hurt.*

"Aries, can I have a word?" I say.

She nods and slips off the stool, still in that over-sized t-shirt without a bra. I pace up the stairs and she follows me to the study. I close the door behind us.

"Sit down," I say, gesturing to the chair.

A look of alarm passes over Aries' face as she lowers into the chair. I'm emotionally closed off; I can feel it. I'm not even doing it on purpose, but I can't handle the guilt of what happened earlier. Charlie coming home, me with Aries still on my face. I cannot risk getting caught with her by one of my children. Tonight, the call was far too close. Next time, we won't be so lucky.

I sit behind the desk, opposite her. "I want you to book Charlie into tennis camp." I open a drawer and pull out the flyer and put it on the desk between us. Aries presses a finger to it and drags it towards her. "Book the whole summer, except the ten days that we'll spend on the boat. You'll have to make sure he gets there. To camp, I mean. He can walk himself, but I don't trust him not to play truant. Make sure he goes."

Aries nods, her features hardening. She doesn't like my professional demeanor, and although I can tell it pains her, I can't always be what she wants me to be.

I take a deep breath, run my tongue over my molars, and keep my eyes on her. *She's gorgeous.* "You need to wear a bra to work."

She flinches. *This wasn't what she was expecting.* "What?"

"In the house, you wear a bra at all times. I have a teenage son."

"Of course," she says, but the dejection on her face tears at my heart. She crosses her arms over her chest.

"I'm sorry."

She looks directly at me. "Why? It's your home. You make the rules."

She sounds as cold as I do, and I don't like it. *Christ, this is difficult.* I swallow hard before I speak. "I don't mean to insult you."

"I'm not insulted. If you wanted me to wear a uniform, I'd wear a uniform. You're the boss. It's your prerogative. Besides, I know you're only asking because you want to keep these"—she briefly cups a breast in each hand—"all to yourself." Her delivery is toneless, but there's a shimmer to her gaze that tells me she's trying to reach me through this façade I've put up.

I want to reach across the desk and grab her, and whisper in her ear that she's absolutely right. She's *mine*, and the idea that my teenage son might be attracted to her would torment me if I gave it space to grow. But I can't indulge her on this. "It's not about the bra. I mean, it is. But not just the bra. It's about us."

Aries' lips part the tiniest bit, and she draws in shallow breaths. Her eyebrows lower, her green eyes darkening as she awaits whatever I'm about to decree.

Until this moment, we've never had a conversation about us. Not properly. Not about what we are or might be or where we might go.

"Now that Charlie's home, we can't keep this up," I tell her flatly, but I don't miss the flare of hurt that blazes across her face. She douses it fast, and I'm ridiculously grateful for that. "I can't risk him finding out about us. It's not fair. Not after what happened with his mother."

Aries nods, and I briefly wonder what she knows. Whether Alec told her. "So this is over?" she asks.

"I don't see how it can't be." *Jesus.* Pain sears across my chest, the words like a blade that cuts straight through my heart. *What the fuck am I doing?* "I'm sorry."

"Stop saying you're sorry." She stands. "It's all right."

All right? That's it? The fact she's giving in so easily kills a small part of me... it's only now I realise I'd hoped for her to fight for this. For us.

She walks towards the door, but when she's about to reach for the handle she glances at me over her shoulder. "You said you liked me." Her voice is soft, but it comes with an edge of accusation.

My chest tightens. "I do. That's not the issue."

She lets this hang in the air a moment. "Am I the only woman you've had sex with, aside from your ex-wife?"

"I don't see how that's rel—"

"Am I?"

Something blisters through me. Shame. Vulnerability. Whatever it is, it's fucking unpleasant. "Yes."

Aries absorbs the information as though it's deadly serious, but then her eyes take on that gleam I know so well, and in spite of myself I feel a throb in my dick. "In that case, it seems a shame..." Her index finger strokes along her bottom lip. "To end things before you've laid me out and fucked me on your desk."

The comment draws a smile from me, and I drop my forehead into my hand. "You are unbelievable," I say, but my heart is leaping, fucking *rejoicing*, in the depths of my chest.

"Mr Hawkston," she says, fully turning to me. "You'd be neglecting your duties as my employer not to give me at least one orgasm in your office."

The way she's looking at me, sexual tension leaking out of her pores and coiling its way around my dick, makes up my mind for me. "Lock the door."

She smirks and turns the lock. I shouldn't be doing this, but I get up, walk around the desk and haul her towards me.

Her beautiful mouth opens. "Is this break-up s—"

I swallow the rest of her sentence with a punishing kiss. I don't care what this is, but I want this woman so much it hurts my cock to even think about denying it the pleasure of her body.

Her hands tear at my hair, yanking at the strands at my nape. Her tongue thrusts against mine, like we could fucking eat each other. White-hot desire spirals from my mouth to my dick, and I pull her hips flush against me.

She gasps into my mouth as my erection presses against her, and she rears back. "Are we safe?"

I pull her back against me, feeling her breasts against my chest. "I don't fucking care. This is it. The last fuck. Make it count. And keep the noise down."

I yank the t-shirt over her head, throwing it in a heap on the floor. *Shit, those breasts. Is this the last time I'll see them?* I push the thought away, taking one into my mouth and sucking hard.

Aries' hands clench against my shoulders. "Oh, shit," she murmurs, her back bowing like she wants me to take more of her breast in my mouth.

I don't. I focus on her jeans, unbuttoning them, pulling them down. Pulling down her underwear too. She steps out of them until she's fully naked again.

Having this woman exposed like this while I'm still in my suit is the biggest fucking turn on; like she's mine to control, to dominate.

I spin her in my arms, forcing her over the desk, pressing a hand against her lower back. She moans as the side of her face hits the wood, her arms splayed out in front.

Her arse is so round, so delicious, exposed to me this way. I run a finger between her cheeks, dusting over her puckered hole. She gasps, and I chuckle at the way her body pulls away from me.

My fingers slide lower, to her exposed pussy lips. I let out a groan of appreciation as I slide a finger into her softness.

"Drenched," I murmur. "So wet for me."

How the fuck am I going to give this woman up?

I slide another finger in, thrusting into her. Those little gasping moans she makes begin. I reach around and muffle her mouth with my free hand, then lean over her, my other hand still in her wet cunt.

"Don't make a fucking sound," I whisper. "Or I'll spank your arse so hard you won't be able to sit down for a week."

A moan, dripping with desire, rumbles against my palm.

The fucking disobedience...

I rip my hand from her pussy and strike her arse hard.

In response she bites down on the side of my hand; admittedly not as hard as I struck her but enough to make me wince.

I remove my hand from her mouth and shake it out. "Not a sound," I demand. "Are we clear?"

She nods against the desk, shaking her bright mane of hair so it ripples over her back.

I undo my trousers, letting my painful hard-on spring free. The head escapes the waistband of my boxers, glistening with pre-cum.

I shift my underwear down and guide the head of my cock along her entrance, sliding in her juices. She pushes back against me, like her pussy wants to swallow my cock whole.

"Patience." With one hand on her back to hold her in place, I edge my cock inside her wet warmth. "So tight, baby. So fucking tight."

I begin to drive deeper, thrusting in and out, drilling my cock right to the hilt with every thrust, my balls slapping against her arse.

The office fills with the sounds of our bodies slamming against one another. It's feral and raw and turns me on even more.

Aries begins to moan again. Her voice is so full of desire that it only drives me to pound her harder. "I. Said. Be. Quiet," I say, thrusting hard on each word, then driving my hand down on her arse cheek, which only increases the fervour of her moans.

I spank her again, the pale flesh turning pink. "I wasn't joking, Aries."

She's quiet, but I can tell she's close, given how she thrusts back against me, her fingers tense and pressing flat against the desk.

I slide a hand around her hips to find her swollen clit, and run circles over it, faster and faster, building the pressure.

Her cunt tightens around my dick, pulsing with the approaching orgasm, and I thrust deeper still, matching my movement with the circling of her clit until her legs are shaking and she's jerking against the desk in the throes of pleasure she's desperately trying to silence.

"Aries... Aries..." My voice is a low rasp, her name like a chant on my lips. Sparks of pleasure shoot through me, cutting me off as my orgasm approaches. The sensation spreads up my length as I spurt thick cords of cum into her. "Fuuuuck," I groan.

When the blast of my orgasm fades, I lean over her naked back, pressing my shirt and suit jacket against her bare skin. I gently rub my palm against her arse where I struck her, soothing the inflamed skin. I want to stay buried inside her, keep her soft flesh beneath my palms. Trap her here between my desk and my body forever.

I rest my lips against her ear. "If that was break-up sex, we need to break up more often."

"I'll do this again if you will," she murmurs.

An excruciating pain tears at the space behind my sternum, and when I speak my tone is full of regret. "I can't. This was reckless. Anything else would be plain fucking stupid."

I kiss the space between her shoulder blades, letting my lips linger there for a moment that stretches too long. I swear I can hear her heart beating; I'm that fucking close to it.

I slide my cock out of her, reaching over for some tissues from a box on the desk to catch our combined cum that leaks from her. I clean her up and toss the tissues in the bin.

I don't want to walk away. I don't want to leave this woman. But the risk is too huge, and I've already risked too much with her.

I fix my trousers and tuck my shirt in, hiding my sins beneath a suit for the second time in one evening.

A million things I want to say to her bubble up on my tongue, but I swallow back every single one until all that's left is, "Good night, Aries."

I let myself out of the room. I know it's a shitty move to leave her naked and bent over my desk, but she knew what this was... she *asked* for it. And it was great, but if I don't leave right this fucking second, I won't be able to walk away at all.

24
ARIES

His cum is still leaking down my thigh when the door closes. I lie with my hands on the desktop for a few moments before I can bring myself to move. I'm like a rag doll, slumped naked across the desk, the cool air touching the wet warmth of my empty pussy.

I can't process what's happened. All I know is the bliss of the orgasm he ripped from me has well and truly faded, leaving a quiet ache in its place that's threatening to break into something far more painful. *If this relationship was just sex, surely I wouldn't feel like something inside me is dying?*

I asked for this... I know I did, but it still feels terrible now that he's gone. I grab another handful of tissues and clean myself up some more, although I know I won't get it all. More of him will seep from my pussy until I shower and go to bed. It's brutal, like pus seeping from a wound that won't heal.

I will myself to hold it together. I can't afford to fall apart over this. I need this job. I pull my t-shirt over my head, covering up that spot he kissed on my back, which still burns from the touch of his lips as though he branded me with his goodbye. Of all the places he's kissed me and touched me tonight, that one hurts the most.

It's faster to gather my clothes than my thoughts, and I'm dressed and leaving the room before I've made head or tail of what's going on or what happens next. I take one step into the darkened hallway.

"What are you doing in my dad's study?"

I jump, spinning to find Charlie standing in the hall, hands on his hips, staring at me like he's caught me in the middle of a robbery. I blink for a second, desperately hoping he didn't see Matt leave. *Holy hell*, maybe Matt's right. We can't do this. Shouldn't have done this. Talking to his teenage son who thinks I'm 'just the nanny', while Matt's cum is leaking, warm and sticky, down my thigh, feels wrong. So horribly, *horribly* wrong.

A rampage of thoughts battle through my mind as I stand in the beam of Charlie's accusatory glare. I filter through them, hoping to hook onto something that will suffice as a viable excuse.

I slide my hands into the back pocket of my jeans, touching the brochure I slipped in there earlier. I pull it out and flash it at him.

"Summer camp," I tell him. "I'm going to book you in."

His eyes narrow a fraction before he nods.

"Welcome home, Charlie."

"Thanks," he mutters, before pushing past me towards the lift.

The heat scorches as we stand beside the boat on a narrow strip of concrete in Valletta. The sky is bright blue and cloudless, and the air so hot the warmth spreads up my nose when I inhale. There's a whole group of us—me, Matt, the kids, Matt's brothers and Kate—and even though I'm trying my hardest to avoid looking at Matt, I'm failing. It's only been a couple of days since he bent me over his desk and I came so hard I saw stars, but I'm finding it hard to come to terms with the fact that it's over between us. I'm in agony. My body is wracked with pain, and all I want to do is crawl into a ball and hide. To make matters worse, Matt's brothers keep giving me weird, assessing looks, which makes me wonder what he's told them. Not that it matters now he's ended our arrangement.

I try to tell myself it's okay... that this was only ever meant to be a casual thing, which is exactly how I like it. Better that it ends now before I get more attached.

Bullshit.

This wasn't casual, and there's something unbearably cruel about being here with him, so close I could reach out and touch him, and yet knowing I can't. Might never get to again. And traveling together, making small talk, discussing the details of the journey all while my heart feels shredded, is a challenge I hadn't foreseen.

To make matters worse, I can still feel the sexual tension fizzing off him, sparking at my skin like unearthed wiring every time I accidentally catch his eye. He might have made a decision with his brain, but his dick is not on board. You can cancel an arrangement, but you cannot cancel sexual attraction. Not like this. It doesn't go away that easily.

But it's not just about sex, is it?

I shift my thoughts away from the pain of this ridiculous scenario and take in the sight before me. I don't know anything about boats, but this one is something special. It's absolutely huge. There are uniformed staff waiting for us to board, and the railing along the bow is so highly polished it looks like no one's ever touched it. The whole thing is beautiful; it looks brand new.

It's hard to process displays of wealth like this. My mind was already blown after the private jet we took. It had bedrooms and bathrooms and the largest, plushest leather seats I'd ever seen. I've been containing gasps of shock all day, whereas everyone else takes it completely for granted. It's normal for them. Even Lucie and Charlie are completely at ease with the extreme luxury.

"Ready?"

I stiffen at the sound of Matt's voice so close to me, but when I look round, he's staring at Lucie, holding out his hand for her to take. She grabs it eagerly, and only when he's about to lead her onto the boat does he glance at me. The heat in his casual stare is undeniable. I'm sure it's unintentional, but it blindsides me and I miscalculate my next step.

"Need a hand there?" Matt's brother, Seb, takes hold of my elbow to steady my reeling.

I like him the most because his manner is more open and friendly. Nico's a tad uptight by comparison, but I'm delighted to see his girlfriend, Kate, again. We might not have spoken much, but because she was there after Lucie fell in the river, I feel a kind of bond with her. It's almost like having a friend here, which I know is deluded.

The guys are all ridiculously handsome. It makes me wonder what their parents look like. Matt and Nico look the most similar, with their dark hair and eyes, whereas Seb is softer somehow. Lighter hair, blue eyes. A warmth to his resting expression that the others lack. He's more carefree... at least it seems that way.

"Thanks," I say. "Getting dizzy staring up at this enormous yacht."

"Yup. Big boat. Matt picked it out to compensate for his small dick."

I frown. "He doesn't—"

"Gotcha," he says, a dimple appearing on his cheek as he smiles at me. Embarrassment flares through me, and I press a hand to my face, knowing I'm turning red. Pain crashes in behind the humiliation. *It doesn't matter how big his dick is, because I'll never see it again.*

I pull my sunglasses down to cover my eyes, and Seb breaks out into a loud laugh. Were he anyone else, I'd feel teased and mocked, but somehow I don't. His laughter is friendly, even if I am dying inside. He doesn't know that.

"What's so funny?" Charlie asks, coming up beside us.

Seb's handsome features fall into neutral. "I was making a bad joke," he says, with a little bow of the head. "Sorry, Aries. Didn't mean to make you uncomfortable."

I shrug. "You didn't." *Not much, anyway.*

We file onto the boat, welcomed by the crew, one of whom leads me to my cabin. She's an athletic-looking woman in her mid-thirties, dressed in a white uniform of a polo shirt and trousers.

I follow her down a series of steps and corridors, and she points out other rooms as we pass. My cabin is nowhere near the others. It's even a walk around the deck to get to the kids' room from mine. And it's tiny.

"Spacious," I joke, poking my head in to take a look around.

"This is luxury. You've got your own room. We're all in together," says the woman. "Do you want me to unpack for you?"

"What? Er, no. Thank you."

"Thought I'd check. We do it for all the other guests and I have time before things really kick off."

"That's okay. Thanks."

She leaves and I sit down on the small bed, stroking my hand over the sheets.

There's a knock on the door. "Aries?"

My heart is in my throat. It's Matt. Hope swirls like a whirlwind through my entire body. A moment alone with him would be enough to soothe the awful ache in my chest that being separated from him has caused. The strain of pretending everything's fine is twisting my insides into a knot.

I stand, brushing down my dress, fluffing my hair, trying to look as casual as possible. I open the door and every fluttering hope in my chest is crushed. It's not Matt at all. It's Charlie, holding Lucie's hand.

I try to conceal my disappointment, but Charlie's eyebrow quirks up. I'm not about to explain that I thought he was his dad, so I crouch and focus on Lucie. "Hey sweetie, what's up?"

"We want to show you around, don't we, Charlie?"

Charlie shrugs as if he had no part in this plan.

"There's a hot-tub," Lucie announces. "And I can see the sea out of my window. Oh, and the swimming pool."

"There's a pool *on the boat*?" I ask, half in shock.

"Yes. At the back. We're going for a swim. You have to come, because I can't swim." She stares up at me with her little hands on her hips. "Not without my armpits."

I try to contain my laughter when I repeat, "Armpits?"

"Armbands," Charlie explains. "She means armbands."

I smile widely. "Okay, let me get changed. Wait here."

I close the door, rip open my suitcase and pull out a bikini and a cover-up. I grab a hat and a bottle of factor 50, and then I'm ready to go.

The boat is insane. It's like a floating hotel. The carpets are as lush as the ones in the London house. There's a cinema room here too. A full dining room, both inside and outside—there's a deck with an outdoor dining table. Lucie's bedroom is a luxury suite, and I'm wondering why my bedroom is so small, when every other part of this boat is spectacular. I'm just the nanny, I guess, but somehow, after Matt breaking things off, my separation from everyone else hurts even more. I breathe out the anguish and focus on how grateful I am to be here. *I'm so lucky.* I mentally repeat the words, hoping they'll break through my heartbreak and shift my mood. After all, it really is amazing. The pool is the best bit though. It's an infinity pool on the back of the boat, surrounded by loungers, and the water sparkles under the hot sun.

We're already sailing out to sea by the time Lucie demands to get in. I slip off my cover-up and help her into the water.

There's noise from above; the sound of men talking and laughing. I glance up to see all three Hawkston brothers on the terrace above the pool with beers in hand.

My gaze lingers on Matt, and like he senses it, he turns to me. His attention hits like a missile launched right into my chest. The impact would take me down if I wasn't holding his daughter in the pool already.

His eyes scoop down my neck, taking in my full breasts in the bikini top. *He still wants me.* He looks away, staring so intently into his beer you'd think there was something growing in the bottom of it.

It's strange, knowing that someone's full attention is occupied by you, even when they aren't looking. That's how I feel right now, and every one of my movements becomes laden and thick, my limbs heavy. *How the hell am I going to survive ten days out here, when one glance is burning me up and I get no release?*

I glance back up, only now it's Nico and Seb staring down at the pool, not Matt. Seb smiles, and gives me a little salute.

"Look, Lucie, your uncles and daddy are up there," I say, pointing. I turn her in the water so she can see, and she looks up and waves. All three of them return the gesture, and Lucie goes back to kicking her feet in the water while I hold her under the arms.

Charlie stays on the lounger. He changed into trunks and a rash vest with full sleeves. It'll protect him from the sun, but he must be boiling in it.

He doesn't get in the water. He's too busy focusing on his Kindle. God knows what he's reading, but it's obviously preferable to socialising with me or his little sister. Or anyone else, for that matter.

"Hi." Kate is standing at the side of the pool, shielding her eyes with her hand, despite the fact she's also wearing an enormous floppy-brimmed hat. "Can I join you?"

"Of course," I say, wondering why she's even asking.

"Auntie Kit-Kat," Lucy squeals, splashing excitedly in her attempt to swim over to Kate.

"Not quite an auntie yet," Kate replies. "But if you want to speak to your uncle Nico about making me one..." She breaks off her conspiratorial whisper and laughs, winking at me, and in turn I break into a smile too, aware that I feel a warm kinship with her. While the sensation is flowing through me, I get the oddest flash of a life where she has Nico and I have Matt, and we're equals... *friends*, even. It's so vivid, so intense, that I frown and blink.

"Is it the sun?" she asks, querying my facial expression, although her tone suggests she suspects it's not the sun at all. What she thinks it might be, I have no idea. "It's bright. Did you bring sunglasses? I can lend you some if not."

"No, I'm fine. Thank you," I reply, indicating where I've left mine on the nearby lounger.

"Oh," Kate muses, and I can tell she's wondering what she missed. "If there is anything you've forgotten to bring, ask me. Nico made me pack more than I could ever wear on one holiday."

I thank her for the kind offer, but I know I'll never take her up on it. It feels like a transgression of boundaries I can't make. Kate on one side, and me the other, and no amount of kindness or generosity will bring us closer together, although I'm grateful for the effort.

25
ARIES

By the end of the first day, I'm half-roasted and my pale skin is burnt. Apparently even factor 50 isn't enough to protect me, and added to the fact I lost track of time playing with Lucie and Kate in the pool, my shoulders are an unhealthy shade of red. I've slathered myself in aloe vera.

I'm not sure how it will work out as the week goes on, but today I ate early with Lucie. The rest of the family, including Charlie, are having a later dinner.

It's awkward, but I have to remember I'm not a guest on this boat; I'm a member of staff. They're kind to me, Matt's brothers and Kate, but I'm not really with them. Matt might have fucked me senseless, but the line between family and staff is heavily marked, and everything about this holiday makes me feel it intensely.

I'm lying on my bed reading. Lucie's asleep. A knock on the door breaks the silence. I sit up and check the time. *Eleven thirty.*

"Aries?"

My heart hitches at the harsh whisper of my name. It sounds like Matt, but it can't be. I consciously try to tamp down my excitement. The crushing blow when I found Charlie outside earlier isn't something I want to repeat.

I get up and open the door.

Matt stands on the threshold, large and handsome in his navy shorts and casual white linen shirt. He leans against the open frame, dominating the space, looking me over.

The tension hits me like a wall.

"Hi," I say, my voice already breathless.

His gaze, so heavy and lust-filled it strokes like a fingertip, drops to my mouth before he drags his eyes back to mine. "I made a mistake."

"Oh, yeah?"

"I can't quit. I'm fucking addicted to you, and the withdrawal symptoms are killing me."

My heart feels like it's about to burst. I've never heard such wonderful words in my entire life. Matt rakes his teeth over his bottom lip, and all the blood in my body pulses to my pussy. He must know it because with one step he's in my tiny room, his arms around me, shunting the door closed with his foot.

His kiss is desperate, and my own desperation rises to meet his, crashing against it with every harried brush of tongue against tongue, lip against lip.

Wetness floods from my core, soaking the gusset of my tiny shorts. My body is oh-so-ready for this man, like I've spent the last few days waiting for this moment. I can feel the hard length of him against my hip as his fingers tease at my pyjamas.

"I've missed these ridiculous shorts," he says, sliding his fingers over my exposed arse cheeks, "but I've missed what's underneath more."

I should be questioning him, but I don't. I want whatever he's willing to give me too much to risk saying anything that might put him off.

I wriggle out of my shorts and no sooner than they've hit the floor are Matt's fingers sliding into me, claiming me, thrusting hard.

"I want you naked," he murmurs, and I slip off my top as he keeps his fingers inside me. *Oh, God.* I want him so much, but the unease lurking below my desire snakes its way to the surface. I need to know if he's just here for sex. If that's all this is.

"Wait... wait," I gasp, and inside me his fingers stop moving. "What is this? What's happening?"

"Everything. It's everything," he whispers back, and my heart does another crazy leap. *Everything*. His eyes lock onto mine as though he's searching for an answer to a question he hasn't asked, but a response pours from me anyway.

"Yes. *Yes*," I breathe.

"It's you. *You*," he murmurs, as though I'm the eighth wonder of the world. "You're all I want."

I push him away, just a fraction, and his brow arches. "Would you want me in a different body?"

He splutters a laugh. "What?"

"Would you?"

Something seems to click, and he knows I'm serious. "Yes. God, yes. But I fucking love this one." His hand tightens on me, then he pauses, watching for my reaction. "Is that okay?"

"Yes."

He nods as though this explains everything either of us might ever need to say, and the look on his face is pure adoration.

"Fuck, Aries. What have you done to me?" he questions softly, and his gaze rakes over my flesh like he wants to bury himself inside it. His eyes are so greedy, so full of want and need that they stoke the fire in me. I hook my arms around his neck, jumping up to swing my legs around his hips. His fingers slide out of me to hold my thighs. His hands are so big, so warm. I didn't realise just how much I missed him holding me like this until he was touching me.

Crack.

Matt's back slams against a shelf as he manoeuvres us. "Ow. Fuck, this room is tiny."

"It's made for small people like me."

He lies me on the bed, spread out for him like a dessert trolley, inspecting me just as greedily. He fists both his hands in his hair. "What the hell are we doing here?"

It's on the tip of my tongue to say 'everything' again, or to tell him there's a damn good chance I'm falling in love with him, but instead I say, "You think too much. Shut up and fuck me."

I sleep in Matt's arms, both of us naked, entwined in my tiny bed. I never want to move. My muscles are plagued with a slight ache, but it's a pleasant throbbing that reminds me how hard I worked last night. It was after four when we finally fell asleep.

My eyes are bleary when Matt kisses my temple. "Hey, beautiful," he says. "I'm so sorry."

"For fucking my brains out last night?"

"No. For messing you around. Charlie coming back threw me off. I didn't want to hurt you. I'd never want—"

"You're allowed to prioritize your kids. That's kinda the whole point of being a parent."

He sighs. "I know. I kept thinking, what if he'd come home a few minutes earlier? Walked in on us? I can't do that to him. It felt like too big a risk."

"Okay... so why did you change your mind?"

He kisses my temple again, his lips lingering there longer. "Because I decided you're worth the risk." He peppers the side of my face with kisses, his lips dancing over my skin. "You're worth every risk."

My chest swells as though he's pumped the words right inside me. "So... what now?" I whisper.

"We'll have to be extra careful."

"On a boat? With all your family around?"

"It's a big boat."

I laugh, then remember Seb's comment. "You told your brothers, didn't you? About us?"

Slowly, Matt nods. "How did you—"

"Seb made a joke about the boat compensating for the size of your dick. I contradicted him without thinking."

Matt laughs. "Fuck. I can't even say I'm sorry. Seb can be an arse, but most of the time, he's a joker. Life's a game to him."

Matt leans over me to grab his watch from the nightstand. "Shit. We've got to get going. We're headed to an exclusive beach today, but the boat can only take us if we're there on time."

I reach out and cup his balls. "So I can't give you a little extra energy healing?"

He laughs and moves my hand. "Are you sure you're really a nanny?"

"I'm a lot of things. My mum home-schooled me. We didn't exactly stick to the regular syllabus."

Matt rears off the bed. "You were home-schooled?"

"Is that so shocking?"

He relaxes back against the sheets as he straps his watch to his wrist. "Actually, no. That fits." He rubs the back of two fingers over his mouth. "I want to meet this mother of yours. Anyone who could home-school you deserves a trophy. I bet you were an unruly kid."

I laugh. "My mum was an unruly mother. But in the best way." My voice catches in my throat and I clear it, but Matt's gaze has turned wary, so he must have noticed the blip.

"You want to see her?" he asks. "Because we could do that."

"We?"

He shrugs and looks away. "I don't have to come. I thought you might want to spend time with her. I feel bad having you all to myself. If you want time off to go and visit, then please take it. But seriously"—he turns to look at me—"whoever raised you did a stellar job." He kisses my cheek and even though it's an innocent peck, my blood turns hot. "Did you like it? This homeschooling thing? My parents sent us all off to boarding school when we were eight."

I catch a glimpse of little Matt in the grown man's face and wonder if he minded that his parents sent him away from home. But then, he's chosen it for his own son so he can't have hated it. "Hmmm," I say, drawing my focus back to his original question. "It was still learning, and some of that is always tedious. The bits you don't want to do. But it did the job in the end. I got to uni."

Matt's body jerks like he's brushed against something sharp, and I can tell he's surprised by this information. I could be irritated by his reaction, but I'm not. I knew he must have an 'idea' of me—some jumbled bunch of assumptions he'd made. But until right now, I hadn't considered what that idea might be, and it's very apparent that going to uni was not part of it. "What did you study?"

"Social anthropology at St Andrews."

He whistles. "Really? How did I not know this?" He props himself up on one elbow. "Shit, I've been sleeping with you for weeks and I didn't know this. I'm a terrible human being."

"No, you aren't. We were somewhat preoccupied most of the time."

"No excuse," he mutters. "Christ, I thought you were this kooky energy healer's kid, who wanted to work with children."

"I am." I narrow my eyes at him. "Didn't you read my CV?"

He frowns. "Obviously not. I mean, I glanced at it. But Mrs Minter sorts all the house stuff out. I trust her. She normally picks nannies who are *nannies*. You know? Career nannies." He scratches his forehead. "I thought that's what you were. I assumed. Have I been duped here?"

The more he speaks, the more his surprise seems to escalate, which makes me laugh. "No. You haven't been duped, stupid. I've worked as a nanny for years. I enjoy it. I like it more than anything else I've ever done. And don't feel bad about not knowing. I have no idea what you studied or where you went."

"Google didn't tell you?"

I snort. "No. And I really don't care. It makes no difference to me. It doesn't change who you are."

"God"—he drags a palm down his face—"I feel like such an arse right now."

For a few moments, we hold eye contact, then I lean in, making a show of examining his face. "You're looking at me differently."

"What? No, I'm not."

I wave my index finger in spiraling circles over his face. "Yeah, you are. I can see it. You think I'm different now, because you know I have a degree. You're re-evaluating."

He rolls onto his back and blows out a breath, fingers interlinked, hands resting on his broad chest.

"Aren't you going to say anything?" I ask him.

He glances sideways at me. "That's a trick question. Whatever I say, you're going to accuse me of judging you. But you know what? This is what humans do. We form judgments based on the little pieces of information we gather, and as we learn, our perception changes. So yeah, you do look different now."

"Different, better?"

He smiles to himself. "I'm not answering that."

"Okay. Fine. But I can tell you like it more than thinking I'm 'just a nanny'."

He sits up. "You aren't 'just a nanny'. No one is 'just' anything."

I chuckle. "Wow. Such wisdom. You should print that on tea towels."

One side of his mouth ticks up like he wants to smile but isn't sure he's allowed. "You think I'm an arse."

"Maybe a little bit," I say, smiling. But then my tone shifts. "There is one thing I do need to say…" He rolls his eyes in a plea that seems to say *'don't make me feel worse than I already do'*. "If you don't want to be an arse, then you can't mess me around. None of this 'it's over', 'it's not over', bullshit. You could have run with it being over if you hadn't come in here last night and fucked me like the world was ending. But you did, and if you pull back a second time, then you are a shitty arsehole, no question." I feel his gaze burning against the side of my face, and I know I'm blushing. "I should have said this before you kissed me, but… I didn't want to stop you."

He nods as though this is all perfectly acceptable. "I love how forthright you are. I'm very glad you didn't stop me." His gaze turns heavy. "I don't want to mess you around, but the kids cannot find out. When I was a teenager, I walked in on my father screwing the housekeeper. It's fucking seared on my retinas, even now." He grimaces. "I won't do that to my kids." He stares into the distance for a moment, unfocused, and I've lost him to whatever thought is crossing his mind. He drags his gaze back to mine. "It was Oxford, by the way. PPE. Balliol College. In case you were wondering."

"I wasn't."

His eyes narrow like he doesn't believe me, but he smiles and glances at his wristwatch. "We need to get up." He nuzzles his nose against my neck and presses a kiss to my throat. "Can you go check the kids? Make sure they're up? Bring them to breakfast on deck. Charlie, especially. He has a tendency to fuck about. Waste time. You know what it was like trying to get him here." He stares at the ceiling of the tiny room, probably recalling Charlie snoozing his alarm clock yesterday morning before we left, having only half-packed his suitcase. The kid wasn't remotely prepared to head to the airport. It was like he was already in a different time zone. I thought Matt was going to lose his shit, but he didn't.

"We're on a tight schedule," he says. "Boat's leaving at half 9."

"Yes, sir."

He stands and pulls on his clothes from last night, having to bend to avoid the overhead beam. "I'm going to shower. And I'm moving you into a bigger room. This is fucking ridiculous."

I run to the kids' rooms, waking Lucie first. She bounds out of bed, hugs me and leaps to the floor, pushing the interconnecting door to Charlie's room open. I'm right behind her when the door swings wide, revealing Charlie standing in the middle of the room, a towel wrapped about his waist.

His eyes flare with alarm when he sees me, but I'm sure mine are the same because Charlie's torso is covered with livid bruises, some fading, some still dark.

"Get the fuck out of my room." His tone is hard, angry, and it reminds me so much of his father that a sickening sensation crawls up my throat.

Lucie begins to cry and I scoop her up, carrying her back to her own room. Charlie slams the interconnecting door behind me, and I hear the lock fall into place.

My heart hammers as I stroke Lucie's hair, soothing her hiccupping tears. I kiss the top of her head. "That was scary, wasn't it?"

She nods against my chest.

"It'll be all right. Charlie wanted some privacy. That's all."

I'm trying to be present with Lucie, to focus on her as she burrows against me, but I keep thinking of the bruises over Charlie's chest. No wonder he didn't take off his rash vest at the pool yesterday.

My mind spins with ideas about what might have happened to him. Rough sport? A beating? Is he being bullied? Did he get attacked and never tell his dad?

An unpleasant sensation settles in my gut. What the hell do I tell Matt about this?

26
MATT

Aries is a drug. She must have coated her skin in cocaine, because I cannot get enough. Watching her cavort in the pool all day in that bikini was torture. That, and Seb bullying me into getting the most out of the situation.

I stand in front of the breakfast buffet, plate in hand. I can feel the heat of the day on the back of my neck. It's only 8 am, and it's already boiling.

"Good night?" Seb asks, coming up behind me with a platter of food piled so high it's obscene.

I grab a croissant. "Erm, yeah."

"You weren't in your room. I checked," he says before giving me the most salacious, suggestive wink.

"What were you doing in my room?"

Seb laughs. "Checking. Duh." He saunters to the outside table, pulls down his sunglasses and takes a seat.

I follow him out. "That's an invasion of privacy. I did not give you permission to go wandering around in my quarters." A boyish grin still decorates Seb's face, irritating the fuck out of me. "I get that this amuses you, but my kids are on this boat. They could come up here at any moment. I don't want them finding out."

"Finding out what?" Kate says, coming over with a steaming cup of coffee in one hand. She's wearing a blue dress that falls just below her knee, her dark hair tied up in a knot on top of her head.

"Matt's screwing the nanny," Seb answers.

Kate freezes, glances at Seb and then back at me, no doubt trying to decipher whether or not this is a prank. "Are you?" she asks in a stage whisper.

I roll my eyes and shake my head, dismissing the entire conversation rather than denying it as I bite into the croissant.

"She's gorgeous," Kate says. "And lovely too. We had a good chat at the pool yesterday. It's obvious she really cares about Lucie. You could do a lot worse."

"I'll say," Seb agrees.

"Stupid though," Nico muses, stepping out into the glaring sun to join us.

"She's not stupid," I say, far too fast.

Seb and Kate share an amused glance, and Nico's lips curve too, although he's not sharing his amusement with anyone else. He pours a glass of fresh orange juice and sips it thoughtfully. "I didn't mean her. I meant the whole"—he raises his glass of OJ and moves it round in the air like he's stirring a cauldron with it—"thing. You're blurring all the boundaries. If she's a good nanny and it doesn't work out, you'll have to let her go. If it does work out..." He shrugs, like he doesn't know what happens next.

"Let the old bugger have some fun," Seb says. "If he wants to get his nuts off with the staff, why not let him fuck the nanny? At least she's hot."

A primal urge to smash my fist into Seb's face rises up.

"Daddy!"

I spin to the voice so fast I nearly choke on my croissant. Lucie is sprinting towards me, Aries just behind her. They're far too close, and I know by the look on Aries' face that she heard exactly what Seb just said. Her expression tears at my heart; she looks humiliated. Uncertain green eyes dart between the four of us like she's trying to gauge who's going to launch the next attack.

I scoop Lucie into my arms. No one else moves. We're all standing, trapped in this horrendously awkward moment until Kate moves towards Aries.

"Did you sleep well?" Kate asks, then immediately shakes her head and curses under her breath as though she wishes she hadn't mentioned last night at all, while Aries looks stunned. Seb's eyebrows shoot into his hairline. "Sorry," Kate says. "Come and get some food. Sit with us. Come on Lucie, come choose some food," she adds, holding out her hand to my daughter. "There are fresh pastries."

I put Lucie down, and she skips off to grab Kate's hand. With one quick, unhappy glance at me, Aries moves off with Kate back inside to the buffet spread.

I turn to Seb. "You're a fucking twat, you know that?"

Nico slowly sits down next to Seb, making no comment.

"I'm sorry," Seb replies. "But come on. You're a walking stereotype. The sad old divorcé fucking his hot nanny."

"Fuck you. Yesterday you were badgering me not to waste the opportunity."

"And I stand by that. Your nanny looks like she stepped off the stage of the Moulin fucking Rouge. But that doesn't change what this is. It's a midlife crisis if ever I saw—"

"You don't know what this is," I fire back. "And you just made her feel like shit. She's a human being, Seb."

He stills, scanning my face. When he's found whatever he's searching for, he breaks into an enormous smile and thumps his palm against the white tablecloth, making the orange juice slop around in the glass jug. "You really like her. It's not just sex, is it?"

Something in my chest locks down. "We are not fucking talking about this."

"No, we aren't," Nico says, like his is the final word on the matter. He turns to me. "But you need to think about it. Because this has repercussions for a lot of people, not least your kids. And you"—Nico turns on Seb—"need to go and apologise to that woman in there."

"Aries. Her fucking name is Aries," I say, swallowing my orange juice in one gulp.

Seb rises from the table, nodding his head at both of us, his expression far more solemn than I'm used to seeing, and goes back inside to find Aries.

I can't sit down, not right now. Not riled up this way. I want to fucking hit something, I'm so mad. This is my business, my *life*, not some topic of discussion or source of amusement for everyone else. *Fuck's sake.*

I pace along the deck, staring out into the calm blue of the Mediterranean Sea, spending a few minutes clinging to the rail, letting frustration pound through me. *I should never have told my brothers about Aries. Why the fuck did I mention it at all?*

I don't know what this is with her, what I'm doing, what this could be, and now they're all waiting for me to make some kind of declaration. To admit that this is more than a fling. *Is it?* I don't fucking know. I don't do this... I don't have affairs; I don't mess around. *Fuck.* I can't feel my way through it anymore, because of damn Seb and his niggling. How can he be both so fucking childish and so uncannily perceptive at the same time?

I need some space to work this shit out, but how can I get that on a boat with all my family?

When I head back towards the dining deck, feeling no better for my self-imposed time-out, Aries is sitting next to Lucie, with Kate on her other side. Nico and Seb are reading the broadsheets, discussing some business story. There's no sign of Charlie.

"Where's Charlie?" I ask, directing the question to Aries. There's a hint of anger in my voice, and I don't know why I'm throwing it at her. I can't talk to her the way I want to, because of the pressure of all these fucking eyes on us, knowing things they shouldn't know that I'm trying to hide from my kids. Judging me. Judging Aries. Like my life is some spectacle they can look at from the safety of their own happy lives. It's a fucking mess and the frustration of it fills my chest like I'm being pumped full of hydrogen on the cusp of exploding.

Seb and Nico are watching me over the top of their newspapers. Seb throws a wary glance at Nico then dips his eyes back to the paper. *They think I'm going to lose it.*

"He's in his room," Aries replies. "He's getting changed."

"I told you to prioritise him. Make sure he was at breakfast on time. We're leaving soon." The anger is louder now, bigger. *Fuck.* I don't know where it's coming from, but it's been there since I sat down to breakfast, and walking along the deck just now did nothing to alleviate it. *I don't have it under control.*

I can't see Seb behind his suspiciously erect newspaper, but I feel his attention so strongly his gaze might as well be burning two peepholes through the small print.

Nico lowers his paper, unashamedly staring like he's trying to warn me off. Talk me down with only his eyes. *Damn condescending prick.*

Fuck. This pressure is unbearable...

Aries stands up. "I need to talk to you about something."

"Not now." *They're all watching me.* "Go and get Charlie."

Aries sets her chin. "It's important."

"No." Aries pulls back, but I can't stop. All the anger rushes up in a torrent of fire through my torso. "Go. And. Get. Charlie. Like I damn well asked you to. How fucking hard is it to follow a simple instruction?"

Kate inhales sharply, straightens her sunglass and stares at the table. Seb shrinks down behind his newspaper. Nico folds his up and lays it flat on the table. I feel his glare most harshly of all. His unspoken *I told you so* booms so loud in my head that he might as well have screamed it.

Nico nods subtly, from me to Aries, in a silent bid for an apology.

I don't fucking need Nico to tell me what to do. I know I should apologise. I want to, but the words are stuck, lodged in my throat. I can't do it, not here, not in front of everyone, their gazes on me like I'm some specimen in a zoo. *What's he going to do next? What's the creature going to do to fix this fuck up?*

And Aries... she *did* ignore my instruction. Again. Maybe Nico's right. This is stupid. This blurring of lines... of *roles*. I've fucked up and I'm losing control of this situation.

Lucie sobs, and it's only now I realise she was at the table at all. I'd forgotten. She's cowering in her seat, and Kate puts an arm around her and pulls her into a hug.

The bitterness in Aries' gaze is a tonic that strips my skin. If we were alone, I know she'd dress me down for the way I've just spoken to her, but she says nothing. She excuses herself from the table, throwing her napkin down in a heap over her half-eaten food.

I watch her storm back downstairs to fetch Charlie, her red hair swinging down her back.

Nico stands, fixing that infuriating older brother glare on me. "And you wonder why you have such a high staff turnover."

I point at Seb. "When he stops f—" I catch myself on the cusp of swearing, biting back the expletive. "Winding me up, I'll be just fine. I need a coffee."

Seb raises both hands like he's under fire. "Don't put your shit on me. This is all you."

Nico shakes his head, walks around the table, and offers his hand to Lucie. "Come on, grab your croissant. We're going to go stand at the bow and yell about being King of the World."

Lucie nods, a little hesitant, but Nico curls his fingers in encouragement, and she slips her tiny hand in his. "Okay. But I don't want to be a king," she says. "I want to be a Princess."

Nico smiles. "You can be whatever you want. Let's go."

Relief spills through me as Nico and Kate walk my little girl along the deck, letting her pretend to be a princess, and giving her a little bit of magic all kids deserve, which I seem incapable of delivering.

They each take one of her hands and begin to count, "One... Two... three..." and on 'whee' they swing her between them and she squeals, and then giggles, calling, "again, again."

Everyone, it seems, is better at this parenting thing than I am.

27
ARIES

How does a perfect morning take such a turn? I woke up in the arms of my handsome boss, feeling a little sleep-deprived but otherwise entirely sated, and dare I say it... *happy*, only to start work and find out his teenage son has clearly been beaten up, and overhearing his brother referring to me as little more than a slutty employee...

If he wants to get his nuts off with the staff, why not let him fuck the nanny? At least she's hot.

...to being sworn at by said boss in front of his four-year-old daughter and his brothers. How can he be the same man who kissed me so tenderly earlier?

I was really starting to believe that maybe Matt and I could have something real. Something *more than passion and breathlessness and orgasms that you can walk away from when the night is over.*

I scratch Mum's words about love from my mind and thump on Charlie's door, the sting in my palm after I hit the wood signalling I'm hitting a bit too hard, but I don't care.

"What?" Charlie's voice comes from the other side of the closed door.

"You need to come to breakfast." All the frustration of my morning rakes through my tone, making my voice sound screechy. "We're going to the beach."

"I'll stay here. I don't want to visit the beach. I fucking hate sand."

I swallow down my irritation at him dismissing Matt's carefully made plans so easily and change tack, leaning closer against the door and speaking more softly. "Can I come in?"

"No."

"Charlie, please let me in. I need to know what happened."

"No you fucking don't."

I heave a sigh and slump against the door. "Charlie—"

"Fuck off."

Right, that's enough for one morning. I am done taking other people's bullshit. "Do not talk to me that way. If you don't open this door, I'm going to get your father and bring him down—"

The door swings open, revealing a fully dressed Charlie, face like thunder, eyes glowering. "It was rugby. Bad tackle."

"Rugby? In the summer term?" I might not be particularly athletic, but even I know rugby's a winter sport.

"Yes. Rugby. I practise with a group in the morning. I'm not very good, so I always take the hits. That's it."

"Charlie, be serious. You look like you've been beaten up. And on more than one occasion. You need to talk to me. Whoever's doing it knows what they're doing because they haven't touched your face. Don't collude in this. Who is it?"

He glares at me, and the hope that I might break through to him begins to ebb. Then, all of a sudden, he relents. "Older boys. They've left now. This was their last term. Please don't tell Dad. I'll never see them again."

"Give me names."

He shakes his head. "No."

"Why not?"

"Because it's not relevant anymore. They're gone. They won't be at school next term. This" —he pulls up his shirt and I wince at the bruises—"was goodbye."

He's so angry that his face is red beneath the teenage pimples. He has his father's bone structure and despite the gawky disproportion of his teenage face, he's a handsome young man. But more than that, there's a well of pain inside him that sends a tremor through my bones.

"Please." His voice breaks a little, and sadness tugs at my larynx, as if I'm the one about to cry. "Don't tell my dad. I don't want to ruin this holiday for no good reason."

"I don't want to keep secrets," I tell him, but I look away as I speak, knowing I'm keeping my own secrets from him. Knowing Matt and I will have to come clean at some point if our relationship is going anywhere.

Although, perhaps it isn't. Perhaps he's a man in his thirties having a breakdown after a divorce. Perhaps all I am to him is a distraction. Maybe that's why he was able to speak to me like that in front of his brothers... Maybe that whispered *everything* last night didn't really mean 'everything' at all.

Charlie pouts his bottom lip, tossing his head like he doesn't care either way, but the pain in his eyes gives him away. "Tell him if you want. He won't care. He doesn't give a shit. You know what he's like."

"What do you mean?"

"Lucie told me he yelled at you like he used to yell at Mum." He slides his hands into his pockets. "If you tell him about this, either he won't care or he'll yell at me. Like it's my fault. He's not a nice man, Aries. He's an arse."

A shiver goes down my spine. "He loves you. I know he does."

Charlie snorts. "Whatever. I'll make your job easy today, because I'm feeling generous. I'll come and have breakfast. Get on the boat.

Come to the beach. But only if you swear you won't mention this to Dad. It's not going to happen again. I'm not in pain anymore. I'm fine. This is all fine. Deal?"

I know I should say no. I shouldn't be making promises to a teenager. But the echo of Matt swearing at me at the breakfast table in front of everyone hums in my bloodstream. *What if Charlie's right and Matt does take it out on him?* The last thing this kid needs is his father yelling at him the way Matt yelled at me, without listening to what I had to say. It was dismissive and soul-crushing. Luckily, I'm old enough to take it and have enough self-awareness to realise that it's Matt's crap, not mine. But Charlie might not have that perspective...

"Okay. Deal," I say. "But if I see so much as a fingerprint on you when we get back to England, I'm going straight to your dad."

As we're wandering along the idyllic beach, not another person beyond our little group in sight, I have the unnerving sensation that I've made a deal with the devil. What was I thinking, promising not to tell Matt about Charlie's bruises?

It's my job to look after these kids. I owe them a duty of care, and I owe Matt the truth. But I'm still so fucking angry with him, angry with myself for trusting him, letting him in... maybe there's no saving a man like that. One who can't control his temper.

Lucie is on Matt's shoulders as we traipse along the sand, so I'm temporarily free. Charlie is walking between Nico and Seb, and Kate is beside me.

"I'm sorry about this morning," she says. "Matt's been under a lot of pressure for a long time."

"You don't need to make excuses for him. If he wants to apologise, he can."

Kate frowns and adjusts her sunglasses. The lenses are so large they make her look a little like a blue bottle under a microscope. A pretty one, but a large-eyed insect, nonetheless. "I'm sure he will. And about Seb—"

"Please. Stop. Are you going to do the apologising for all the Hawkston brothers? Because that's not your role."

Kate's tongue runs over her top lip and she nods. "You're right. But I wanted to check you were okay."

"I'm fine. Plus Seb already spoke to me, so it's just Matt..."

Kate smiles and leans in, whispering in my ear. "Refuse to sleep with him. You'll have him on his knees in no time."

A mixture of embarrassment and shock surges through my body, and my mouth falls open. Kate, seeing my reaction, laughs a little and shrugs. She moves ahead, calling out to Nico, Charlie and Seb. "You boys, come with me. There's a little alcove just along here where we can set up for lunch. It's like a mermaid cave. Lucie will love it." Matt moves to follow but Kate shakes her head. "You're not invited. You should show Aries around instead. If you head in the other direction, there's a beautiful little bay. Come back to meet us for lunch." She winks. "Here, let me take Lucie."

She holds out her arms, and Lucie lets go of her dad's hair which she's been grabbing like reins. Matt lifts her down and Kate takes her hand, the two of them sinking into the sand with each step as they run to catch up with the others.

Matt pulls on his earlobe, staring at me awkwardly. A warm breeze ruffles the hair around my face, but I'm anchored in place by the force of his gaze.

"I'm sorry," he says. "I—"

I turn and begin to walk uphill. I have no idea where I'm going—and I'm definitely not headed where Kate pointed—but I need to get away from him.

"Aries, would you wait a minute?" He grabs my elbow and spins me to him. "Where are you—"

"I had a perfect night with you. Perfect. The sex, the sleeping, your apology... all of it. Fucking perfect, and you went and ruined it. You swore at me in front of your family. Your brothers, who already think I'm 'just the nanny'"—I raise my index fingers to air quote—"you happen to be fucking because you're having a midlife crisis. Is that what this is?"

His irises move frantically over me, his chest rising and falling under his linen shirt. "Do you need to know what it is? Can't we just enjoy it?"

"I don't know. Can we?"

A flicker of something I think is guilt crosses his face. "I'm sorry."

"We're lying to your children."

"We're not lying. We're protecting them from information they don't need to know. Christ, everyone's getting at me to define this thing between us even though it's only been a few weeks. As if this is some life-defining relationship, when it's not. It's sex. It's just sex. It's not as though we're going to get married."

His last sentence is spoken with such disdain, such disparagement that I can feel the words scraping my heart.

Just sex? "Wow, Matt. You really know how to make a girl feel good. Well done." I start clapping, slowly, mostly because I know it's fucking annoying and I can tell by the look on his face that he thinks so too. But his expression shifts quickly.

"Shit. Aries, I'm sorry," he says, reaching out to me, but I turn away and start walking quickly up the hill again. Away from the beach, the water. I don't know why; my brain is too fogged with anger to think straight. I keep marching until my legs ache. I'm practically running, and the sand is turning to tufted grass, prickling the soles of my bare feet. There's no one else here. I ought to go back down, to find the others, to look after Lucie and do my job. Not fight with my boss about what ought to have been casual sex, but never was.

I spin back to find Matt right behind me, a worried, almost panicked expression on his handsome face. For a second, it gives me pause, but I have to say what I have to say. I can't keep quiet. "Last night, you said it was *everything*. Is it just sex, or is it everything? Which is it?"

"Everything."

The word buries itself right inside me—a treasure to be unearthed later—but right now, it's not enough. I haven't finished. *Not yet.* "My parents used to fight. Before they got divorced. My dad would talk to my mother like she didn't matter. Like he wasn't thinking about anything other than his own temper. And I swore I would never, *never* have that in my life. When he left, I was relieved. I was six years old, and I *rejoiced* that my daddy had gone. No more hiding under the stairs. Cowering under my duvet, waiting for the screams to stop."

Matt's eyes are on me, his expression so pained it makes the ache in my heart worse, but I'm not going to hold back to save either of us a little discomfort.

"When Alec told me about you and Gemma, and when I met her, I thought maybe it wasn't your fault. Maybe she *was* a bitch, just like you said." My gaze lingers on the scar, that thin white line through his eyebrow. He watches me intently and, noticing where I'm looking, he rubs a finger along it.

"But you aren't a victim. You aren't the good guy, who got stuck in a bad marriage." I shake my head. "Everything is a co-creation. Every relationship is two people muddling their way through. You were in it together, just like we are. And you *aren't* the good guy." My voice is so quiet, I can barely hear it above the sound of gulls and the rhythmic thump of the waves on the shore. "And I so wanted you to be. I wanted it so badly. I wanted this to be *everything*."

His eyelids droop, and beneath them his dark eyes are full of sorrow. My heart is so wrung out with the pain of seeing him like this. I can hardly meet his gaze.

"I never said I was a good guy," he says, and the words seem to break him. "I'm a lot of things, but that's not something I can claim." He drops his head into his palm, then drags his hand over the back of his head, pulling dark swathes of hair clear of his forehead. "Fuck, Aries. If you're looking for some perfect man, some perfect prince, then that's not me. And you might as well scrap the fucking illusion, because I don't want to disappoint you. I hate feeling this way, like I can't be good enough, like you're another person I'm letting down. Another person I'm hurting."

"Then stop doing stupid shit."

The tiniest smile pulls at his gorgeous mouth, then he drops his gaze, looks to the ground. "I'm an idiot."

"Yes."

We stand, breathing, watching one another.

"You know what?" I say. "I like having sex with you. I like it so much, I'd put up with a lot of your crap. And I hate myself for it, because I know you'll swear at me or yell like a madman or walk away from me when I'm bent over your desk, and in spite of all that, if you say one nice thing to me... If you look at me like that"—I wave at his face, where his eyes are so full of care, so remorseful, so *troubled*—"I'll do anything you want. Because to me, this is more than just the sex. More than the passion and the breathlessness... this is..."

My words trail off. I can't bring myself to say 'love' because that would be insane. *Wouldn't it?*

"Aries," he says softly as he reaches out to take my hand, but I snap it away.

"Just give me one more minute being angry with you. One more. Before you tear it all down."

His hand falls to his side, and he stands opposite me as I count in my head. *One Mississippi, Two Mississipi...* I count all the way to sixty before Matt moves.

Then, like he's been counting too, he drops to his knees there in the grassy sandbank and looks up at me.

It's so unexpected that heat blasts through my body. I glance around to check whether any of the others can see this ridiculous scenario play out, but no one is here. It's just us and the breeze and the sand and the sea.

"What are you doing?" I whisper.

"I don't deserve you. I know that. I don't want to marry you. I don't want to marry anyone, ever again, because marriage is a bullshit load of paperwork and heartache that made my life a whole lot worse. But I should never have shouted at you. Never. You're the most wonderful woman I've ever met. I can't believe you exist at all, let alone that you might want to be with me. I'm pinching myself the whole fucking time. And I really like having sex with you too. I really fucking love it. But it's not just sex. I don't know why I said that. I'm so sorry." He cups a hand over his mouth, but there's a hesitancy in his gaze, like he thinks he might not win me over this time.

"I knew from that first night that this was something more, and it scared the shit out of me. It still does. I love how you call me on all my bullshit, always asking the hard questions, pushing me to places

I'd otherwise refuse to go." He takes a long, shuddering breath, before he speaks again.

"I want to be better than this, Aries. I want to be better, for you, so we can see how far this thing between us can run. We can tell the kids about us at the end of the summer, if that's what you want. You can fucking resign and I'll get a new nanny. We'll tell the kids in October. Let's just wait until then, okay? First of October. We'll break it to them then."

It's on the tip of my tongue to say '*if we last that long*', but I don't want to ruin the moment, because I have the most devastatingly handsome man in the world on his knees for me, and I'm savouring it for as long as I can.

"I don't want you to do anything you don't want to do," he continues. "If this is as far as we go, then I'll thank God for every second I had you in my life, and I'll walk away. I want you to know that I'm sorry. And I swear, I will never raise my voice to you again. Even if you never fucking listen to me and you ignore every rule I've put in place."

I laugh, sniffling a little, wiping my nose on the back of my hand. I don't know if I'm crying or my nose is running or what. "You're allowed to be angry. But it's the way you handle it that matters."

Matt's lips tip up, a little tension leaving his shoulders. "Do you forgive me?"

I do an exaggerated eye-roll. Of course I forgive him, but I'll make him wait for it. Just a wee bit longer.

From his knees, voice church-sermon serious, he says, "If you don't, how can we have more of that great sex we've been having?"

I laugh. "How could I not forgive you? I *really* like having sex with you. More than with anyone else, *ever*. And you're on your knees on the beach." *And I think I love you, you grumpy bastard.*

He smiles. "So that's a yes? Because there are stones down here. It's killing my patellas."

"Get up, you idiot."

He stands up, holding both my hands in his. "Thank fuck, because I…" His voice drops away, like whatever he was going to say plunged off a cliff.

My heart hammers. "Because you?"

"Like you. I like you."

"God, you are just so English. Save me from your stuffy English charm." A smile pulls at my lips against my will, and Matt's eyes light up as he notices. "Don't get ahead of yourself," I say, referencing his obvious relief. "We need to add to the list of things you can't do."

He squeezes my hands in his, his eyes bright and eager to please. "Okay."

"You can't swear at me, or shout unreasonably. Oh, and you need to move me into a bigger bedroom."

He chuckles. "That's in hand. All your things will be moved by the crew by the time we get back on board."

"And the rest?"

"I'll try. I have a bad temper. It's stress. It's—"

"It's you. Don't make excuses. Those are your emotions. Don't throw them at me unless it's really warranted. Unless it's really *me* that's made you angry. No random swearing because you're frustrated by your son or your brothers or whatever. If it's because I've done something wrong, I'll take it. But otherwise, no. It's not acceptable."

Charlie pops into my mind, pleading with me not to tell his dad about his bruises. *Do I even have a right to demand this of Matt, when I'm concealing things from him about his son's welfare?*

"Okay," he says, and I believe he means it. His heated gaze strays from my eyes to my lips. "Can I kiss you now?" He looks at the time on his watch. "It's been at least five hours and that's far too long."

He leans in, and I put one hand to his hard, firm chest, holding him off. "October first?"

He gives a lop-sided smile, and he looks so handsome that longing shoots straight through my belly. "October first," he agrees. "It's a date."

And then his lips are on me, and everything around me blurs as I lose myself in his kiss.

28
MATT

The holiday was a great success. Ten days of heat and sun and the sea, and sweltering afternoons and ice cream and balmy evenings. And the kids, laughing. Even Charlie loosened up by the last few days.

And best of all, Aries. The salty tang of her skin after a day in the sun. The warm sweetness of her kisses. Her soft curves... the stolen whispers and orgasms that blazed a path through my entire body. Aries' stifled cries as she came undone. It was divine.

"I cannot believe you wouldn't let me bring a date when you spent ten days secretly screwing the nann—" Seb falls silent as I raise my eyebrow. We're in my office, both more tanned than any Caucasian British man has any right to be. "Aries," he corrects as he runs his fingertip along the edge of my desk. "You should lock her down, you know."

"Huh?"

"She's smart, funny. Gorgeous. Great with the kids. And she likes you. She must be mad, but"—he lifts his hands in a gesture of helpless confusion—"what are the chances of that combination coming along in one hot package?"

"I'm not locking anyone down, ever. I've spent my adult life in the shackles of marriage. I'm done."

"Fair," Seb concedes. "I guess you'll have to stick to 'nanny-with-benefits' then." He scratches his temple, then his eyes spark and I know he's had some new, probably inappropriate, thought. "There's a latent market there. I could start a side hustle pairing up single dads with hot nannies. It's like a two-for-one deal. Childcare and bedroom—"

"Shut the fuck up and get out of my office."

Seb chuckles, straightening his tie as he paces towards the door.

"Oh, and Seb?"

He pauses, his hand on his tie knot, the other in his perfectly coiffed hair, checking his reflection in the window to put a strand back in place. "Yeah?" he says, without looking away from his own reflection.

"If you don't grow up, you aren't going to find anyone to lock down."

He looks affronted for all of half a second before he grins at me. "Who says I want to lock anyone down? I'm free as a bird, brother. Free as a mother-fucking bird." He puts his hands on his hips and lets out a peal of laughter so wholesome that even I want to join in. "Want to come for a beer?"

I shake my head, and he tilts his as if to say, '*fine, you old bore*'. The door closes behind him, and I glance out the window. We're pretty high up here on the twentieth floor. High for London, at least. It's still light, given it's mid July. I glance at the time. 8 pm.

Lucie will be asleep. We've been home for five days and Aries and I haven't had sex. We've barely even kissed. I can't with Charlie in the house. I don't know why the boat seemed better. Maybe it was the sun or the salt air, or the fact the kids were in their own section and there was the noise of the engine, the sea. The house is fucking quiet at night by comparison.

I pick up my phone and call Aries. She answers on the third ring.

"Mr Hawkston, what can I do for you?"

The sound of her voice makes me smile. "Dinner. Have you eaten?"

"No."

"Do you want to go out?"

She's silent a moment. "Like, on a date?"

"Yeah. Tonight. Can you come?"

She's quiet again, and I can almost hear her thinking. I know she wants to say yes. I can *feel* it. "Who's going to look after the kids?"

"Ask Alec. Scratch that. *Tell* him. He's there, isn't he? Get him to wait in the main house. I'll pay him extra."

"You want the chef to babysit so we can go out?"

"Yes. Don't say that though. Tell him you have to run an errand for me. I assume Mrs Minter's left already?"

"Yeah, she left half an hour ago."

"Okay. Tell Alec I'll pay him five hundred quid—"

"Woah. You rich people have no idea about the value of money, do you?" I cringe at the shock in her tone. "He'd do it for fifty."

"Whatever. He's there making dinner now, isn't he? Tell him I'm eating out and he can sleep on the sofa if I'm back late."

"You sure?"

"Yes, I'm fucking sure. Get over here, now. Come to the Hawkston building in the city."

She chuckles lightly, and the sound settles right in my heart. I want to be where she is. *Now*. "That doesn't sound like a restaurant, Mr Hawkston."

"It's not. But it has a wonderful roof terrace. And it's warm out. And I already know exactly what I want to eat. And I'm ninety-nine per cent sure you're going to want me to indulge in private."

She laughs, loudly this time. "I need to change."

"Don't. Come as you are. Get in a cab, now."

"Phew," she says on an exhale, as though I've ordered her to run a marathon. "Yes, sir," she adds, and I can tell by her tone that she's smiling.

"Wow," Aries says, one hand clasping the railing that runs around the roof terrace of the Hawkston building. "This view is insane."

It won't be totally dark for another hour or so, but already some lights across the city are sparkling like fireflies. "You get used to it," I say, but she frowns at me like I'm an idiot and slaps my forearm.

"Don't pretend to be old and jaded. You know this is amazing. Otherwise, you wouldn't have asked me up here." My grin is as much affirmative as she needs before she continues, "You know there are still people in the office? Not many, but some."

"I locked the door. No one can get out here."

She visibly relaxes, her shoulders sinking and the tension fading from her face.

I stand behind her, caging her in with my arms, a hand on the railing either side of her. She smells like fresh laundry and something sweet, like honey. The combination is pure Aries. I nuzzle into her neck, inhaling deeply.

"Fuck," I groan. "You are my kryptonite, Aries McClennon."

She laughs and I spin her round to face me, taking in her features in the evening sunlight: the fine bridge of her nose, the freckles scattered over it like a sprinkling of pepper. She's *perfect*.

Our eyes connect like magnet and steel, and I feel that deep tug, as if merely looking at Aries affects some inner part of me that I can't keep from her. I'm more bound to this woman than I've ever been to anyone else. *No secrets.*

"What are you thinking?" she whispers.

"I'm thinking how much I want to fuck you out here."

She shoots me a look as though she knows that wasn't *all* I was thinking. "On the roof?"

I nod, lowering my lips to hers, feeling the soft, wet warmth of her mouth. "Mmm, hmm," I hum, the sound vibrating mouth-to-mouth.

Her tongue sweeps through my lips, so willing that it sends a thrill to my dick. I pull back. "Is that a yes?"

"Always yes," she replies. "But I'm really hungry so can you make it quick?"

This draws a chuckle from me, and I spin her back round to face the railing, my hands on her hips. I reach one around to meet the soft flesh of her stomach and unbutton her jeans. No matter how many times we do this, I still feel like an excited teenager who's finally been allowed access after months of wanting. I slide my hand into her waistband until my finger grazes through her pubic hair. She's bare beneath the jeans, and lust pulses through me with more demand.

"No underwear?"

She glances over her shoulder, her lips parting into a beautiful smile. "Like I said, I'm really hungry. Didn't want to waste time with unnecessary layers."

She shuffles her jeans down so they rest mid thigh, leaving her exposed. Needing no more encouragement, I slide my hand further between her legs. Her sweet lips are wet... *dripping*, and my fingers slide into her cunt with no resistance. Her back arches, her arse pressing against me.

"You're always so ready for me," I breathe in her ear. "Do you know how hot that is?"

She nods, her hair brushing against my cheek as I lean against her. Her arse rubs against my erection. "I do know, because you're always so ready for me, too," she teases. "And I love that you are."

The slick sounds of her soft, wet cunt being fucked by my fingers slice the evening air. Little sensuous moans fall from her mouth, and she throws her head back as the heel of my hand rubs against her clit.

"I didn't lock the door," I admit in a hoarse whisper.

"You lied?" Aries says, a hint of concern edging through her arousal. "So anyone could come out here?"

"Do you like that idea?"

She moans as I keep playing with her pussy, and I know she does. I can't get enough of her, of how turned on she is. "But... but... you could get in trouble. You could get fired."

"No one is firing me, Aries," I growl in her ear. "My name is on the building."

I increase the pressure against her clit, and she lets out a series of stuttered gasps. *She's getting close.* "What about me?" she pants.

"Be a good girl, and you can keep this job forever." I finger-fuck her harder and faster, pressing on that spot inside until small shudders ripple through her body. Her hands cling tight to the railing in front of her and her back arches.

"Oh, oh, shit," she mutters. "Matt..."

Her body goes rigid, and warm wetness gushes from her, pooling in my hand, streaming down my wrist. "Fuck," I groan. "You just... shit. That went everywhere..."

Aries lets out a delightful sigh, sounding utterly blissed out as her body relaxes. "I squirted," she admits as thought it's a completely regular occurrence. Clearly I'm more surprised by it than she is. "Are my jeans wet?"

"Your jeans? No. I think I got it."

"Phew." She huffs the tiniest laugh. "Sorry."

I kiss her neck, flicking my hand so her juices spray the paving at our feet. "Don't be fucking sorry. That's the hottest thing I've ever seen. Can you keep going?"

"Don't you dare stop," she says, and I can hear the smile in her voice.

My cock is achingly hard, and as I return my wet hand to her pussy, I use the other to undo my trousers.

"Fuck, Aries," I murmur, sliding one hand around the base of my hard cock, and up to the tip, where a bead of pre-cum nestles. *Always so ready.*

I slide her jeans right to the floor and she steps out of them, exposing her soft curves to the night air. I grab her hips, manoeuvring her so I can slide my cock through the lips of her wet pussy. She's shorter than I am, so my thighs will burn with the effort of holding this position, but it'll be worth it.

"Fuck me," she moans. "I'm ready. Fuck me hard with that huge dick."

I laugh, making her laugh, and something about how ridiculous we are, and yet how hot this still manages to be, has warmth spreading through my chest.

I do exactly as she asks, slamming into her, our skin slapping together as I simultaneously tease her swollen clit.

"Fuck, that's good," she murmurs, her hips writhing against my fingers. "Right there. Yes. Keep that—"

I rail into her harder, cutting off her words. I speed up the circular movements over her clit and she moans, louder now—*oh, oh, oh, oh*—over and over. With each of her delirious moans, pleasure sparks up my shaft.

I drive into her harder, seeking out my orgasm, *her* orgasm, like my survival depends on it.

With an explosive cry, and a sound that's almost a scream, Aries' walls pulse around my dick as uncontrollable jerks of pleasure take over her body.

I hold her up as I take my final thrusts, my orgasm unspooling at the base of my spine and erupting.

My muscles tense and my jaw tightens as my cum spurts into Aries' perfect pussy, even as she's still whimpering and clenching around my dick.

As our breathing returns to normal, Aries leans her head down between her shoulders. "I'm definitely having a dessert," she pants. "I think I've earned it."

"Indeed," I agree, pulling a cotton handkerchief from my pocket. It's perfectly ironed and folded into a square. I pass it to her and she stares at it for a moment before a burst of laughter escapes her. "How old are you?" she asks, as she runs her fingertip over the monogrammed corner. "This is such an old man handkerchief."

"Hey." I slap her exposed arse gently. "My father got them for all of us."

"What's the J stand for?" Her fingernail flicks at the embroidered middle initial.

"James."

"Matthew James Hawkston. Nice." She unfolds the fabric and places it between her thighs. "Ready," she says, and I slide out as she catches the mess and wipes herself down.

When we're both dressed, she holds out the scrunched up bit of fabric. "What do you want to do with this?"

I take it from her and throw it into the bin. "Never liked it anyway."

She puts a hand on her hip and looks me up and down. "You suddenly seem so much younger, Matthew James Hawkston. Let's go eat."

29
ARIES

The evening is unusually balmy for the UK as we drift hand in hand through Covent Garden. I'm thankful I'm wearing trainers, because these cobblestones would be lethal otherwise.

This whole evening has been surreal, from sex on the roof, to strolling around like a real couple, as if we're on holiday. Even when we were actually away, on the boat, we couldn't do this. We were so stealthy, stealing kisses and glances and touches like we'd be sent down for life if anyone caught us.

This is reckless in comparison, but the feel of Matt's large fingers interlinked with my smaller ones, while we're out in public, is a sensation I didn't know would give me so much pleasure.

We eat at a little restaurant called Clos Maggiore, which might be the most romantic restaurant I've ever been in. The ceiling is decorated in greenery and blossom and the place is lit with tiny lights. It's like eating in a fairy dell.

Matt orders the wine, which is delicious. I eat so much I'm positively bursting, and then we share a pudding. A chocolate fondant that's warm and melting and sickly sweet.

Matt takes a few bites and pushes it towards me. "All yours. Too sweet for me."

"Yum. Thanks."

I scoop up the rest and chow it down as Matt sips on the rest of his wine. There's a heated look in his eyes.

"What?" I ask, my spoon, laden with chocolate sauce, halfway to my mouth.

He smiles. "I want to eat you as much as you want to eat that pudding."

"Wow." I pop the final spoonful in my mouth and then, before I've even chewed, I say, "You must want to eat me a hell of a lot."

"I do. Let's get out of here." He waves to the waiter with one lazy raise of his hand, not taking his eyes off me.

A few minutes later, we're back outside, only now it's dark. Groups of tourists and youngsters cross the market place, and their loud joyous voices fill the air. There's a hum of excitement in Covent Garden, as if only good things happen here; things that speak of the promise of life and happiness and unlimited possibilities. My heart is burgeoning with the sensation, and my head is swirling with expensive wine, and I'm giddy at the proximity of Matt. I'm so high, I feel like I'm on drugs.

Matt tugs on my hand, pulling me into an alcove.

"What—"

In seconds, his hands are around me, his lips warm and desperate over mine, swallowing my weak protests.

His hot palms and strong fingers are all over me, in my hair, down my back, squeezing my bum. It's like he's touching me everywhere at once, pulling me against him, the thick erection at his groin pushing against me. I gasp.

"Always ready," he mutters, then shakes his head like he's disappointed somehow. "Fuck, you make me so hard. I'm like a teenager around you." He kisses me again, the rough stubble on his chin grazing my skin. He drives his tongue deeper into my mouth, and warmth spills through me, desire coiling low between my legs.

I slide my hand over his erection and he groans. It's such a feral noise, as if he's only half-human in this moment, and full of such need that I can't help sliding my hand into his trousers to grip the hard, hot length of it. I begin to stroke up and down the soft skin of his hard dick.

Bang!

My body contracts in fear, and I whip my hand out of Matt's trousers so fast I catch it on the zipper.

"What the fuck?" Matt says, cradling me against the broad strength of his chest. He holds me like I'm precious, smothering me against his hard muscle, the scent of him engulfing me. *Protecting me.* My heart pounds and I can feel the quickened beat of his heart too.

A crumpled can lies on the ground next to us.

"Get a room," calls a male voice.

I twist out of Matt's grip to see who's shouting at us. A group of teenage boys, probably eighteen or nineteen, are stumbling around in the square behind us. They look drunk. One of them kicks another empty beer can in our direction.

Matt lurches away from me like he means to go after them. "That's it—"

"Please, leave it," I beg, tugging him back.

"Whore," comes a voice.

Matt's features shift, and for a second its like he barely sees me, lost to a sudden onslaught of rage. He tries to head towards the boys, but at the idea of him leaving me, I cling harder to him, my fingers pressing into his biceps.

"Stop. Please."

He looks down at me, then at the group of boys. There's such danger flickering in his eyes that I know he wants to yell at them. Maybe even hit them. But I can't let him go around unleashing his temper on drunken kids. "They don't get to do that," he growls. "To call you that—"

"I don't care. Let's just go home."

He breathes heavily through flared nostrils, the strong line of his jaw firm like he's clenching his teeth. His hand slides to my waist, tightening against me.

I glance up at the group of boys, and one of them catches my eye. A shiver courses over my skin. There's something familiar about the kid, but I can't place it. A horrible feeling settles low in my stomach, and I know I won't be able to shake it off until I work out what has disturbed me.

"Those little shits," Matt mutters.

"Please," I say. "They're just drunk."

I hold eye contact, my fingers fixed tight to his arm, until finally the anger seeps out of his gaze. "Fine. Let's go."

Matt calls his driver, and we walk hand in hand to where the car is parked down a side street, but somehow I don't feel the comfort from Matt's touch that I did before.

"All okay?" he asks as we reach the car and he opens the door for me.

I nod. "Thank you for dinner."

I gnaw on my thumbnail and stare out the car window all the way home. Something isn't right, but I don't know what it is. I suspect Matt senses it too because he doesn't speak or touch me, keeping his hands firmly planted on each of his thighs.

Perhaps it's guilt... the inevitability of getting caught doing something we shouldn't that's really hitting home right now. Whatever it is, the fine balance of our little world has been knocked askew, and I don't know how to put it right.

Back in my room at home, I wait all night for a message from Matt to come through on my phone, but nothing does. I can't shake the eerie sensation that something ended tonight, and a panicked pressure swells in my chest with no relief, until I'm so tired I can't keep my eyes open anymore.

When I wake the following morning, I find Matt sitting on the edge of my tiny bed, dressed in his suit. A particularly dapper navy linen suit. Fuck, he looks good. Any worries I had about last night dissolve as he smiles at me and runs his fingers through my hair, watching the red strands filter across his palm before dropping onto the pillow.

"I love your hair," he says, still mesmerized by it as he continues to play with the strands. I let him do it a while longer before I rub my eyes, giving him a deliberate once-over.

"Why are you in a suit? Isn't it Saturday?"

He curls a lock of my hair around his finger, keeping his gaze on it like I haven't spoken. "I thought this whole Scottish redhead thing was an urban legend."

"Do you mean stereotype? Because yes, it's a stereotype. I'm a stereotype." Irritation has my words coming out a little too fast. "Just what every girl wants to hear. And yes, I've heard it before."

Matt's eyes glint at me, all dark and mischievous. "Are you talking to me, or having an argument with yourself?"

I huff. "Why are you wearing a suit?"

He smiles, rubbing his hands down his muscular thighs and leaning forward as he says, "Because we're taking a trip."

I sit up, alarmed. "What? Who is?"

"Me and you."

I must be dreaming. "We only just came back from holiday. And who's looking after the kids? We can't ask Alec again."

"Nico and Kate are coming over to babysit. In fact, they're probably downstairs already. They're great with Lucie. She'll be fine."

"Where are we going?"

"Scotland."

My mouth drops open. "Are you having a laugh?"

"No. We'll be back for dinner. You don't need to pack. Just get dressed."

"Why?"

He stands up. "Your mum. We're going to see her."

Oh, my God. A million thoughts zing in my brain. Mum. I get to see my mum. Scotland. Matt. *He wants to meet my mother. Shit.* I never thought he'd actually follow through on that vague discussion about meeting her.

"Wait." I push the covers off the bed and swing my legs over the side, bare feet hitting the floor. "Don't tell me you're wearing that suit—looks great, by the way—to see my mum?"

He gives me the most disarming lopsided smile on his way out the door, and my insides instantly reach melting point. Or boiling. Hard to tell. "Only get to make a first impression once, Aries."

"You're crazy," I call. "We can't just show up at her door. We need to tell her we're coming."

"All in hand. Get dressed," he replies before his deep chuckle fades down the corridor.

God, that man is soooo sexy. I want to race after him in my tiny pyjamas and jump on his back like a monkey. Nibble his neck. Make him carry me back to bed. But I do none of those things. I squeal and jump up and down on my tiptoes in the safety of my room. I'm going to see my mum. And she's going to meet Matt.

I hope she keeps all her woo-woo stuff locked down. If she starts talking about me and Matt having some other-worldly soul-deep connection that spans lifetimes, I might need to abort the visit early. There's only so much of that stuff a man like Matt can take.

I get dressed and ready in record time, and when I get downstairs Matt hands me a coffee and a croissant. I'm still half-convinced I'm dreaming when he says, "All set?"

"Yup."

"Morning, Aries," Nico greets, and it's only then I notice him and Kate standing behind me.

"Oh, hi. Thanks. For this... you know..." I'm waving my hand around to indicate the house, but I'm so inarticulate and obviously flustered that Kate giggles and Nico shoots her a disapproving look.

"Come on, you," Matt says, putting his arm around me and ushering me towards the front door, but not before I've seen Nico raise his eyebrows and glance at Kate, who answers with a smirk and a shrug. I can't help smiling, because the way Matt said 'you' before he grabbed me warmed me all the way from my toes to the crown of my head. And the fact he did it right in front of his brother and Kate somehow makes it *better*. As if them witnessing it, witnessing *us*, validates whatever this relationship is.

The car is waiting outside, driver at the wheel. Matt opens my door, and I shuffle across the leather and buckle in.

"We're not driving, are we?" I question as Matt enters the other side of the car. "Because you know we won't be back by dinner if we are."

"God, no. I'm not sitting on the A1 all the way up to Scotland."

"Okay, so... Easyjet?" I wink.

"Nooooo," he says, long and slow, teasing me for teasing him.

"Prince Harry travelled on Easyjet. Pretty sure Wills and Kate did too."

"Publicity stunt. I'm not into that bullshit."

I laugh, and he smiles as he slides his fingers between mine. Linked together, we sit in the back of the car.

After a while, the car slows, and I peer out the window. *We're in Battersea. The London Heliport.*

I let out a noise that's somewhere between a squeak and a chirrup. *This is insane. A helicopter, so I can see my mum for the day?*

I glance over at Matt, but he's staring out of the window. "You don't have to do this, you know," I tell him.

He turns to me, smiling. "I know. I want to do it. I want to meet this superhero mother of yours who raised the woman I..."

My heart beats frantically, my mind not daring to fill in the blanks. "The woman you what?"

He presses his lips together and my heart sinks at the idea that he's not going to reply at all, when he says, "The woman I like the most of all women in the world."

My insides turn to goo. It's not quite 'love', but it's somewhere close.

"I like you the best too." I'm grinning so hard that my cheeks ache.

"Right, well." He gives a stiff nod, like we've just negotiated the world's most awkward business deal. "Good." He heaves a breath, then, "Plus, I can't bear the thought that you're wasting your time with me and my children when your mother is sick."

This silences me, and I realise all of a sudden how much of my energy I expend locking away my feelings about Mum's sickness. It's been relentlessly hard, all the rounds of chemo and how sick they made her. Losing her hair. Not being able to keep down any food, and then not being able to taste it when she finally could. I grit my teeth. Perhaps if I keep my mouth shut tight I can keep everything locked inside a little longer.

I stare out of the car window, forcing my thoughts away by focusing on the view. "I've never been in a helicopter. Is it safe? I've never thought those things looked safe. And there was that story about the one—"

He squeezes my hand. "Stop. It's safe." He lifts my hand and kisses the back of it. It's such a small, tender gesture that I'm entirely distracted from my helicopter-induced anxiety and my concerns about Mum.

It only takes twenty minutes to park the car, get out, pass through the lobby of the Heliport where Matt stops to sign a few documents, and out onto the tarmac. The helicopter blades aren't moving, but I lower my head just in case.

Matt laughs, pulling me close. "You don't have to duck. You're not that tall."

Inside, the seats are cream leather, the floor a rich blue carpet. It's more spacious than I expected; I can stretch my legs out. There's a fully stocked hamper set out in front of us, with a bottle of chilled champagne and two glasses at the top.

Matt helps me fix my headset, his fingers stroking the skin of my face as he gets it in place.

It's terrifying when we lift off. So noisy. It feels like I'm rattling around like a bean in a can. I reach for Matt's hand and grip it so tight he lets out a surprised chortle. "Ow. I need that hand for later." I hear his voice through the headset; it's too loud to have a regular conversation.

I giggle and let go, but he immediately takes my hand again and squeezes. My fingers tingle and I wonder if his do too.

When we're in the air, I stare out the window at the sights of London below. I can make out the Hawkston Mayfair hotel from here, and I get a strange reality shock. I'm in a helicopter with one of the richest men in the world, and I can see one of his hotels from the sky.

What the hell is going on?

By the time we arrive at Mum's, I'm still buzzing with adrenaline from the flight. Overhead, the sky is dense with grey cloud. Oppressive. Matt stands next to me, looking devilishly handsome and completely out of place in my mother's little cul-de-sac.

I dig into my pocket and remove my keys for the small, pebbled-dash semi. The glass in the PVC front door is thick with frosted patterns across it. I go to unlock it, but I pause.

"What are you to me? I mean, what am I telling my mother?" I ask, realising I have no idea what the story here is.

Matt looks down at me from his position on the doorstep. "What do you want to tell her?"

"Boss. You're my boss. My incredibly handsome—"

He cuts me off with a kiss and I melt like ice cream on a hot day. A puddle held together only by the cone. His lips on mine, his tongue in my mouth. My brain sizzles.

"Hello, Aries," comes my mother's voice. We break apart to find her in the doorway, smiling as she looks between me and Matt. I'm delighted to find her amused, but she looks so frail that my heart aches. A purple and turquoise turban is wrapped around her head, no doubt hiding what remains of her hair. *Maybe I shouldn't have left at all...*

"London's treating you well then?" she asks, barely holding in her laughter.

"Mrs McClennon," Matt says, "I'm—"

"You're London. Yes."

Matt's eyes dart to me, one eyebrow raised, like he has no idea what to make of this response. "I'm—

"I know who you are," Mum replies, pulling me into a hug. She's so thin, she feels like a bird in my arms. Tiny bones. "You're the hotel man," she says to Matt over my shoulder. Then she steps aside, indicating we should follow her into the house. "This is the most wonderful surprise. I'd say it's romantic, bringing Aries up here, but I don't suppose it is. Coming to sit with a sick woman for the afternoon isn't my idea of romance. And I'm quite sure it's not yours."

Matt half-smiles, half-frowns, clearly unsure what to say to that. He slides an arm around my lower back and together we walk inside. The narrow hallway seems even smaller than I remember when Matt's tall frame fills the space. He wrinkles his nose a fraction, noticing the smell in the air. It's incense, white sage if I'm not mistaken, but beneath it there's something else... ham soup, perhaps. Maybe a touch of bleach too. It's not unpleasant, but there's something about it that reminds me of hospitals or old people's homes and an edge of panic bubbles up in me. What if Matt hates this... my family home... What if he thinks that none of this is good enough for him?

Guilt and shame strangle my panic. *What am I thinking?* I love my mum and I love this house, and if it's not enough for him, then that's his problem.

Just then, as if he knows what's flashing though my mind, he squeezes me tighter, and presses a kiss against my hair causing a sense of calm to flood me.

I smile up at him and extricate myself from his embrace so I can help Mum, who is weakly walking ahead, one hand on the wall for balance. She's so much frailer than she was when I left and its only been a few weeks.

"Can I use the bathroom?" Matt asks.

I nod towards the stairs.

He raises his eyebrows as if to say, '*Really? Upstairs?*'

"There is no downstairs toilet," I whisper.

His lips form a quiet 'oh' of sudden understanding. *Has he ever been in a house that doesn't have a downstairs bathroom?* He heads up the stairs, leaving me wondering if this is the smallest house he's ever been in.

Mum is panting by the time I get her back to the sitting room, where a bed is set up in front of the TV. Lizzie, the carer we interviewed and employed before I left, is fussing over the sheets.

"Aries, so lovely to see you." She hugs me. "Your mother wanted to answer the door herself. I said not to, but she was having none of it."

"I'm not dead yet," Mum says with a laugh that sounds genuinely amused, but it makes me inwardly wince as I help her lower to the sofa and sit next to her. "You should see this man she's brought with her, Lizzie. Looks like Clark Gable. Just like I suspected." She winks at me.

"I saw him," Lizzie says, nodding at the open door we've just come though. She must have caught a glimpse of Matt on the way in. "I wouldn't say Clark Gable though." She screws up her face as she thinks. "Maybe Gregory Peck. Actually, no—"

I scoff. "Don't tell me Mum's sucked you into watching those old movies?"

Lizzie smiles, and Mum says, "Those are classics. I'm reliving my youth. They say it keeps you young." She leans in and winks at me. "Keeps you alive." Sitting back, she looks me over, lips a tight smile, eyes delighted. "Anyway, doesn't matter what he looks like when he's making you look this happy."

Lizzie and Mum both stare at me, grinning, and my face grows hot. I dip my head and tuck my hair behind my ear. Mum strokes my cheek with the back of her hand, her skin cool against mine. "It's okay to be happy, Aries." Out of nowhere a lump expands in my throat and I try to swallow it down. "I want you to be. I'm not afraid of dying—"

"Mum, please."

But Mum's attention is on the door, where Matt is standing, leaning against the frame. Not even the threat of tears pricking my eyes can blind me to how incredibly handsome he is.

"You really should be in the movies," Mum says to him.

I cover my eyes with my hand and groan. *She did not just say that.*

Matt frowns. "Thank you... I think. Can I get anyone a cup of tea?" For some unknown reason, we all laugh and he looks at us like we're a bunch of unruly groupies, which makes it even funnier.

"I like him," Mum whispers. "He's got a little anger though..." She waves her hand in the air, indicating Matt's heart area. "But that can all be released, with a little work."

Matt gives me a quizzical look, aware Mum is talking about him but clearly unable to hear what she's saying. I'm glad because he'd think her energy chat is insane. I shrug in a '*I can't control my mother, but I love her*' type way.

"Tea for everyone, then," he says before he turns towards the kitchen. A moment later, I hear him fill the kettle and flip it on, opening cupboards and searching for mugs.

There's something delightful about a small house. You can walk inside as a total stranger and know your way round in ten steps. And oddly enough, it feels even more like home knowing Matt is in the next room.

30
MATT

After we've finished tea and eaten half a packet of cheap biscuits, Aries excuses herself to use the bathroom, leaving me with her mother. Mrs McClennon is younger than I expected, but her illness has drained her. She's putting on a good show, smiling and laughing, but I can tell she's already wiped out. I feel a bit bad for having sprung this visit on everyone, but when I called last night, she sounded delighted by the idea.

Lizzie, the carer, is arranging flowers on the table, paying us no attention.

The house smells like a yoga studio, and incense puffs away from a slowly dwindling joss stick on the dining table. There are more crystals in here than have any right to exist in one house. On every table there are little circles of the damn things, like Mrs McClennon has been casting spells with them. I've never been in a house like this, but it's exactly the kind of place I would have imagined for Aries. From the outside, it looks totally ordinary, but inside, it's bursting with magic.

Mrs McClennon stares at me, saying nothing.

Fuck, this is awkward. I'm tensing up, and not even the heavy scent of incense is calming me. I'm pretty sure the whole point of incense is to put you at ease. Doesn't fucking work, not when Aries' Mum is inspecting me like I'm in a display case. A fucking taxidermy of a man.

What is she searching for? She's staring so intently that she can't possibly just be examining my suit, my shoes, my face. It's as though she's seeing right through to the core of my being; my thoughts and feelings and emotions, and assessing every single one. I'm not sure anyone has ever paid as close attention to me as this woman is doing now.

The only sound in the room is the clock on the wall. I hadn't noticed it ticking before, but now each movement of the second hand is thunderously loud. I break eye contact with Mrs McClennon to look up at it. On the large, cream face is written, 'Relax. Time is an illusion'.

"It is, you know," Mrs McClennon says, and I turn back to find her piercing blue eyes still fixed on me. "An illusion. All we have is the ever present now. No past, no future."

I clench my teeth to stop my eye-roll in its tracks and then have the almost irresistible urge to check the time on my watch. I dig my fingertips into my thigh to prevent it. "Right." The word spins out, elongated, like I think she's a madwoman. "You should get rid of the clock then."

Fuck. Shouldn't have said that.

I begin to worry I've offended her when a cacophony of phlegmy laughter sounds from her mouth. "You're something."

I have no idea what to say to that. I'm not even sure she expects a response. Her tone is assessing, as if she's weighing me up and finding me... not quite wanting, but something less than complete. It's unnerving. If she were anyone else, I would have walked away already, or at least told her to stop staring. As it is, I'm sitting here waiting for her to give me some insight into her thoughts while simultaneously hoping Aries returns before she says anything else.

She leans towards me, eyes suddenly serious. "You'll be good to my wee girl, won't you?"

My heart performs an awkward kick-start. "Yes."

"Good." She waves a bony-fingered hand at my chest, her eyes going all unfocused. "You've got stuff trapped here. Pain. Sadness. Anger."

I sit back a little in the chair. I didn't like the way she was examining me before, but this is worse. It's like she's sliced into me and is checking through the layers of my body. "Doesn't everyone?"

"Some. Most, probably. But not everyone." She slurps at her tea. It must be cold by now. "It's hard, if you've had a lot of disappointment in life. We build walls. Block people out. Some people never take them down."

What the fuck is she talking about? Is she still talking about me, or people in general? I have no clue.

"It can be hard to let go of the pain," she adds.

My body grows rigid. I'm not comfortable with this. I glance at the door. *Where the fuck is Aries?*

"She's strong, you know. Passionate. A true Aries." Mrs McClennon laughs. "My little ram." Then her lips form a tight line. "But she's not strong enough for both of you."

Jesus. What the fuck is this conversation? Even Lizzie over by the table has grown still, listening in.

"You have to feel your own pain, Mr Hawkston. Release it. She can't do that for you. She's a wonderful girl, but she's not a solution. Not a bandage for all your wounds."

"I'm not... that's not what... Christ, I'm not expecting Aries to fix me. Is that what you're getting at here?" Frustration simmers beneath my skin, and at the same time an awareness surfaces that this is exactly what this woman is talking about. I inhale, long and slow, then exhale the same way. My fingers tighten on the arms of the chair.

Mrs McClennon sits back, her expression softening. "Let me help you."

I scoff, and when her eyes widen, I immediately regret it. "Sorry. I don't need help."

"You do." Her voice is gentle, but there's an edge to it that has the hair on the back of my neck rising. A noise sounds out in the hall. Thank fuck, Aries must be coming back. "No. Really, I'm fine."

"Bullshit." The word catches me off guard, my breath stalling in my throat for a second. Lizzie glances over at us, like a dog hearing a shot in the distance, then goes back to arranging the flowers. "I'm dying, Mr Hawkston. You can faff and bluster around as much as you want, avoiding the truth. Your time is your time. Your now is your now. But it doesn't pay for me to waste mine not saying what I mean. Aries likes you. A lot. I can sense it, and I don't want to leave this world knowing I didn't do everything or say everything to protect my only child. So shut up and listen to me."

Wow. This woman's directness is so intense that I want to laugh, but not because it's funny. It's overwhelming, and laughter would be a release. And yet, her directness is not surprising at all. Aries is such a live-wire that she must have been raised by someone with spunk. "All right. I'm listening."

"Do you give me permission to send you healing, every night until I die?"

A shiver ripples through my whole body. "I'm not sure what you're offering."

"You don't have to do anything. Nothing at all. You won't even know. I just need your permission to work in your energy field."

This is a load of fucking rubbish. As if this woman could have any impact on me from up here, across the border, when I'm back home.

"It's like prayer," she adds, evidently having taken my silence as confusion. "Can I pray for you?"

Might as well humour her. "Sure. Whatever. If you want to."

"Excellent." She clasps her skeletal hands together and rests them in her lap. "Thank you."

Just then, the door opens, and Aries, all beautiful smiles and red hair, comes back in. "What are you two talking about?" she asks, glancing suspiciously between the two of us.

"I think your mother was reading my energy," I tell her, unable to keep the ridicule out of my voice and the scepticism off my face.

"Ah. Was it awful, Mum?"

Mrs McClennon's eyes gleam, her thin lips almost smiling. "No. Not at all, actually."

The answer surprises me and, if I'm not mistaken, delights me too because a smile is stretching my mouth. Even if all this talk of energy and healing is way beyond anything I'm familiar with, or would ever take seriously, she's still Aries' mother, and if me being 'not awful' is the best she can come up with, then I'll take it.

"Not awful," Aries muses. "That's just what I think too." She grins at me, and any lingering irritation I feel fades away entirely.

"Oh, good," I deadpan, exaggerating an eye roll.

"Yes." Aries walks towards me and kisses me on the mouth. Not explicitly. It's chaste, even, but I can feel the thrum of passion behind it. "Very good." She brings her mouth to my ear and whispers, "She likes you. I can tell."

Mrs McClennon's sharp eyes are on me, even as Aries' breath is cooling against my neck. Her gaze is watchful, but not unkind. As if she knows I'm trying to work her out, she winks and smiles, and unbidden, I laugh.

"Maybe," I whisper back to Aries.

"Definitely."

And again that unnerving warm sensation flows through me as though, in spite of everything Mrs McClennon said and warned me against, Aries is shining light into my darkest corners, healing parts of me I've long kept hidden.

I want to cling to her, hold her against me, and make this sensation of wholeness last as long as I fucking can.

31
ARIES

We've settled into a rhythm of sorts, now we're all back in the London house. We have slightly less sex because Matt's still worried about Charlie finding out, given his bedroom is up on the top floor with me and Lucie. Matt won't come anywhere near my space, and I can tell he's anxious if I go to his room.

The distance only makes me long for him. Each secret touch at the table or in the hall is charged with electricity that could bring the house down. I know he feels it, because he grabs me when no one's around and whispers things like, "God, I want to fuck you. Can I?"

Sometimes, I laugh. Other times, if we can steal a moment, we do exactly that. Fuck. Hard and fast. So damn satisfying. In the pantry, a cupboard, the boot room. Reckless, but addictive. And every time we do, I feel my heart opening that little bit more.

I know to the core of my being that Mum's statement—*You don't like men*—doesn't hold up anymore. Because this man—Matthew Hawkston—I like very, *very* much. I'm fiercely attached to him in every way; spiritually, emotionally and, of course, physically. I just haven't managed to admit it yet. I've come close, but I haven't come out and told him I'm falling in love with him. Have fallen, perhaps. Just the thought makes me feel both vulnerable and buoyant, as though I'm floating on a cloud that could vanish at any moment.

Today, Lucie and I are in the park, waiting for Charlie's tennis camp to finish. Ordinarily, he walks himself home, but this afternoon Lucie wanted to come down here to play, so I figured we might as well pick him up. I'm trying to put the whole affair with Matt out of my mind, but it's not working. October first. That's the end game, but I really don't know what the end game means. I push Lucie on the swing, half a mind on how we'll explain to a four-year-old that I'm... what? Her daddy's girlfriend?

I'm keeping an eye on the time, so after negotiating Lucie off the swing, we head down to the tennis courts. We're a little late, and for a moment I wonder if we've missed Charlie entirely. Then I catch sight of him off to one side, with two other boys. They're bigger than Charlie, both in height and breadth; older than him too.

I frown. There's something about the interaction that doesn't look altogether friendly. They're jostling him between them, shoving him from each side. It reminds me of something I can't place, but whatever it is, it makes me feel uncomfortable.

Maybe it's just banter. Joking around.

"Come on, Lucie, let's get a bit closer." She takes my hand and we traipse down the grassy bank to the courts.

Charlie and the boys have their backs to us, but one of the boys turns sideways and I get a glimpse of his profile.

I recognise him instantly from Charlie's Speech Day. One of the Charlton twins—the sons of the man Charlie's mum is dating. It takes me a fraction of a second to realise the other boy is the twin.

As I watch the interaction, my mind whirs. Charlie said the kids who beat him up had left school. The knowledge that I withheld the incident from Matt churns malevolently in my mind. I'd managed to convince myself I didn't need to say anything because it was over, and I'd promised Charlie I wouldn't. Stupid, maybe. But I did it. Now, seeing the way they're shoving him, I know it's not over, and I'm certain that these are the kids who beat Charlie up.

He isn't fighting back. He's taking it, his body limp, resigned, his tennis racket dangling from one hand as the two older boys shove him between them.

Anger rises in me, and I find myself letting go of Lucie's hand, bidding her to stay put, as I rush towards Charlie.

One of the boys shoves him, harder this time, and the other grabs him by the shoulders when he's doubled over and brings his knee up into his chest.

"Hey," I yell. "Stop that."

The boys look at me, and the twins release Charlie, who stands upright, wiping the back of his hand across his mouth. *Is he bleeding?*

"Well, look who it is," one of them says, grinning at me, and my skin crawls at the sleaze in his tone. *Why is he speaking to me like that?*

Charlie's staring at me like he wishes the ground would swallow me up.

"Saved by a girl, eh, Charlie?" the other says.

"By a slut, more like," the first one adds.

Shock bolts through me. *What the fuck?* Whatever I was expecting when I raced down here to protect Charlie, it wasn't a slut-shaming. Something jabs in the back of my mind, like a fragment of memory I can't hold onto.

Charlie's fingers clench around his tennis racket.

"Yeah," the same twin continues, nodding at me. "Saw you with your hand down Mr Hawkston's trousers in Covent Garden."

Oh, fuck.

It slots into place. The weight of doom that's been in my gut since we saw those kids in Covent Garden. The face, the *eyes*, of that boy in the street...

"You know she's fucking your dad, right?" He starts to laugh as Charlie's cheeks blanch and his eyes widen in a question I don't want to answer.

I glance over my shoulder. Lucie's tottering down the bank towards me.

Shit.

"Yeah. Hand right down his fucking trousers," says the other, joining in with a disgusting grin that makes the contents of my stomach curdle, and I press a hand to my belly. *Am I going to throw up?*

Charlie still isn't speaking. He's staring at me, then at the two Charlton boys, like there is no safe place for him.

One of them jolts him, pushing his shoulder and Charlie stumbles a few steps to the side with no resistance, as if their words about me and his dad have leeched all the strength right out of him.

"Touch him again, and I'll call the police," I say, stepping right up to them. All three of them are bigger than me, and my heart is racing so fast it might explode.

One of the twins snorts a laugh, then deliberately looks me up and down. "Got to hand it to him though," he says, tossing a wink over his shoulder at Charlie. "He's a lucky bastard, your dad. I'd do her." He turns back to me. "If you're switching things up for a younger model, I'm game."

"Does he pay you extra?" says the other.

Heat floods my body, but I try my best to ignore it, looking directly at Charlie when I say, "We're leaving. Now."

One of the twins takes a step towards me, and I steel myself, planting my feet on the ground. "Don't come any closer." He halts at my words and cocks his head in amusement. "What you're doing here is not acceptable. Harassing another boy. Leave him alone."

The twins are smirking, but my speech seems to be the final straw for Charlie. He slams his racket onto the ground and marches up the grassy bank towards Lucie.

The twins' mocking gaze runs over me. It's so invasive that each sweep of their eyes is like a grabbing touch I haven't consented to. I bend to pick up the racket, feeling vulnerable in this position. They're laughing, muttering words I can't discern. My body is on fire. I'm angry and humiliated and the pit of doom in my belly is growing ever larger by the second, swelling with the sensation that I've fucked up on multiple counts.

"You're fit as fuck, you know that?" calls one of the twins.

I need to get away. My heart is pounding. Out of the corner of my eye, I swear I see one of them coming towards me. If he fucking touches me, I'll scream.

I run to catch up with Charlie, leaving the twins back by the tennis courts. I can still hear them laughing, but I'm focused only on Charlie. He doesn't acknowledge me, but his scowl is enough to communicate that he's aware I'm right beside him.

"Are they the boys who beat you up?" Charlie says nothing, so I try again. "Charlie? Was it them?"

He keeps walking, and I hurry my steps to keep up, then suddenly he stops and turns to me. Lucie's still a few paces away, her little worried face evidence that she knows whatever's going on isn't good. I want to pick her up and reassure her, but Charlie feels like the most pressing issue right now.

"Are you?" he spits. His breaths are fast and angry, his entire torso heaving with the force of them. My blood beats a heavy pulse, and for a few seconds, it's all I'm aware of. That, and Charlie's ferocious glare bearing down on me. "Are you fucking my dad?" he hisses, just as Lucie reaches us and grabs my hand.

"Can we go home?" she pleads, looking anxiously between me and Charlie.

"Yes, honey," I tell her, giving her hand a squeeze.

Charlie rolls his eyes, then fixes his gaze back on me. Hard. Angry. "Are you going to answer the question?"

Lucie's tiny fingers grip tighter to mine at the furious resonance in her brother's voice.

I take a deep breath. "This is a conversation you should have with your dad—"

"Oh, my God." His hands come to either side of his face before falling away just as fast. "You are. You're fucking him," he cries, then storms off before I can reprimand him for his language.

"Why did Charlie use the f-word?" Lucie whispers, tugging on my hand. I turn to see her big brown eyes peering up at me.

"He had a bad day at tennis camp," I say, adding yet another lie to the mound I've already told.

We turn and follow Charlie as he marches up Kensington High Street like a thundercloud, me and Lucie trailing behind.

Halfway up the street, Charlie stops again, then marches forward, then stops. It's as if the intensity of whatever thoughts are passing through his mind drive him on, then hold him back, alternately gripping and letting go. Shoppers and pedestrians begin swerving him, casting him confused looks. As if he knows we've nearly reached him, he spins round.

"Why?" he yells. "Why did you do it? Is it the money?"

"What? No. Of cour—"

"Do you think he's going to marry you or something? Because he won't."

I haul Lucie into my arms, settling her on my hip because she can't keep up with Charlie's pace, and hurry forward until I'm alongside him.

"This is not appropriate," I whisper-hiss. "Not in front of Lucie. And not in the street."

"Ha!" Charlie's voice is loud and brash. "And jerking my dad off in the middle of Covent Garden is appropriate?"

Fuck. *Fuck, fuck, fuck.*

People are actively staring now, appalled at the scene. My throat is swelling, and tears well up behind my eyes as Lucie burrows her head into my shoulder. I feel so helpless, so stupid... so completely ashamed that I'm at a loss as to what to do.

"Charlie, please. Let's get back to the house. We can talk then."

He laughs, but the sound is bitter. "I actually thought you were nice. Maybe Mrs Minter picked a good nanny this time. But no. Just another gold-digging slut."

Each word off his tongue is like another strike of the whip, flaying bits of my heart. I don't even know what to say to defend myself.

"That's not true," I reply eventually, restraining the urge to fight back. This isn't what he thinks it is, and I want to yell that in his face.

I force myself to remember that Charlie's a boy... One who feels betrayed by his dad. By me. By every adult figure he's had in his life. This isn't personal. But his words cut like a blade honed specifically for me.

"I'm sorry." There's a tremor in my voice. It's pathetic, and I hate it, but I can't hold it steady. "But it's not like that. You don't know what's going on. I like your dad. This isn't some seedy—"

"Oh, fuck off." He rolls his eyes hard and tosses his hair off his forehead, scowling at me before continuing his march down the street.

Panic sears through me, but I try not to let it show as Lucie's arms tighten around my shoulders.

"He said a bad word again," she says. "He's just like Daddy."

And I swear, a piece of my heart actually breaks right off and drops onto the street like a lost button. No matter how hard I look for it, I know I'll never find it.

32
MATT

The minute I step into the kitchen, I know something's wrong. It's late, so Lucie must be asleep, but Charlie and Aries are sitting opposite one another at the table in complete silence. Aries' forearms are on the table, her head hangs low, a curtain of red hair hiding her expression. Charlie is glaring at her.

The sight makes my heart drop. "What's going on?"

Aries' hair ripples like she's shaking her head, and when she looks up what I see in her face makes my heart plummet right through the fucking floor. Her eyes are ringed with red like she's been crying, or wants to cry and hasn't let the tears fall. Her normally flawless skin is red and blotchy. She touches her lips with her fingertips.

"Is anyone going to answer me?" The question drags rough along my tongue, because I'm pretty sure I don't want to hear anything they're going to tell me.

Charlie's jaw flexes, and I know he has no intention of speaking to me.

"Aries?" I ask.

She raises those big, beautiful green eyes at me. "Covent Garden..." are all the words she manages.

A horrible pressure swells in my chest as I try to sift through possible explanations. There's no way Charlie was in Covent Garden. He couldn't have seen us. He was at home with Alec. I know for sure because Alec sent me pictures of the two of them playing Mario Kart in the cinema room downstairs. And Charlie was asleep when we got back. If not Charlie, then who?

Shit.

The group of boys who kicked cans at us. I frown, trying to remember their faces, but it was so dark, and I'd been more worried about Aries than anything else.

And then, like a cruel flash of lightning in a midnight sky, I remember. "Ben Charlton?"

Aries swallows and says, "Yes. And Hugo. Both of them."

Charlie pushes his chair away from the table and tosses me a scowl that looks like he wants to murder me and feed my body piece by piece to the pigeons.

"Fuck you, Dad. Fuck. You," he spits, before striding up to me, his shoulder glancing mine as he pushes past.

The impact jolts me, but I don't shift. Instead, I grab him by the shoulder, and although he tries to shrug me off, he can't. "Watch your language. Do you want to talk, or do you want to run away?"

"The latter."

"Tough. Sit down." I can hear the threat in my voice, and Charlie resentfully holds my gaze, me physically pinning him in place, until the resistance in his muscles melts, and he takes his seat opposite Aries.

Silence crackles around the table as I take a seat too. My heartbeat throbs around my body, the rush of blood so loud in my ears I feel dizzy.

"This isn't how I wanted you to find out," I say. "I'm deeply sorry. But Aries and I..." I break off, searching for the right words, but all that come to mind are inappropriate phrases that would only add crap to this shitfest.

A wry chuckle sounds from Charlie. "I'm not a child, Dad. I get it. And I don't care."

"You don't?"

He shakes his head. "No. I don't care what you do. But I do care that you gave the Charlton twins another reason to..." His voice fades.

"To what?"

Charlie says nothing, his eyes flicking to Aries, but this time it looks like he's pleading with her for help.

"They beat him up," she says. "After the boat race. Said it was his fault they lost. Because of Lucie falling in. Because Charlie jumped out the boat. Because—"

"You knew about this?"

Aries nods, closes her eyes and drags a hand through her long hair. "I only found out who did it today..." She falters, pinning her bottom lip with her teeth as tears well in her eyes. It takes a few seconds before she can continue. "But I knew he'd been beaten up before that."

Before? She fucking knew before? How could she have kept something like this from me? "How long?"

"Since the holiday." Her voice is weak; a little broken. "On the boat."

Fucking hell. I'm torn between wanting to hold Charlie in my arms and yell at Aries for hiding this. *What was she thinking?* "Why didn't you tell me?"

Charlie scoffs. "Like you'd give a fuck."

"If they hurt you, I care. How often was it happening? At school?"

"Yes, at school," Charlie says. "And often enough."

"The weed?" I ask.

"Yes," Charlie says. "They planted it. Made it look like it was mine."

This is a total shitshow. "Why didn't you tell anyone? Why didn't you say something? Barney called me. Said he thought something was wrong."

Charlie stiffens, just slightly. He says nothing.

"We can sort this out," I reassure him, straining to keep my anger in check. Charlie doesn't need me losing it right now. "I'll speak to your mother."

Charlie drags breaths through flared nostrils. "She definitely won't give a shit. I don't want you to do anything about it. I'm fine. This is why I didn't tell you in the first place. Do you really think anything you can do or say is going to make a difference? You only make things worse. Like this." He waves a hand between me and Aries, disgust warping his lips. "Can I go now?"

I know I shouldn't let him swear at me, or talk about his mother like that, even though she deserves every word of it. But I don't feel like I can reprimand him... not when my actions have caused him pain. Not when I've allowed my feelings for Aries to dictate my behaviour.

And he has a point; not to excuse the twins, but my recklessness, my *infatuation* with Aries, gave them fodder to tease my son. If I felt like a bad father before, I feel worse now.

All that sneaking around... hiding it all from him on the boat... on the holiday. What was the point? Maybe we should've come clean back then. Or not done it at all.

And the whole time she was keeping something this important from me...

"Can I go?" Charlie repeats.

I nod my head and Charlie gets up.

Aries shrivels in her seat, and the sight of her makes anger boil in my blood, but it's tempered by the acidic flavour of disappointment, eating away at my organs like a bitter type of sadness. *How could she have hidden this from me?* If she respected me, cared about me, wouldn't she have told me?

I wait until Charlie's footsteps have disappeared up the stairs before I speak. "Your job is to take care of my kids," I say, very, *very* slowly. "You have a duty of care to them. To me. You've known someone was hurting my son for what... three weeks? A month?"

Aries' chin trembles and a single tear rolls down her cheek as she nods. "I'm sorry."

In spite of everything, all I want to do is wipe that tear from her face, hold her in my arms, and kiss her. *I want to make all of this go away.* But I can't, because this time, sorry isn't good enough. "Tell me everything."

She drags her eyes to mine, and I know whatever she's about to say she doesn't want to admit. "I walked in on him after you told me to bring him to breakfast on the deck. He was covered in bruises, but he promised me it would never happen again. That the boys who did it had left the school. He'd never see them again. He said it was over. I had no idea he was talking about Mark Charlton's kids. I didn't know it was boys he'd see again, boys he would have to live with when he stays with his mother. I wanted to tell you at the time, but you wouldn't let me talk. You swore at me in front of your brothers and Kate. I was angry with you. And when I went back to fetch Charlie, he wanted me to promise not to tell you. He didn't want to ruin the holiday. I didn't think..."

How could she hold this back? I close my eyes, fisting my left hand over my mouth. When I open my eyes again, Aries' tearful gaze meets mine. "I'm really trying not to lose my temper with you right now, but those excuses are paper fucking thin, Aries."

"I know." Tears are rolling freely down her cheeks. "I'm so sorry."

I sigh and run my tongue over my top teeth. "What happens now? What do I do now?"

She stares at me across the table, looking like she's about to shatter into a thousand pieces. "What do you mean?" she whispers.

Christ, I don't know what I mean. I don't know if I mean with Charlie or with her. With us. With her continuing to work in a role I'm not sure I can trust her to do.

I thought we were building something real here, but this feels like a betrayal.

My chest is tight, each breath a struggle it shouldn't be. "This was a bad call, Aries."

She swallows so hard I can see every muscle working up her neck. "I know."

"What were you thinking?"

She shakes her head, and strands of her hair catch the brutal gleam of the overhead lights, turning into burnished gold. "I'm sorry."

"It's Charlie's birthday party tomorrow," I say. "Let's just get through that, then we can sort this out properly."

"Okay." She stands, and as she passes me, her hand reaches out like she means to touch me, but she doesn't. Her hand falls to her side like she lost her nerve. "I made a mistake. I'm sorry."

"We both made a mistake."

Unspoken words hum in the air, and I know she's wondering the same fucking thing I am. *Is this such a huge breach of trust that we can't get beyond it? Is this over? Are we over?*

Every fibre of my being wants to reach out and pull her to me; tell her I don't care, that I want her more than this... need her more than this. But I can't because I'm not sure it's true anymore, and the thought breaks my fucking heart.

33
ARIES

*G**et through the party.*
   And then what?

I spent half of last night staving off the need to cry into my pillow, the other half tossing in light sleep that leaves me foggy-headed when I wake.

Why did I let a teenager eke a promise out of me that was not at all in his best interest, or mine now I come to think of it? I'd been so angry at Matt... so furious that he treated me so badly in front of his family that I neglected my duty. But in my defence, Charlie had been very convincing, and I hadn't wanted to sour the holiday either.

Today, that sense of doom that has been plaguing me since Covent Garden is shackled round my ankles, weighing me down. I messed up. It was a massive error in judgment and I'm surprised Matt hasn't fired me.

Maybe that's what he meant by '*Get through the party'*. Get through the party, and then I'll fire you. My mind's been so off the job, I've left Lucie settled in front of the cinema screen watching The Little Mermaid again while I help Alec with party preparations for later.

"What's wrong?" Alec says as he adds the finishing touches to the birthday cake. "You look beyond miserable."

Matt's words rattle around in my empty skull, even as I try to stay present and focus on Alec. *We both made a mistake.*

What does he mean? Does he think we... *us*... is a mistake? Am I his mistake?

I force a smile. "It's nothing."

He raises an eyebrow. "Like hell it is. Is it him? Is it Mr Hawkston? Need me to have a word?" He puffs out his chest like he can be man enough to stand up to Matt Hawkston, but a smile teases at his lips, and I know he'd never dare.

"Thanks, but I'll be okay."

He adds a final icing flourish to the cake and stands back to admire his work. It's an epic two-tier cake that looks more like a wedding cake than a birthday cake.

On top, it says *Happy 17th Birthday Charlie* in a gorgeous chocolate icing scrawl.

"Help me lift it into the pantry?" he says.

"No way. I can't be responsible for something like that."

"Come on. I can't leave it out here. Lucie will stick her fingers in it," he says.

I laugh and help him move the cake. We place it down on the table in the pantry, and I eye it greedily. "Maybe if I take a small bite, right here"—I dip my head down to one side—"no one will notice."

Alec grins and swipes at my hand, which is reaching out to the cake. "Get your hands—"

"Sleeping with the nanny. Really classy, Matthew. Really fucking classy."

Gemma's voice cuts through Alec's words, and the two of us freeze. Her footsteps click down the stairs, followed by Matt's heavier ones.

Alec's eyes go wide, and he holds a finger to his lips, using his other hand to pull the door of the pantry closed a little more so we're concealed.

"Not that it's any of your business." Matt's deep, serious voice seeps through the gap in the door, caressing me like his touch. I can't see them through the gap, but their voices are so clear I know they're just outside. "But it's over."

It's over?

The words drive a blade through my windpipe. I'm choking and gasping all at once, but trying my hardest to do neither while Alec is standing right next to me. Shock spirals into sadness, tugging me down like an undercurrent I didn't expect. I cover my mouth with my cupped hand.

I will not cry. I will *not* cry.

"I'm glad to hear it. I assume you'll let her go? You aren't intending to continue seeing the girl after you fire her, are you?"

"Mmm," is Matt's only reply.

"I sincerely hope not. Because—"

"Gemma, this is none of your fucking business."

"I disagree. Mark's boys saw the two of you fumbling in public like horny school children. That directly affects me. It has an impact on my life." Gemma blows out an exasperated sigh. "A hand job, in the middle of Covent Garden. You're a grown man, Matthew. With a public profile. You're lucky it was only the twins and not some member of the paparazzi. Or the police. It's disgraceful."

I can feel Alec's attentive stare and I use both hands to cover my eyes. I can't bear the scrutiny. In the darkness, Alec's hand falls to my shoulder, and he pulls me towards him, enveloping me in a hug. He's scrawny compared to Matt, and he smells like buttercream icing and flour, but the comfort his hold gives me is exactly what I need. I cling to him, desperately trying to stave off the tears prickling behind my eyelids.

"I don't owe you an apology if that's what you're waiting for," Matt says. "And speaking of Mark's boys, they've been bullying Charlie. He was black and blue at the end of term."

"Pffft, what a load of nonsense. The boys wouldn't touch a hair on Charlie's head. Who told you that?"

"Aries. Charlie confirmed it."

"I absolutely don't believe it. The boys are angels. They adore Charlie. In fact, they've made him a cake for this afternoon."

Alec pulls back from me, gesturing at the elaborate cake he's slaved over and mouthing, '*What the fuck*?', his face twisting with exaggerated outrage.

Why on earth would they have baked him a cake? Nothing feels right about that scenario...

The doorbell sounds.

"Ah," Gemma says. "They're here. I'll have them put the cake upstairs."

Panic roars loud and clear. We cannot serve that cake to Charlie. I'd bet my life on it they've poisoned the bloody thing with strawberry jam, hoping Charlie will have an allergic reaction.

Before I can think twice, I'm slamming out of the pantry, Alec's desperate hand clutching at air in an attempt to stop me.

"No." The word explodes, crazed and uncontrolled.

Both Gemma and Matt turn to look at me. Matt's anguished gaze meets mine, then shifts over my shoulder to the pantry. His face hardens as Alec steps out sheepishly.

Gemma guffaws. "Looks like you aren't that special after all, Matthew." Her gaze drifts lazily over my form. "Your little nanny here clearly likes to cop a feel of any man in the vicinity."

Matt's eyes flutter closed a fraction of a second too long, but I'm not going to be deterred by whatever mistaken idea he has about what I've been doing hiding in the pantry with Alec.

"You can't serve the cake the twins made," I blurt. "Alec's made a beautiful one. And those boys... they'll have filled it with strawberries." Gemma's eyes pop, and I turn to Matt. "I swear it, Matt. The bruises on Charlie, you ought to have seen them—"

"If you'd told me, I would have," Matt says, his voice slow and deep and full of a rumbling menace.

I should back down right now. Run away. But I don't. "There's no way they'd bake a cake that'll be any good."

Gemma cackles, casting her gaze to Matt. "She's delusional. If you think for a second I'd let the boys make a cake with strawberries in it for Charlie, then you're just as mad." Her voice is light, frothy, like all this is inconsequential. "Where is the birthday boy, anyway?" When no one responds, Gemma turns and heads up the stairs. "Guess I'll go and find him."

"Please, Matt. Serve Alec's cake," I plead when Gemma is gone, tilting my head to where Alec is still standing by the pantry door, his hands clasped before him.

Matt looks from me to Alec and back again. The cut of his jaw is so severe, it makes me want to weep. There isn't an ounce of softness in his expression. "You think those boys are going to poison my son?"

It sounds horrendous, what I'm accusing them off. They're barely adults, boys only just grown up, no matter how horrible they are.

"Yes."

He shakes his head, "Fuck, Aries." The words hang on a slow exhalation, as though this is all too much for him. "Why didn't you tell me at the time?" I know he means on the boat, when I first saw the bruises. His voice is so full of sorrow that my heart aches for him. "Why didn't you tell me?"

"I'm telling you now."

He runs a hand through his thick, dark hair, leaving it casually tousled. He looks so sexy that even amidst the turmoil in my body, my attraction to him breaks through as strong as ever. I take the smallest step towards him, but he makes no move to close the distance between us.

"Is this... is this over?" My words come out sharp but fragile, like shards of glass. "You said it was over."

"Fuck." He drives both hands over his scalp, tugging fistfuls of dark hair. His harried gaze darts to Alec before settling on me, and I know he's uncomfortable that this is being witnessed. "I don't know. I'm not going to tell Gemma what's going on, am I? None of her fucking business."

This does nothing to reassure me and my heart races in a wild panic. *I'm losing him.* I can't stand still, but I don't know where to go. What to do with my hands, my arms, my feet. Everything is shaking. "Matt, please—"

"Stop. Not now." He swallows, his eyes like stone. Then, without another word, he follows his ex-wife back up the stairs.

I can't breathe, I can't think. I want to rush up the stairs after him.

A heavy silence descends, broken only when Alec whispers, "Did you really toss him off in the middle of Covent Garden?"

34
MATT

The cake sits high and proud on the dining room table. A catastrophic three-tier leaning tower of vanilla icing. It looks like a lump of wax that's been attacked with a blow torch. The twins stand either side of it, grinning like a pair of fucking idiots. I can barely take it in because my thoughts keep returning to Aries.

Is this... is this over?

"Isn't it great?" Gemma says, waving at the iced monstrosity, her gaze flicking between me and the cake, waiting for some kind of reaction.

I say nothing, and Gemma brushes past me, calling up the stairs. "Charlie, get down here. Come and see the cake the twins made for you."

There's no response from upstairs, and as we wait for Charlie, my attention settles on Mark Charlton, who's standing with his sons, staring at me. *Why the fuck are they here so early?*

Mark has this look on his face that makes bile rise up my throat... It's like he's secretly delighted by something he knows I won't like and is bursting to talk about it.

"You brought the whole family?" I query, displeasure evident in my tone. "The party's not for hours."

"Of course. We wanted to bring the cake in person," Gemma replies. "The boys were keen to be here to witness Charlie's reaction."

The silence that follows crackles with tension. Unfortunately, it's Mark Charlton who breaks it.

"Hear you gave the boys an eyeful," he says, all friendly jocularity, but I know there's a viper beneath the words. *Fucking arsehole*. I scowl at him, warning him to stop, but Mark can't read the room for shit. "Lost all sense of decorum in the presence of a good pair of tits, did you?" He chortles like we're all in on a good joke. This is why the prick is here. This is the reaction he's been wanting to see. Nothing to do with Charlie and the fucking birthday cake. "Not that I blame you. She's quite the looker, that nanny of yours. Where can I get one for the boys?"

There's a leery smile on his face. The twins chuckle too, their awful laughs and smarmy smiles replicas of their dad's. The three of them standing there grinning at me like skittles waiting to be knocked down.

Anger rushes through me so violently that a pulse starts beating just above my left cheekbone. An irritating twitch in my peripheral vision.

Footsteps distract me from the Charltons. I turn to find Aries standing in the doorway. *Did she hear what they said?* My stomach tightens at the thought.

"Here she is," Mark announces, eyes brightening as he looks over my shoulder. "How much extra do you charge for a hand job? Or is it an all-inclusive package?"

Charlie appears in the doorway, but none of us acknowledge him hovering there like a ghost.

"Mark," Gemma exclaims, feigning shock, but I know she's amused. Enjoying the spectacle, even. "Do behave."

Mark laughs aloud, and the rage I've been struggling to control bursts through me. Before I know it, I'm on the other side of the table, grabbing the grey-haired arsehole round the neck.

I push him against the wall and his hands flap, his face a caricature of alarm. "Apologise to her, Charlton. Or you'll lose your teeth." My voice is hard and raw; unfamiliar.

My fingers are crushing the man's windpipe. He's turning red, eyes popping, little red veins spreading over the whites, but I don't give a fuck. It's satisfying to see the prick frightened like this.

"Matthew!" Gemma's sharp cry has me digging my fingers tighter into his throat. "Get off him. Let go."

I'm lost to the fucking rage, the frustration, the idea that this man's kids have hurt mine. *He deserves it.*

"Matt." Aries's voice is calm, her small hand daring to rest on my forearm. I don't know how or when she got so close to me. I glance down at her tiny fingers against my sleeve, then up to my own large ones, still wrapped around Mark's throat. "That's enough."

Her presence soothes me like nothing else in the world could. My body softens and I step back, flexing my fingers and wiping my palm on my trousers.

Mark lurches forward, spluttering, a hand to his neck.

The twins close in on either side of their father, propping him up. I know my anger should be directed at them too, but they're teenagers. Barely older than Charlie, although they look like men.

"What the hell are you doing?" Gemma squeaks. "You lunatic."

"He was being disrespectful." I glare at Mark, who's still coughing, hand still resting on his throat. Between his fingers, the skin is red, and I feel a disturbing flush of satisfaction at the sight. "Did you know your sons have been attacking Charlie at school? Beating him up? Bullying him?" I snarl at Mark.

He coughs, bent over, and looks up at me. "What are you talking about?"

"He came home at the end of term covered in bruises. They did it." I nod at the twins.

Charlie's probably furious that I'm raising all this so publicly, but I don't look at him to check. I should, I know I should. I ought to have consulted him before I started spouting off, but it's too fucking late now.

"Dad—" he begins.

"Cut the cake," I say, jerking my chin at the cake.

"What? Matthew, no. Don't be crazy about this," Gemma says. "The cake is fine. Don't cut it yet. The party— "

"Cut the fucking cake," I roar, and somehow Alec is scuttling forward with a cake knife, holding it out but he doesn't know who to give it to and I don't know either.

"Matt, please," Aries hisses, tugging on my arm. "Let's talk about this."

Somehow the cake knife is in Charlie's hand and he's stepping up to cut the world's ugliest cake. He glances at me and I nod. *Cut the damn thing.*

"He's lost his fucking mind," one of the twins mutters, and I know he's speaking about me, but I'm too enraged to even bother acknowledging it.

Charlie angles the cake knife over the cake; the blade trembles in his shaking grip.

"Are you sure about this?" I ask Gemma. "You're sure you trust those two little cunts?"

Gemma draws in a quick, fast breath. Then she nods.

Charlie grimaces, but he doesn't look at me again. He keeps his gaze on the cake. My heart is racing and my mind conjures memories of TV shows where bomb disposal units attempt to dismantle explosives, because that's exactly what this feels like. We're all waiting for disaster.

Charlie lowers the cake knife, letting it hover over the icing. It's only seconds, but it feels like eras go by before he presses it into the cake, digging through the mess of the icing, the metal disappearing into the sponge.

We're all holding our breaths, not a sound in the room but the tick of the grandfather clock in the corner.

Charlie raises the knife and makes another incision. He pulls the first slice out, revealing the interior of the cake. There isn't a hint of strawberry. Not anywhere. No jam at all.

It's a fucking sponge cake. Pale yellow butter-cream between the layers. There's nothing wrong with it.

Charlie breathes a sigh of relief, his upper body slumping as if the only thing keeping him upright was fear.

"Told you he'd lost his mind," one of the twins says in a stage whisper.

Gemma's jaw clenches, and she stares me down. "I think you owe the boys an apology."

All eyes are on me. Expectant. Waiting. "The fuck I do."

I slam my fist so hard into the cake the whole thing splits in half and icing splatters over everyone.

I storm out of the room and head to the basement. Raw fury fuels my every moment, burning through my veins like lit petrol. I don't even know who I'm angry at. Mostly myself, for going off like an idiot upstairs. I'd half hoped a shit ton of strawberries would pour out of the cake, just so my bout of madness might have been justified.

The self-hatred that's rolling around my head right now is unbearable. Mark Charlton's an arse, but I lost it over a cake because Aries put the idea in my head.

I check the time. I have three hours to cool off before I have to pretend to be the happy father of a newly seventeen-year-old. I don't know if Charlie will ever forgive me for making a scene like that. I can't think about it now, though.

I slam open the door to the gym and rip off my cake-covered t-shirt, throwing it to the floor. I go to the sink and wash the cake off my hand, my forearm, and scrub myself dry with a towel. I'm not dressed for a workout, but I kick off my loafers and turn on the treadmill, running in my bare feet and shorts. All I need right now is to blast away my anger, my frustration, and this is as good a way as any.

I've broken a sweat when I hear a knock on the door. I can see Aries's red hair through the glass. *What the fuck does she want?* I beckon her in and she pushes the door open, lingering on the threshold. She's so fucking beautiful, her face so full of remorse, that a deep soulful rage comes over me.

This woman... she's the reason everything's coming apart at the seams. Her hair, her face, her lips... God, the curves of her. Her smell, her taste...

I'm losing myself in her.

I slow down the treadmill and push my hair off my face. "What do you want?"

"We need to talk. I'm sorry. I panicked. I thought they'd try to hurt Charlie. I didn't want to fuck up again. I thought—"

"Don't fucking talk." I get off the treadmill, pacing towards her, reaching her in seconds. I pull her into the room, slamming the door behind her. "I've had enough of you talking." She gasps, but before she can speak I've pushed her against the wall. "Do you know how fucking angry I am?"

She shakes her head, blinking rapidly. "No," she whispers.

I press my body against hers and my cock begins to harden, desire pooling through the pit of rage that threatens to suck me up and spit me out. "Do you want me to show you how fucking angry I am?"

She nods, the tiniest whimper sliding out from between those full, pink lips. On her next breath, I press my lips to hers, kissing her hard, invading her mouth with my tongue, not giving her a second to rethink her answer. I fist a hand in her hair, gripping it tight, tugging so hard it must hurt, but she doesn't make a sound.

I force the kiss, deepen it, ravage her mouth with mine. The stubble on my jaw will make her skin raw, but I'm past caring. If I can take what I need from her, it might kill this obsession that's turning me into a monster.

She pulls back, speaking against my mouth. "You said it was over. You said—"

"How can it be over? You're in my fucking bloodstream, Aries. Every passing moment, you're there. In my mind, my head, my heart. *Fuck*. I can't get rid of you."

I kiss her again, hard. It's not romantic. Not careful. My hand fumbles at her jeans, hauling them halfway down her thighs with a rough yank. Every movement I make is full of rage. I slide my fingers between her legs, where she's already so wet, so slick, that I drive two fingers, three, into her with ease.

She wants me even when I hate her, even when I'm so mad I can't think straight.

I finger-fuck her, thrusting into her like I could tear her pussy apart.

Small moans burrow from her mouth into my shoulder, and I can't be sure they're pleasurable. I could be hurting her.

I freeze, Aries still between my arms, caged against the wall. My breathing is heavy, laboured from the run, from Aries, from not knowing if I want to fuck her or hurt her.

I pull back, watching her as I slowly slide my fingers out of her cunt, the slick sucking sounds of her wetness filling the gym. My dick is painfully hard, just as desperate for her as I am.

There are tears in her eyes, rolling down her cheeks. Her eyelashes are wet with them and mascara makes slippery tracks over her cheekbones.

"Did I hurt you?" I whisper, my voice sounding dangerously close to breaking.

She shakes her head, then strikes her heart with her fist. "Only here. I love you. I fucking love you."

Turmoil thrashes through my chest; a torment of feeling that blazes the rage right out of me. *How could I ever want to hurt this woman?*

I fucking love you.

Her eyes flicker anxiously over mine, and she must see something in my reaction because a sob breaks through and her shoulders shake. "Please Matt, please…" She digs her head into my shoulder, her hair rippling like she's shaking her head against me.

"Please what?" I murmur, amazed at how cool my voice sounds, even as some deep part of me splinters right along with her.

"Please fuck me. One last time. Please."

Her words wrench my heart right out of its resting place, tearing it up my throat. I don't know what's happening here. I don't know how everything got so out of control or why she's begging me. I don't know why she's calling this the last time or why it feels like it *is* with a cruel certainty that rings through my bones.

"Please," she whimpers.

I nod and slide her jeans to the floor so she can step out of them.

I ease my hard, aching cock free from my shorts and slide into her like she's the only place I've ever belonged. I thrust in and out, slow and gentle, and she clings to me, crying against my shoulder.

It's such a sweet, painful agony to feel pleasure while her heart is breaking. While mine is breaking. We're together but falling apart all at once, and the pain of it hovers just at the brink of bearable. I keep going, her hips grinding against mine, her swollen clit finding purchase against me until her orgasm finally explodes, her pussy pulsing around me, her juices running down her thighs, covering my dick.

She's so warm, so soft, and she smells so fucking good. I want to stay like this forever, holding her against my chest, feeling the swell of her breasts against me as she breathes. But even now, as a violent orgasm rockets along my shaft, spilling through my hips and up my spine, I know this is exactly what's wrong. I'm taking risks I shouldn't, lying to people, missing the signs my teenage son is being bullied, and then overreacting like I'm a brute with no self-control.

I press my forehead to hers, the two of us breathing in tandem, her confession of love hovering in the air, and mine unspoken on my tongue, like a pill I've yet to swallow. Physically, we're so close I can't tell whether the sweat that slicks her skin is hers or mine, but emotionally I've never felt further from her.

There's a canyon between us, and I don't know how to cross to the other side. I don't know how to pull her back, or if I even want to.

I slide out of her, fetching tissues from a dispenser on the wall and handing her some. Without meeting my eye, she cleans herself up, throws the tissues in the bin, and tugs on her jeans, all while I ache at the idea that this might be the last time I see her body. The last time I touch her. The last time I spend an intimate moment with her.

"You were right," she croaks. "We both made a mistake." She pulls the smartphone out of her pocket and holds it out to me along with the credit card I gave her that day at the Natural History Museum.

"What's this?" I question.

"I'm resigning. I can't stay here. There's no room for me in your life."

As I take them from her, a tingling numbness swells behind my lower ribs, spreading upwards. Beneath it, a core of pain. *You are my life.* "Your notice period..."

She shakes her head. "If you need me, I'll stay until you've found a replacement. But don't hold me to a notice period when we both know it'll be excruciating for me to stay in this house."

I don't contradict her. I can't.

Because this is already excruciating.

"The party. Stay for the party."

Aries nods. "Yes. Do you need me to stay longer?"

A lump, thick and heavy, lodges in my throat. I want to say yes. "No. Mrs Minter can get someone new for Monday."

"All right." She looks at her toes. Bare. Nails painted yellow like little suns. The sight of them sends a piercing pain right through me, and I clench my jaw to hold it back. Make sure it doesn't show.

"Where will you go?"

Her eyes are ringed with red, and she wipes at tears, smudging her mascara. Her lips press together, hiding their fullness as she shakes her head and backs out of the door. "Home. I'll go home."

35
MATT

Music is blasting from the speakers built into the ceilings. The house is full. A handful of Charlie's friends, surly teenagers with dubious facial hair and limbs too long for their scrawny bodies, stand awkwardly around the room, mingling with their parents, Charlie's godparents and our extended family: Nico, Seb, Kate and her brother Jack Lansen and his girlfriend. After I smashed the cake, Gemma, Mark and the twins left so that the staff could clean everything away and set up for the party. Now, Gemma and the twins are back, but not Mark. He, at least, had the decency to stay home.

Alec's cake is spectacular. Delicious too, but that's to be expected. Thank goodness he'd made it because what remained of the twins' cake wasn't salvageable.

Charlie looks miserable, and Lucie is clinging to Aries' legs like she knows this is their last evening together.

It's what I would be doing if I could. But here I am, dressed in a fucking tailored suit, drinking champagne with my ex-wife and pretending everything's all right on Charlie your-son-is-a-wreck's seventeenth birthday.

"Delicious cake," Seb mumbles as he stuffs another forkful into his mouth and chews it down. "Bloody good chef you've got."

I nod, but I don't care. I don't give a fuck about anything Seb says right now.

"She was home-schooled, you know," I say, although I don't know why.

Seb pauses, fork midway between his mouth and the plate. "Who was? What are you talking about?"

"Aries. Her mother educated her. On the road, mostly."

"No shit. That sounds like a hell of a lot of work." He stuffs another lump of cake in his mouth and swallows it down. "Maybe you should sack off the business and do it for Lucie." He chortles like the idea of me giving up my work to dedicate my life to Lucie is ridiculous. I suppose it is, and at the thought, pain pokes the inside of my chest like nails being hammered through my heart. I'll never be the type of parent that Mrs McClennon was to Aries. But Aries... she could be like that. She's devoted to my little girl, but leaving me means leaving Lucie too...

Shit. When Aries leaves, the heartbreak is going to resonate through my entire family...

Across the room, Charlie picks crumbs off his plate, popping them into his mouth one by one. He's chatting to a friend and his mother. Thank God he's at least engaging with people. That's got to be a good sign.

I glance back over at the door, where Aries was standing with Lucie only moments ago, but she's gone. It's seven thirty. Lucie's bedtime.

I'm a jangle of nerves. Aries is here, still inside my house, upstairs, putting my daughter to bed. But then she'll be gone. Whisked away north of the border to live a life without me in it. And I have to stand here and ignore the fact that it feels like my heart is falling out of me in a bloodied mess that no one else can see.

Hugo Charlton is moving across the room, glass of champagne in hand. He stops at Charlie, exchanges a few words, slaps him on the back and hands him the glass. Then he saunters off, looking delighted.

What the hell is he looked so chuffed about? A sinking sensation tugs at my gut.

Fuck. Aries has made me paranoid. I know I didn't see the bruises on Charlie's torso, but if the twins would do that to Charlie, how can anything they do be well meaning? Did they really bake him a fucking cake out of the goodness of their hearts? I doubt it. But there's no evidence to the contrary, and my explosion earlier made me look like the bad guy.

I grip the stem of my champagne glass and stride towards Charlie, leaving Seb sucking icing off his fork.

I step right into the middle of Charlie's conversation, not caring that I'm interrupting. My manners have gone to shit, if I ever had any in the first place. "Give me your glass," I order, taking Charlie's before he can object.

The friend and his mother are standing there, staring at me like I'm the jerk who has stood up and blocked the screen in the middle of the cinema.

"What the fuck, Dad?" Charlie hisses. This is as much as I've got out of him since I smashed the birthday cake, but I wasn't expecting more.

"Have mine," I say, swapping them over. "And don't drink more than one."

Then, without a word of apology or explanation, I take the drink and walk out of the room. Seb, still licking icing off his fork, calls after me, but I don't respond.

I pace down to the kitchen, setting the champagne glass on the granite-topped island. I place my palms flat either side of the glass and stare at it. Bubbles rise, non-stop streams, oblivious patterns. Meaningless.

Maybe I have gone mad. Lost the plot. *What the hell am I doing with Charlie's champagne? What do I think Hugo Charlton did to it?* Damn Aries and her panic. It's infected me. I'm itchy all over with it.

"You all right?"

I turn to find Jack Lansen standing at the bottom of the stairs. Kate's brother. Nico's best friend. Handsome fucker. His girlfriend hovers behind him, golden curls free-falling over her shoulders, and for a painful second I'm reminded of Aries.

I was so swept up in my own thoughts that I didn't know anyone had followed me. Nico and Kate are behind, and the four of them peer at me.

"Charlie told us what happened with the cake the Charlton twins made," Jack says.

I nod, focusing on the bubbles in the glass. My skin is beginning to heat up, knowing there are multiple pairs of worried eyes on me, wondering if I'm in the middle of some kind of crisis. Maybe I am.

"There's probably some left somewhere. If you want to try it," I say. "I didn't smash the whole thing. I'm sure what's left is perfectly edible."

They're silent, but I swear I can hear the rustle of their clothing, like they don't know whether to stay or go.

"You drinking that champagne?" Nico says, stepping around Jack and coming towards me.

"I think it's poisoned." My voice is emotionless, like I'm dead inside. I know, without looking over, that the four of them are sharing looks like I'm insane.

I pick the glass up, swill the liquid and take a huge gulp.

Kate gasps.

I rinse my mouth with it, then swallow. Wait for a moment. Tastes fine. A little sweet, perhaps. I drink the rest and set the empty glass down and turn to face them.

"Should we... call an ambulance?" Jack asks, sounding as though he doesn't know whether to laugh or not.

"No. It's fine. The champagne is fine."

"Do you need help?" Nico asks.

Jesus. All these people, watching me, worrying about me, all the fucking time. I go to the cupboard, grab a glass and fill it with water. I take a gulp, rinse and spit in the sink and that's when I see it: the tiniest little piece of yellow.

I stare at it. Prod it with my finger so it sticks to the tip and bring it closer so I can see it.

A fucking strawberry seed.

I knew it. Rage rises like a beast as I turn back to the others, and I know Nico can see it, because his eyes flare and he sticks an arm out to shield Kate, or stop her approaching me. I'd never hurt Kate, but I must look feral enough that Nico thinks he needs to protect her.

"Strawberries," I explain. "Those fucking boys put strawberries in Charlie's drink."

"Shit," Nico mutters, but I don't hang about to hear his thoughts on the matter, and the four of them blur as I push past, making my way up the stairs. They're swearing and cursing behind me, muttering amongst themselves. Nico calls out to me. "Wait, Matt."

I spin back to face them all, crowded on the stairs behind me like something from a comedy sketch. "Let me handle this."

"Don't lose it. The party—" Jack urges.

"I've got this," I growl, and they must accept it because they don't immediately follow as I barge back into the drawing room, scanning it quickly for the twins. Neither of them are here, but Charlie's still talking to his friend and the mother, and this time I grab him by the arm. "With me," I command, and Charlie barely has a second to excuse himself before I drag him away.

"Dad, what—"

"Where are they?" I whisper. "Ben and Hugo. Where the fuck are they?"

"I don't know. How would I know?"

They must be here somewhere. I know it. I stride into another room just off the drawing room, where the staff are pouring out champagne, lining glasses on tables, preparing to serve them.

I hear a noise; a loud, malicious sounding chuckle, and I know it's them. *The fuckers.* Still dragging Charlie with me, I enter the boot room, where coats hang from the walls, and shoes are lined up neatly beneath. More shoes than we'd ever need.

Standing in the corner of the room are the twins, huddled over, conspiratorial. Hugo has a glass of champagne in each hand, and Ben is holding a punnet of strawberries. He's running one around the edge of a glass, and in the liquid itself a lone strawberry floats.

"What the fuck are you doing?" My voice booms in the small room, and next to me, Charlie shudders.

The twins jerk their heads up at the same moment, like a pair of rabbits in the headlights, and a brutal, murderous impulse to run them down in one of my cars blasts through me like a heartbeat.

I storm over and grab the strawberries, the plastic box crunching in my hand. "Get out of my house. Get the fuck out before I throw you out."

"Mr Hawkston," Ben begins. "We aren't doing—"

"Don't give me that bullshit. I know exactly what you're doing. What you've already done." I'm simmering with anger, struggling to hold it together. Charlie is still standing at the door, trying to make himself smaller. "You've hurt my son. Tried to harm him. And I will not allow it. You will never, *ever*, enter this house again. And if you dare come near him, I will personally make you regret that you were ever born." My voice is shaking with the effort of holding myself back from beating the two of them to a pulp. "Get your stuff and get out right now."

There's a moment of stillness where the twins are still frozen in place, but then it breaks like someone pressed play on a film, and everything moves at double speed. Hugo places the champagne glasses on a side table, and they grab their coats, shuffling into them.

"Charlie, mate," one of them starts, his voice weak and fearful. "It was all in good fun. We—"

"Don't fucking talk to him. You'll leave, now, in silence, or I will drag you both into that party and publicly shame you for what you've done. There is nothing you could say that could excuse this. Out. Now." My empty hand is a solid fist at my side, the other still clenching the strawberries, juice dripping between my knuckles and down my fingers. Charlie's head is lowered, but his eyes are huge, peering at all of us from beneath his hair.

I focus on trying to control my breathing as the Charlton twins sheepishly leave the room, hunched over and—hopefully—ashamed of themselves.

When they've gone, Charlie and I are left alone, and I'm still struggling to hold myself in check. I slam the strawberries down next to the champagne.

"Dad—"

"What?" I snap, all that tightly held anger bursting out. Charlie jerks away, and I'm immediately regretful, covering my eyes with the heels of my hands as I speak, juice and strawberry pulp leaking over my face. "Shit. Sorry. God, I'm so sorry, Charlie. I'm not angry with you. Christ, I'm not angry with—"

"Thank you."

My frustration fizzles out at the sound of Charlie's soft voice. I lower my hands to find him, in spite of everything, staring at me with a look I haven't seen for years. It's how he used to gaze at me, before he hit double-digits, whenever I did something to help him without being asked, like tied his shoelaces or wiped toothpaste off his face; wide-eyed and worshipful, as though he believed I was an omnipotent saviour in his small world.

Back then, I reveled in it that glorious expression, but now it chokes me, and I see in an instant how much my son has needed me to be that man for him, and I haven't been there.

I want to hug him, but I don't dare; not covered in the remains of the strawberries. I hold my hands up. "Let me wash up. Wait here."

Charlie smiles, a cute, hesitant grin, as though he's not sure he's allowed to smile, but he really fucking wants to.

I walk to the cloakroom and wash my hands and face, but when I go back into the boot room, Charlie has disappeared, and Seb is standing in the doorway.

"What's going on?" he asks, gesturing over his shoulder with his thumb. "I saw the twins leaving. Gemma went with them."

Of course she fucking did. "Good riddance." I'm still breathing heavily, aware I must look crazed. "They're never coming back. Not to this house."

Seb's gaze lights upon the crushed strawberries, and I can see him putting the pieces together. "Fuck," he whispers, looking a little shocked, then he shrugs it off and says, "Whatever happened in here, it must have been good because Charlie's out there looking pleased as punch. Haven't seen him smiling like that in an age."

Thank God. "Where's Aries?" I need to tell her she was right about the twins, about the strawberries.

"She left," Seb says.

A horrific sensation occurs in my chest, like a vast hand is clutching my heart, squeezing it the way I just crushed those fucking strawberries. "When?"

"A few minutes ago."

Fuck. If it hadn't been for the twins and their actions, I might have caught her. Might have seen her, held her, one last time.

My heart is beating way too fast; it can't be healthy. I shove past Seb and go back into the drawing room, which is thick with people, but none of them are the person I want. The person I need. *How far has she gone? Where is she? Can I still catch her?*

I dash out into the hall, not giving a shit that the speed of my movement is attracting attention. I open the front door and trot down the steps. It's still light. The air is cool, only the mildest trace of the summer heat lingers. I can see Gemma and the twins walking down the street, but they don't notice me and I don't fucking care about them.

I still can't see Aries.

There's a taxi outside the gates, its orange indicator flicking on and off. I run across the lawn towards it. Press the button to release the pedestrian gate. It clicks open as the taxi pulls away.

I wrench the gate's heavy weight and pass through the gap into the street. Begin to run again. But the taxi is faster than I am, and it takes a turn at the crossroads ahead. I'm sprinting now. Running like a madman through Kensington. The taxi turns again, disappearing from view.

When I reach the corner, it's long gone. The street is empty. I double over, hands on my thighs. Breathless. And then I throw up, right there on the pavement, until I'm empty too.

Later, when everyone has gone home and Charlie's in his room, I go up to the fourth floor. Light-headed. Heartbroken. A mess.

Lucie is asleep. Has been for hours. There's no strip of light from Aries' room. I push the door open and immediately wonder why I'm here, because the sight of the bare room splits me open: a wound carved right down my torso. I grip the door handle and think about sinking to the floor for a moment, but decide to sit on the bed. If Lucie wakes up, I don't want her to find me in a crumpled heap on the threshold of Aries' empty room.

She's stripped the sheets; the bare duvet is curled up like an over-sized cinnamon roll on the mattress. Her scent lingers in the air. Coconut. Sweet. Like the promise of sun.

On the pillow, there's a small card with a neat, hand-written note.
Dear Matt,
I knew you'd come up here. I'm sorry.
I wish this could have ended differently.
I love you.
Aries.

I cover my eyes with my hand for a second. My breath shakes and bone-crushing pain shudders in my chest. *Fuck.* This *hurts*. It hurts worse than divorce. Pressure shimmers behind my eyes, pulses in my throat.

I scrunch up Aries' note, feeling the edges of the card biting into my palm, then stuff it deep into my pocket. Behind my ribs, there's a splintering sensation as if part of me is shattering. I don't cry. I never fucking cry, but right now I know I could. Unshed tears burn like acid at the back of my eyeballs.

Fuck this shit. I can't sit in here, wishing she was still here, wondering how the fuck it all went wrong.

I push off the bed and walk out of the room, closing the door behind me. An attempt to shut it all away. To shut *her* away. A chuckle, entirely devoid of humour, escapes me; as if I could ever shut her away.

You're in my bloodstream.

I go to my own room, but memories of Aries are even worse here. I see her everywhere, ghosts of her against the cupboards, splayed on the bed, smiling, laughing. Images of red hair strewn across my sheets are superimposed over the emptiness beneath.

I sink to the floor, dropping my head into my hands, bracing to hold back the pain I know is right there, knocking at the edges of my awareness, but I refuse to let it in. This will not be the thing that breaks me.

Not yet...

36

ARIES

I could hardly breathe in the taxi. In the airport, I sat in a café on a high stool with a takeout cup of shitty tea on the bar next to me. I couldn't even begin to drink it because I was crying so much that I was almost hyperventilating.

Now, back home, I'm numb as I unlock the front door. The familiar white PVC, thick frosted glass in the upper half, is so different from Matt's glamorous house. World's apart. Lifetimes.

The thought breaks my heart afresh. *He's so far away.*

I step inside, toeing off my shoes, feet sinking onto the threadbare carpet with its swirling paisley patterns. I bet Matt had never even seen a carpet that looks like this before he came here.

An electric oil diffuser on the hall table bubbles away, changing colour like the lights in a cheap disco, scented air spilling out in clouds. Around it are large tower crystals that Mum has set out in a circle, selenite, rose quartz, citrine and amethyst.

I quietly lower my suitcase to the floor so as not to wake Mum if she's asleep. Matt hovers in my mind's eye as I replay memories of him being here, dominating the house. Lowering his head on the way up the stairs, leaning against the doorframe and offering us all tea...

I loved that he brought me here and wanted to meet my mum, but now I wish he'd never come because I can't get rid of his image hanging over the space, an eerie hologram haunting my mind.

"Lizzie?" comes my mother's voice.

"It's me."

"Aries?"

I don't answer. Instead, I walk into the sitting room. The sight pains me. Tubes. A ventilator. Oxygen tank. There's no scent of incense in here because the diffuser from the hall doesn't penetrate this far. Instead, it smells sour, like death is seeping out of the walls.

Mum is couched on the bed, the duvet pulled up, two frail arms lying atop. Her skin is waxy, like she's already dead. Cheeks hollow, lips thin and cracked. She didn't tell me it was this bad. I didn't know. *She got so much worse, so fast.* My knees weaken and my hand reaches out for the wall, fingertips pressing into unyielding plaster.

I want to yell at her, to scream at her for not telling me how bad it had got, but all I say is, "Hi, Mum." My voice is timid, and the large, sorrowful eyes Mum turns on me tell me she's reading every thought that passes through my mind.

"I wasn't expecting you," she whispers, and although she looks like she's about to cry, it's me who sobs. The sound splits through me, dragging a pain behind it like a knife being drawn through my flesh from hip to shoulder. I cover my mouth with one hand, stifling anything else that might leak out.

"I'm sorry," she croaks. "I wanted you to enjoy London." And by London, I know she doesn't just mean the city. She means Matt and everything he meant to me, and my heart rips clean in two. I press my hands against my chest as though that might keep it together, but it makes no difference.

She lifts a hand from the floral bedspread, her frail, withered fingers reaching out. She glances beyond me, as if she expects to see Matt.

"Aries, honey," she says. "Are you alone?"

I force a smile onto my face, but it's so difficult to perform it wouldn't convince anyone, least of all Mum. "I am."

"Your lovely man isn't with you?"

Lovely man. "It didn't work out."

She glances at the ceiling for a second, then back to me. "He'll be back. Men don't look at women the way he looked at you if they don't mean to stick around," she tells me, and a phantom flicker ignites in my heart, fading a moment later. *Ever hopeful, my mum.*

I shake my head and make my way over to her. I take her hand in mine. Her fingers are thin and her grip so fragile it feels like she could disappear at any moment. I want to squeeze tighter, but I don't want to break her. I sit beside her on the bed, gently cradling her hand in mine. "I don't think so. Not this time."

Eyes full of motherly concern meet my own, and I sense her weighing everything up, as though she's comparing this version of me against an older, past version, and noting the changes. "Oh, honey." Tears rise in her bloodshot eyes. "You did it. You fell in love."

Searing pain crashes through me. My chin begins to tremble, my lower lip soon joining the dance. *I'm going to break.* I pin my lip with my teeth, biting so hard I taste blood.

"Do you need to cry?" Mum asks softly, as a tear runs down her own cheek. "I'm here if you need to cry. Let it out, honey. Let it all out."

I snort, the sound halfway between a sob and a laugh. I can't bear the way she's looking at me, like I'm the one who needs to be looked after. "I cried at the airport," I say, as if that's enough. As if that could ever be enough for Matt. For Mum. For all of it. As if I could ever cry enough tears when I'm staring down the barrel of a life where I have no one.

Mum watches me, analysing everything until she knows exactly what I need to hear. "I'll always be here, Aries. Even after…"

After I'm dead.

I close my eyes and grit my teeth to halt the choking sensation rising up my throat. Without meaning to, I tighten my fingers around Mum's, but I can't speak. Can't form a single word.

"Just imagine I'm with you, and I will be," Mum whispers in her most soothing voice. "That's how it works. You can talk to me anytime. Wherever you are. Wherever I am."

No, Mum. It's not the same. It won't be the same. You'll be gone, and I won't be able to reach you.

I feel a rush of anger that maybe all this time Mum's been feeding me lies. The energy, the bonds across space and time… maybe it's all bullshit, and I'll be utterly alone. But whatever anger I feel is doused by the knowledge that it doesn't matter either way. I can believe it's true, and if it's not, I'll never, *ever* know. All I have is now, *right fucking now*, and I want to hold onto it and never let go.

Mum strokes the back of my knuckles with her free hand. "Anyway, you're here, and I'm glad you're home early."

Her fingers shift against mine. She closes her eyes and rests her head against the pillow. She's not wearing a turban today and her hair is thin, each strand frail. It never grew back the same after the chemo. The first time, it came back curly. But the second time, it hasn't had a chance.

When I was little, her hair used to be like mine. Thick and red. I thought she was the most beautiful woman in the world. All powerful. A goddess. Immortal. She taught me how to be human. How to love. I thought she'd last forever.

But nothing is forever…

This reality is cruel. It's splitting me open, and I'm pulling at every ounce of my energy to hold it together so Mum doesn't have to see what it's doing to me.

"I'm not early. I'm late. I should have been here," I say, struggling to keep my voice from cracking.

Mum opens her eyes; pale blue. The only thing that's the same as it used to be. "No, Aries, honey. You were where you were meant to be."

I scrunch my face, trying to contain the tears. "I'm so sorry. I didn't want to leave you. But I didn't want to disappoint you either." My next inhale is an uneven wrench that filters into my lungs in jerks. Little whimpering sounds pop out of my mouth.

"Let it come," Mum soothes. "It's all right. I'm here. You could never disappoint me."

Her words make it worse, and my upper body collapses, my spine curling over, protecting my heart like I can stop it breaking into a million pieces. Waves of uncontrollable emotion surge through me, and even though a voice in my head is screaming, *don't do this to her, don't let her see this*, I can't stop. "I'm too late—"

"No," she says, more firmly now. A little more like her old self. "You're not. You're exactly where you should be. Exactly when you should be. We always are. It's universal law. That's—"

"How it works," I finish, sucking in air and wiping at my eyes with the palms of my hands.

She shifts her other hand over mine, so she has my hand between both of hers. "Exactly. We are always perfectly on time."

I really wish I could believe her.

37
MATT

The last week has been a disaster. I haven't been able to work. Aries whirled into my life, blew the whole thing into pieces, and then vanished.

I don't know what to do without her. There's a yawning chasm in every moment of my day, knowing when I get home, she won't be there.

Lucie is distraught. Heartbroken. Even now, in the drawing room, offering biscuits to Seb and Nico and Kate, she doesn't look her usual happy self.

"Thanks so much, sweetie," Kate says, taking a biscuit that Lucie has licked all over. She's possibly even sucked it.

When Lucie moves to Nico, Kate puts the biscuit down on the side-table, tucking it behind a lamp so Lucie won't see. It's considerate, and it makes me think of Aries. It's the kind of thing she would do. *No.* Aries would have eaten the whole damn biscuit and smiled doing it.

"Go on then," Seb says, nodding at Nico and Kate. "Tell us how he did it."

Kate grins, and the diamond sparkling on her finger catches the light. "In the London Eye," she says. "Got down on one knee—"

"Mate," Seb interrupts while staring at Nico. "You did it in one of those bubble capsules?" Seb tucks his chin, one eyebrow arcing over a disapproving blue eye. "Bit cliché, isn't it?"

"I'm memorising that expression"—Nico points at Seb's face—"so that I can replicate it when you propose to someone."

"Just thought you'd have gone for something more private."

"It was private," Nico retorts.

"It was very romantic," Kate says in a pacifying tone. She smiles at Nico like he's the best thing since sliced bread, and he puts his arm around her on the sofa and kisses her temple. They're sickeningly perfect together, and I don't think either of them would have given a shit where the proposal took place. The answer was a forgone conclusion. There's a hard lump of envy nestling at the base of my throat that I'm trying to bury.

"Are you going to have babies now?" Lucie asks. "Daddy says that's the only reason people get married."

A sudden chill ripples through the room, and Seb fists his hand and brings it to his lips. Kate's raised teacup is halfway to her lips as her nervous gaze shoots sideways to Nico, whose gaze is flicking from me to Seb and back again.

"People get married for all sorts of reasons," Seb says, and I'm surprised he's the one segueing us out of this awkwardness.

Kate, who has managed to collect herself, leans towards Lucie and adds, "We might have babies. But we're choosing to get married because we love each other, and we want to celebrate that with all our friends and family."

"Oh," Lucie whispers, like this is a piece of conflicting information she doesn't have context for.

I clench my jaw and swallow. *Shitty father.*

"How've you been?" Nico asks, looking at me.

The air crackles with awkward tension, and when I don't answer immediately, Seb chips in. "You cancelled all your fucking meetings."

Lucie pricks up, looking at me. "Uncle Seb said a bad word."

Seb slaps a hand over his mouth and stares at Lucie. "Sorry. Uncle Seb is a very naughty man."

Lucie laughs and gives him a biscuit, which he immediately eats even though she's definitely chewed half of it off already. He might be a bit of an arse sometimes, but he has a heart of fucking gold.

The doorbell rings and I get up, thankful not to have them all staring at me like I'm broken and they don't know how to put me back together. Or to have to respond to Seb's non-question about my meetings. I'll reschedule them at some point.

I find Mrs Minter in the hall, having buzzed a courier in. She signs for a package, which she hands to me. "For Lucie."

"For meeee?" Lucie must have followed me into the hall, because she's nipping at my heels, grabbing my trousers, her voice high-pitched and excited.

I glance at the package. It's from one of those internet photo companies. "Let's see what's in it, shall we?"

I lead her back to the drawing room, where Nico and Seb and Kate are talking in hushed tones, perched on the edge of the sofas, leaning in so their heads are close together, like school kids keeping secrets. They fall silent when we enter, and I suspect they're talking about me... probably about how I'm falling apart, or perhaps they're plotting an intervention. Something to save me from myself. I ignore them and sit on the floor with Lucie as she rips open the package.

She squeals when she sees what's inside, whereas I immediately feel nauseous. A photo book, hardcover, with a picture of Aries and Lucie on the front.

"Look, Daddy," Lucie cries, thrusting the thing in my face, "It's Ariel." Then she presses the book to her lips and gives the image of Aries a big smack on the lips. "I love her."

If it's possible, the others sitting on the sofa have gone even quieter. All I can sense is the thunderous beating of my heart and a constriction around my lungs.

Lucie begins flicking through the pages, which are printed with photos Aries must have taken while she was here on the damn smartphone I gave her. She must have uploaded all the photos to her laptop before she handed it back to me.

"When I'm five, I want to have hair just like Ariel." Lucie strokes the picture of Aries, and I clench my fists to prevent doing the same. "Can you buy it for me, Daddy?"

I swallow, disturbed by the lump that's risen in my throat. "We'll see about that," I say, my voice rough like someone's hacked the edges off.

Lucie keeps turning page after page. Aries and Lucie in the park, in the garden. Aries doing a handstand, her t-shirt falling and exposing an expanse of skin, her feet cut off because Lucie must have taken it and couldn't frame the picture. There are even pictures of us all on the boat. I look disturbingly happy, and staring at my smiling face is like looking at a different man.

I can't do this. I can't fucking sit here when each picture is ripping at my insides, yanking at my heart, threatening to drag it up my throat and out of my body.

I ruffle Lucie's hair with one hand and get up. "I have to check something... Outside." Lamest excuse ever, and I feel everyone's eyes on me, apart from Lucie's, whose attention has been sucked into the pleasure of her gift.

Kate gets up off the sofa and sits on the floor with Lucie. "That was when we went to the beach," I hear her saying, pointing at one of the pictures. "And we threw stones in the sea. Do you remember?"

Their voices fade as I make my way through the house and out into the back garden. *Fuck, I can't breathe.* The pain in my chest is so acute, I wonder if I'm having a heart attack.

I lean one hand on the wall and hang my head. I've never felt this way. I didn't give a shit about losing Gemma. Our relationship was long dead, if there had ever been a decent one in the first place. And apart from Gemma, there's been no one else until Aries.

How the fuck do I get through this? My whole body is poisoned with it. With her. With the absence of her.

"Matt?"

I glance up to see Seb standing on the back step. The wall of the house is covered in a climbing vine, the leaves of which have been vibrant green all summer. But now, they're turning wine-red. I hadn't registered the change until I saw him standing there, framed by all the fucking leaves.

"You okay?" he asks.

I push off the wall and drop onto a nearby bench, head falling into my hands.

I don't look, but I hear Seb step down and come towards me, taking a seat beside me. "What can I do?"

I shake my head. "Nothing. Everything is just... fucked."

"It's not."

I turn to look at him. "I'm thirty-five. Divorced. I've got two kids I'm struggling to relate to—"

"Those kids love you."

I snort. "Sure they do."

"Don't be a dick. You're not a bad father. Trust me, I know a bad father when I see one. We had one."

"Have," I correct. "We have one."

"Yeah."

We're silent for a few moments, and I'm sure Seb's running through a montage of shitty childhood memories, just like I am.

"It's Aries, isn't it?" he asks.

Something pinches in my chest, and my feet tingle inside my shoes, toes almost throbbing. I lean forward and stare down at them, my fingers steepled between my knees.

"You miss her." Seb makes the statement so softly that the pinch in my chest increases.

He watches me intently. Not just my face, but the entirety of me, right down to my feet, as if any movement I make might give something away. Reveal some hidden part of me. I force myself not to move at all.

It's not exactly silent out here, but it's close. The breeze rustles the vine leaves, and there's the droning background noise of cars passing on the street outside. There's even birdsong in the trees, and the sun hits the top of my head with a pleasing warmth.

"You can admit it," he whispers. "I won't think any less of you."

"No—" My voice catches. Sounds weak. I hate it. "She left. I can't—"

"Fuck, Matt." He pauses and I focus on trying to control the range of emotions that are swirling in my chest. "You love her, don't you?"

I break right then. Something in the middle of me, shattering like glass, each shard spearing my heart, my lungs.

As though he knows what's happening inside me, Seb slides a hand over my back and rests it between my shoulder blades. "You gonna cry?" he asks, and when I don't respond he adds, "Because I might have to film it. Never seen you cry before."

A strangled groan escapes me, but there's a hint of laughter under there. "Fuck you." I rub my eyes. They're definitely wet. "It's not just Aries. It's the whole fucking thing. Gemma cheating on me, the divorce, Charlie, Lucie. I'm failing everyone around me."

Seb opens and closes his mouth, as if he's unsure whether he should commit to whatever he intended to say. He pauses for a moment before he speaks, and when he does, there's an unfamiliar gravity to his voice. "And the one person who made it all better left you."

I click my tongue against my teeth and shake my head. "When did you become such a hopeless romantic?"

"I'm not the one who just ran away from a photo album."

I close my eyes, tears welling right behind my lids, and let out a long exhalation. Pain leaches through every organ in my body until it rises up my throat. Next to me, Seb shuffles, getting something out of his pocket.

"Put your phone away," I warn him.

He lets out an amused sigh. "Here," he says, and when I open my eyes, there's no sign of his phone, but he's handing me a handkerchief. Neatly pressed, with his monogrammed initials in the corner. Memories of that night with Aries on the balcony at the Hawkston Building rush in and I scrunch the bit of cotton up in my palm. *Is every little fucking thing always going to make me think of her?*

The sadness crests to a peak, pain surging right beneath it. I can't fucking hold this back anymore. I have seconds before it breaks me.

"You know what?" I say, so low I can barely hear my own voice.

"Yeah?"

"I'd like you to go inside."

Seb stills for a moment, as though he's running through his options. He taps his hand against my back again and leaves without another word.

And then, when I'm certain I'm alone, I fucking weep.

38
MATT

The new nanny is older than I am. Efficient, upright, spine like a steel rod. Her plummy English accent pisses me off. Thinks she's Mary fucking Poppins.

We're all in the front hall. Charlie's back from school for the weekend and we're ready to play tennis. The nanny is fixing Lucie's hair. My daughter looks pristine. Little patent Mary Janes, frilly white ankle socks. But she doesn't look happy; not the way she did when Aries was caring for her.

My heart does that squeezing thing, a numbness spreading over my shoulders that I try to shrug off, but it doesn't work. It's been a month since Aries left, and I still think about her all the time. Every minute of every fucking day. I've come to accept that maybe it's not something that's going to go away.

Apart from the lingering pain of missing her, everything else feels better. Calmer. It's as though my anger has somehow settled or dissipated since that day the photo album arrived for Lucie. As if facing the pain of it all unlocked something inside me. Aries, I think, would be pleased about this, if she knew.

I've noticed that I have more space for the kids, emotionally. The irritation and anger that were so ready to flare up don't rise the way they used to. It takes a lot more to rile me. In fact, I can't remember the last time I raised my voice. Probably not since Charlie's birthday.

Aries, I think, would be pleased by this too.

Fuck. It hurts to think about her and yet I do it almost constantly. Can't fucking help it. Tormenting myself, as if thinking of her might bring her back. *Futile.*

Every night I take out my phone and write her the same message. Three words. Then I delete it. Pointless. Meaningless. What does it matter how I feel now?

"Daddy, can we come and watch?" Lucie takes my hand, tugging on it a little. Her brown eyes are bright, shining with hope so vivid that it's almost contagious. *Almost.*

Beside me, Charlie lifts one foot behind him, knocks his tennis racket against the heel of his shoe, then repeats the motion on the other side. The strings twang against his rubber soles.

"Sure." Lucie bounces on her toes and I ruffle her hair. Glancing up at the nanny, I add, "Will you walk her over?"

"Of course, Mr Hawkston."

"Great. We'll see you later."

Charlie and I make our way to the courts in the large private square garden opposite the house. It's early evening, but still bright enough that the light won't mask the ball in that strange way summer evenings do, as if there's a gauzy film over the world. We have about forty-five minutes until that point, but before then we'll be able to play.

Charlie's as good a tennis player as I am, if not better. A skilled racket-sportsman. Highly coached, I supposed you'd say. A beautiful, graceful serve. Powerful forehand. He's been a good player since he was eight years old.

He stops halfway to the grass courts, beneath a magnolia tree, its waxy green leaves arcing over his head. "I don't want to play."

I keep walking, looking over my shoulder at him. "We don't have long before the light changes. Lucie's coming to watch."

Charlie's lips fold inward, turning downward at the edges like a melancholy rainbow. "Have you heard from Aries?"

The question yanks against me, as though Charlie has hooked his finger in the back of my shirt to keep me in place. I stop walking and turn to face him. "No."

"Have you contacted her?"

"No."

"You didn't tell her?"

A prescient tingle runs down my spine. "About what?"

"The strawberries. The party." Charlie kicks the heel of his shoe into the ground.

"No." I thought about it, but I didn't want to drag her back into my family drama, not when she'd managed to extricate herself from me and all my baggage.

Charlie absorbs my answer for a few moments, fidgeting with the grip on his tennis racket. "I knew what they were doing before you threw them out."

"You did?"

"Yes. I saw Hugo fishing a strawberry out of a glass of champagne in the boot room. Ben was there too. They were both at it, eating the strawberries as they talked about it. What they were planning."

"What did you do?"

"Nothing. I left. They didn't see me. He came back a while later and gave me a glass of champagne. I wouldn't have drunk it." My heart thuds and Charlie looks right at me. "But you took it off me. Even after the cake, and everyone saying what a fucking delirious prick you were, you still took it off me." We stare at one another, the breeze rustling the leaves over our heads. "You still thought she was right." For a second, I don't follow, and Charlie adds, "Aries."

I think of the moment I'd seen Hugo hand Charlie that glass of champagne, and how I'd known something was wrong, even before I spat that strawberry seed out in the sink. "Yes. I believed her."

Charlie inhales, long and slow. "She *was* right. Not about the cake, but about the twins. She thought they'd try and mess the party up, and they did."

I think back to that night. "When I asked you where they were, you said you didn't know."

"I didn't want you to make another scene. I thought you'd kill them."

"I wanted to. I'd want to kill anyone who hurt you. I love you. You kids are more important to me than anything."

Charlie looks at the ground, unblinking, but when he looks up and meets my eye, there's an imploring look on his face. "I don't want to live with Mum again. Not with Mark and Hugo and Ben."

"God, of course not. I already spoke to your mum. I told her everything. There's no way you'll ever have to be with them again. I told her I'd call the police if they came anywhere near you. You can stay with your mum at her house if you want to, but not if she's with Mark and the boys."

"She still wants to be with Mark?" Charlie asks, his voice near breaking.

"She does," I confirm, and the sadness that wells up in me is a mirror of Charlie's. *We've let him down so many times...*

Charlie nods. He's quiet, but then he looks at me, his expression serious. "Did you love her?"

"Your mother?"

He gives me a sad little smile, as though he already knows the answer to that question. "No. Aries. Did you love her?"

The question is a tiny dagger tearing at a wound I've been trying so hard to heal, and in seconds the blood is flowing freely from it once more, and standing here opposite my son, I find myself unable to staunch it. The life drains out of me, swirling into the ground, and although I haven't moved, I'm suddenly empty, amazed that, somehow, I'm still standing.

I can't talk about her. Not here, not now.

"Let's play." I thrust the head of my tennis racket towards the courts. "We won't be able to see the ball soon."

I pace across the grass, faster than I need to, despite the dimming of the day.

"Dad?"

I turn to find Charlie right behind me. For a beat, he doesn't move, then he throws his arms around me and squeezes tight. My mind becomes a vacuum. Shock. It must be. We stand like that for a few stretched-out seconds and then, when I gather myself enough to realise what the fuck is happening, I fold my arms around him, feeling the sharp points of his shoulder blades against my wrists.

"I love you too," he whispers.

Thank God. My throat shrinks, and my next inhalation feels like I'm dragging air through the eye of a needle. I hold him tighter, hardly able to breathe as I say, "I love you. I always loved you, even when it felt like I didn't. And when I didn't know how to tell you. Always."

"I know," he replies.

"Family hug!"

Lucie's voice screeches across the lawn, and Charlie and I pull apart to see her running towards us, arms out. We share a quick look and Charlie grins, and something inside me warms as we crouch down to her level at the same time, both replicating her outstretched arms. When she reaches us, she throws herself between us, one hand around each of our necks. The smell of baby shampoo wafts off her. I kiss her on the cheek, and she squeals.

"Family hug, family hug," she chants.

Fuck, I want to cry again.

Behind Lucie, the nanny approaches. "She couldn't wait," she explains.

"That's okay," I say, standing. Charlie takes Lucie's hand and together we walk towards the tennis court.

When we finally start our match, I'm relaxed. So is Charlie. He strikes the ball perfectly, and the rhythmic back and forth of our rally is like a Wimbledon soundtrack. The noise of a carefree summer. Straw hats and sandals. And, if we were another family, strawberries and cream. But I don't miss them. We have raspberries, and those are just as good.

Lucie runs about the court fetching the tennis balls while the nanny looks on. Seeing her there, leaning against the netted wall of the court, I think of Aries. Of how beautiful her hair would look against the green. How it would shimmer in the light. She really did have the most incredible hair.

But more important than any of that, Aries felt like part of my family.

God, I miss her so, so much.

When we arrive back at the house, Mrs Minter is waiting for me.

"Can I have word, sir?" she asks. Prim, proper. More so than normal, and I wonder if it's the effect of this new nanny, spreading her uptight manner like the vines creeping up the walls of the house.

I nod, and Mrs Minter and I step into the drawing room, trusting the nanny to take the kids upstairs.

I stare at the sofa, remembering how I made Aries come on the floor behind it the night Charlie came back from school. I'm replaying it in my mind—her soft pale flesh, freckles on her arms, her nose; that hair, spread across the carpet—when Mrs Minter clears her throat.

"Sorry," I say. "What did you want to talk about?"

She assesses me as if trying to work out if I can handle whatever she's about to tell me. A sinking sensation occurs in my stomach. She fishes into her handbag and pulls out a letter. "This is for you."

She holds it out towards me, but when I don't take it, she flutters it. A small encouragement.

My mind buzzes. Never has Mrs Minter handed me a letter with this much ceremony. Post is left on my desk. This, whatever it is, is different.

I take it from her, noting my name—*Matt*—written on the envelope. My heart lurches, thoughts immediately rushing to Aries. But it's not her handwriting. *Foolish*.

"Thank you," I say, and wait for her to leave, but she doesn't move.

"Open it."

I frown. "Right now?"

"Yes. I have instructions to stay while you read it."

"Instructions? From whom?"

Mrs Minter's lips squeeze together as though I'm testing her patience. She's got to be twenty years older than me, and right now I feel every one of them, like she's a school mistress reprimanding me for some mistake I'm not aware I've made. "Read it," she repeats.

"Fine." I prop my tennis racket against the sofa and rip the letter open.

Matt,

Thank you for allowing me to send you healing. I've done it every night since you visited, and in a curious way—as it always goes with energy healing—I feel I know you much better than our one-time meeting allowed.

You're a sceptic, and that's fine. You don't need to believe for this kind of thing to work. Even when we can't see it, things are changing in the unseen dimension. Shifting. Altering. The power of intention cannot be underestimated. I have felt the discharge of your anger and know the burden of pain has lessened. Do you feel changed, Matt?

Aries is different. Heartbroken, but also changed on a soul level. I know, you see. I can feel it. Sense it. I used to worry she might never be able to love or let herself fall, but I was wrong. There have been tears, of course, but tears aren't always a bad thing. We must grieve before we can heal.

I know your heart is broken as clearly as I know Aries' is. This will seem far-fetched to a man like you, but there it is. I truly hope the two of you can work out whatever came between you. When there is a connection like the one you have, I know you will. If not in this lifetime, then in the next.

I wish you well, whatever the future holds. And thank you for letting me get to know you better.

Josephine McClennon

My mind spins. Pins and needles prickle over my skin, like I'm going numb, yet pain spikes between my ribs at the same time. My hand hits my breastbone before I have a moment to question the motion.

Never in my life have I received such a bizarre letter. Every line reads like a joke. If I hadn't met Aries' mother, I'd think this was a prank. But at the same time, there's an accuracy to it I can't deny. I do feel different. And my heart... *fuck*. Yes. It's fucking broken and I'm doing my best to ignore it. To carry on.

Mrs Minter clears her throat, reminding me I'm not alone. I glance up to find her staring, a concerned expression on her face.

"Where did you get this?" I ask, holding the letter out to her.

"Aries' mother sent it to me. It arrived yesterday. I don't know why it's so late."

Late? "Is she expecting an answer? Do I write back?"

Mrs Minter swallows. "Matt," she says my name slowly, and a sense of foreboding spreads across my shoulders, creeping all the way down to my lower back. "Aries's mother died. Much sooner than we expected."

"When?"

"Last week. The funeral is on Wednesday. First of October."

We'll tell the kids in October. A horrid, sinking sensation plunges through me, stealing my breath and making me dizzy. I want to grab onto something, to find something to anchor me. I rest my hand on the back of the sofa, digging my fingertips into Gemma's fucking designer fabric. "Thank you for telling me."

39
ARIES

October first. The day we put my mother in the ground.

As the coffin is lowered, it begins to rain. Smir, as we call it in Scotland. A hazy drizzle that feels like the soul of the west coast. It cools my skin, soothing the tearing pain in my chest as I take out my wallet and pull out the folded up note Mum gave me before I went to London. It's soft with wear, the paper splitting in the folds. I read it one last time.

Aries' London To Do List.

1. Live

2. Dream

3. Live the Dream

4. Fall in Love.

I raise my eyes to the sky. *I gave it my best shot, Mum. Ticked them all off. What's next, eh?*

The response is a resounding silence that breaks my heart.

I thought I would keep this note forever, but it feels suddenly pointless to hold onto it, and I let the piece of paper flutter into the grave until it settles on the coffin. I take a handful of dirt and throw it on top. The hole is deeper than I imagined it would be. I wouldn't be able to climb out of it, and the inescapability of it all... of loss, of death, of burial, of the grave itself, fucking terrifies me, but I force myself to hold it together. For Mum.

Turns out, she was right. We're exactly where we're meant to be, when we're meant to be there. Leaving Matt broke my heart, but it meant I got to spend time with her. By the end, she would sometimes forget who I was. She was bloated. Swollen. And yet somehow withered and hollow at the same time. Unrecognisable. But I wouldn't have traded being able to be there for her at the end for anything in the world, as painful as it was to witness.

"Who is here for you, Aries?" she whispered to me one night, near the end, her fingertips cold and still in my palm. "Who is holding your hand?"

"You are," I whispered back, and she only smiled, but we both knew I hadn't answered the real question. Had it been another day, another conversation, before she'd got really sick, she would have said, "No, you wee monkey. When I'm gone, I mean. Who will be here for you then?"

But this wasn't another day, so she only smiled and squeezed my fingers. I'd wept at her side, breaking, grieving, even while she was still alive, knowing I couldn't make her stay. No matter how hard I held her hand, I couldn't keep her here.

I stayed by her side until that shift in breathing occurred, and I knew the end was near. They'd warned me to listen for it; the change in the way we take in air, rattling in the throat, when our body is struggling to perform its most basic, most essential task, for the last time.

In the end, it was she who held *my* hand. It was only afterwards that I was alone.

Earlier today, the church was full. Mum touched a lot of lives, spreading all that positive energy all over the place. She believed that every time you made someone smile you were healing a tiny fraction of their soul. Maybe it's true, maybe it's nonsense. I don't know. But either way, I'm not sure as many people would have turned up for me.

There aren't nearly as many people here for the burial itself. They'll all have gone ahead to the wake. Beside me, Lizzie throws a handful of dirt into the grave, and then she puts her arm around my shoulder and squeezes. She says nothing, retreating from my side as though she senses my need to be alone.

Slowly, everyone else leaves. I don't follow, but instead wait until the very end, seeking a private moment with my mother, wondering if I did enough. If I was there enough. If, perhaps, I shouldn't have gone to London at all. But then I remember that pull... that gut instinct that had told me to take the job. That, for some reason, I was meant to go.

What was it all for?

I pull my coat tighter around me. It already feels like autumn, the leaves on the trees turning red and gold. It won't be long before they fall.

"Bye, Mum. I love you," I whisper. Then, finally, I turn, but the cemetery isn't empty as I expect it to be. *I'm not alone.* A man stands behind me on the path that runs through the neat rows of headstones. Tall, dark hair, dark coat, collar popped, hands deep in his pockets. He's been watching... waiting.

Matt Hawkston. *He's here.*

The sight of him steals my breath. His presence is a surprise, and yet... expected. As though part of me knew he'd come. Pieces of my broken heart cleave together, but somehow the fusing hurts just as much as the breaking.

His expression is serious, but there's a flicker to his lips, his mouth, like he might have smiled if it had been appropriate. It's just enough to let me know he's glad to be here. Relieved to see me, even on a day like this.

I pace up the slope, and he comes down towards me, the two of us drawn together like an inevitability. We stop a few feet apart; my heart racing, breaths catching in my throat.

The intensity of his eyes, fixed on me, makes my insides begin to glow. *Hope.*

"I'm so sorry, Aries."

Without realising, I've stepped up so close to him that I can smell him. The familiar richness of his scent. It makes me ache. "Thank you."

"Are you all right? I mean, obviously not." He glances to the open grave behind us, endearingly flustered as he speaks. "But... are you doing okay?"

"I suppose so. I had some time to prepare."

We're quiet for a few moments, the drizzle doing its slow work to soak us both, little pearls of it glistening on his coat sleeves, his shoulders. "I wasn't sure you'd want me to come. Didn't know if I ought to be here."

The hesitation in his words makes me want to reach out and touch him. To tell him that, of course, I want him to be here more than anyone else. I long to feel his arms around me. To let him comfort me, hold half my pain. But I can't. The energy between us, the memories of the things we said, of everything that happened, hang too heavy in the air. I'm not sure I can push through it. Not today.

"I'm glad you came." It's not enough to invite him closer, and he knows it. He swallows, pressing his lips together as his gaze dips to the ground.

"I'll be here," he says when he looks up again. "If you need me. I'm staying at the—"

"Hawkston?"

He nods. Only a few weeks ago, I'd have laughed at this. So obvious. So funny to stay in a hotel with your name over the door. But not now. There's no humour in this moment, or this day, and frankly, I can't imagine laughing ever again.

His eyes are full of care, full of pain, and I know he wants to take me in his arms just as much as I want to be held. But I hold back. I don't know what he is to me anymore. He's not my boss, and he's not my friend. We haven't spoken in weeks.

And yet, seeing him standing there, it feels like he's the other part of my soul, offering himself up to me. So close, and yet still so far away. I can't breech the gap between us, but I desperately long to do exactly that. "I need time."

His hands burrow deeper into his pockets, his shoulders hunching. "Of course. Take as long as you need. I'm not going anywhere." He frowns. "Actually, right now I'm going to go. But I won't be far away. I'll be—"

"At the Hawkston. I know."

He gives me a sad little smile. "Yeah."

The wake is held in a dingy room in the basement of a local hotel. Perhaps I should have invited Matt, but what I said was true. I do need time. I don't know what to think or what to feel. I need to say goodbye to my mother first.

There are a hundred people here, all condoling me. I've heard the same phrases over and over again, so many times that they're already rolling into one blurry memory. Meaningless noise in the background of my grief.

I'm sorry for your loss.
Your mother was a wonderful woman.
Time is a great healer.

I want to scream. My ability to accept the kind words of others has run dry. I know they mean well, but it feels like they're handing me condolences the way parents give children sweets at a party; to numb their emotions with sugar, keeping them quiet so they don't cause a scene or make anyone else uncomfortable. I drink a couple of glasses of cheap red wine that sticks to my teeth, and make an effort to smile at a few more people, have a few more empty conversations. It's only after an hour of the same that I realise I don't have to stay here. I'm allowed to leave.

I say my goodbyes as calmly as I can and push through the other mourners out into the bleak, grey car park. Overhead, the clouds rumble and the heavens open, and rain pours down, as though every tear I've held back today is spilling from the sky, soaking me in seconds.

I run all the way home, fueled by a barrage of angry thoughts. *Why did it have to be Mum? Why couldn't Dad have been the one to die? Dad who never gave a shit. Dad who abandoned us and never cared that Mum was sick, beyond thinking of what he might get out of her death. Why couldn't it have been him?*

I don't even have it in me to feel guilty about wishing him dead. I'd do anything to bring Mum back, but I can't, and powerlessness rages inside me like a violent storm.

I'm splashing through the puddles in my Doc Martin boots. The only black shoes I own. Cars roar past, waves of rainwater splashing me, drenching me. But I'm past caring. I don't even notice them.

I unlock the door to Mum's house, and then silence engulfs me. "Mum?" I call. "Mum?"

I begin to run through the house, smashing doors open as I rocket from room to room, calling her name. I know she's gone. I know she's not here, but I can't bear it. *I refuse to accept it.* Mum always said we make our own reality. Well, I'm making mine now. *She's here. She's fucking here. She should be here. If she's not... where is she?*

I begin to scream, running up and down the stairs, beating my fists on the walls, smashing whatever I can lay my hands on. In the background of my mind, I know I'm losing it. But maybe if I scream enough, break enough things, the pain will go. Maybe I can purge it out of me if I make enough noise; drag it out through a raw throat.

But it doesn't work. The pain doesn't lessen. I'm breaking, shattering, dying with it. Even after I'm hoarse and weak and shaking, the pain is still there, tearing at my heart, weakening my limbs.

I sink onto the floor outside Mum's bedroom, pulling my knees up to my chest as sobs wrench their way from my lungs, great spasms of pain I can't control. I'm lost to it... lost to the grief and the pain and helplessness of it all.

How will I survive this?

A screaming sound ricochets around my skull. My mother. Dying. Dead. I put my arms around her, trying to soothe her, but she keeps screaming. I can't do anything to stop it.

The sound stops. Begins again. Stops. Repeats, dragging me from the dreamworld.

I'm still on the floor, curled in a ball, wearing the same damp clothes from the funeral. Everything aches.

What is that noise?

The doorbell. I ease myself out of my scrunched position and make my way downstairs. Through the frosted glass of the front door, I can make out a hazy figure. Tall. Dark clothes. If it's someone trying to sell me something, I'll murder them right there on the doorstep.

But it's not.

It's Matt, all gorgeous in his peacoat, popped collar, polished dress shoes. He takes one look at me and his expression falls into something approaching horror. He steps inside and closes the door.

"Jesus, Aries." His hands are on my shoulders, and he's stooping down, peering into my face, his dark eyes seeking out mine. "Your clothes. They're wet. Have you slept at all?"

I shrug, but suddenly Matt's intent focus isn't on me at all. It's beyond me, staring deeper into the house, the concern on his face etching its marks deeper still.

"What happened here?"

I turn, only now noticing the mess I made last night. Everything is broken, pieces of Mum's stuff strewn all over the floor. The crystals. The oil diffuser. "Me. I did. I—"

He folds me into the embrace I longed for yesterday, and squeezes me tight, like I'm broken too and he can put me back together.

A great rush of emotion surges upwards, scraping at my insides, tearing at my lungs. It's striving to pour out of me, to spill itself on the floor at his feet. I can't let it happen. It will destroy me. I can't... I can't... it's too much...

I push against his embrace, loosening it. He draws back but my fingers grab at him, pulling at his shirt, his coat. Anything I can get my hands on. If I can get them off... get all his clothes off...

"Aries—"

But I don't stop. Can't stop. If I can have him, *fuck him*, I can block out everything else. My hands are round his neck, on his face, pulling him towards me. I kiss him hard, but he's unresponsive, and when I break away, his eyes search mine for an explanation.

"Aries." He says my name like a plea. "We can just talk—"

"I don't want to talk. I talked to a hundred people yesterday. I don't want to talk anymore." I grab his coat and pull him closer, my breaths coming in rushed gasps. *This isn't me.* I don't know what I'm doing.

His eyes move frantically over me, and although he looks worried, I can see that he's tempted. If I try a little harder, I can win him over. Drown it all out with kisses and sex and Matt. "Aries—"

"Please." I kiss him again, his stubble rough against my skin. I try to tug his coat off his shoulders, but there's a reluctance to his movements, like he doesn't trust me to know what I want right now. I give up and begin to pull his shirt out of his trousers instead.

"*Please,*" I repeat, desperate. My fingers fumbling, ineffective. "Please, don't deny me right now. I need this. I need you."

His jaw flexes as he looks down at me, and whatever he sees in my face has him pulling me flush against him, one hand cradling the back of my skull against his chest. "I'm here for you, Aries. I've got you."

And then, like he turned on the fucking tap, I cry, great wracking sobs that make my ribcage shudder, causing tears to fall that soak right through his shirt.

He holds me again, warm and tight against him, as I fall apart. And he doesn't let go until I haven't a tear left to cry.

Later, Matt carries me up to the bathroom and runs a hot bath. He peels off my wet clothes, easing me out of them as though he's removing the bandages from a gaping wound, which I suppose he is. I get into the tub, and he sits on the floor beside me, running the warm water from the shower over my back.

I hug my knees up to my chest and tell him about Mum and the sickness and her dying, and how hard it was to hold it together at the wake. I even tell him how I wished that Dad had died instead, and that I'm not even ashamed of wanting it. I tighten my hold on my raised knees, curling over them as I speak. For some reason, keeping myself small makes it all seem a fraction more manageable. Like I can contain all the grieving, angry parts of me.

Matt washes my hair, massages my scalp, rinses the soap, and I'm reminded of how I put bubbles on his chin that first night in his house. How reserved he was, and it occurs to me that back then, I could never have imagined this current scenario playing out.

"Do you think you'll forgive him? Your dad?" Matt asks as his fingers move through my hair, teasing apart the strands. His voice is hesitant, as though he might take my answer and make it mean something else in his mind.

"Maybe. But we'll never have a relationship. And I wouldn't want one with him anyway—he was a terrible parent."

Matt's gaze slides off me, brows drawn together. "Hmm."

I watch him for a few moments, and my heart aches. "You're not a bad father." His eyes snap to mine, the movement as quick as a shot. "I know you think you are, but you aren't. Not even close."

He turns off the shower, fixes the shower head back in place, and sits back on his heels. "Thank you. I'm trying my best." His sleeves are rolled to the elbow, and he leans over the tub, drawing spirals on my bare shoulder with a fingertip.

"Why did you come here this morning?"

"I wasn't going to. I know you asked for time—"

"So why did you come?"

He starts to roll his eyes, smiling as his lids sink. "If I told you it was my intuition, would you believe me?"

A warmth ignites in my chest, like a solitary candle in a darkened room. "Of course."

He snorts a laugh. "Sounds fucking weird, but I heard this voice inside my head telling me to come. So I got in the car and I drove right here. I don't know what you've done to me, but I'm all in on this shit now."

A wave of love for him rushes through me with such force, my breath catches. I want to tell him I love him, want to say the words, but I told him before and he never said them back. "I'm glad you came."

He smiles, trailing his index finger up my neck, spreading tingles through my body. "I didn't know whether you'd want to see me."

"You know what my mother would say?" I ask, and he waits, quietly staring. "We're always exactly where we should be. Exactly when we should be."

His lips curve upwards. "She was a very smart woman, your mother."

For the first time today, I smile too. Broad. Real. *Happy.* "She was."

We're quiet for a few minutes, and Matt lets his fingertips trail in the bath water. "If this tub wasn't so small, I'd get in with you."

I glance at him, then the tub, pretending to assess the dimensions. "It's definitely too small."

"I have a very large bathtub in London."

My heart lurches. *Is that an invitation?* I glance at him, but he's following the motion of his fingers in the water.

"There's something I meant to tell you," he continues. "And I know this really isn't the moment, but if I wait, I might not say it and I've written this message over and over on my phone and never sent it, and I'm starting to feel like a damn, gutless fool." His tongue swipes over his bottom lip and for every second of the pause that follows, my heart beats wildly, as though my ribs are the only thing stopping it from taking flight. "I'm in love with you."

My heart catapults into my mouth, then slides slowly back down my throat. "Took you a while."

"The saying of it, maybe. But not the feeling."

Heat rises through me so intense that if we turned the lights off, I'm pretty sure I would be shining like the sun. "That makes it a wee bit better."

"Just a wee bit," he teases, and I laugh, but he keeps talking. "I know you have things to sort out here, but if you want to, I'd like you to come back to London. Live with me. Be with me. No rush. Take as much time as you want, but I'd really like you to make my home your home and fuck me until I can't walk."

I flick water at him, grinning. "So romantic."

The side of his lips twitch up. "I just told you I love you. I love you more than I've ever loved a woman, and I let you leave me once. I don't intend to do it again. I fucking love you. And I love fucking you. So please, come and live with me and let me do both until I'm old and grey. And even when I'm too old to fuck, I'll still love you." His finger slides across my shoulder and down my upper arm, making me hotter than the bathwater. "I've never met anyone like you, and I'm sure I never will again. I haven't stopped thinking about you since you left. I've missed you so much, there were times I thought the pain might get the best of me. That I couldn't go on without you, because you'd clearly stolen my heart and tucked it inside that giant suitcase of yours and taken it to Scotland." He blows out a beleaguered breath. "I love you, Aries. I've never loved anyone the way I love you. I don't want to lose you. I don't want to go through that again."

I've wanted to hear these words for so long, but actually hearing them makes my throat swell. *I'm going to cry.* "I don't either," I whisper.

"So, it's a deal? Because I'm not the only one who thought we were meant to be." Tears sting my eyes, and even before he confirms it, I know who he means. "Your mother wrote me a letter." He sounds serious, but his eyebrow quirks and a teasing smile touches his lips. "Said we have a connection. And that if we don't work it out in this lifetime, we will in the next one."

I gasp, covering my mouth with my hand, a confusing mix of happiness and sadness assailing me as I think of Mum secretly penning such a letter, refusing to hold back on her convictions, even though she must have known they'd sound outlandish to Matt. *Looking out for me, right until the very end.* "She did not," I squeal.

He laughs, so loud and happy that my heart warms, the heat of it rising up my throat and melting away the lump that formed there.

"She absolutely did. And I think she might be right, so you can come home with me for this lifetime, or you can wait until the next one. I'm easy."

"You're easy?"

He nods. "Time is an illusion, right?"

Laughter splutters out of my mouth. "Oh, dear Lord. I need to get you out of this house before you turn into a different man entirely."

"I think it might be too late for that. But I'd really rather we sorted our shit out this lifetime, right now, so I don't have to wait." He pauses and looks upwards like he's reflecting on what he just said. "Fuck, I didn't come here with the intention of forcing you into anything, or suggesting things while you're... vulnerable." He drags wet fingers through his hair, clumping the strands. "I'm making a mess of this. I don't want to do anything if you aren't ready—"

I cut him off with a kiss, leaning out of the bath, throwing my wet arms around him, soaking his shirt.

He chuckles into my mouth. "Is that a yes?"

"It's a hell yes."

Matt stays with me all night, cradling me in his arms, stroking my hair. And in the morning, we make love. Slow and passionate, and with each kiss, with each deliberate thrust of him into me, I feel my broken heart begin to heal. Afterwards, in the shower, I close my eyes and tell my mother I'm going to be all right, because there's someone holding my hand now.

And then, even through the thrumming of the hot water around me, I swear I hear her whisper, 'I know'.

EPILOGUE

"I am not wearing a kilt. Absolutely not." Matt is standing in the middle of the bedroom, looking devastatingly handsome in his black-tie suit. "It's too fucking cold outside. I think it's going to snow tonight."

"Please?" I hold out the kilt, waggling the hanger. "You'd look so good. Get your legs out. Take your boxers off."

He shakes his head, lips tightly closed, but his eyes are laughing. "No. Plus Nico wouldn't be happy if I showed up to his engagement drinks wearing that. I'd upstage him. This is their night, not ours."

"Fine. Maybe we can use it for dress up, later," I say, throwing it down onto Matt's huge bed; the big bed where I now sleep every night, snuggled up next to him after we've come so hard and so frequently we've exhausted ourselves.

Matt eyes the kilt sceptically. "That doesn't even look like it would fit. Where did you get it?"

"A charity shop on Earl's Court Road."

He closes his eyes and pinches the bridge of his nose. "You've got to get rid of it. It probably has moths. It'll destroy my suits. My cashmere."

I begin to laugh.

"I'm serious." He grabs it from the bed and I laugh harder, wiping tears from my eyes. "Not on the fucking sheets," he adds, marching the undesirable item into the bathroom where I hear him throw it in the bin.

He comes out slapping his hands, looking delighted with himself.

"You know I'm getting that out later," I say. "I'll wash it. But there is no way I'm not getting you into a kilt one day."

"I'm not Scottish."

"So?"

He shakes his head at me, his gorgeous mouth splitting to reveal perfect teeth. The motion slows as he appraises me, his gaze scooping upwards from my feet, lingering at my hips, my breasts, my lips, until finally he meets my gaze. I'm tingling everywhere. It's amazing that even after all these months, he still has this effect without laying a finger on me.

I brush a hand down my green silk evening dress, the fingers of my other hand tangling in my hair, which is all blow-dried and perfect. I'm probably messing up the effect—it's different... good, even. I'm normally in jeans and a t-shirt, my hair tucked up in a messy bun, so this evening's attire is a huge change, and from the look on Matt's face I can tell he appreciates the effort.

He paces towards me, sliding his hands to my hips. "God, you're beautiful."

"You too."

He rolls his eyes. "What every man wants to hear."

"Shut up."

He kisses me, slowly, like he wants to experience every second of it fully. I melt in his arms, my body liquefying beneath his touch.

"Do we have time—"

"No." He cuts me off, and we stare at one another for a few heated seconds. "Fuck," he groans, shaking his head as though not taking me here and now, in all my evening finery, is a very difficult choice to make. "I don't want to ruin your hair."

I laugh, lightly tapping his arm as I move towards the door so we can head out, but he grabs my hand and spins me back into his embrace. "I love you," he says, his voice deep and sincere. "So, so much."

Every time he says it, I feel like a field of blossoming flowers as new parts of me open up. "I love you too."

"Daddy? Ariel?" Lucie's excited voice comes from outside the bedroom.

We share a glance, knowing that if we let her in, the chance of any fooling around slides to zero. Matt sighs, and I grant him a conciliatory smile as I ease out of his arms to open the door.

Lucie's mouth falls open as she takes me in. "You look like a real mermaid." She turns to Matt. "Oh, Daddy. She's the most beautiful lady in all the whole world."

I crouch down and give her a hug. "Not as beautiful as you," I whisper, and she giggles.

"I love you," she mumbles softly in my ear. "I'm so glad we got to keep you."

I get a little choked up, and raise my gaze to Matt's over Lucie's head as I say, "Me too, honey, me too."

By the time we arrive at the engagement party, I'm feeling buoyant with happiness. I never imagined I could feel like this—whole, complete, and fully supported by a man I cannot get enough of—and I know that Mum, if she's out there somewhere, must be delighted too.

The party is glamorous, the room teaming with well-dressed guests. And tonight, all made up and elegant, I fit in, but there are so many people here that I doubt anyone is looking at me. Except Matt, of course. His gaze always lingers on me, his eyes seeking me out, latching on, even when we're talking to other people.

We're standing in a little group, congratulating Nico and Kate on the impressive party.

"I never thought he'd step up," Seb says to Kate whilst nodding at Nico. "Thought he'd string you along forever."

Kate glares at Seb, then smiles. "Liar." She's so pretty, the sparkling overhead lights making her skin look dewy and her jewellery glitter. The diamond ring on her finger looks like the iceberg that sank the Titanic.

Seb laughs and that little dimple appears to the side of his mouth. "Fine. I admit it. I'm surprised it took him this long. He was *that* desperate to put a ring on it."

"You're a prick," Nico says, averting his gaze as he drains the rest of his champagne.

Even in the face of his brother's cussing, Seb's smile doesn't dim. He gestures to Matt. "What about this one? Finally got his act together. We should drink to that." He casts a wide smile in my direction, which I mirror without hesitation.

Seb raises his glass, and Nico summons a server over to top him up before joining in the toast.

"To true love," Seb says.

Nico splutters, only just managing to hold his champagne in his mouth before he swallows. "Hearing you toast to true love is just wrong. Sorry."

"Oh, fuck off," Seb jibes, and they begin to bicker, while Kate laughs.

I drown them out as Matt's arm tightens around me and he dips his head to whisper in my ear.

"You sure you're keen to stick with me when we have to spend time with this lot?"

"I like your family."

He pulls back to raise a sceptical brow.

"Okay, fine. They're growing on me. But I like you enough to put up with anything." Right at that moment, Seb bursts out laughing, spraying champagne across the floor, narrowly missing the silk of my dress. He swears, wiping his mouth with the back of his hand, cursing Nico for something he said and apologising profusely to me.

I glance at the ceiling. "Almost anything," I add.

Charlie appears beside us, a glass of champagne in hand. He's so different now that he's living permanently with us. The strain on his face has vanished, and he looks much more the carefree kid he always ought to have been.

"Only one glass," Matt instructs, indicating Charlie's drink.

"Yes, Dad."

God knows how Matt worked it all out with Charlie and Gemma. I think part of him wanted to charge the twins with attempted murder for putting that strawberry in the champagne. As it is, Gemma agreed to only see Charlie when the twins aren't around. It's a peculiar arrangement, and I can't even begin to understand it. But, most importantly, everyone I care about seems happier.

Alec is babysitting Lucie tonight, so we could all be here to celebrate with Nico and Kate. Alec says it's a bit weird now that I'm officially with Matt... as if I've been promoted above him. I told him not to be ridiculous. I'm still me, and I still go and hang out with him in the staff block. He's trialling at the Hawkston Mayfair next week, and he's so nervous. Nervous, but excited. A whole new chapter.

Up on the stage, a beautiful blonde woman with wild curls begins to sing. I recognise her from Charlie's birthday party. Elly, I think her name is. Kate's brother's girlfriend. Apparently, there was a lot of hoo-hah about her on social media not so long ago, but I'm not into that sort of stuff, so I don't know. Her voice is beautiful, and for a moment I tune in, and the music makes me feel as though I'm living a dream. *Everything is perfect.*

The others are so busy chatting that they hardly notice when Matt squeezes my hand and leads me away, pushing through the guests until we reach a door that leads out to a balcony. He opens it and lets me pass through in front of him. I have no idea why he wants to go outside, given how chilly it is, but I'm used to him seeking out quiet places to kiss me. *Fuck* me. I smile at the idea, anticipating his hands on me.

The door closes, and we're alone. A full-body shiver rips through me. "Holy crap, it's freezing." My breath fogs out into the night. "We're not having alfresco sex on the balcony, if that's why we're out here."

Matt smiles, amused. "It's not. Sorry." He takes my champagne glass from my hand and puts it on a nearby table, next to his own. Then he removes his jacket and wraps it around me. I snuggle into it as he says, "I'm going to make this quick. There's something I want to ask you."

My heart races. He sounds serious. "Yes?"

"Do you want this?" He gestures back to the party inside.

"A party?"

"To get engaged. Married. All of it."

My heart momentarily pauses, then resumes its beat. I know this isn't something Matt wants. Not again. A little muffled throb of pain makes itself known in my chest because, as soon as I knew I was in love with Matt, this *is* something I wanted. But he already had it all, and I chose him over that experience. His family. His life. His kids. I love Lucie and Charlie, but I've avoided thinking about what being with a man who had his own family might mean for me. For my future.

"I just want to be with you," I say.

His brow creases, which puzzles me. I thought he'd be relieved, but he doesn't look it.

"Is something wrong?" I ask.

"No." He takes both my hands in his. "I want to be with you too, but I don't want you to have to compromise on anything you might want. Marriage. Kids. Any of it. I'd do it all again if I could do it with you."

Oh, my heart. "I hadn't thought—"

"I had. You're young. You must have thought about having your own family. Kids. Marriage. A wedding."

Nerves bubble up in my stomach. I can't speak. Don't know what to say.

He's staring at me, the divot between his brows deepening. "Aries?"

"Yes. I wanted those things," I admit, heart hammering. "But I want you more. I'd give it all up, just to be with you. I love you. I love your kids. Your house feels like home to me now."

His features soften. "It's as much your home as it is mine. You chose every bit of furniture and every piece of fabric in it."

I can't help smiling. He let me change *everything*. The house is barely recognizable.

And then, right there on the balcony, he drops to one knee.

My hand flies to my mouth. "What are you doing? Matt? Don't... wait... what are you doing? Get up. Get *up*."

He pulls a velvet ring box from the pocket of his trousers and presents it to me. He flips it open, and inside there's a yellow diamond surrounded by smaller white ones. It's stunning. It's perfect. It's ex actly what I would have chosen if I had ever dared to think about a moment like this.

I think I stop breathing for a moment.

"Aries McClennon, will you marry me?"

My knees weaken, and I sink to the ground opposite him, throwing my arms round his neck. "Holy shit, you're an idiot. You're an idiot. You're an idiot," I chant.

"Well, this isn't how I imagined it would go," he says, chuckling against my cheek. He eases me off him so he can look at my face, which is already streaming with tears.

"I don't want to misinterpret this abuse," he says. "Is this a yes?"

"Yes. Yes. *Yes*."

He takes the ring from the box and slides it onto my finger. It sticks on my knuckle. "Fuck, this was going to be so perfect," he mumbles with a disbelieving snort.

"It is. It is," I reassure him as he eases the ring the rest of the way.

He stands, helps me up, and gives me my champagne. He raises a toast with his glass, tilting it towards mine.

"To true love," he says, and my mouth can't stretch wide enough to contain my smile. It feels like my entire body is grinning. We take a sip, and then he kisses me, his mouth warm and soft, and tasting like champagne.

"Oh, fuck," comes a voice, and we look up to see Seb standing in the doorway, his expression twisted with mock-distress. "Not you too."

We all laugh, and I know for sure this is exactly where we're meant to be.

THE END

Want more Matt and Aries?

Want to know what happens when Aries finally gives Matt that energy orgasm?

You can find the bonus scene here:

https://dl.bookfunnel.com/dn4cal17od

Seb's Book

If you want more from the Hawkston Billionaires, you can preorder the ebook of Book 4, Seb's Story, using the QR code below. I can't wait for you to experience Seb getting his Happily Every After.

Afterword

Thank you so much for reading Worth Every Risk. I truly appreciate every reader who takes the time to read my work. Without you, I wouldn't be able to do this. If you do have a moment to review the book, it would mean a lot to me. Reviews are still one of the most effective ways of convincing new readers to try my work. Whether it's Amazon, social media, Goodreads or anywhere else – even just telling your friends that these books exist – it all helps.

I wrote this book immediately after Worth Every Penny because I wanted to tell Matt's story. As far as the plot turned out, this one flowed a lot more than Worth Every Penny or Worth Every Game, and was easier for me to write. I hope that made it easier to read, despite the tough topics and emotional situations I put the characters through.

If you want to keep in touch, you can join my newsletter here:

KEEP IN TOUCH WITH RAE

Join my Facebook reader group, Rae's Romantics, where you can discuss my books, characters, and get information about upcoming releases.

You can also find me at my website
www.raeryder.com
And on Instagram and Tiktok
@raeryderauthor

Acknowledgements

This book wouldn't be what it is without my Developmental Editor, Emily Maher, and my Line Editor, Sarah Baker, as well as the numerous early readers who took a look at it, gave me suggestions, and pulled out typos. (Aries was a Manny in there for a little bit. Oops).

I have to say a huge thank you once again to my husband and kids, who put up with me being totally distracted and living in a made-up world most of the time.

Finally, thank you to everyone who has read this book. Without you, I wouldn't be able to do this every day. I am so very grateful for your time.

Rae x

Printed in Great Britain
by Amazon